THE GILDED CAGE

THE GILDED CAGE

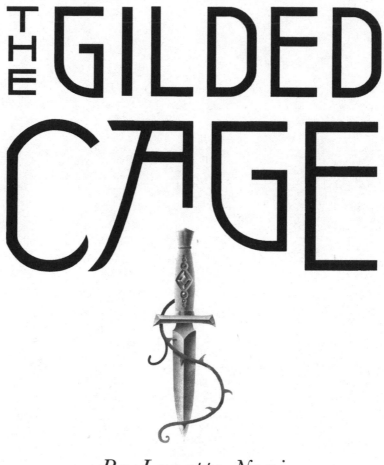

By *Lynette Noni*

HOUGHTON MIFFLIN HARCOURT

BOSTON   NEW YORK

hmhbooks.com

The text was set in Baskerville.
Jacket art © 2021 Jim Tierney
Jacket and interior design by Mary Claire Cruz and David Hastings

Library of Congress Cataloging-in-Publication Data is on file.
ISBN: 978-0-358-43459-7

Manufactured in the United States of America
1 2021
4500832773

CV 06.28.2021 1057

To Mum—

For the penguin.

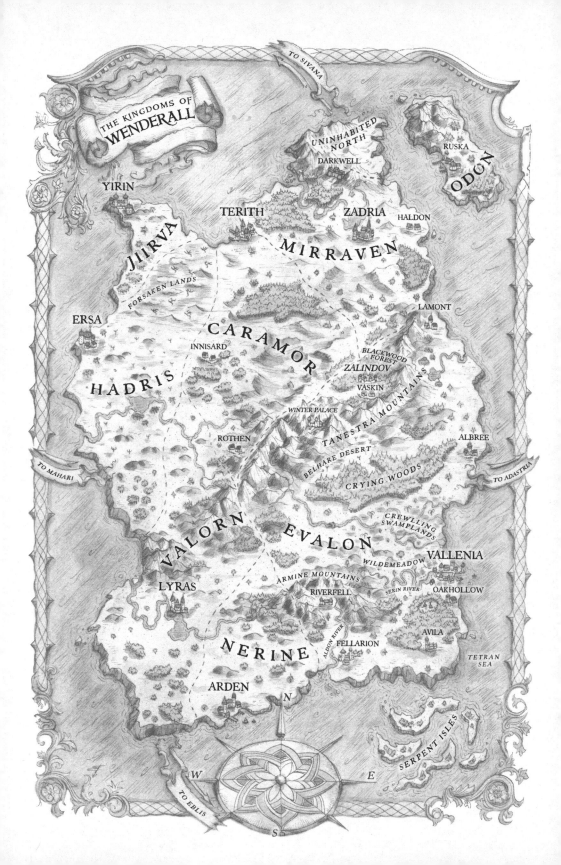

Running.

They had to keep running.

The night was dark, the cold so bitter that it pierced straight through to their bones, but still, they couldn't stop. Not when death itself chased their heels.

"Mama, where are we—"

"Quiet, sweetheart," the woman hushed her daughter, looking over her shoulder for any sign of pursuit.

"But what about Papa?" the little boy whispered. "What about—"

"Shhh," the woman cut him off, gripping his hand tighter and hastening his steps.

Neither the little boy nor his older sister uttered another word, both sensing their mother's urgency, both seeing the silent tears that slid down her face, shining in the moonlight.

On they ran, none speaking of who they had left behind and everything they had lost that night.

The woman couldn't bear to close her eyes lest she recall the image of her family's cottage in flames, her husband and youngest daughter being dragged away by the Royal Guard, her youngest son—

A sob left her mouth before she could stifle it.

Her son was dead.

He was *dead*.

The woman clamped down on her tongue to halt another sob, grateful that her two eldest children had heeded her command to stay hidden when she'd crept back to investigate, sparing them from the sight that would forever haunt her nightmares.

A sword piercing his small chest.

Her husband begging for help.

Her daughter screaming, trying to reach him, desperate to save him.

But it was too late.

"Mama, you're hurting me."

Her son's quiet whimper had her easing her grip and whispering an apology. It was all she could manage, too choked by what she was feeling to offer anything more.

Hours passed as they followed the twisting Aldon River, never slowing, always looking back to see if they were being followed. There was no sign of the guards, but the woman didn't risk stopping until they were deep in the foothills of the Armine Mountains, far from any civilization. A safe house, she had been told. A place where she might find sanctuary, should the worst ever fall upon her and her loved ones.

When the invitation had come from a cloaked stranger in the marketplace, she'd laughed as if it were a joke, claiming to have no idea why her family would ever be in such danger. They were but humble servants of the people, she'd said, her husband the village healer, she herself a devoted wife and mother.

How they had tracked her down, she had no idea. For years she had remained in hiding, after a lifetime of denying whose blood ran in her veins.

Some called it the blood of traitors.

Others, the blood of kings.

Or—in her case—queens.

The woman had done everything she could to ignore the rumors of the growing rebel group searching for descendants of their long-lost monarch. She'd taken a new name and become a new person, wanting nothing more than a quiet life with her beloved family.

Tonight, half of that family had been ripped from her.

Something vital within her had shattered as she'd watched, helpless to do anything.

She never wanted to feel that helpless again.

She would never *allow* herself to feel that helpless again.

And so, as she and her two remaining children approached the safe house—a thatched cottage hidden deep in the snow-dusted woods—the woman made a decision.

Three short raps of her numb fist against the wooden door was all it took before it opened, the cloaked figure from the marketplace illuminated by the luminium beacons shining from within, along with a small group of others reclining by the fireplace and peering curiously in her direction.

"This is a surprise," the cloaked man said, his hood pulled back enough to reveal his weathered features as he took in the woman and her two shivering children.

The woman raised her emerald eyes to his, gripping her son and daughter tighter as she said, "We're here to join you."

Those in the room beyond froze like statues, but the man merely angled his head and repeated, "Join us?"

"I know who you are and what you're after," she stated baldly. "You won't succeed without me."

The man arched an eyebrow as everyone behind him seemed to hold their collective breaths. "And what would you want in return?"

The woman recalled everything she had suffered through that night, still hearing the screams, still seeing the *blood,* and whispered one word: "Vengeance."

A slow smile stretched across the man's face before he sank into a deep bow. "Then please come in, Tilda Corentine," he said, as those in the room stood and bowed in turn. "Your rebels have long been waiting for you."

Swallowing back her doubt, the woman and what remained of her family stepped over the threshold. No longer would she be called Tilda Meridan, no longer would she or her children deny their bloodline.

The blood of traitors.

And the blood of queens.

Tilda planned to be both—to betray a lifetime of convictions to claim what was rightfully hers.

Nothing would change what had happened that night. But Tilda Corentine would be damned if she didn't spend the rest of her life making those who were responsible pay.

One way or another, no matter what it cost, she would have her revenge.

TEN YEARS LATER

CHAPTER ONE

The man was dead.

Kiva Meridan—known to a select few as Kiva Corentine—stared down at the body, noting his sunken cheeks and ashen skin. Given his state of bloating, he'd likely passed into the everworld three or four days ago. Long enough for the scent of death to emanate from him, even if he was yet to show physical signs of decomposition.

"Middle-aged male, average height and build, pulled out of the Serin River early this morning," Healer Maddis said, her crisp voice enunciating every word perfectly. "Who can speculate as to the cause of death?"

Kiva kept her mouth shut, fully aware that she'd been granted entrance into the sterile examination room as an observer only.

"No one?" Healer Maddis prompted her students, all of whom were crowded around the body resting on a metal slab in the center of the small space. "Novice Waldon?"

A young man wearing large spectacles blinked owlishly and answered, "Uh, he drowned?"

"Marvelous deductive reasoning," Maddis said dryly, before turning to the student beside him. "Novice Quinn?"

The young woman hunched in on herself, her voice barely a whisper as she said, "Maybe a heart attack? Or—Or a stroke?"

Healer Maddis tapped a fingernail against her lips. "Perhaps. Anyone else?"

Kiva shifted on her feet, catching the healer's attention.

"What about our visitor?" Maddis asked, drawing all eyes to Kiva. "Miss Meridan, isn't it?"

Seeing the open, inviting challenge in the elderly healer's gaze, Kiva shook off her trepidation and stepped closer to the corpse, picking up his limp hand to reveal the smudges beneath his nails.

"This discoloration indicates he was suffering from an immune disorder, most likely syphinus or cretamot," Kiva said, having diagnosed similar cases in the past. "If left untreated, both can lead to the rapid swelling of blood vessels." She glanced toward the two novices who had been called upon. "Waldon and Quinn are both right—he most likely had a heart attack or a stroke, caused by his underlying medical condition, then fell into the river to drown." She released the man's hand. "But only a full examination will be able to say for sure."

An approving smile stretched across the Matron Healer's dark, wrinkled face. "Well spotted." She then launched into a lecture about common immune disorders, but Kiva was only half listening, still marveling over where she stood.

Silverthorn Academy—the most renowned healing academy in all of Evalon. Some would argue in all of Wenderall.

When Kiva was a child, her father had spoken often about Silverthorn. Having grown up in the city of Fellarion, he'd used any excuse to visit Vallenia and sneak into the academy's classes. His greatest regret was that he'd never relocated to study on campus full-time, instead accepting an apprenticeship from a master healer nearer to his home—an honored position, but one that paled in comparison to being a Silverthorn student.

Faran had made it his life's purpose to help people, something Kiva had inherited to the point that, even when she'd been locked away in a nightmare, she'd still used everything he'd taught her to make the lives of others better.

A shadowy feeling overtook Kiva as she thought of the long years that were now behind her. A decade of her life spent behind thick limestone walls and impenetrable iron gates.

Zalindov prison.

It was a death sentence for most, but Kiva had survived.

And now she was here, standing at the heart of her father's dream, when she should have been somewhere else. *Anywhere* else.

There was no excuse for her actions today. But when the opportunity to visit Silverthorn had presented itself, she hadn't been able to say no, even knowing that her own desires should have been at the bottom of her priorities.

It had been six weeks since Kiva had escaped Zalindov. Six weeks since she'd discovered that the crown prince had helped keep her alive through the deadly Trial by Ordeal, a set of four elemental challenges she'd undertaken in order to save the life of the Rebel Queen, Tilda Corentine.

Kiva's mother.

Her efforts had been in vain, with a violent prison riot ending Tilda's life. But even in death, her purpose remained, inherited by Kiva and her two older siblings. Together, the three of them would seek vengeance for what had been stolen generations ago; together, they would reclaim Evalon's throne for the Corentine bloodline.

The problem was, Kiva had no idea how to find her brother and sister. The only hint she had was a coded note she'd received before leaving Zalindov, containing a single word: *Oakhollow*.

The village was barely half an hour's ride away from Vallenia, but Kiva hadn't had a spare moment to explore since arriving in the city two days ago, having spent the previous weeks holed up in the Tanestra Mountains waiting for the spring thaws. The first chance she'd had to sneak away was today. But instead of using the opportunity to seek out her long-lost siblings, she was indulging in her own dreams.

Tilda Corentine would have been livid.

Faran Meridan would have been delighted.

Kiva chose to side with her father, deciding that her mother's mission could wait another day.

Guilt had simmered within her when she'd made her choice that morning, but a knot of anxiety had also eased in her stomach. She had no reason to be nervous about a reunion with her siblings, and yet . . . ten years was a long time. Kiva wasn't the same carefree child anymore, and she could only assume the same must be true for them. Too much had happened—to them all.

And then there was what the three of them intended to *do* . . .

The sound of chiming bells interrupted her thoughts, the noise making her jump, a lingering effect of the years she'd spent listening for the smallest of sounds that could herald her death. But she was no longer in Zalindov, the peaceful chimes merely echoing through the walls of the sterile examination room to signal the end of class.

The students, all clad in pristine white robes, scrambled to finish writing their lesson notes as Healer Maddis dismissed them.

"And remember," she called as they started toward the door, "for those heading to the festival this weekend, there will be no mercy come Monday should you partake of excessive libations. Consider yourselves warned."

There was a twinkle in her gray eyes as she uttered her half-hearted threat, with some of the braver students grinning in response as they headed out the door, Kiva following in their footsteps.

"Miss Meridan, a word?"

Kiva halted at the threshold of the small examination room. "Yes, Matron Healer?" she asked, using the honorific owed to the woman, not only because of her age and experience, but because she was the head of Silverthorn Academy.

"Few people would have noted the discolored nailbeds as quickly as you did," Maddis said, covering the deceased man with a sheet. "And even fewer without proper training." She looked up, their eyes meeting. "You impressed me."

Kiva squirmed and mumbled, "Thank you."

"Faran Meridan once impressed me, too."

Kiva stopped squirming in an instant.

Healer Maddis's wrinkles deepened as she smiled. "I knew whose daughter you were the moment you walked through the door."

Unsure whether she should flee or wait to see what the healer said next, the choice was taken from Kiva when Maddis asked, "How is your father? Still saving the world, one patient at a time?"

A million responses came to Kiva's mind, but she settled on simply saying, "He died. Nine years ago."

Maddis's face fell. "Oh. I'm sorry to hear that."

Kiva only nodded, seeing no reason to reveal how he had died. Or where.

The Matron Healer cleared her throat. "Your father was my best student—ignoring the fact that he wasn't a Silverthorn student at all. Young Faran Meridan was always sneaking into my classes, acting like an innocent novice." Maddis huffed with amusement. "He showed enough promise that I never reported him to the Matron Healer at the time, knowing he'd be banned from the grounds. Someone with such natural, intuitive talent deserved the chance to hone his skills. I believed that then." She paused. "And I believe it now."

The look Maddis sent Kiva caused her breath to catch.

"Faran's death is devastating, but I'm thrilled to learn his passion was passed on," the healer said. "Should you wish it, you would be welcome to study here at Silverthorn. No sneaking in necessary."

Kiva's mouth opened and closed like a fish. Studying at Silverthorn would be a dream come true. The things she would learn . . . Tears welled in her eyes at the very thought.

And they welled even more because she knew she couldn't accept.

Mother is dead.

I'm on my way to Vallenia.

It's time to reclaim our kingdom.

Kiva had written those words to her brother and sister upon leaving Zalindov, and she had to see them through, denying her own ambitions in order to put her family first.

"Think on it," Healer Maddis said, when Kiva remained quiet. "Take however long you need. The offer will remain open."

Blinking back more tears, Kiva prepared to utter a polite refusal. But when she finally spoke, what she said was, "I'll consider it."

Despite her words, Kiva knew Silverthorn wasn't in her future. As soon as Maddis learned where she'd practiced her skills for the last decade, the invitation would be withdrawn. All Kiva had to do was raise her sleeve and uncover the Z scar on her hand.

But she couldn't do it. Couldn't sabotage herself with such finality. Instead, she uttered a quiet farewell and stepped out of the examination room into the sterile hallway beyond.

Mind reeling, Kiva paid little attention as she walked down the long corridor, passing white-robed healers and students, along with a mixture of plain-clothed visitors and patients. She'd already had a tour of the campus earlier that day, learning that there were three large infirmaries—one for psychological trauma and healing, one for long-term patient care and rehabilitation, and this one, which was for diagnosing and treating physical ailments specific to illnesses and injuries. There were also a handful of smaller buildings dotted across the campus, like the apothecaries' workshop, the quarantine block, the morgue, and the healer residences. Only the main infirmaries were accessible to the public, all connected by outdoor pathways with arched stone sides offering views of the gardens at the center of the grounds. The Silverthorn Sanctuary, as those gardens were known—a place where patients and healers could retreat and relax, enjoying the tranquility of the bubbling brook and aromatic wildflowers all from atop a hill that overlooked the city, straight down to where the meandering Serin River met the Tetran Sea.

It was to the sanctuary that Kiva headed once she left the largest of the infirmaries, walking along the stone path a short way before stepping off it, her sandals sinking into the lush grass, the late afternoon sunshine warming the chill from her bones. She kept moving aimlessly until she reached a small footbridge affording safe passage over the trickling stream, pausing to lean on the wooden railing in an attempt to gather her thoughts.

"Uh-oh, you're wearing your serious face."

Kiva stilled at the familiar voice, ignoring how it made her feel — *all* that it made her feel. She braced herself and turned to see the approaching figure just as he came close enough to stop beside her.

Jaren Vallentis — or Prince Deverick, as most of the world knew him. Her fellow escaped inmate, her traveling companion, her once-friend — and once-potentially-more-than-that — and her family's sworn enemy.

Her sworn enemy.

"This is my normal face," Kiva said, struggling not to stare. His deep blue shirt with gold embroidery along the collar looked far too good on him, as did his tailored black jacket and pants. It took a supreme effort of will for her to cast her gaze away.

"Yes, and it's much too serious," Jaren stated, reaching out to tuck a strand of dark, windswept hair behind her ear.

Kiva's stomach gave a traitorous leap, and she frowned inwardly at herself. Casual affection from Jaren wasn't uncommon. Even when they'd been in Zalindov together, he'd been overly friendly toward her. Since they'd escaped, Kiva had sought to keep him at arm's length, but her will was beginning to crumble. It was as if he'd been born for the sole purpose of tempting her, of distracting her from her task.

And that was unacceptable.

"Did you have a good day?" he asked, his unique blue-gold eyes capturing hers.

Kiva smoothed her outfit — a simple green dress paired with a thin white cardigan — and weighed her response. Jaren was the reason she was even at Silverthorn; he'd called in a favor, resulting in her being awakened at dawn and bustled out of the River Palace for the once-in-a-lifetime opportunity to spend a day at the best healing academy in the kingdom.

There were so many reasons for Kiva to hate the crown prince, but she couldn't summon the burning resentment that should have consumed her. She blamed Jaren for that. From the moment they'd met, he'd been caring and thoughtful and wholly devoted to her. Even when she'd learned that he'd lied about who he really was, she still hadn't been able to turn her back and leave him to die of his injuries down in the tunnels beneath Zalindov. She'd tried—*desperately*—to harden her heart toward him in the weeks they'd spent at his family's palace in the Tanestra Mountains, and then during their long days of travel to Vallenia, but it was useless. He was just too gods-damned *likeable*. It made everything Kiva planned to do to him and his family that much more difficult.

Not that she'd ever admit as much—even to herself.

"It was . . ." she started, unsure how to answer. Her day had been amazing, incredible, everything she'd ever hoped for. But knowing what she did about her future, and how she would have to turn down Maddis's offer, all she said was, "Interesting."

Jaren's golden eyebrows inched upward. "A glowing commendation."

Kiva ignored his sarcasm and asked, "What're you doing here?"

There was no one near where they stood leaning against the footbridge, but she still peered nervously at those spaced further out in the sanctuary, and the spattering of people walking along the arched stone pathways between the infirmaries.

"I came to pick you up," Jaren said with a merry wink. "First day of school, and all that."

Kiva shook her head at him. "You shouldn't be here."

"Ouch," Jaren said, pressing a hand to his heart. "That hurts. Right here."

"If someone recognizes you—"

Jaren had the audacity to chuckle. "People in Vallenia are used to me and my family wandering freely among them. We only wear masks during special events, so we're easily recognizable the rest of the time. Don't worry—we're not as much of a novelty as you'd think."

"I doubt Naari would agree with you," Kiva argued, looking past him. "Where is she?"

Since leaving Zalindov—and in the time they'd been there together—it was rare to see Jaren without his most loyal Royal Guard, his Golden Shield. That Naari Arell was absent now meant one of two things: either she was giving them space and watching from a distance, or—

"Would you be impressed if I said I managed to give her the slip?"

The self-satisfied grin Jaren wore had Kiva tilting her head to the side, a smirk playing at her lips as she replied, "I'd be impressed if you managed to survive her wrath afterward."

Jaren's grin fled, a wince taking its place. "Yes. Well." He straightened his shoulders and rallied. "That's a problem for later."

"I'll say something nice at your funeral," Kiva promised.

Jaren huffed out a laugh. "You're too kind." He then grabbed her hand and started leading her back toward the arched pathway. "Come on, we have to get moving if we don't want to miss it."

Kiva tried to free herself from his grip, but his fingers only tightened around hers, so she gave in, resolutely ignoring how nice it felt, and sought to keep up with his long strides. "Miss what?"

"Sunset," Jaren answered.

When he said no more, Kiva dryly observed, "This may come as a shock, but there'll be another one tomorrow."

Jaren gave her a gentle tug. "Smart ass." The amused look he shot her warmed her insides—and *that* she ignored, too.

She was ignoring a lot these days, when it came to Jaren.

"The annual River Festival kicks off at sunset *today*," he said. "It lasts all weekend, but the first night is always the best, so we want to make sure we have a good view."

"Of what?"

"You'll see," Jaren said mysteriously.

Kiva made a quick decision. She would allow herself one more night—a night to experience the River Festival and enjoy being in Jaren's company, knowing that their days together were numbered.

One night, and then she would set out for Oakhollow, where she would finally follow through with what she'd determined upon leaving Zalindov.

No matter how she might feel, no matter how the crown prince had wormed his way into her heart, it was time for the Vallentis family to fall.

CHAPTER TWO

Vallenia was known as the River City, Kiva had learned upon her arrival two days earlier. With numerous meandering waterways, none was more impressive than the mighty Serin River, which twisted and turned like a serpent throughout the capital.

It was to the river that Jaren was leading Kiva, an easy downhill walk from Silverthorn until they reached the main thoroughfare, where people were already beginning to crowd the sidewalks bordering the water, the thrill of anticipation heavy in the air.

As they wove their way through the masses, Kiva assumed Jaren was taking her back to the River Palace—a feat of architecture split in half by the Serin, the two sides connected by a gilded bridge. Not even Kiva could deny the magnificence of the royal residence, the luminium threaded into its outer walls creating a glittering effect that was dazzling.

So far, Kiva had only set foot in the eastern palace, where Jaren had a whole wing to himself—including guest quarters, inside which Kiva had been allocated a lavish suite. His siblings, Mirryn and Oriel, also resided in the eastern palace, but their parents lived on the western side of the river. Kiva had yet to lay eyes on the king or queen, but given how she felt about the monarchs, she wasn't in a rush to meet them.

The crowds became uncomfortably thick as they approached the River Palace, offering a valid excuse for Kiva to free her hand from Jaren's. She refused to acknowledge the loss she felt once their connection was severed, focusing instead on the back of his tousled gold-brown head as he led her off the main street and into a grimy alleyway well before they reached the guarded palace gates. The dilapidated buildings on both sides were tall enough to block out the quickly setting sun, casting deep shadows across their path.

"Is this the part where you kill me and hide my body?" Kiva asked, squinting into the gloom.

"Don't be ridiculous," Jaren said, before adding, "I have people to do that kind of thing for me."

Kiva was grateful for the darkness hiding her smile. "I guess you wouldn't want to get your royal hands dirty."

Jaren snorted. "My *royal hands* are busy doing other things." He guided her around a puddle, remaining close enough that their arms brushed as they walked. "Not much further—it's just up here."

"What is?" Kiva asked.

"I told you—we want a good view."

"Of the river?"

"And the palace," Jaren said, halting beside a decrepit-looking doorway, the brass knob falling uselessly off the wood at the turn of his hand.

"You're not serious," Kiva said flatly when she looked inside and saw the staircase—or rather, the slats of rotten wood that rose from the empty room and ascended around the corner out of sight.

"Where's your sense of adventure?" Jaren asked, dragging her through the doorway.

If not for the faintest trace of light trickling in from somewhere high above them, Kiva wouldn't have been able to see anything. "I've had enough adventure for one lifetime, thanks," she said, even as he began leading her toward the stairs and nudged her upward in front of him.

"It's just a few little steps," Jaren coaxed, as she climbed one, two, three, and continued higher. "See? They're perfectly safe."

No sooner had he uttered the words than the wood she'd just placed her weight on splintered. A squeak of fear left her, but rather than crashing back down to the ground, her foot was caught and held aloft midair.

Gaping at the empty space beneath her, Kiva turned back to find

Jaren shaking his head with fond amusement. "You really need to learn to trust me."

A weightless feeling overcame Kiva until suddenly she was hovering *above* the rotten steps, Jaren's elemental magic floating them both up to the top of the staircase, bypassing any further danger.

Kiva waited until she was standing on her own again before she said, "You could have done that from the beginning."

"Magic always has a cost," Jaren said, ushering her through another battered door that led out to an open-air rooftop. "Only a fool would waste power for no reason."

"What does it cost you?" Kiva asked, curious.

"Depends on how much I use. Something like that" — he indicated the staircase behind them — "doesn't require much. But larger things can become exhausting."

Kiva cocked her head to the side. "So it's like an energy transference?"

Jaren nodded and steered her around a stone chimney top. "As far as I understand it. The more energy I have, the stronger my magic. And vice versa."

"Have you ever run out? Of magic, I mean."

"A couple of times, when I was younger," Jaren admitted. "I try to avoid that happening now, since it leaves me feeling strange, like a piece of me is missing. My magic is . . ." He paused, thinking. "It's a part of me, you know? Like an arm or a leg. If I use too much too fast, it's like I've cut off a limb and have to wait for it to regrow. Does that make sense?"

Kiva nodded, recognizing the similarities with her own magic — the forbidden healing power in her veins, a mark of the Corentine bloodline.

Unlike Jaren, however, Kiva couldn't relate to his wistful tone, the joy and contentment in his voice as he spoke about his magic. For her own safety, she'd had to keep hers hidden deep within her. She'd come to consider it more a burden than a gift, something to deny at all costs, lest she risk exposure. In the last decade, she'd used it just the once, during a moment of true desperation to save—

"K-Kiva! You're h-h-here!"

Jaren came to a dead halt and muttered a curse under his breath when he saw who stood before them. Kiva's eyes softened at the young redheaded boy skipping their way, but then she snickered when she saw the reason for Jaren's distress—his Golden Shield standing with her arms crossed, her dark face frowning with displeasure.

Before anyone could say anything—or shout anything, judging by Naari's expression—Tipp reached Kiva and wrapped his arms around her in a quick hug. While it was brief, she reveled in the embrace, painfully aware that he'd nearly died six weeks earlier. Had she not arrived at the infirmary in time, had she not been able to use her long-suppressed magic to heal him . . .

But Tipp hadn't died. He was alive and well, and just as effervescent as he'd always been.

Kiva had worried, the first few days after his near-death experience. He'd been disoriented when he'd finally awoken, even terrified. It had taken some quick lies to convince him that he'd bumped his head and anything he remembered couldn't be trusted. When she'd assured him that he was all right, that he was *free,* he'd bounced back to his joyous self, ready to take on the world and experience life to the fullest. He hadn't even blinked at hearing Jaren was a prince, but was simply all the more excited for what adventures they might find once they reached Vallenia.

"Come on, c-c-come on, *come on,*" Tipp said, yanking her toward the far edge of the building.

Kiva noted that there was a blanket resting on the ground, an open hamper beside it with fruit and pastries all laid out invitingly. But she only spared them a half glance as Tipp brought her to a screeching halt, her attention diverted by the view of the city.

"Wow," Kiva breathed. It wasn't just the shining River Palace that left her awestruck; with luminium threaded into the pale-colored rooftops of many of Vallenia's homes, the entire city appeared to be glowing as the final kiss of sunshine faded beyond the horizon.

"Right?" Tipp said, jigging from foot to foot. "N-Naari said it's one of the b-best views in the whole c-capital."

"She's not wrong," Kiva agreed, glancing back to see the guard having a heated conversation with Jaren. The prince looked like he was fighting a grin, which was doing nothing to soothe Naari's temper.

"Do you think w-we should save him?" Tipp whispered, following Kiva's gaze. "Naari was really m-m-mad when she realized he'd l-left without her."

"He survived Zalindov," Kiva said, sitting cross-legged on the blanket, the panoramic view unobstructed before her. "He can survive Naari."

"—and if you ever run off like that again, I'll lock you in the dungeons myself, do you hear me?"

Naari's irate voice floated over to them, prompting Kiva to wince and amend her previous statement. "Probably."

Tipp snickered, but quickly shoved a pastry in his mouth when Naari stomped their way, rearranging her weapons so she could sit. She speared a look at Kiva and threatened, "If I find out you had anything to do with—"

Kiva quickly raised her hands. "I was innocently minding my own business before he dragged me here."

"Thanks for the solidarity," Jaren muttered, collapsing beside Kiva, close enough for her to feel his body warmth. She contemplated shifting away, but she hadn't dressed with a nighttime outing in mind when she'd left that morning, her thin cardigan doing little to ward off the evening chill.

One night, she reminded herself. It would do little harm for her to remain where she was.

"At least we have p-plenty of food," Tipp said, reaching for some grapes.

"What a relief," Jaren said, his tone dry.

Kiva realized something then: Jaren had cursed upon seeing Naari and Tipp, as if he hadn't expected them to be there. All of this—the view, the blanket, the hamper—he'd set it up for her.

She turned to find a sheepish expression on his face. He shrugged slightly, as if to say that he'd tried, and something within her melted. But then she reminded herself of who he was and what she planned to do to him—what she *had* to do to him—and she looked away, slamming a wall around her heart.

"For future reference," Naari declared, "the next time the two of you sneak off for some alone time, please do so *inside* the palace grounds."

Kiva opened her mouth to deny her involvement, but Jaren jumped in first by saying, "Where's the fun in that?" He tossed an apple to the guard. "Eat something, Naari. You're grumpier than usual when you're hungry."

The look she sent him promised retribution, but she raised the fruit to her lips and bit into it.

"Not long to go," Jaren told Kiva, offering her a plate of pastries. "Eat up and get comfortable."

Nibbling on a custard tart, Kiva marveled at the novelty of being able to eat freely. For the first time since she was a child, she actually had flesh on her bones, not to mention curves that had been previously non-existent. Tipp, too, had flourished in the time since leaving Zalindov and its meager rations, his boyish frame filling out, his freckled skin glowing with youthful radiance.

Kiva wondered how she'd ever survived for so long on so little. But Zalindov was behind her. One day, she would seek justice for the crimes committed by Warden Rooke, the man responsible for her father's death and so many others. But that day, she knew, would have to wait.

"Any second now," Jaren said, just as the last of the sun's rays sank below the horizon.

Tipp rose eagerly onto his knees, while Naari continued chewing on her apple, her alert amber eyes darting around the rooftop. Kiva squinted into the twilight, having no idea what she was supposed to be looking for, especially with the darkness quickly setting in.

"Will we—" Kiva broke off with a gasp as a kaleidoscope of color lit the night, accompanied by an orchestral symphony amplified throughout the city. The music's origin was impossible to pinpoint, but the rainbow spotlights streamed from the palace's gilded bridge right into the heart of the Serin River, reflecting off the water in a psychedelic haze.

The crowd cheered loud enough to make Kiva's ears ring even from a distance. The noise transported her straight back to Zalindov, to the moment she'd volunteered to take her mother's sentence, and the resulting roar from the gathered inmates. Her palms began to sweat, but the city crowd was celebrating, not jeering, the sound joyful enough to ease the sudden constriction around her chest.

"Here we go," Jaren said from Kiva's side as the colored lights began to spiral. He was unaware of the mental battlefield she'd just navigated, but he of all people would understand her lingering trauma, especially since she knew he was suffering in his own way, having heard his restless nightmares through the walls during their weeks at the winter palace. She'd acted oblivious, never revealing that she'd lain awake until his distressed sounds had faded, never sharing that she endured her own torturous dreams.

Shoving away her thoughts, Kiva rose onto her knees beside Tipp, waiting to see the reason for Jaren's declaration.

Mere seconds later, a small boat appeared in the center of the lights, the multicolored streaks shifting to form a perfect circle around the vessel. A single figure stood on the stern of the boat, dressed in white with their hood pulled over their face, a glint of a gold mask peeking out from beneath it.

The music rose into a crescendo, and with it, the figure's arms stretched high into the air, the lights moving again, more erratically this time. The river began to swirl and gurgle, a whirlpool forming around the boat, which remained perfectly still at the center of it. And then—

"No w-way!" Tipp exclaimed as a swan burst out of the whirlpool, three times the size of the boat—and made entirely of water. Rainbow lights streaked from the bridge to highlight the bird as it rose into the air, water-wings flapping and dripping straight back into the Serin below.

"L-Look!" Tipp cried, drawing Kiva's stunned gaze back to the figure on the boat, who was twirling their hands to the music and pointing at the water again.

This time, it was a pod of dolphins that emerged, all similarly magnified in size. Numerous spotlights touched on them as they skipped over the surface of the river, diving deep and reappearing to leap high in a series of aerial acrobatics.

When the figure on the boat pointed their finger again, an entire section of the Serin began to bubble, with long, straight lines shooting up into the air, the tops budding into perfect sunflowers emphasized by bright yellow lights from the bridge. Then, as Kiva watched, the sunflowers parted as a herd of horses galloped through them, tossing their wind-whipped manes and trailing water in their wake.

"What is all this?" Kiva breathed.

"The River Festival celebrates life," Jaren answered as a massive oak tree formed out of the whirlpool, rising high into the sky. Iridescent birds appeared and launched off the branches, joining the swan still circling above the river, all dripping water back to the surface. "Centuries ago, it offered a reminder that our lives are seasonal, and that those who survived the winter could relax and enjoy the pleasures of spring. But these days, it's essentially just an excuse for a party." The orchestra increased in volume, so Jaren raised his voice to continue, "We have four of these festivals throughout the year: the River Festival in spring, the Carnival of Flowers in summer, the Ember Rite in the fall, and the Crystal Gales in winter. Each focuses on a different elemental power—water for spring, earth for summer, fire for fall, and wind for winter—and acts as a reminder to our people of the magic we have and the protection we afford them."

Kiva squinted at the figure on the boat. "That's the queen down there, isn't it?"

It had to be, since the king had married into the Vallentis family and therefore had no magic, Princess Mirryn was a wind elemental with a slight affinity for fire, and young Prince Oriel was most adept at earth magic. Jaren alone was capable of wielding all four elements—the reason he'd been named heir, despite Mirryn being the elder sibling—but to the world, he was considered to be only a powerful fire elemental, with some control over wind. His people believed the succession had fallen to him because of the strength of his magic, with very few knowing what he was truly capable of—Kiva being one of them.

"Yes, that's my mother," Jaren confirmed. Nothing in his voice revealed how he felt toward the woman who had abused him repeatedly over the years, her addiction to angeldust unknown to the general public.

"She has a lot of power," Kiva observed carefully.

Before Jaren could respond, a colossal serpent formed out of the Serin and swallowed the oak tree in one bite before slithering toward the field of sunflowers and ingesting them, too. It then struck upward like an asp, and the birds vanished within its watery maw, followed by the acrobatic dolphins and prancing horses. Soon only the serpent remained, circling the boat in place of the whirlpool, which had dissolved back into stillness.

"Believe it or not, these kinds of tricks don't take much effort," Jaren said. "She'll feel a little tired afterward, but that's about it." He indicated the water. "She's nearly done now—you'll like this part."

It was difficult not to ask more questions, but Kiva refocused on the serpent rising high above the river, like a wingless dragon flying through the air. As the orchestra reached its climax, Queen Ariana clapped her hands together and the serpent exploded, turning into millions of water droplets suspended like glittering diamonds.

"Oh," Kiva couldn't help gasping as the River Palace came alive, the luminium glowing so brightly that she had to raise a hand to shield her eyes.

As if it offered some kind of sign, the crowd roared even louder than before, with those closest to the water lighting lotus-shaped lanterns and placing them onto the surface, first dozens, then hundreds, then thousands floating along the river.

"It's even b-better than I imagined," Tipp whispered, his voice filled with awe.

The young boy wasn't wrong—the combination of rainbow droplets and floating lanterns all backlit by the shining palace was easily the most beautiful thing Kiva had ever seen.

And then came the fireworks.

Tipp let out a *whoop* as they exploded high above the palace, and Kiva jumped at how loud the first crackle of them was. The music helped drown out the noise, the orchestra still playing as the masses screamed with delight.

"Did you say this lasts all weekend?" Kiva had to nearly shout at Jaren to be heard over the booms.

"The next two days will be quieter," he said, also close to yelling.

"It'll be more about art, culture, and community, and not so much about the drama."

Drama was a good word for it, Kiva thought. The show had been a spectacle from the moment the boat appeared on the water—a boat that had now vanished, the queen having returned to the palace, leaving her people to enjoy the festivities.

Kiva settled in to watch the pyrotechnical display, oohing and ahhing along with Tipp. Only when the last ember dissolved did the hovering water droplets trickle back into the Serin, the palace slowly fading to normal. The lotus lanterns, however, remained lighting up the water, and while the orchestra had silenced with the finale of the fireworks, street musicians began to play upbeat tunes, continuing the festivities now that the official celebration had ended.

"We should go," Naari said, standing and dusting pastry flakes off her leathery armor, a near-identical outfit to what she'd worn at Zalindov. "I want us back at the palace before things get too rowdy down there. I'd rather not have to explain to the king and queen why their son and his friends were caught up in a drunken street brawl."

"I'd like t-to see a street b-brawl!" Tipp said, jumping up beside her.

Naari slung her arm around his neck. "Another time, kiddo."

His face fell, but then he brightened again and said, "Ori's g-going to be so jealous. I can't wait to get b-back and tell him what it was like w-watching from out here."

"Where *is* Oriel?" Kiva asked. The vivacious young prince had been joined at the hip with Tipp since their meeting two days earlier. Where one went, the other followed, at least until tonight.

"The royal family usually watches the opening of each seasonal festival from inside the palace," Naari said. She looked at Jaren and emphasized, *"Together."*

Kiva's eyes moved to him as well. "You really did sneak away, didn't you?" After six weeks spent living and traveling with the haughty Princess Mirryn and the flirtatious Prince Caldon, Kiva couldn't blame him.

"It's not the first time, and it won't be the last," Jaren said with an unrepentant grin. "How do you think I found this place to begin with? I've been coming here for years."

Naari grumbled inaudibly before saying, "Pack up. We're leaving."

Since the light show was over, no one fought the guard's terse order. Tipp helped refill the hamper with the leftover food, shoving handfuls of crackers and cheese into his mouth as if afraid he'd never see another meal. Kiva understood that feeling of desperation, wondering how long it would take for it to fade — in both of them.

A gust of wind hit the top of the roof, causing her to shiver and rub her arms. Noting her reaction, Jaren removed his jacket and laid it over her shoulders. Warmth instantly seeped into her as she slid her arms into the sleeves, the comforting scent of fresh earth, sea salt, morning dew, and wood smoke tickling her nose. Earth, wind, water, and fire — a smell perfectly unique to Jaren.

"Thank you," she whispered, staunchly ignoring how his shirt caught tantalizingly on his muscles.

"Anything for you," Jaren said, winking as he bent to collect the last of their things. The move only threw his physique into sharper relief under the moonlight, his body so flawless that —

"Ahem." Naari cleared her throat, her face stern but her amber eyes laughing.

Willing the heat from her cheeks, Kiva folded the picnic blanket into squares and passed it to Jaren, who had already claimed the heavy hamper from the too-eager Tipp.

"Ready," Jaren told Naari. She didn't bat an eyelash at the crown prince bearing their goods like a packhorse, having experienced years of him acting in a manner well beneath his station. The Z scar on his hand was proof of that—proof of his service to his people, the lengths he would go to in order to keep them safe.

Guilt bubbled in Kiva's stomach, but she ignored it and followed Naari across the roof, continuing on past the decrepit doorway and heading instead to a stairway that led right down to the street. Kiva shot a look at Jaren, wondering why he hadn't brought her up using the much more stable entry, but he studiously avoided eye contact.

You really need to learn to trust me, he'd told her earlier.

Kiva nearly snorted, realizing his intention had been to remind her that she was safe with him—always.

Not that she didn't already know that.

"Let's get a move on," Naari urged, interrupting Kiva's treacherous thoughts and hurrying them down into the alleyway. There was a dangerous feel to the air now, almost as if they were being watched, but Kiva's concerns eased slightly as they approached the main thoroughfare, the lights and sounds of the festival growing with every step nearer to the river.

Naari cursed when they finally exited the side street to find swarms of people standing shoulder to shoulder, dancing, laughing, and singing along to the music. So much revelry—and all of it blocking the road, right up to the palace gates.

"I don't like this," the guard said, her lips pursed.

Kiva barely heard her over the raucous sounds of the street party.

"They'll be at it until dawn," Jaren pointed out, which didn't improve Naari's mood. "Unless you're happy for us to stay out here all night—"

He quickly shut his mouth at the look she sent him.

"I'll forge us a path. You three stay *directly* behind me," Naari ordered, one hand tensing around the hilt of her blade, as if she intended to cut through anyone who got in their way. "No stopping, no looking around. Straight to the gates."

She waited until she had Tipp's attention, since he was staring at the chaos with wide, longing eyes. When he finally realized what she wanted, he uttered his reluctant agreement.

Stepping into the masses, Naari was swallowed in an instant, but Kiva gave Tipp a hearty push to keep him close behind the guard. Jaren nudged Kiva forward so that he could take up the rear—something Naari wouldn't like, but Jaren had been right earlier: no one seemed to care that the crown prince was in their midst. To the festivalgoers, they were just four citizens trying to carve a path.

When they were halfway to the palace, the music shifted and an emphatic cry rose up around them, the stamping of feet followed by the jumping of sweaty bodies shaking the ground. Kiva couldn't hear anything over the delighted shrieks, and could barely make out the figure of Naari being engulfed by the swelling crowd. Somewhere along the line, Jaren had abandoned the hamper and blanket, instead keeping both hands free to hold on to Kiva and clear a path for her, much like she was trying to do for Tipp.

Another almighty cry sounded, and the jumping increased, bodies ramming into them from all angles. Claustrophobia clawed at Kiva as a wayward carouser shoved her hard to the side, ripping her fingers from Tipp. She stumbled violently, only managing to stay upright because of Jaren's firm grip on her. Even so, the two of them slammed into a group of people, all of whom were too lost in the revelry to care.

One quick glance up was all it took for Kiva to realize that she could still see Naari—but she couldn't see Tipp.

Her claustrophobia instantly forgotten, Kiva yelled his name over the music, Jaren doing the same by her ear. They surged forward together, their urgency growing when they caught sight of the young boy on the ground, struggling to rise.

"He'll be trampled!" Kiva cried, her heart lodging in her throat.

She'd barely finished the words when Jaren pushed past her and shoved his way through the suffocating masses, reaching Tipp at the same time as Naari, the two of them hauling the boy up to his feet.

Someone bumped into Kiva from behind, a hand latching on to her arm and stopping her from joining her friends. She tried to free herself, but the grip tightened, yanking her roughly backwards. The space around her was so tightly packed that she couldn't turn to see who held her, her panic growing for a different reason now. She could just make out Jaren and Naari checking Tipp for injuries, feeling a momentary relief when it appeared he was unharmed, but then the hand gripping her gave another vicious tug, trapping her against a hard body. She struggled anew, but before she could so much as scream, a cloth was shoved over her face, the pungent smells of whitlock and tamadrin making her eyes water. Knowing that a deep enough inhalation would render her unconscious, she held her breath and fought harder, willing Jaren or Naari to turn her way.

A masculine oath came from her captor when he realized she wasn't going down easily, and he removed the cloth, giving Kiva hope that he'd decided she wasn't worth the trouble. But the next thing she knew, a spike of pain caused starbursts to explode in her vision, and she crumpled in his arms, out like a light.

CHAPTER THREE

". . . didn't leave me with any choice."

"Are you *mad?* You see the bruise on her face? The general's gonna bury you."

There was a sound of shifting feet, followed by a mumbled, "The commander said to do whatever it took to get her here alone."

A strained laugh. "Good luck using that as an excuse."

Slowly, Kiva opened her eyes, biting back a groan at the steady pounding in her temple. She tried to move, only to find that she was tied to a wooden chair in the middle of a grimy room, ropes chafing against her wrists and ankles, a gag over her mouth. A single door in the corner opened to a brightly lit hallway, revealing shadows cast by two guards standing just out of sight—the owners of the foggy voices that had awoken her.

Carefully testing her bonds, Kiva only succeeded in digging the ropes deeper into her flesh, earning herself a few splinters from the chair in the process. She wouldn't be escaping anytime soon. Not without help.

Kiva had been in Vallenia barely two days. It was nowhere near enough time to have made enemies, let alone ones powerful enough for orders to come directly from a "commander." But . . . if someone had seen her walking with Jaren . . . He was heir to the richest kingdom in Wenderall, his enemies innumerable and hailing from every territory across the continent. Should a rival court wish to harm him, a sure way to do so would be to target those close to him.

Kiva swallowed, before reminding herself that Jaren and Naari would find her. They would get Tipp to the palace, then tear the city apart to make sure she was safe. She just had to buy them time. Buy *herself* time.

Footsteps echoed in the hallway, prompting Kiva to freeze, her gaze darting to the open door.

"You got her?" came a hard female voice.

One of the male guards offered a response too low for Kiva to hear, continuing for much longer than a simple yes or no.

"You're right, he won't be pleased," the woman muttered, before sighing loudly. "He's on his way. I'll deal with him when he arrives."

A thousand questions flooded Kiva's mind, but every single one fled at the sight of the young woman who strode confidently through the open doorway.

"Uurreega," Kiva gasped, the gag over her mouth making the word, the *name,* indistinguishable.

But there was no denying who it was.

No denying that Zuleeka Meridan—Zuleeka *Corentine*—had just stepped into the room.

With dark hair braided over her shoulder, eyes the color of liquid gold mixed with honey—their father's eyes—and moon-pale skin, she looked so similar to when Kiva had last seen her ten years ago. But Zuleeka was no longer an innocent, wide-eyed eleven-year-old child. There was a harshness about her now, her angular features set, her hands resting on weapons belted to her leather-clad waist. Her stance was both casual and threatening, the latter becoming more evident when a slow, dangerous smile stretched across her hawkish face. "Hello, sister."

Kiva could only stare, having no idea how to respond even if she'd been capable of doing so around the gag.

Stepping closer, Zuleeka tugged the cloth away from her mouth. "I hear you gave Borin some trouble." She made a tsking noise. "He was only doing his job. We've had eyes on you since you arrived two days ago, but you've made it tricky for him to grab you."

Kiva's voice was hoarse with emotion. "He could have asked nicely."

A bark of laughter came from Zuleeka, but Kiva found nothing about this to be funny.

She waited a beat, but when her sister made no further move, Kiva asked, "Are you going to untie me?"

"In a minute," Zuleeka said, drumming her fingers against her thigh. "First I want to ask you some questions." A calculated pause. "I hear you've made some powerful friends."

Kiva's blood turned to ice.

Ten years.

Ten years she'd been locked away in a godsforsaken death prison. Their parents had died there, and Kiva herself had gone through hell to survive long enough to escape. But instead of showing any indication that she was pleased to see her, Zuleeka wanted to *interrogate* her?

Kiva drew in a deep breath and made herself consider how she might have acted in her sister's place, realizing that perhaps she would be just as careful to test her allegiances. But even so, she couldn't help feeling a sting of disappointment.

"We have spies everywhere, you know," Zuleeka said conversationally when Kiva remained silent. "They've been watching since you left Zalindov, following your progress all the way here. Your note arrived weeks before you did—*I'm on my way to Vallenia. It's time to reclaim our kingdom.* You penned that yourself, your hunger for what is rightfully ours literally written in your own blood."

She was wrong about that—it wasn't Kiva's blood that the note had been written in. And that wasn't all she had written.

Mother is dead.

Zuleeka had yet to mention the first line of Kiva's letter. Had her spies—her *rebel* spies—already shared the details of Tilda's death, or did she simply not care to know?

"It seems you've been busy, little sister," Zuleeka continued, cocking her head to the side. "Surviving the unsurvivable Trial by Ordeal, escaping the inescapable Zalindov prison, and somehow growing close enough to the crown prince that he'd invite you to live with him and his precious family at the River Palace." She smirked. "Now, *that* is a bold move. I applaud you for your strategy. And your acting skills."

With every word that came out of Zuleeka's mouth, a burning feeling grew inside Kiva. She squashed it down, not allowing herself to consider the reason for it.

"Unless," Zuleeka said, drawing the word out. "It wasn't *all* an act."

Kiva sat stiffly in her chair, holding her sister's narrowed gaze.

"I hear he's very handsome, Prince Deverick." Zuleeka flicked the edge of Kiva's sleeve in a silent observation of whose jacket she wore. "But you don't call him that, do you? People he cares about use his middle name. Jaren, isn't it?"

"What exactly are you accusing me of?" Kiva asked tersely.

Zuleeka pressed a hand to her chest in mock innocence. "No accusations here, little sister. I'm merely trying to assess your priorities."

"My priorities are the same as they've always been," Kiva said in a firm voice. "First and foremost, they're to my family." After everything she'd been through for them, she couldn't understand how that was even in question.

"It's time to reclaim our kingdom." Zuleeka repeated Kiva's note again. Her expression turned cunning, even vicious, as she went on, "Forgive me, but I can't help wondering how you plan on doing that while rolling in the prince's bedsheets."

The burning in Kiva's chest rose to her face, but it wasn't from embarrassment.

"I don't know where your information is coming from," Kiva said in a cold voice, "but you should have a word with your spies about getting their facts right."

Zuleeka's dark eyebrows rose. "You deny that—"

"I'm not denying anything," Kiva said, bubbling with anger, "because I shouldn't *have* to. I'm your sister. That alone should be enough for you to trust me."

"I don't trust anyone," Zuleeka shot back. "Least of all someone who might as well have been dead for a decade."

Kiva's head jerked as if she'd been slapped, her reaction violent enough that Zuleeka's features softened for the first time since she'd set foot in the room. She opened her mouth, looking like she was about to apologize, but was interrupted by the approach of loud, fast footsteps and a male voice demanding, "Where is she?"

A stuttered response came from the guards, and seconds later, a young man stormed through the door, coming to a dead halt when his eyes landed on Kiva.

Emerald eyes — the exact same shade as hers.

And the exact same shade as their late mother's.

"Kiva," her brother Torell breathed, saying her name like a prayer.

Throat tightening, Kiva whispered back, "Hey, Tor."

He took another step forward, his gaze still locked on hers, but then it narrowed as he noticed the gag, the ropes, and what she could already feel was a nasty bruise blossoming on her left temple.

"What the *hell?*" Torell growled, spearing their sister with a look that had Kiva's knees trembling.

"Calm down, brother," Zuleeka said. "Kiva and I were just getting reacquainted."

Tor's face darkened further, his jaw clenching as if to bite back words. Unsheathing a dagger, he knelt before Kiva and began sawing at her bonds. Once she was free, he stood and pulled her up to her feet, straight into his arms.

"Kiva," he breathed again, his grip forcing the air from her lungs. But she didn't complain, holding him just as fiercely, tears welling in her eyes.

This was the reunion she'd imagined. The reunion she'd longed for.

As her second-eldest sibling, Torell had been nearly ten the last time Kiva had seen him, a skinny little boy with perpetually scraped knees. There was nothing of that child in the young man who now towered over her, his black hair and piercing eyes complemented by a rich bronze tan, broad shoulders, and a hard body indicating years of careful discipline. With dark clothes and enough weapons to make Naari green with envy, everything about Tor screamed that he was a fighter, a warrior. It was enough for Kiva to know that he, like Zuleeka, had changed much in the last ten years.

"Gods, Kiva, you have no idea how much I missed you," Tor said, using one hand to wipe her tears before tilting her chin and examining the bruise on her temple. His handsome features hardened as he asked in a lethal voice, "Who did this?"

"It's just a little bump," Zuleeka said dismissively, before Kiva could answer. "There was some trouble separating her from her friends, and with the festival being so crowded, things got out of hand. But look at her — she's fine."

As much as Kiva wanted to see the brutish Borin reprimanded, she sensed it was more important to talk her brother down, so she placed her hand over his on the unhurt side of her face and said, "Don't worry, I've had worse."

It was the wrong thing to say, his emerald eyes filling with shadows as he realized why — and where — she'd felt such pain.

His throat bobbed, the anger bleeding out of him as he whispered in a rough voice, "I almost had you."

Seeing his anguish, Kiva uttered a confused, "Sorry?"

"We were so close," he continued, his gaze unfocused, his mind a thousand miles away. "My best fighters were with me, all of us ready to do whatever it took to get you and Mother out."

Kiva sucked in a breath, suddenly understanding.

"We were hiding in the mountains, taunting the Warden and his guards," Torell went on. "We feigned a rescue, prompting him to double his sentries. It was a distraction, something to keep them busy so they wouldn't notice our true intentions."

Kiva remembered—she'd been walking through the refectory the night before her second Trial and had overheard a group of prisoners talking about the rebels' failed rescue attempt. But . . . if Tor was saying it *hadn't* failed, that it had just been an act . . .

"Everything was in place," he said, sounding hollow now. "We were all set to strike, but then—"

"Then I sent an order for them to stand down," Zuleeka interrupted. She eyed Kiva warily as if making a decision, then nodded to herself and shared, much more openly than before, "As general of the rebel forces, Tor has the same level of authority as I do, but since Mother named me interim commander before she left for Zalindov, it does no one any good to see us challenging each other. I left him little choice but to withdraw, even if he wasn't happy about it."

That seemed like an understatement, given the haunted look on Tor's face.

"Did you say Mother *left* for Zalindov?" The word tasted strange on Kiva's tongue, the implication that Tilda had willingly chosen imprisonment. "Wasn't she—Wasn't she captured? In Mirraven?"

Before anyone could reply, three loud knocks sounded on the ceiling above their heads, prompting dust and plaster to rain down on them.

"We're running out of time," Zuleeka said, brushing white speckles from her leathery clothes. "Seems your *friends* have better tracking skills than I anticipated."

Kiva ignored the sneer in her tone—just as she ignored how it felt to know that Jaren and Naari were on their way. *They* hadn't waited ten years to try and rescue her.

"You need to answer me," she said, her voice trembling slightly. "I need to know——"

"There's a lot you need to know," Zuleeka said, and while the words were taunting, her face was serious. "But you're going to have to wait."

Tor sighed, giving Kiva's shoulders a comforting squeeze. "Zulee's right. I've heard about the company you keep these days——we need to be well and truly gone before they arrive."

Kiva braced herself for more of the accusations Zuleeka had slung at her, but Torell only grinned and added, "Befriending the crown prince and his Golden Shield? Very clever. I can't think of a more effective way to gain privileged information."

Though his words were full of praise, there was something in his eyes that Kiva couldn't identify. It wasn't judgment or suspicion or anything remotely similar to how Zuleeka had looked at her. But something about it tugged at Kiva, almost like she was looking into a mirror. Before she could examine it further, Torell blinked and it was gone.

Another three knocks came from above their heads, followed by one more a moment later.

"Time to go," Zuleeka said, before pointing a finger at Kiva. "Get back in the chair."

Kiva looked at the chair and back to her sister. "Pardon?"

Zuleeka collected the ropes Torell had cut, giving a low whistle. One of the men guarding the door entered the room and took them from her, handing over a fresh set before leaving again.

"Back in the chair," Zuleeka repeated her order. "You were abducted, remember? You have a role to play, so put on your acting boots."

"I——" Kiva didn't know what to say. She'd planned to travel to Oakhollow in search of her siblings the next day, but now there was no need. Zuleeka and Torell were standing before her, the three of them finally reunited. She had so many questions for them, so many things they needed to discuss, which was why she croaked out a confused, "Aren't I coming with you?"

Zuleeka snorted. "You can hardly spy on your prince from the rebel camp."

Kiva stilled.

Dark eyebrows rose as Zuleeka said, "Don't tell me you're surprised. We have people inside the palace already, but Deverick—sorry, *Jaren* —has bigger trust issues than I do. There are things he doesn't even share with the Royal Council, with his *family,* or so my sources claim. But you have his ear. *You* can get to him in a way no one else can, learn things about him, about his plans, about where he's most vulnerable. You can learn his secrets." She paused before finishing, "And then we can use them against him."

Schooling her expression, Kiva said nothing. Jaren *did* trust her— and because of that, she already knew some of his greatest secrets. But for some reason, she held back on revealing anything. Now wasn't the time, she told herself, almost convincingly.

"I hate to say it, but I agree with Zulee," Torell said. "For now, you need to stay here. It's safer for you this way, with them believing you were taken against your will."

His gaze flicked to the bruise on her face, then traveled to the chafed and splintered skin around her wrists, his lips pressing together when he realized she wouldn't have to lie to convince anyone.

Unlike Zuleeka, Tor didn't say more about her spying, nor did he imply that she was only as useful as the information she gleaned. Instead, he wrapped her in another quick hug and whispered, "I'll see you again soon. Promise."

Stepping away, he pulled what appeared to be a silver mask from inside his cloak. Kiva didn't get a good look at it before he turned to Zuleeka and said, "I'll make sure our exit is clear. You finish up here— *gently*—then meet me in the alley. Be ready to run."

Zuleeka gave a short nod, and Torell took off after one final glance at Kiva, silently reassuring her that he would keep his promise.

"Sit," Zuleeka ordered Kiva, and this time she did as she was told.

With hurried motions, Zuleeka bound her with the fresh ropes and pulled the gag up until it covered her mouth once more.

More knocks sounded above them, conveying enough urgency that even Kiva understood her sister would risk discovery by staying any longer.

"Tor doesn't know this, but I've ordered a handful of our people to stay behind, just enough to put up a believable fight," Zuleeka said. She tilted her head to the side and finished, "I'm sorry about this. He told me to be gentle, but this part needs to be believable, too."

Kiva's eyes scrunched with confusion, but then they widened with alarm when her sister unsheathed a dagger and, with no further warning, slammed the pommel into the side of her already injured face. Pain burst anew . . . and then she succumbed to darkness once more.

CHAPTER FOUR

Clashing steel and heavy thumps from the hallway met Kiva's ears as she slowly returned to consciousness. She uttered a quiet whimper, her sister's parting gift feeling like a blade had pierced straight through her brain.

Nausea turned her stomach as the grimy room spun around her, the sensation easing only slightly by the time another loud *thump* came from just beyond the doorway, right before a figure rushed through it.

"Gods, Sweet Cheeks, you're a mess."

Relief and disappointment flooded Kiva at the sight of Jaren's cousin, Prince Caldon, standing before her.

"I know, I know," he said, moving quickly forward and reaching for her bindings, his golden hair shining in the dim light, his broad shoulders casting their own shadows. "You're thrilled to see me. Delighted. Couldn't imagine anyone you'd rather have here in my place. It pains me to say this, Sunshine, but you need to rein in your excitement. It's embarrassing."

Kiva groaned when all the ropes were cut away and he finally removed the gag. Unable to offer even the briefest of warnings, she leaned over the side of the chair — and vomited all over the moldy carpet.

Caldon swore and jumped away, sidestepping behind her to hold back her hair. "Usually people have a different reaction upon seeing me. I'll try not to take offense."

"Sorry," Kiva said weakly, wiping her mouth and pressing a hand to the side of her head, the flesh hot and swollen and throbbing.

"Not your fault," Caldon said, returning to face her. "That's quite the shiner you've got yourself. But don't worry, it only brings out your pretty eyes."

Kiva groaned a second time. "Stop flirting with me, or I'll be sick again."

Caldon raised his arms in surrender, and Kiva's vision finally focused enough to take in the blood splattering his body.

"Are you hurt?" she asked, inspecting him closely.

Caldon snorted. "It'll take more than a few lousy rebels to cause me any real damage." A distant sound had him cocking his head and listening intently, before adding, "But there are others on the way, and since you're more damsel-in-distress-y than usual, we should go."

Kiva was in too much pain to argue about his damsel comment as Caldon carefully helped her to her feet, steadying her until she could hold her own weight.

"You good, Sunshine?" he asked, repeating the nickname he'd come up with during their time at the winter palace, a mockery of her less-than-sunny personality, he'd claimed.

"Good enough," she said, having long since given up on asking him to call her by her actual name—especially when he'd responded that if she didn't like Sunshine, then he could always call her Felon. She'd taken great delight in throwing a toss pillow into his laughing face.

When he'd shared the reason for her other nickname—Sweet Cheeks—she'd thrown something much heavier.

"I wish I could say we'll take it slow, but I try to avoid lying to beautiful women," Caldon said, supporting her with an arm around her waist as they moved toward the door, his other hand clenched around the hilt of his bloodied sword. "We need to get you back to the palace and send word to the others that you're safe."

"Where *are* the others?" Kiva asked as they entered the shabby hallway, the brighter lights making her wince.

"We had to split up," Caldon said, toeing aside the body of a man he'd carved his way through to get to her. She glanced away quickly, partly to ward off memories of the last time she'd seen such violence — the bloodthirsty prison riot — and partly because the dead man had been ordered by Zuleeka to remain behind, giving his life for the rebel cause. Her *family's* cause.

"Your abductors were clever," Caldon went on. "They laid a number of false trails, making it hard for us to pinpoint which direction they'd really taken you, especially amid the festival chaos. Jaren and Naari took the eastern side of the city, Captain Veris and a contingent of guards are covering the south and north, and I came west." He sent her a cocky grin. "I've always been the better tracker. You're welcome, by the way."

"We're not out of here yet," Kiva said. Remembering the role she had to play, she added, "And it'd be nice to know why they took me to begin with."

"They didn't say anything?" Caldon asked dubiously as he pulled her into a large, high-ceilinged room that looked like it had once been a kitchen.

"I only woke up seconds before you came through the door," Kiva said. It wasn't a lie, even if it wasn't the whole truth. She continued playing her part, asking, "You mentioned before that it was the rebels — what would they want with me?"

Caldon's cobalt eyes flashed and his jaw tightened, but he relaxed it to say, "Your guess is as good as mine, Sweet Cheeks." He reached across and tapped her nose with his sword hand. "But I think it's safe to assume you're just very tasty bait for a much larger fish."

Kiva swatted at his arm, but he'd already moved it back to his side, his body tensing as he brought them to a quick halt. His gaze narrowed in the direction of the door at the far end of the kitchen, his attention on something beyond Kiva's senses.

"What——"

Caldon shoved a hand over her mouth and pushed her behind a freestanding bench in the middle of the run-down room.

"Quiet," he hissed, tugging her into a crouch. "We've got company."

Zuleeka had said she was leaving a handful of people behind, but Kiva had assumed Caldon had already seen to those. Just how many more would have to fight—and *die*—to make this ruse believable?

"Seems our luck has run out," Caldon said, unsheathing a second sword for himself along with a sharp dagger, which he held out to Kiva. "Do you know how to use this?"

Kiva grasped the pommel awkwardly between her thumb and fore-finger. "I, um . . . maybe?"

Caldon muttered something under his breath that sounded a lot like, "Gods spare me."

"Believe it or not," Kiva said defensively, "they didn't teach us how to handle weapons *in prison*."

The prince huffed with amusement before a noise in the next room caused a rare seriousness to overtake his features.

Grabbing her hand, he repositioned her fingers around the hilt, closed them tightly, and whispered, "If things get heated, run and hide, and I'll find you afterward. Only use this"—he indicated the blade—"if absolutely necessary. But whatever you do, don't stab yourself. Jaren will kill me." As an afterthought, he added, "Don't stab me either, obvi-ously."

Kiva sent him a bland look and didn't bother to confirm that she had no intention of stabbing *anyone*.

"By the sounds of it, there's half a dozen of them waiting for us, maybe a few more," he said, listening for something only he could hear.

"Can't we go another way?" Kiva asked.

"They'll have more people watching the back," Caldon said. "The front door is right through this next room, which makes it our easiest path out." He ruffled her hair. "Don't worry, Sunshine. Half a dozen is nothing. I'll keep you safe."

Caldon might have been an incorrigible flirt, but something Kiva had learned in the last six weeks was that he wasn't a spoiled prince who sat around playing courtier all day — even if, for reasons she'd yet to uncover, he made it so people believed that was true. His weapons weren't for decoration; she'd seen him training with Jaren at the winter palace, the two of them sparring with lightning-fast speed, strength, and skill. Kiva believed Caldon when he said he would keep her safe, but it wasn't *her* life she was worried about. Those were rebels he was about to fight a path through, all so she could keep up her ruse.

"Do me a favor and try not to puke again," Caldon said, gripping his swords and rising from his crouch. "With you behind me, I'll be right in your trajectory. You'll ruin my outfit."

His fitted green jacket was already speckled with blood, the silver embroidery now a rusty red, so she knew he was only speaking in an effort to keep her calm.

Bracing herself for what was about to happen, Kiva hurried forward with Caldon, but they barely made it halfway to the next room before the rebel group flew into the kitchen with raucous yells, their weapons held high.

Caldon cursed and shoved Kiva back, swinging his two swords to meet their attackers strike for strike. It wasn't like when she'd watched him practicing with Jaren. That had been almost beautiful, with calculated, nimble steps. This was different; it was messy and chaotic, with an underlying fury coming from the rebels, and a cold calmness emanating from the warrior prince.

The first rebel fell before Kiva had even regained her balance, the second was down before she'd raised her dagger uselessly in the air. She was a healer, her sole mission in life to help people, not hurt them. But she didn't know how much Zuleeka had told these rebels—whether they knew she was one of them, or if they believed she was the enemy.

Caldon dispatched the third and fourth attackers with ease, his blades blurring as he ducked and parried in quick succession. Five more rebels ran through the doorway, three of whom went straight for the prince, but the last two burly men bypassed the skirmish, their eyes locked on Kiva.

She backed away, clutching her dagger tight enough to make her fingers hurt. The men prowled toward her, licking their lips and sharing meaningful glances, dark anticipation spreading across their faces.

"I think we'll have some fun with you," the one in the lead said, his accent marking him as a native of Mirraven. Kiva had heard the rebels were recruiting from outside of Evalon, but seeing the evidence came as a surprise. "Don't worry, poppet. We'll show you a good time."

Bile rose within Kiva at the lecherous look on their faces, at the mirth touching their eyes as they took in her pathetic figure. Her dagger trembled, but she kept it aloft, her knuckles turning white around the pommel.

A quick glance revealed that Caldon still faced two opponents, both more skilled than those littering the moldy floor, demanding his full attention. But that didn't keep him from peering back toward Kiva and noting the large men stalking her way.

"What are you waiting for?" he yelled, blocking an overhead swipe that would have split his skull in two. *"Run!"*

The command unfroze her brain, prompting her to turn and flee from the kitchen. She sprinted down the hallway in search of a hiding place, two pairs of heavy footfalls chasing after her. The pain in her head was secondary to the panicked awareness that she was in no condition to fight *anyone,* let alone her hulking pursuers. She couldn't reveal who she was with Caldon so close, but she stood no chance if they—

There. An open door, halfway down the hall.

Kiva ran straight through it and into a dark room lit by a sliver of moonlight peeking through a filthy window. Seeing no other exit, she slammed the door shut and slid the bolt into place, praying the lock would hold.

The doorknob rattled, a heavy *thump* sounding as one of the men shoved his weight against it.

"You really think this will stop us, poppet?" he called, the hinges groaning.

His next shove had enough force to crack a line through the rotten wood. Kiva leapt forward to brace her body against it, her heart hammering and her grip on the dagger tightening as she realized she had mere seconds before the door failed entirely.

The loudest *thump* yet echoed in her ears, followed by a muted oath and a *thud* that had the very walls shuddering, and she knew the time had come. There was no way for her to communicate that she was on their side, nor would they believe her if she tried. She had only one choice: she had to fight.

A solid boot smashed into the door, splintering the wood around the bolt, and another kick thrust it open, sending Kiva flying. Not allowing herself to hesitate, she spun and roared into the face of the figure bearing down on her in the darkness, slashing out blindly with her dagger and feeling a sickening lurch when the blade sank through flesh.

"Dammit, Kiva, *what the hell?*"

In less than a second she was disarmed and yanked roughly back into the brighter hallway, only to see Caldon glaring furiously at her, a hand pressed to his bleeding shoulder.

"I told you not to stab me," he said angrily. "You had *one job.*"

"Caldon," she gasped, automatically reaching toward his wound. "I'm so sorry. I—"

She inhaled sharply and snatched her hands away, shoving them behind her back.

No.

No, no, no.

It was just a trick of her eyes, that was all. Just the adrenaline flooding her veins, just the head wound making her see things — making her see the golden light start to glow from her fingers when she'd reached for the prince.

The golden light of healing magic.

Magic no one could know she wielded.

Especially not a Vallentis prince.

Kiva fisted her hands so hard that her nails pricked her skin, daring to look up and meet Caldon's gaze. A relieved breath whooshed out of her when she found him scowling at his wound, offering no indication that he'd seen anything strange.

"Are you all right?" Kiva asked feebly.

Caldon's cobalt eyes speared hers. *"This"* — he indicated his shoulder — "is not how you make friends. And it's definitely not how you keep them."

"I'm sorry," Kiva repeated, her voice thick with regret. She kept her hands behind her back, even if her healer instincts urged her to inspect his injury. "I thought you were —"

"I know what you thought," Caldon said, jerking his chin toward the two men on the ground. At the paling of her face, he sighed and visibly shook off his anger, holding out his hand. "Come on, let's get you out of here."

Kiva stared at his palm, her chest tightening with renewed fear.

Caldon's features softened, misinterpreting her reaction. "You're safe now, I promise." He wiggled his fingers, and Kiva had no choice but to unfist her hands, breathing another quiet sound of relief at finding them perfectly normal.

Maybe she'd imagined the glow, after all.

But . . . she couldn't ignore the sense of power thrumming just beneath her skin, an electric, addictive feeling begging for release. It took all of her strength to bury it deep down, forcing the tingling sensation to fade. Only then did she risk taking Caldon's hand, his grip strong and steady as they set off down the hallway again and out into the night.

CHAPTER FIVE

After exiting the dilapidated building, Caldon led Kiva through a narrow alleyway, his hand still entwined with hers. There was nothing romantic about his hold, but rather it was like he was lending her his strength, his reminder that she was safe with him.

"Thank you," Kiva said quietly. "For coming to get me."

"By 'get you,' I assume you mean 'save your ass,'" he muttered, turning them down a dark side street. "You owe me a new jacket, by the way."

"I didn't throw up on you," Kiva defended.

"No, you just *stabbed* me," he shot back. "There's a hole two inches wide, right through the embroidery. It's completely ruined."

Kiva bit her lip, since it wasn't just the fabric that was damaged. "Are you in a lot of pain?"

Registering her concern, Caldon dropped his attitude. "It's just a flesh wound, Sunshine," he said in a soothing voice. "You barely scratched me."

She knew he was lying—she'd *felt* the blade sink into his flesh—but she was grateful for the reassuring look he sent her.

They turned down another side street, this one brighter than the others, the distant sounds of the River Festival reaching Kiva's ears. She felt like years had passed since she'd witnessed the queen's magic show. Exhaustion flooded her, the increased throbbing of her head making her desperate for a long, hot soak in the palace's massive bathing tubs, after which she would happily sleep for the next three months.

"The rebels did us a favor by dragging you over to this side of the river," Caldon said conversationally. "From here we can take the back entrance into the palace, avoiding the crowds entirely."

Kiva wondered if her sister had planned that, like an ironic gift to ease the blow of everything she'd suffered through that night.

"We're nearly there now," the prince continued. "Are you good to keep going? We can stop and rest if you need a minute?"

Kiva hadn't realized that Caldon had slowed his steps for her. "I'm fine," she said, picking up her pace.

"You have a bump the size of Wenderall on the side of your head," Caldon said dryly. "I'm pretty sure that's the definition of *not fine*."

Kiva grimaced, but returned, "And you're bleeding from multiple wounds. If anyone needs to rest, it's you."

"Just the one wound, actually," Caldon said with a pointed look.

Kiva didn't say anything to that, feeling guilty all over again.

Caldon squeezed her fingers and relented, "You're forgiven, Sunshine. I know you didn't mean it."

He was right. And that, Kiva realized, was a problem. Because Caldon was a Vallentis. Not even her favorite Vallentis, if she was being truthful. And yet, knowing she'd caused him pain made her feel physically ill.

Compassion was a healer's most intrinsic quality, she reminded herself. What she was feeling was normal, a part of her fundamental makeup. But she could control it. She *would* control it. For ten years, all she'd wanted was to seek vengeance on the royal family—*his* family. Nothing would stop her from her mission, least of all herself.

"Home sweet home," Caldon said when they turned the next corner to find the Serin River spread out before them, lapping gently against the stone wall bordering the rear of the palace. Both the eastern and western sides had much more picturesque views from the front—ornamental fences with cast iron gates overlaid with gold—but their backs were more military in appearance, fortified and intimidating, a strong contrast to the welcoming allure of the main entrances.

Caldon's strides didn't falter as he led Kiva straight to where a group of armed guards stood near a wall opening large enough to be used for deliveries and the movements of palace workers.

"Evening," Caldon greeted the sentries.

"Prince Caldon, is everything all right?" a young female guard asked, noting his bloodied appearance.

"Never better," he lied. "Can you send word to the search parties that they can return to the palace? Our little felon is safe and sound."

Kiva not so subtly stomped on his foot.

The woman smiled coyly and offered a breathy, "At once, Your Highness."

To Kiva's shock, Caldon didn't react to the invitation in the guard's eyes, instead bidding the group a good night before tugging Kiva past them and up the narrow gravel road toward the palace.

"I'm surprised you didn't flirt with her," Kiva couldn't resist saying as they trudged along the path. Freestanding luminium beacons lit their way, the manicured gardens beyond looking like an enchanted parkland under the soft light of the moon.

"Careful, judgy," Caldon said, swinging their hands like children, "or I'll think you're jealous."

Grinning, Kiva shook her head and replied, "Keep dreaming, *Your Highness.*" There was no mistaking her mocking tone as she copied the guard's breathy words.

Humor lit Caldon's eyes. "I think my cousin underestimates you."

That was exactly what Kiva was counting on.

And it was also something that made her insides roil unpleasantly.

Reaching the end of the path, Caldon guided Kiva into the western palace, a place she'd yet to set foot in, the residence of the king and queen. They'd barely stepped through the back entrance before a servant appeared, bobbed into a curtsey, and informed Caldon that his aunt was waiting for them in the River Room.

His aunt—Queen Ariana.

Nerves bubbled in Kiva's stomach as Caldon shuffled her down a long hallway peppered with artwork that she barely paid any attention to, nor did she notice the gold finishing on the walls, the white marble floor, the sweeping staircases lined with red carpet. All of it she'd already seen in the eastern half of the palace, both sides equal in grandeur. Just as she'd already seen the River Room on the opposite side of the Serin. It was her favorite room, small enough to be intimate, but with floor-to-ceiling windows that looked straight out over the water and into the city beyond.

Upon arriving in the western River Room, Kiva saw it was identical to its eastern counterpart, right down to the elegant luminium chandelier dangling at the heart of the inviting space. The only difference was who sat on the comfortable plush lounge awaiting their arrival.

Kiva sucked in a breath at her first close look at Evalon's ruling monarch.

With golden hair coifed perfectly atop her head and eyes like shining sapphires, there was no denying the queen's beauty. But what brought Kiva up short was the look on Ariana's face as she moved quickly toward them, the relief, the warmth, the *kindness*. Her expression radiated genuine concern as she took in the wound on Kiva's head, the blood on Caldon's clothes, and she didn't waste a second before asking a lingering servant to call for a healer. Only then did she reach out her hands—but not to her nephew. Instead, she drew Kiva away from Caldon, giving her fingers a squeeze of comfort and saying, "I'm so glad you're safe, Kiva. Please, come and sit. I can't imagine what you've been through tonight."

"What about me?" Caldon asked with fake affront. "Your favorite nephew is standing here, bleeding freely. Just in case you didn't notice."

"Favorite nephew?" Ariana arched a golden brow. "Who's been lying to you?"

Caldon laughed. "That's just mean."

The queen's face gentled—even more, if that were possible. She released one of Kiva's hands so she could touch Caldon's cheek, heedless of the dried blood that speckled his flesh. "Thank you for finding her, darling. As always, you make me proud."

"That's more like it," Caldon said, satisfied.

Something was happening inside Kiva, something she didn't understand. *None* of this was what she had expected upon meeting the near mythical Ariana Vallentis. The Queen of Evalon was supposed to be haughty and cold, vicious and unforgiving. She was the face in Kiva's nightmares, the person responsible for all of her family's suffering.

But Ariana was nothing like what Kiva had imagined. Even with Jaren's warning in the back of her mind, how his mother's angeldust addiction had resulted in untold abuse over the years, none of that added up to the person standing before her with bare feet and kind eyes.

"I have hot cocoa on the way," Ariana said, turning back to Kiva. "And we have fresh blueberry muffins already waiting." Another squeeze of her soft hands. "Let's get you off your feet and resting until the healer arrives to take a look at that nasty bump."

Kiva moved stiffly as the queen led her deeper into the room, her mind struggling to comprehend Ariana's reaction to their meeting. The queen knew exactly who Kiva was—and where she'd come from. Surely Ariana couldn't be so accepting of an escaped criminal, even if Kiva had earned her freedom. No monarch would want an ex-felon living in their home, and they definitely wouldn't want one befriending their children, their *heir*. And yet . . . there was no mistaking how genuine the queen's expression was as she smiled at Kiva before turning her attention to her nephew.

"Caldon, be a dear and try not to get blood on the lounge," Ariana said over her shoulder. "Last time the servants had to replace the upholstery, and I'm rather fond of this fabric."

Caldon uttered a dry reply that Kiva didn't hear, too numb to what was happening. That feeling only grew when she rounded the side of one couch to see Tipp curled up in a ball, snoring softly.

Ariana reached down to run her fingers through his glossy red hair, quietly telling Kiva, "The poor darling was so distressed that we had to give him a moradine tonic to keep him from joining the search parties. I couldn't bear to move him, not until you'd had a chance to see him and know he was all right."

Kiva's heart clutched. She hated that Tipp had been so afraid for her, and was reluctantly grateful for the queen's intervention. Moradine was a strong sedative, prompting a swift and dreamless sleep. The young boy would likely be out until morning.

Not wanting to disturb him, Kiva followed the queen toward a second lounge, where a tray of food was waiting. Her stomach rumbled as Ariana prepared a muffin for her, loading it with cream before handing it over.

Seeing the Queen of Evalon wait on her like a servant, Kiva's mind blanked of thought, leaving her with nothing to do but raise the muffin to her mouth as Ariana began questioning Caldon about how he'd found her. They were interrupted partway through by the arrival of a young woman, perhaps a year or two older than Kiva, dressed in the familiar white robe of a Silverthorn healer.

"Your Majesty," she said, offering a respectful curtsey. Her pale skin had a rosy glow to it, and while her features were too sharp to be considered classically beautiful, her heart-shaped face, russet-colored eyes, and ashy blond hair pulled back into a messy bun were captivating enough to make Caldon watch her with keen interest.

"Thank you for coming so quickly," Ariana said, standing and beckoning the healer closer. "I know it's late."

"A healer never sleeps," the young woman said amicably, her smile lighting up the room. She glanced from Caldon to Kiva, before she made a clucking sound with her tongue. "Looks like we had too much fun at the festival."

"Not enough fun, if you ask me," Caldon said, leaning back and sending her a lazy grin full of promise. "But there's plenty of night left."

Kiva fought to control her gag reflex. She pulled a face at Caldon when the healer opened her medical bag, causing his eyes to light with amusement.

"I'm Rhessinda Lorin," the young woman said. Her gaze locked with Kiva's as she added, "Friends call me Rhess."

"Lovely to meet you, Rhess," Caldon said, all but purring her name. Kiva wasn't sure whether to laugh or groan, her respect for the healer growing when she seemed oblivious to the prince's attention and instead focused on pulling out her supplies.

"Who wants to go first?" Rhessinda asked.

"She does," Caldon said, and Kiva didn't have the energy to argue as the healer took the seat vacated by Ariana, who hovered but kept her distance so as to not smother them.

Rhessinda tipped Kiva's face toward the light and prodded at the bump. "Can you tell me your name?"

"Kiva."

"Age?"

"Seventeen."

"What day is it?"

"Friday."

"Favorite color?"

Rhessinda's questions continued until she was satisfied, after which she withdrew a handheld luminium torch and shone it straight into Kiva's eyes, causing her to hiss and jerk away.

"Ouch," Rhess said. "That looked painful."

Kiva shot her a look, and then transferred it to Caldon when he coughed, failing to hide his humor.

"You have a nasty concussion, but I don't think we need to worry about anything more serious," Rhessinda declared, dabbing on some aloeweed gel to help with the inflammation, her callused fingers scratching slightly against Kiva's sensitive skin. "I'll leave you something for the pain, so you should be feeling a lot better by morning. If your discomfort grows or you start to have problems with vision, balance, nausea, and the like, send word to Silverthorn."

Kiva nodded her understanding, knowing enough about head injuries to not need—or want—further mollycoddling.

"Your turn," Rhess said, relocating to sit beside Caldon. "Clothes off, if you please."

"I thought you'd never ask," Caldon drawled, flexing his muscles as he removed both his green jacket and white shirt, leaving him wearing only dark pants and a pair of boots.

Once again, his attempted seduction flew straight over Rhessinda's head—as did his impressive body being on display—with her focus being solely on her task. Kiva leaned forward to look at his injury, distracted for a moment by the other scars lacing his torso, one in particular looking as if someone had tried very hard to gut him. But then she shifted her gaze to the fresh stab wound near his shoulder, the flesh around it puffy and red, the blood already clotted. Some disinfecting and a few stitches, and he would be fine.

Rhess reached the same conclusion, unstoppering a vial as she said, "This isn't too bad."

Kiva breathed easier at the confirmation, but then her attention was diverted by quick footsteps and low voices heralding the arrival of a small group of guards bursting through the doors to the River Room. In their lead was Jaren, the look of relief on his face when he caught sight of Kiva making her stomach flip in an undeniably pleasant way.

With long strides eating up the space between them, Jaren reached her just as she stood to greet him and drew her straight into his arms.

"I was so worried," he whispered.

Kiva knew she should push him away, but try as she might, she simply couldn't do it. Instead, she returned his embrace, wishing she felt repulsed or disgusted — anything other than protected and cherished.

"I'm all right," she said quietly.

He leaned back enough to see her face, his gaze landing on her head wound, his expression tightening.

"It's just a little bump," she said quickly. "I can barely feel it."

Caldon snorted, drawing Jaren's eyes, and shared with brutal honesty, "It's actually a concussion bad enough to make her pass out, puke her guts up, and struggle to stand on her own, with even the dimmest of lights causing her acute agony." The prince shrugged his uninjured shoulder. "But, sure, *it's just a little bump.*"

At the tension refilling Jaren's body, Kiva hissed at Caldon, "Would you shut up? You're not helping."

Amusement flittered across Caldon's face, but it turned into a wince when Rhess dabbed his wound with silverseed oil, a bitter antiseptic smell flooding the room.

"What happened to you?" Jaren asked his cousin.

With a sly look at Kiva, Caldon answered, "Your girlfriend stabbed me."

Kiva flushed as everyone turned to her — the guards, the royals, and the healer. "It was an accident," she said, ignoring the girlfriend remark entirely. Frowning at Caldon, she warned, "But at this rate, the next time won't be."

The cocky prince grinned widely, and Jaren's chuckle sounded in Kiva's ear, prompting her to turn back and see the humor lighting his eyes.

Distance — she needed to put some distance between them. It was the only way she'd survive all that was coming.

Clearing her throat and stepping out of his arms, Kiva glanced over at the new arrivals. Naari was there, showing vivid relief at seeing Kiva safe. Behind her stood a handful of Royal Guards and Captain Veris, the latter of whom Kiva had been introduced to during her first Trial at Zalindov, though in reality she'd met him ten years earlier. It was hard for her to look at him now, part of her fearing he might suddenly recognize her, and the other part unable to repress the memories of that horrific winter's night when her life had changed forever.

"Well," the queen said loudly, smiling benevolently at the guards. "What an evening we've all had. Thank you for your help in searching for our guest—we're all very grateful."

Her dismissal was kind but clear. In response, Veris gave a respectful dip of his head and ushered his troops back out the door. No doubt he would receive a full report later, but Kiva was thankful the queen was limiting her own involvement in that.

With the guards gone, Jaren, Naari, and Ariana waited for Rhessinda to leave before asking any questions. Sensing their impatience, the healer finished her sutures quickly and covered Caldon's wound with a bandage, declaring her work done. On her way out of the room, she handed Kiva a small vial of poppymilk, warning her to awaken every few hours during the night and send for help if needed.

Alone with the royals and Naari—and the still-sleeping Tipp— Kiva had little choice but to share the events of her night, starting with how she'd been knocked unconscious in the middle of the festival crowd, leaving out the middle part with her siblings, and ending with Caldon's rescue, the prince chiming in with his own details.

When she was done, her audience began debating what the rebels had sought to achieve with their abduction. Caldon offered some interesting—and incorrect—theories, stating that it might not have been *just* rebels and claiming to be concerned by the presence of Mirravens during the final attack. Jaren then reminded him that the rebels were re-cruiting from other kingdoms, but Caldon remained unconvinced, look-ing to Kiva as if hoping she would jump in and agree with him. But all she could do was shrug and say that she'd been locked away for a decade, so she knew nothing about how the rebels operated.

It wasn't even a lie.

As their conversation continued, Kiva knew Zuleeka and Torell would want to hear thorough details, but the last few hours were swiftly catching up to her enough that she was having trouble keeping her eyes open.

The next thing she knew, gentle fingers were tracing her cheekbone, lulling her from her doze. She blinked awake to find Jaren crouching beside where she'd unconsciously curled up on the couch.

"Time for bed," he whispered.

Kiva didn't push him away when he helped her up to her feet, nor did she argue when he handed her the vial of poppymilk. She swallowed it in one go, knowing she'd have just enough time to return to the eastern side of the palace and fall into bed before it took effect.

"We'll see each other again soon," Queen Ariana told Kiva quietly, kissing her on the cheek.

Kiva was so groggy that she didn't panic at the show of affection from her sworn enemy, instead mumbling, "Good night," and watching blearily as Jaren gathered Tipp into his arms.

"Come on, Sunshine, let's get you to your room before one of us has to carry you across the river," Caldon said, nudging Kiva toward the door.

Barely able to walk in a straight line, Kiva paid little attention to what Caldon continued saying as he led the way through the palace halls toward the private bridge. But she did wake up just enough to hear him state, "And just in case you missed it earlier, I'm dragging you to the training yard at dawn to work on your nonexistent fighting skills. Next time you hold a blade, I don't plan on becoming collateral damage."

Anything he said after that was lost as the poppymilk took hold, the rest of the walk a blur, until Kiva finally collapsed onto her bed fully clothed and fell instantly back to sleep.

CHAPTER SIX

The next morning, Kiva was rudely awakened. *Twice.*

The first was when Tipp burst into her room, his panic only easing upon seeing she was all right. Kiva murmured something comforting before tugging him onto her bed and telling him to go back to sleep.

Her next awakening was much less pleasant.

"Wakey, wakey, Sunshine," Caldon's voice came from beside her ear.

"Go 'way," she mumbled sleepily.

"No can do, Sweet Cheeks. It's time to get you fighting fit."

He prodded her shoulder, and Kiva swatted at him. As her consciousness returned, she began to recall what he'd said before the poppymilk had kicked in hours ago, something about her working with him in the training yard.

Her eyes shot open to see his smirking face.

"I didn't agree to anything," she said.

"I didn't give you a choice."

And then he was yanking her out of bed and away from the still-snoring Tipp, who was hugging one of Kiva's pillows, oblivious to everything around him.

"You've got five minutes to get dressed," Caldon said. "If I have to come back in, I won't knock first. Feel free not to have any clothes on."

Kiva tried to hit him with a cushion, but he ducked out of the way, laughing as he left her room.

As much as she wanted to go back to sleep, Kiva decided not to risk the obnoxious prince storming in to dress her himself. Instead, she stumbled to her wardrobe, her vision limited because dawn was barely peeking through her balcony overlooking the Serin River.

Groaning at the early hour, Kiva tried to be grateful that her head, at least, was no longer pounding, the deep slumber having done her a world of good.

She quickly rifled through her clothes, some having been loaned by Princess Mirryn at the winter palace, and more having been waiting upon her arrival in Vallenia. It had been strange at first, wearing anything other than her gray prison tunic. For too long she'd been denied the luxury of choosing her own clothes; even after six weeks of doing so, she still cherished such freedom. But with Caldon's warning ringing in her ears, she didn't dally, grabbing a pair of leggings and a loose beige sweater, figuring the basic outfit would serve her best.

Hurrying to her private bathroom—another luxury, particularly the hot running water—she went about her business, admiring the gold and pearl tones of the room. Her bedroom had the same color scheme, as did the rest of the palace, all of it elegant, classy, and peaceful.

After splashing water onto her face, Kiva grabbed a pair of boots and left her bedroom, moving into the sitting room at the center of her suite. The space was simple but comfortable, with large windows looking out at the river, a door opposite her room leading straight into Tipp's bedroom, and another door opening into the palace hallway.

"That was six minutes," Caldon drawled from the couch. "I'm adding a minute to your training."

"About this 'training'—" Kiva started.

"Nope," Caldon interrupted, jumping up and shooing her toward the door. "It's already decided. I get you first thing every morning, rain, hail, or shine. No arguments."

While Kiva had no desire to partake in whatever he had planned, she also knew it was something she shouldn't miss, especially since she was meant to be gathering information. Zuleeka and Torell would have her hide if they learned she'd let this opportunity pass her by. Zuleeka, especially.

The palace was large enough that it took Kiva and Caldon some time to reach the ground floor, after which they stepped outside and kept a brisk pace to ward off the cool morning air. Caldon hummed merrily under his breath as they approached the barracks, an impressive compound with sleeping quarters for the guards, a mess hall, a small infirmary, a stable, an armory, and even a weapons forge complete with on-site blacksmith. At the very center stood the expansive training yard, the grassy area sweeping out beyond the barracks and deeper into the palace grounds.

As they approached the training yard, Kiva marveled at how many people were already out practicing unarmed combat, swordplay, archery, dagger throwing, and countless other lethal practices.

Naari was, for once, not watching Jaren like a hawk, and instead was shooting arrows into targets an impossible distance away, one after the other, reloading her bow so fast that her hands were a blur.

Jaren was also in the yard, his sweat-slicked shirt indicating he'd been there for some time. Only six weeks earlier, he'd barely been able to *move*, let alone spar with anyone, but their extended stay at the winter palace had healed all the injuries he'd sustained inside the prison. His quick, powerful movements showed just how swiftly he'd returned to health, with him currently facing off in a robust clash of swords against the formidable Captain Veris.

Kiva couldn't keep her eyes off the crown prince. There was just something so compelling about him, something so addictive about watching the way he moved, the graceful, strong lines of his body, the intense focus, the perfect—

"You've got a little drool happening. Right there."

Kiva shoved Caldon's hand away and scowled at him. Attempting to cover her embarrassment, she grumbled, "Why are so many people up at this ungodly hour?"

"This may come as a shock, but there's an entire world of people who start their day before eight a.m.," Caldon commented dryly. Nudging her forward, he added, "I think it's best if we keep a certain someone out of your direct line of sight, or we'll never get anything done."

Kiva remained silent, trying to keep some small shred of dignity intact.

Leading her to the far side of the training yard, Caldon finally came to a stop at an empty space near the corner and said, "Wait here, I'll be back."

He took off, leaving Kiva to watch a group of guards sparring close enough for her to marvel at their quick, daring moves. The sight catapulted her back to the bloodthirsty riot in Zalindov, where the inmates had taken up arms against the prison guards. Their laboring tools had been used as weapons; unwieldy pickaxes, hammers, and chisels fighting against much more lethal blades. Even now, Kiva could picture it vividly, her palms turning clammy as she recalled the screams, the blood, the *death*.

Sucking in a breath, Kiva wiped her hands on her leggings and willed her heartbeat to settle. She'd only just managed to calm down when Caldon came up behind her and dropped a wooden box on the ground, causing her to jump, her pulse racing anew.

The prince cocked an eyebrow at her overreaction, but then his features softened as he took in her pale face, as if he understood what memories were battling for her attention. To her relief, he didn't comment on it, only saying, "Let's start with some stretches."

After completing a set of exercises to loosen her muscles, Kiva looked at the nearest pair of guards, their clashing swords screeching with each strike, and asked, "Is that what we'll be doing?"

Caldon threw back his head and laughed. "You're crazy if you think I'm letting you anywhere *near* a blade anytime soon."

Kiva crossed her arms.

His chuckles waning, Caldon said, "I need to see what I'm working with here. Stand up as straight as you can."

She did as ordered, his eyes trailing down her body, but not in his usual flirtatious way. There was a seriousness about him, enough for Kiva to realize this was important to him — the art of training, and the discipline required for it.

"It's worse than I feared," Caldon muttered.

"Excuse me?"

"Are you sure you're standing up straight?"

"Of course I'm —"

"May I?" Caldon didn't wait for her permission before he pushed her shoulders back, kicked her legs apart, braced her spine, and tilted her chin up. "Better," he said. "Now hold that position."

Barely seconds passed before her shoulders began to curl inward and her chin drifted down, neither of which she would have noticed if Caldon hadn't corrected them. A slight ache began in her lower back, the burn spreading both higher and lower the longer she remained in the one position, her neck beginning to scream.

"What's the point of this?" Kiva asked, gritting her teeth when he pushed her shoulders into place yet again.

"We need to improve your balance and strengthen your core," Caldon said, tapping his sword against her stomach. "You have seventeen years of bad habits to break, but those two are important. There's no point in learning how to do anything more challenging" — he indicated the sparring swordsmen — "until your foundation is in place."

"But I'm just *standing* here."

"The way you stand affects the way you move," he said. "If you can't stand correctly, you'll never move to the best of your ability."

Kiva grumbled under her breath, but in the back of her mind, she saw the logic in what he was saying.

When Caldon called time, Kiva took great effort not to slump over. She ignored the dull ache in her back and neck, instead holding Caldon's amused look and hating that he seemed to know about her physical discomfort anyway.

"Now that you know what your posture *should* be," he said, moving the wooden box closer, "step up."

Wondering if it was some kind of trick, Kiva tentatively did as instructed. The box wasn't very high, but she still felt her muscles tighten with the stretch.

"Now do that again, but hold your straight-backed position," Caldon said.

Kiva repeated her actions, but this time with the correct posture, prompting a burning sensation to ricochet all the way down her body.

"Good," Caldon said. "Again."

And so Kiva did it again.

And again.

And again.

While continuing the mindless task, she tried to glance around the training yard in search of anything her brother or sister would want to know. But she had no idea how to describe the fighting techniques that were being practiced, and soon enough it took all of her concentration just to keep her legs under her as she stepped up and down, over and over again.

Her thighs were on fire, the rest of her body equally inflamed, sweat dripping from places she didn't know *could* sweat, when Caldon finally told her to stop.

"How's that feel?" he asked as she collapsed on top of the box.

"Like I want to murder you," Kiva panted, massaging her legs.

"Perfect," he said. "We're making progress."

She didn't even have the energy to scowl at him.

A water canteen entered her line of sight, and she eagerly grabbed for it.

"Take it easy," Caldon said, pulling it away before she could drain it all. "You'll regret it if you drink too much. We haven't finished yet."

Kiva bit down on a whimper as Caldon tugged her back up to her feet.

"Balance and core strength are important," he said. "But right now, you have no fighting skills, and that won't change overnight. So if something were to happen to you, like, say, if someone tried to abduct you— *again*—then your best bet for staying alive is simple: run away."

Dread began to well within Kiva.

"Your fitness levels are nonexistent thanks to your time in Zalindov, so we need to work on your endurance." A grin stretched across Caldon's face. "If you want to murder me now, just wait to see how you feel after what's next."

Half an hour later, Kiva wondered if *hatred* was too kind a word for how she felt toward Caldon, especially as she vomited for the third time into the bushes bordering the training yard.

"I told you not to drink all that water," he said, not even winded.

"It wasn't the water," she half moaned, half panted. "It was the sadistic asshole of a prince—"

"Language," Caldon tutted.

"—who wouldn't let me stop even when I said I was about to die."

"And yet, here you are, still alive," he said. "How's the head?"

Last night's head wound was the least of Kiva's troubles, the rest of her body screaming after being forced to run around the expansive training yard three times, pausing for only a minute between laps—just long enough for her to expel the contents of her stomach.

Rather than admit how miserable she felt, she turned the question around on Caldon. "How's the shoulder?" she asked, having seen him press a hand to it during their second lap, grimacing as their rapid steps jolted his upper body.

"I've felt better," he admitted.

Kiva moved closer. "Let me see."

Caldon didn't object, shifting his collar until his blood-splattered bandage was revealed.

Pulling back the dressing, Kiva was relieved to find that he hadn't ripped his stitches. She was careful not to touch the raw skin with her unwashed hands, only prodding the swollen edges to check for infection.

"You're fine," she told him. "You'll be tender for a while, but if you keep it clean, you should heal quickly enough."

"It's not my first stab wound, Sunshine, or my worst," Caldon said, reminding her of the older scars she'd seen on his torso last night. "It likely won't be my last, either. I know what I'm in for."

Kiva quashed the alarm she felt and began to rewrap the dressing.

. . . Until her hands started glowing.

No.

Her nausea returned with a vengeance—this time prompted by terror—as Kiva urged the magic away, praying the bright sunshine was enough to keep anyone from noticing. Caldon, thankfully, was focused on a nearby sparring match, unaware of the golden healing light flowing from Kiva's fingertips right under his nose.

No, no, no.

Kiva gritted her teeth against the tingling sensation, her hands trembling as she fought for control over her power. It was an effort of sheer will to keep from panicking as she made herself methodically finish bandaging Caldon's wound, the light fading just in time for his attention to return to her.

"You have the magic touch."

Kiva nearly fainted. "What?" she breathed, heart thundering in her chest.

Caldon rotated his shoulder. "Whatever you did, it's already feeling much better. Thanks, Sunshine."

"I—" Kiva cut herself off, before weakly saying, "I really didn't do much."

In truth, she hadn't done anything *at all*. Nothing mundane, at least. But . . . her magic . . .

Kiva wouldn't think about it, fearing that doing so might encourage the golden light to return.

It was a fluke, she told herself. Last night and today, both unfortunate coincidences, the result of fatigue and stress, and nothing else. For ten years, she'd managed to hide her power. There was no reason to fear that anything had changed, not when —

"How was your first day of training?"

Kiva gave a quiet yelp as Jaren stepped up beside her, even sweatier than when she'd last seen him. Unlike how she felt, he appeared invigorated from his exertions, his hair damp, cheeks flushed, and eyes crystal clear in the morning sunshine.

For once, Kiva wasn't distracted by his appearance, instead studying his face to see if he'd witnessed anything strange on approach. He was looking at her no differently from normal, so she pushed away her magical misgivings, reassuring herself that it was nothing a good night's sleep couldn't fix.

"She gets top marks for staying," Caldon answered Jaren. "But there's definite room for improvement."

He was being generous, Kiva thought, fully aware of how much work she had ahead of her.

"Ready to get out of here?" Jaren asked her.

"You have no idea," she replied, meaning every word.

"Same time tomorrow, Sunshine," Caldon said, unsheathing his sword and, heedless of his injured shoulder, starting off toward where Naari waited with her own weapon ready. He winked back at Kiva and finished, "It'll be the highlight of your day."

She watched him walk away before turning to Jaren and asking, "How close are you two?"

He angled his head to the side. "Why?"

"I'm just wondering how you'd feel if something happened to him," Kiva said. "Like an accident." Quickly, she added, "Hypothetically, of course."

"Of course," Jaren repeated, lips twitching.

Kiva toed the dirt with her boot and mumbled, "Never mind."

Jaren chuckled and began leading the way back toward the barracks. "*Hypothetically*, I'd say he probably deserves whatever misfortune comes his way."

Nodding emphatically, Kiva said, "That's my thinking."

Jaren chuckled again, before sobering. "You don't have to train with him, you know."

"Why *am* I training with him?" Kiva asked. "Why not with you or Naari or . . . or . . . anyone else?"

"It's always better to learn from the best," Jaren answered, guiding her around a pair of guards, one male, the other female, locked in unarmed combat. "Cal's one of the greatest warriors in the kingdom. His mother — my mother's sister — was the general of our armies, his father was the commander of our armadas. His childhood was spent learning the art of fighting and strategic warfare. He's been training since he came out of the womb, which makes him the most qualified to teach you. To teach *anyone*."

Kiva frowned. "Are we talking about the same person?"

Jaren shook his head — not in the negative, but as if he found her amusing. "I know he comes across as, well . . ."

"An arrogant, self-absorbed reprobate?" Kiva supplied helpfully.

"And then some," Jaren said, grinning. "But there's a lot more to my cousin than meets the eye."

Kiva was beginning to realize as much. "Did you say his mother *was* the general? And his father *was* the commander?"

Jaren's lingering humor vanished. "Three years ago, my aunt and uncle took a group of elite soldiers out on a ship to practice a training drill in open waters. Cal was meant to be with them, but he woke up violently ill that morning. His sister, Ashlyn, stayed behind to look after him." Jaren's throat bobbed. "That afternoon, a storm came up out of nowhere. It battered the city so badly that we needed months of repairs afterward, but even so, that was on dry land. My aunt and uncle and their soldiers were still out at sea when the storm hit." He swallowed again. "They never made it back."

Kiva came to a sudden stop at the edge of the training yard. "Are you saying——"

"Cal lost both his parents that day," Jaren confirmed, his expression grim. "He'd been groomed since birth to take over as the general once his mother stepped down, with Ash intended to command the armadas once their father did the same, but neither expected the time to come so soon."

"What happened?" Kiva asked quietly, the sparring noises fading into the background as she focused on Jaren's sad tale.

"My uncle had a number of highly competent people under him, all of whom were capable of overseeing the armadas in his stead. But the armies . . . My aunt was so beloved that her lieutenants struggled to maintain order," Jaren said, looking off into the distance. "Cal and Ash were both overwhelmed by grief, but we all knew one of them would have to take charge. It should have been Cal—that had been the plan all along, what he'd *wanted* all along. But not like that."

Jaren blew out a breath and continued, "He wouldn't do it. *Couldn't* do it. So Ashlyn did. She's only a few years older than him, which made her the youngest appointed general in Evalon's history. But the respect our armies have for her—for both of them—is unparalleled. Men and women would not only fight for her, they'd die for her, knowing she'd give all of herself right there alongside them." More quietly, Jaren admitted, "We would have been in real trouble back then without her."

"Would your armies have disbanded?" Kiva asked, wondering how something so strong could break so easily.

"We never would have let it get that bad," Jaren said. "It was more the timing that was problematic. Three years ago, when all this was happening, was around the time the rebels started to become a real nuisance."

Nuisance—Kiva nearly snorted at the term, doubting Torell or Zuleeka would appreciate it.

"Their attacks grew bolder, to the point that they became openly hostile, causing damage to villages and loss of life to those who stood against them. They were always careful to avoid the larger cities—they still are—but the smaller townships were easy targets. It was . . ." Jaren shook his head. "Well, it was a real mess, honestly. And all the worse because our own forces were disorganized and waiting for a leader to step up. So that's what Ashlyn did."

Openly hostile, causing damage to villages and loss of life . . . Kiva pushed the words away, certain there had to be an explanation. Her brother led the rebels' forces, and Tor wouldn't allow senseless violence without good reason.

"Why didn't Ashlyn use your armies to stop the rebels?" Kiva asked.

"It was too late," Jaren said. "They'd had too much time to gain a foothold and build their following. Years and years of quietly adding to their numbers and spreading out over Evalon and beyond made it impossible to hunt them all down and end their movement entirely. But Ash did what she could to defend against them, protecting our people from the worst of their attacks. Protecting the rebels, too, from themselves. Even if they didn't realize. Or didn't care."

Kiva wondered what her siblings would think of Jaren's words, whether they'd offer a defense. But then a familiar sparring pair caught her eye, and her mind was pulled back to Caldon as she watched him and Naari across the training yard, their swords blurring.

"What happened to him?" Kiva asked quietly.

"Nothing," Jaren answered, just as quietly. "And that's the problem. He's doing nothing with his life; he has no purpose, no direction. Before the accident, all his time was spent training and studying to become the next general, but now he won't even set foot in any of the army camps. And he hasn't seen his sister in three years — not since she took up her position. Whenever Ashlyn comes to Vallenia, Cal always finds an excuse to be elsewhere. It's as if he's avoiding anything that might remind him of their parents."

"But he seems so . . ." Kiva searched for the right word, before settling on, "Carefree."

Jaren said nothing for a long moment, watching his cousin spar with Naari. "Sometimes the people who act like they don't care are really the ones who care the most. They feel so much that it overwhelms them, and to keep from falling apart, they hide behind easy smiles and quick laughter, acting like nothing matters. It's a defense mechanism, a way to protect themselves from the world. A way to keep from getting hurt."

"It's unhealthy," Kiva said, though she was hardly one to judge, given that she'd made an art out of pushing people away in order to protect herself.

"Maybe," Jaren said, turning and indicating for Kiva to follow again. "But people process emotions in different ways. Until Cal is ready to deal with what happened, all we can do is be there for him, no matter how much of a pain in the ass he can sometimes be."

"Sometimes?" Kiva murmured, but the insult was only half-hearted. She hated that the rakish prince had lost his parents so young, relating in ways she wished she couldn't. Equally, she hated that she felt such empathy for him, since it would only make her own mission all the more difficult.

What was *with* these Vallentis princes? Why did they have to pull on her heartstrings so deeply? Why did they have to be so . . . so . . .

Kiva didn't allow herself to finish the thought, slamming the door shut on that part of her mind.

"Truly, though," Jaren said, reclaiming her attention, "I meant what I said earlier—you don't have to train with him if you don't want to. You don't have to train with anyone."

"What do you think I should do?" Kiva asked.

Jaren thought over his answer as he led her through the rest of the barracks and out onto the gravel path. "If something like last night ever happens again, I'd feel more comfortable knowing you can defend yourself, or that you can at least run away to safety," he said. "But this isn't about what I want. What do *you* want?"

That wasn't something Kiva could answer honestly, not to Jaren. Perhaps not even to herself. So all she said was, "I agree."

"So you'll keep training with him?" Jaren asked.

It cost her, but Kiva said, "For now."

"I'm glad," Jaren said, visibly relieved. "If Cal becomes too much, let me know, and I'll have a word with him. I don't want you feeling uncomfortable. Ever."

His words warmed Kiva, but she brushed them aside and said, "I can handle your cousin."

"I know you can," Jaren said, and that warmed Kiva, too. "But the offer stands."

Before she could repeat her sentiment, a male servant approached from the direction of the palace and bowed deeply to Jaren, handing over a note and scurrying away again.

Breaking the wax seal, Jaren skimmed the words before turning to Kiva, his expression unreadable.

"What?" she asked.

"My mother has invited you to brunch."

Kiva blinked and repeated, "What?"

"And the Royal Council would like a word with me," Jaren continued, refolding the note. "So it seems you'll get to eat your weight in pastries while I have to sit in a stuffy underground room listening to a group of people who all think they know better than each other."

Unable to curb her curiosity, Kiva asked, "You meet underground?"

"Security," Jaren said. "Less chance of eavesdroppers when there are no windows."

Kiva would have given anything to spy on that meeting, but she could think of no reason to convince Jaren to let her accompany him, especially with the queen's invitation already extended. Forcing a smile, she said, "It'll be a sacrifice, but I'll see to my duty if you see to yours."

Jaren's mouth quirked. "So noble." He then sighed, his goodwill fading. "I'd planned to take you to the stables and show you the grounds on horseback, but I guess it'll have to wait. As you said—duty calls."

CHAPTER SEVEN

Kiva barely had time to clean up and change clothes before a servant arrived to deliver her across to the western palace's River Room. There she found Queen Ariana reclining on one of the comfortable couches, with Princess Mirryn sitting opposite her. Her trepidation grew at the sight of the princess, knowing that Mirryn could be caring and generous, but her mood could quickly turn cynical and biting.

"Kiva, darling, so wonderful you could join us," Queen Ariana said, rising to greet her with a kiss on her cheek. Mirryn offered a chin dip, smoothing her wine-red dress and watching Kiva take a seat. Ariana also wore a gown, hers a navy blue with complicated beading, making Kiva feel significantly underdressed.

"Thank you for inviting me," she said. "It's an honor to be here."

The queen smiled kindly. "No need to be so polite. You're among friends."

Kiva would have felt more comfortable in a pit of snakes, but she made herself return Ariana's smile.

"I wasn't sure what you'd like to eat, so I had the kitchen prepare a selection for us," the queen said, moving toward the table that was near overflowing with food. "Let me get you a plate."

Uncomfortable at the idea of the queen serving her, just like last night all over again, Kiva fidgeted as Ariana went about her task, humming quietly. There was something so gentle about the queen, so *loving*, that Kiva struggled anew to see her as the villain she'd envisioned for a decade. But she couldn't afford to look at her differently. For all Kiva knew, this was some kind of act. The queen had years of experience learning all the airs and graces that came with her title. No matter how she appeared, there was no telling what lay beneath the caring façade.

An hour later, however, Kiva was having trouble remembering that she was in the company of her enemy, especially since the queen had spent the whole time sharing adorable stories from Jaren's childhood.

". . . and he's been terrified of turtles ever since," Ariana finished her latest tale.

Mirryn snickered into her tea. "It's true," she said. "I was there."

"My fearless son," Ariana said with clear affection. She looked at Kiva and added, "He'll be horrified to know we shared that little piece of history with you."

"My lips are sealed," Kiva promised, her grin genuine.

"No, you should definitely use it to embarrass him sometime," Mirryn stated. "It'll do him good to be taken down a peg or two."

Kiva considered the comment, curious how the princess could say that about her brother. If anything, it was *Mirryn* who could use a good ego deflation.

"You must have some interesting stories about my son," Ariana said to Kiva, refilling her dainty teacup. "Jaren has told us hardly anything about his time in Zalindov. How did you two meet? What was it like in there?"

All the delectable food Kiva had ingested during the last hour turned over in her stomach.

Showing uncharacteristic consideration, Mirryn jumped to her rescue and said, "I'd much rather hear about your abduction last night. I can't believe no one came to get me — I missed hearing all about it."

"I can't believe I forgot to ask," the queen said, concern in her gaze as she peered at the side of Kiva's face. "How's your head feeling today?"

"Much better," Kiva answered.

"Those Silverthorn healers are worth their weight in gold," Ariana said.

"Speaking of gold," Mirryn said, her eyes lighting with passion as she turned to her mother. "I'm thinking blue and gold as the color scheme for my party. What do you think?"

Kiva felt as if she'd missed a step, but the queen was nodding slowly, a thoughtful look on her face.

"I'll tell the decorators," Ariana said. Seeing Kiva's confusion, she shared, "It's Mirry's birthday in just under a fortnight. She's having a masquerade here at the palace to celebrate."

"The weather kept us trapped in the mountains longer than expected," Mirryn told Kiva. "I've been running around like a headless chicken since returning, organizing all the details."

"You haven't *only* been organizing the party," Ariana said with a sly smile. "I hear you've also been staying up until all hours writing letters to this mystery girlfriend of yours. Will we finally get to meet her for your birthday?"

Mirryn brushed crumbs off her lap. "Since she's not answering my missives, and her last one said she thought it best if we break up, I can only assume she won't be coming."

Ariana's face fell. "Oh, Mirry. I'm sorry. I know how happy she made you."

"Only fools find their happiness in others," Mirryn said, her expression hard, but Kiva could see how hurt she was. Ariana saw it as well and moved to sit beside the princess, reaching for her hands.

"Be that as it may," the queen said quietly, "there's someone perfect out there for you, my beautiful daughter. I promise you that."

Mirryn looked away, but not before Kiva saw the sheen of tears in her eyes. "I know," she whispered. "And now I've lost her."

"Darling," Ariana whispered, leaning forward to hug her daughter.

Kiva averted her gaze, fighting the sting of jealousy, of *longing*. It had been over ten years since she'd felt the loving touch of a mother. Seeing

Ariana embrace Mirryn left a tightness in her chest, along with the painful knowledge that she would never have that again.

Mirryn cleared her throat and pulled away, wiping under her eyes and reclaiming her teacup. Not looking at anyone, she declared, "I think we should use Chef Laveau for the catering, but I want the cake to come from Euphorium. Nuru is a master when it comes to flavor and design."

Seeing how much her daughter was struggling with her lost love, Ariana allowed the change of topic and simply said, "I agree. They've both proven themselves highly capable at our past celebrations."

Together, the queen and princess launched back into discussing the masquerade, brainstorming ideas for decorations, music, and menus. Kiva remained mostly silent, resolutely ignoring the sympathy she felt at seeing the sadness lurking in Mirryn's eyes, and answering any questions with whatever she thought the royals wanted to hear. She was just considering how best to remove herself from the discussion when the door to the River Room opened and a burst of activity flew inside.

Two bursts, actually.

Tipp and Oriel, on a break from their studies.

Behind them walked Caldon, Naari, and Jaren, the latter of whom looked particularly good in a black shirt with the sleeves rolled up to his elbows, his corded forearms drawing her shameless attention.

"You're h-here!" Tipp cried, running straight for Kiva and interrupting her blatant staring.

"Tipp," she chided when he bounced onto the couch beside her, "remember your manners."

"Oh, r-right," he said, jumping back up to his feet, before sitting down again much slower.

"That's not what I—" Kiva broke off with a sigh. "Never mind."

Everyone over the age of eleven chuckled, but Kiva's attention was snared by Prince Oriel when he shyly held out a flower—a snowblossom.

"For me?" Kiva asked.

Oriel nodded at the ground, his cheeks pink. "I've been practicing my magic, and Jaren said they're your favorite."

Kiva glanced up to find a soft smile on Jaren's face. She'd only shared her love for the winter-white flowers after they'd escaped Zalindov, during a moment of reflection when she'd considered the one he'd created out of nothing down in the tunnels. To this day, she couldn't remember if she'd favored the blossoms before then, or only afterward.

"It's beautiful," Kiva said to Oriel, inhaling the fresh, sweet aroma, before tucking the stem behind her ear.

The young prince's cheeks turned pinker at her actions.

Wanting to ease his discomfort, Kiva leaned in and whispered, "You know what?"

"What?" he whispered back.

She transferred the blossom to his ear, hiding the stem in his soft golden locks. "I think it looks *much* better on you." She touched the tip of her finger to his nose briefly, causing him to giggle. "Will you keep it safe for me?"

Oriel nodded eagerly, a bashful but still bright grin spreading across his face.

"I want one t-too!" Tipp said, bouncing beside Kiva. "P-Please, Ori?"

The prince scrunched up his face in concentration, and seconds later, an identical snowblossom appeared in his hand. Tipp thanked him profusely and shoved it behind his own ear, beaming with pleasure.

"Now we're t-twins!" he said excitedly.

"And very handsome twins," Queen Ariana said, still seated beside her daughter. "The handsomest in the kingdom with those flowers, I daresay."

"Careful, or you'll make Jaren jealous," Mirryn drawled. There was no trace of sorrow in her eyes now, her emotions firmly locked away. "He's not used to having competition."

"Sure he is," Caldon said cockily, prompting Naari to roll her eyes.

"Here you go, Jaren," Oriel said, creating another snowblossom.

"Thanks, Ori, I love it," Jaren said, ruffling his brother's hair.

"Where's mine?" Caldon asked.

Oriel frowned. "You called Flox fat yesterday. He's not fat—he's fluffy."

Caldon arched an eyebrow. "Your point?"

"I'm not making you anything until you apologize to him."

Oriel's beloved pet chose that moment to bound into the room, a silver and white streak heading straight for Jaren. There, he rubbed up against the prince's legs like a cat before collapsing on top of his boots.

Kiva had met Flox upon her arrival at the River Palace, and after some deep consideration, she still had no idea what kind of creature he was. Part fox, part ferret, part racoon was her best guess, combining to form an unholy bundle of mischief. All she knew was that he had as much energy as Tipp and Oriel, and he was absolutely infatuated with Jaren—not that Kiva could blame him.

"You can keep your flower, kiddo," Caldon said, mouth quirking as he watched Jaren try to extricate himself from Flox, only to have the fluffy creature cling to him with fierce desperation. "And I'll keep my apology."

"As much as we appreciate the company," Queen Ariana cut in, "dare I ask why we've been graced with your presence?"

Her question was addressed to the room, but it was Caldon who answered, "Jaren needs to blow off some steam." He glanced from Ariana to Mirryn and asked, "Do you two have time for a quick trip downstairs? We've already cleared it with Ori's tutor."

The queen's expression grew troubled as she looked at her eldest son. "The council meeting didn't go well?"

"It didn't go at all," Jaren answered tightly. "Grand Master Horeth sent a note postponing until this afternoon." He abandoned his attempt at dislodging Flox and picked up the silver fluffball, cradling his squirming body close until he settled. Within seconds, Flox's eyes closed and he fell into a light doze.

Kiva marveled at the sight, something about it so pure, so *wholesome*.

"I have lots of party planning still to do today, so let's make this quick," Mirryn said, standing and starting toward the door, the queen at her side.

Unsure what was happening, Kiva rose to follow, with Tipp hurrying over to Oriel as the young prince collected Flox from Jaren's arms.

Kiva, however, didn't make it two steps before Caldon's fingers wrapped around her elbow.

"Sorry, Sunshine, but you'll have to entertain yourself for the next little while." His gaze flicked over to Tipp. "You too, bud."

Tipp looked crestfallen.

"It's fine. Let them come," Jaren said.

Ariana and Mirryn paused at the doorway, looking at him with raised brows.

Caldon turned to his cousin, a hint of warning in his eyes. "It's one thing for them—or at least her—to know. Another thing for them to see."

His statement perplexed Kiva. Tipp, too. But no one else in the room batted an eyelash.

"Caldon has a point," the queen said slowly.

Surprisingly, it was Mirryn who came to Kiva's defense. "She's already seen a lot of it. And felt it, for that matter."

"That was different," Caldon objected.

"I trust them," Jaren stated. "If any of you have a problem with that, don't come."

Without another word, he strode out of the room.

"He's in a delightful mood," Mirryn murmured.

"Horeth's note implied the council is going to demand answers for his actions of late," Naari informed them, her lips pinched with disapproval. "He's bracing for an unpleasant afternoon."

The queen's expression shifted to concern as she stared after her son, and neither she nor anyone else offered further arguments against Kiva and Tipp accompanying them. Instead, Ariana hurried after Jaren with Mirryn and Naari at her side, and Oriel and Tipp skipping after them.

Alone with Caldon, Kiva waited to see if he would try and stop her again.

Seeing her hesitation, he shot her an apologetic smile, one that didn't quite reach his eyes. "Sorry about that, Sunshine. I can get protective when it comes to my family."

Kiva recalled Jaren sharing the tragic tale about Caldon's parents, her heart catching painfully in her chest. "I understand. Family is everything." Gods, did she know *that*.

A shadow passed over Caldon's face as he held her compassionate gaze. "Not everything. Not always. Sometimes you're better off letting them go."

His sister. Kiva had nearly forgotten. But she doubted Ashlyn Vallentis supported Caldon's decision to avoid her for the last three years.

"And sometimes you need to hold on tight," Kiva returned, unconsciously thinking of the rocky reunion she'd had with her own sister. She hated the idea of that tension remaining between them forever — or worse, that they'd become like Caldon and Ashlyn, deliberately choosing not to see each other. Troubled by the thought, Kiva resolved that the next time they crossed paths, she would try harder to mend whatever had broken between them. Hopefully Zuleeka would recognize the attempt and meet her halfway.

"We'll have to agree to disagree on that, Sweet Cheeks," Caldon said, brushing aside his melancholy and swinging an arm around her shoulders, dragging her toward the doorway. "Come on. Jaren says it's fine for you to watch us training, so let's get moving before you miss all the good stuff."

Kiva stumbled along with him, her forehead scrunching as she repeated a single word. "Training?"

The only answer Caldon gave was, "Hurry up, and you'll see."

CHAPTER EIGHT

Jaren was waiting for Kiva and Caldon at the end of the corridor, the others now slightly ahead. He remained quiet as they headed down to the ground floor, continuing until they were underground.

With the palace split in half by the Serin, Kiva had questioned its defensibility upon her arrival, but Jaren had claimed it would be nearly impossible for an enemy to take. If one side was invaded, the royal family need only flee to the other using their private bridge. Were that to become compromised, there was an entire network of underground passageways spanning beneath the river to connect the eastern and western residences—which was also how the servants and guards traveled between the two sides at all hours of the day.

Kiva had felt mildly ill at learning how well the palace was fortified, having been forced to acknowledge yet another challenge in the way of her family taking the throne. Until today, she hadn't set foot in the tunnels, merely assuming they would be similar to what lay beneath Zalindov: a dark, claustrophobic spiderweb of passages, many of which were at least partially submerged. But she soon discovered that wasn't the case, instead finding a marble-pillared thoroughfare with a paved stone pathway wide enough to fit three carriages side by side. The tunnel was dry, it was clean, and the countless luminium beacons affixed to the pillars flooded the space with a bright, welcoming light.

"Impressive, huh?" Caldon said, reading Kiva's expression.

She nodded mutely in return, following their small group along the path, mentally mapping every doorway and bylane they passed and intending to return later for further exploration.

When they reached a point near to where Kiva guessed the bank of the river sat above them, they turned off down a narrower passageway, this one much more reminiscent of those at Zalindov. Goose bumps rose on Kiva's flesh as the memories assailed her mind, but she pushed them back and breathed deeply, not allowing fear to take root.

The passage ended at a wooden door with an iron keyhole, but rather than producing a key, Mirryn flicked her fingers in an upward direction. A *whoosh* of wind preceded the rattling sound of a lock turning, before the door sprang open on creaky hinges.

"A-Awesome," Tipp whispered, grinning widely.

Beyond the door lay a staircase cut out of the ground itself, this one again traveling downward, but at a much steeper incline. There were no luminium beacons ahead, the path swallowed into blackness, but no one seemed the slightest bit perturbed, with Mirryn, Jaren, and Caldon all reaching for wooden torches that rested in a basket next to the door. At a wave of Jaren's hand, the torches ignited into three bright flames, flooding the staircase with light.

Kiva repressed her apprehension and followed the group downward. Her thighs were screaming by the time they reached the bottom and entered a damp, earthy-smelling chamber, the burn from her morning exercise making itself known all over again. It only vanished when, with another wave of Jaren's hand, fire shot around the chamber and ignited multiple sconces affixed to the stone walls, revealing a space that took Kiva's breath away.

Before her lay a massive underground river cavern. Rich limestone walls rose high above her head, with long stalactites drooping lazily downward and chubby stalagmites climbing upward from the rocky ground. In the middle of the hollow expanse rested a pool of turquoise water that snaked around a bend and out of sight, the surface still but for a gentle lapping at the craggy edges.

"Whoa!" Tipp breathed as he looked around the cave.

"Welcome to our training space," Caldon said, with a flourishing wave of his arm.

"Training for *what?*" Kiva asked, though she was beginning to guess.

"For our magic," Princess Mirryn answered, confirming Kiva's suspicions.

Jaren placed his flaming torch into an empty sconce and approached Kiva. Making a visible effort to shake off his feelings about the upcoming council meeting, he explained, "Most people assume that since we were born with magic, we automatically know how to use it. And that's partly true. I told you last night that it's like another limb, wholly ingrained into who we are. But in that same way, it's also like a muscle. And like any muscle, we need to strengthen it." He indicated the cavern and went on, "To do that, we need a safe space, hidden from the public." He shuffled his feet. "Or I do, anyway."

Kiva's eyes widened with understanding. Only a handful of people knew that Jaren could control all four elements, so of course he would have to practice in secret. A quiet voice in the back of her mind reminded her that she, too, had magic that worked like a muscle, something she needed to use, stretch, grow, but she ignored the voice, refocusing on Jaren when he turned to Tipp and leaned down until they were eye to eye.

"You're about to see some things, and I need to know you won't tell anyone," he said seriously. "I said earlier that I trust you. Was I right?"

More solemn than Kiva had ever seen him, Tipp nodded and said, "I swear it, J-Jaren. You can c-c-count on me."

"Good man," Jaren said, squeezing Tipp's shoulder. He then stepped closer to Kiva and removed the snowblossom from behind his ear, gently transferring it to hers and saying, "Mind this for me, will you? It's precious."

The way he looked at her made her think he wasn't talking about the flower. His thumb brushed her cheek in the softest of touches—just enough to make her legs wobble — and then he turned and strode deeper into the cavern toward the water's edge.

Without a word, Mirryn, Ariana, and Caldon set off after him, Oriel doing the same but only once he'd shifted the still dozing Flox into Kiva's arms.

Looking down at the softly snoring creature, Kiva shook her head with confusion and moved to follow the royals, but Naari held her back.

"Best we keep our distance," the guard said, motioning to a large flat stone that jutted out in a slight overhang and looked straight down the mild slope to the river.

Taking a seat between Naari and Tipp, Kiva remained silent as she waited to see what was about to unfold. Even Tipp was unusually quiet, though Kiva could feel him buzzing with excitement beside her.

Combing her fingers through Flox's soft coat — and earning a sleepy sound of contentment in response — Kiva found that her pulse was picking up speed, anticipation flooding her veins. She had no idea what she was about to witness, but she had a feeling it was something very few people would ever get to experience.

Down at the riverbank, Jaren's back was to the water, his mother, sister, brother, and cousin all facing him, but keeping a large distance from each other. It was only seeing them standing in such a way that prompted Kiva to realize what they represented. Ariana had control over water magic, Mirryn's strongest power was wind, Oriel was an earth elemental, and Caldon, being born to the Vallentis line through his mother's side, had an affinity toward fire magic.

And then there was Jaren, who held sway over all four of the elements.

"What a-are they —" Tipp's whispered question was cut short when, from one second to the next, the cavern exploded with light.

But not just any light.

Caldon's arms were outstretched like a conductor directing an orchestra as he pointed to the wall sconces spaced around the cave, the flames growing higher until they shot away from the limestone, numerous fireballs soaring through the air—and straight toward Jaren.

The crown prince raised his own hands, the water at his back surging out of the river and enveloping him, snuffing out the inferno as the flames struck.

But then the queen stepped forward and wiggled her fingers, causing even more river water to rise and surround Jaren, pushing what was already there inward until he could barely be seen behind the mountain of liquid.

Kiva clutched Flox tight enough for the creature to give a disgruntled squeak, but she couldn't soothe him, too afraid that she was watching Jaren drown inside the body of water.

It soon became clear, however, that Jaren knew what he was doing. With an outward thrust of his hands, the water erupted, bursting into millions of droplets that splattered his family, all the while revealing that he'd remained untouched by the attack, not a hint of dampness on his body.

And that was when the real battle began.

Mirryn flung out a hand, and Jaren made an *oomph* sound as he was flung violently backwards into the air, but he used his own wind magic to come to a stop over the middle of the river. An ear-splitting sound echoed around the cave before he could return to the bank: a stalactite ripping from high above them at Oriel's command and plummeting like a deadly spear. It didn't faze the still-hovering Jaren, who clapped his hands together, causing it to shatter into limestone dust that fell harmlessly into the water below. But he then saw it for the distraction it was, since at the same time, Caldon shot another round of fireballs his way, while Mirryn made a circling motion with her hands and Jaren became caught in a mini tornado, spinning uncontrollably.

Kiva was certain that Caldon's fire was going to scorch Jaren, especially since the crown prince seemed to reach for his water magic but the river didn't rise to his command — instead, it was buckling under the weight of whatever the queen was doing, as if she was pressing it into the earth, keeping it from coming to Jaren's defense.

Suddenly, Kiva couldn't breathe. She thought it was from being so anxious over what she was seeing that her lungs had stalled, but then all the fires in the room spluttered into pitch-blackness, and she realized that Jaren had caused this — that he'd purged all the air from the room to free himself from his sister's tornado while also snuffing out Caldon's flames before they could strike him.

It was clever — so very clever. But Kiva couldn't fully admire his strategy. Blind, suffocating, and alarmed by the same choking sounds from Tipp and Naari beside her, along with the distressed Flox, she was only keeping from full-blown panic because she knew Jaren would never allow any harm to come to his family — or to her.

Sure enough, within seconds, she was sucking in fresh air again, and with it, fire burst back into existence — not only along the walls, but also at Jaren's fingertips, remaining there just long enough for him to thrust it like a javelin toward his cousin.

Caldon ducked the attack, the fire slamming into the limestone behind him in a roar of sparks. A second javelin from Jaren had Caldon scrambling to summon a shield of fire to absorb the flames, which he managed just in time.

"You'll have to try harder than that!" the rakish prince goaded.

Jaren didn't have a chance to respond, because his other family members were still sending their own attacks his way. Wind was buffeting his clothes and hair, but it didn't lift him off the ground, making Kiva realize he was nullifying whatever Mirryn was trying to do. At the same time, water was rising again, forming the shape of a serpent similar to the one from the River Festival last night. The snake moved to strike at Jaren, and he pointed a finger not at the beast, but at the ground near where he stood, an almighty *crack* sounding as a section broke away and rose to shield him from the brunt of the attack. But what Jaren didn't see was Oriel's sneaky move, the young prince directing camouflaged vines to crawl along the ground and wrap around his brother's ankles. With one quick hand gesture from Oriel, Jaren's feet were yanked out from beneath him, his earth shield all that kept the queen's snake from engulfing him as he wrestled now with the creeping plants that were moving swiftly up his body, trapping his limbs and squeezing the air from his lungs.

A flash of light had Kiva flinching backwards as Jaren summoned a sword made of flames, using it to cut through the vines. Freed from their grip, he somersaulted back up to his feet, shooting a proud look at his younger brother for his effort. But the moment was only brief, with Caldon, Mirryn, and Ariana all launching new attacks against Jaren, and Oriel jumping right back into the fight.

Kiva didn't know how long they kept at it, earth, fire, air, and water moving around the cavern in ways she'd never imagined possible. Ice shards were thrown like daggers, a crevasse opened beneath Jaren's feet, a horse and rider made of flames charged him and nearly sent him toppling into the river, and on it went. The attacks grew in creativity and difficulty the longer they continued, prompting Kiva's stomach to tighten with the realization that *this* was what it meant to be a Vallentis —and *this* was what her family would face if they dared challenge them for the crown.

No wonder Caldon had been wary of having witnesses. This kind of magic . . . it was beyond what Kiva had ever envisioned. She'd known the royal family could control the elements, and she'd seen examples from both Jaren and Mirryn over the last few months, but she'd never truly realized what that meant. Not once had she considered that the queen could drown someone with a flick of her fingers, that the princess could force all the air from someone's lungs, that young Oriel could bury someone alive, that Caldon could set someone alight with a thought.

And Jaren . . . he could do all of that and, as Kiva was seeing, much, *much* more.

He was unstoppable. No matter how his family attacked, he found a way to defend himself, whether by using their own element against them or one of the other three powers he had at his disposal.

He was magnificent.

And he was terrifying.

Watching him, there was no doubt in Kiva's mind why the Royal Council had chosen him as the heir in Mirryn's place. As long as Jaren ruled the kingdom, his people would be safe, no enemy force standing a chance at defeating him.

And that presented a problem for Kiva.

For her family.

For the rebels.

Nervous sweat was trickling down her back by the time Jaren finally called a halt to the magical attacks. He was breathing heavily, but the weight that had been hanging over him earlier was gone, his face glowing with contentment as he shared grins with his family, all of whom seemed equally revitalized by their training session. Kiva couldn't hear what they were saying to each other, but she watched as Jaren threw back his head and laughed at something Caldon said, the sight and sound so carefree that her heart clutched in her chest.

Was it the magic that had done that? To all of them? If so, Kiva didn't understand. Her own magic wasn't something she'd ever been able to rejoice in. She'd barely discovered she even *had* it before she'd been carted away to Zalindov, after which she'd promised her father never to use it. She couldn't fathom the lightness emanating from the royals in the wake of their training, the joy they were radiating. But she also couldn't deny that she felt a prickle of envy — and a hint of curiosity. If she trained like they did, would her own power grow like a muscle? Would she stop seeing it as a burden and embrace it as a blessing? She didn't know. And as long as she was living at the palace, she wouldn't have a chance to find out, so she slammed the door shut on her thoughts, resolved to think on it no further.

After the royals shared a few more words among themselves, Jaren led the group over to where Kiva, Naari, and Tipp waited, with Oriel hurrying forward to reclaim the wide awake and mildly agitated Flox.

"He didn't like not being able to breathe," Kiva explained, standing and shooting a pointed look at Jaren, who offered a contrite grimace in return, fully aware that she wasn't talking only about the fluffball.

"Poor Floxie," Oriel cooed, stroking the critter until he made what sounded like a purring noise.

Naari and Tipp had risen beside Kiva, the latter staring at the royal family with stars in his eyes. "That was a-a-a-*mazing*," he breathed.

"Nah, that was nothing. Barely a warm up," Caldon said, dusting ash off his clothes and out of his golden hair. "You should see us when we really let loose."

No one disagreed with him, which told Kiva that he wasn't just boasting. She schooled her features, inwardly horrified by what they might be able to do when really trying.

"If we're done here," Mirryn said, wringing water from her skirt, "I need to go and order my birthday cake."

"I should leave, too," said Queen Ariana. "I have a desk full of paperwork that I've been putting off for days." Her eyes moved to Oriel and Tipp. "And you two need to get back to your studies with Tutor Edna."

Tipp looked as if he might expire on the spot if he didn't ask a million questions about what he'd just seen, but at the queen's stern look, he exhaled loudly with resignation.

"Don't worry, we can write notes to each other when Edna's not looking," Oriel whispered to him.

Ariana made a disapproving sound, and her young son sent her a sheepish look.

"Um, during our break," Oriel quickly added.

Tipp snickered until the queen's eyes came back to him, at which point he bit his lip and looked guiltily at the ground.

"Well, I for one am *starving*," Caldon declared. Turning to Kiva, he said, "We need to get more protein into you, so you're coming with me to the kitchens."

He didn't wait for her to agree before he took off after his family, with Tipp and Naari trailing them. Jaren remained behind, and Kiva hung back with him, sensing there was something on his mind.

Only when the others were out of sight did he clear his throat and say, "Tipp seemed to handle that well. The magic, I mean."

Kiva snorted. "If he didn't already idolize you, he would now."

"And you?"

Her humor fled as she realized Jaren wasn't worried about Tipp's reaction—he was worried about *hers*.

"I already knew about your magic, Jaren," she said slowly.

"Not to that extent."

She eyed him carefully and agreed, "No. I suppose not."

Jaren looked away and ran a hand agitatedly through his hair.

"Hey," she said, reaching for him and pulling back at the last second, clenching her fingers to keep from taking his hand in her own. "What's going on?"

"It's just . . ." he said haltingly. "I don't want you to be afraid of me."

Kiva blinked. "Afraid?"

"Of what I can do," he clarified. "Of whether I'll hurt you."

Taken aback, Kiva didn't know how to respond. But then she saw the fear in this eyes and made herself say, "When you sucked all the air from the room, I nearly panicked. But you know why I didn't?"

Jaren shook his head.

"Because I knew you wouldn't let anything bad happen to your family." Quietly, she added, "Or to me."

His tension faded. "I wouldn't. Not ever."

Kiva was painfully aware that one day soon he might not be able to keep that promise. And yet, she hadn't lied—she wasn't afraid of him. Of his power, absolutely. But not of him. Never of him.

She was in so much trouble.

Biting her lip, Kiva made herself look away, but as she did, the air shifted between them, as if they both suddenly became aware of how close they were standing, how alone they were. Her eyes flicked back to his, warmth flooding her veins when she saw the look on his face.

"Kiva," he whispered, moving closer. "I—"

"Excuse me," came Caldon's loud voice from the entrance to the cavern, causing Kiva to jump backwards, "but did you not hear me say I'm starving?"

Heart thumping, Kiva muttered, "Have I mentioned how much I hate your cousin? Not a little. A lot." Despite the words, she was over-whelmingly grateful for the interruption, fearing what might have happened if Caldon hadn't returned when he did.

Stupid. She was so, *so* stupid. She needed to be more careful, to be *smarter*. What had just happened with Jaren—or *nearly* happened—couldn't happen again.

"Right now, I hate him a lot, too," Jaren agreed under his breath.

"You know the acoustics in here mean I can hear you, right?" Caldon called. "Hurry your asses up!"

Both Jaren and Kiva sighed at the same time, then shared a look of amusement before heading toward the passageway and starting up the endless stairs toward the palace. Each new step made Kiva's muscles scream with pain, offering a reminder of where she was, who she was with—and why she was there to begin with.

She had a role to play. She had a mission to fulfill.

And no matter what, she would not let her family down.

CHAPTER NINE

That afternoon, Kiva returned to the tunnels, striding along the underground thoroughfare with a fake confidence, acting as if she had every right to be there. Her intentions were risky, but with the Royal Council meeting having been rescheduled to later that day, she couldn't pass up the chance to at least try spying on them.

Kiva had watched Jaren carefully during their walk to the training cavern, and there had been one doorway in particular that he'd scowled at as they'd passed by, the expression so foreign on his face that she'd felt a burst of triumph. While she didn't know what time his meeting had been postponed to, she was prepared to linger in the tunnels all afternoon if it meant she might overhear something of value.

Since the crown prince was currently aboveground, there was still time to refine her plan before the council gathered. She'd left him with Caldon after finishing lunch, claiming that her head wound was causing her pain and she wanted to take a nap. His concern had caused a prickle of guilt, but she'd forced herself to ignore it. No matter how she felt when she was around him, no matter how much he clearly cared for her, she had to remember that they were on opposite sides of the throne. And because of their bloodlines, they always would be.

There was no hope for them.

There never had been.

And she couldn't afford to forget that.

Ever.

Silencing her thoughts, Kiva continued down the passageway, resisting the urge to slink along the edges where the light from the luminium beacons faded into shadows. It was quiet, with only a handful of servants and palace workers traveling beneath the river. Thankfully, there were no guards stationed along the path; the only two she saw were covered in sweat and returning from the training yard, both of them young, off duty, and deep enough in conversation to not even glance her way.

With no eyes on her, it was easy for Kiva to reach the doorway that had prompted Jaren's adverse reaction, and she quickly slipped through it, groaning at the sight of yet more stairs.

Similar to the path that had led to the training cavern, before her was another downward tunnel, but this one was lit by small luminium orbs, the glow fading into the distance and all but daring her to investigate.

Kiva hadn't survived as long as she had by acting rashly. There was no telling how far the passage descended or what it led to. And if the council members were to arrive while she was exploring . . . If *Jaren* were to find her sneaking around down there and catch her in her lie . . .

She bit her lip, deliberating for a moment before pushing aside her misgivings and starting downward, cursing at the renewed burn in her legs. When she finally came to the end of the staircase, she felt no relief, since she now faced a fork in the path.

Kiva peered down both tunnels, having no idea which to take. Worse, neither was lit by luminium orbs, so if she continued onward, she would be doing so blind.

Knowing she couldn't afford to dally, Kiva set off along the right fork. Trailing one hand against the rough stone wall, she kept the other raised before her to keep from walking into anything, praying to the long-forgotten gods that there were no more stairs that she might tumble down.

Just as the darkness became too much and she decided to turn back, her foot collided painfully with stone.

Hissing, Kiva jumped up and down, before crouching and running her hands along what she'd walked into, discovering it to be a staircase traveling back upward. Squinting through the gloom, she was able to make out the slightest trace of light up ahead, indicating that the ascent wasn't long.

Reaching the top of the short staircase, Kiva's heart leapt when she hit a dead end and discovered the source of the light. It was stronger now that she was closer—and now that she understood where it came from.

It was sunshine.

She hadn't found the council meeting room. But she wasn't disappointed, because above her head was an iron grate. Through the slits, Kiva could see that it opened up near the bank of the Serin River—and, more importantly, *outside* the palace walls.

Entirely by accident, she'd found what appeared to be an emergency escape route out of the tunnels.

An *unguarded* escape route.

Kiva assumed it was in place should the Royal Council ever need to evacuate in a hurry, and while part of her wanted to test the grate, to step out of the dark passage and return aboveground, she knew her task wasn't yet complete.

Turning from the exit, Kiva made her way carefully back down the staircase and along the pitch-black path, refusing to consider the repercussions of her discovery. If an unmonitored opening could be used to escape, it could also be used to infiltrate—and that was dangerous knowledge. She almost wished she hadn't found it, if only so she wouldn't have to decide what to do with the information, and who to share it with.

Tripping on a loose rock, Kiva cursed her distracted thoughts. The very fact that she was questioning whether or not to reveal what she'd found made her insides churn, but that feeling eased when she remembered that she didn't have to do anything about it yet. She could take the time to consider whether it was worth sharing—and whether she could bear the burden of any consequences.

Clearing her mind—and quieting her traitorous heart—Kiva made her way back to the fork in the path and turned down the blackened left tunnel, walking blindly once more. It was a mercifully short journey before her outstretched hand met a solid surface. She feared it was another dead end, this time without an exit, but then she felt the distinct shape of a door handle and hesitated only briefly before opening it.

Light flooded into the passageway, bright enough that she winced and had to wait for her eyes to adjust. When she could finally make out the room beyond, a victorious smile spread across her face.

Before her was a sealed room boasting a round mahogany table atop a lavish crimson rug, above which hung a luminium chandelier. To the right of the door was an immense bookcase, the titles covering everything from military strategy, political history and trading laws, to foreign religious and cultural traditions.

Stepping into the room, Kiva marveled at the maps strung along the walls, one for each of the eight kingdoms and a ninth detailing the entire continent of Wenderall. But it was the ashwood cabinet opposite where she stood that snared her gaze, an unscrolled parchment resting on the surface begging for her attention.

Wisdom told Kiva to retreat back up the passage and hide in the darkness of the other forked tunnel until she saw Jaren and the council members arrive, after which she could sneak back down and eavesdrop with her ear pressed to the door. The wood wasn't too thick; their words would be muffled, but she should be able to hear them.

But that unscrolled parchment was too tempting to resist.

Listening carefully, Kiva could hear nothing to indicate anyone was heading her way. She had to hurry—she couldn't chance crossing paths with them on her way back to the fork.

Her hands shook as she rushed around the circular table toward the cabinet. She didn't touch the parchment in case someone noticed it had shifted, but she also didn't need to, since a quick glance revealed that it was a handwritten letter—in another language.

Kiva swore under her breath and scanned for any recognizable words. While all of Wenderall's citizens spoke the common tongue, some of the other kingdoms also had their own native languages. She might have kept to herself inside Zalindov, but she'd still picked up a few phrases from her more talkative patients.

Squinting in concentration, Kiva skipped to the bottom of the letter and found the name of the sender: Navok Kildarion.

Shock coursed through her body, and she read the name again, just to be sure.

The Kildarion family were the ruling monarchs of Mirraven. When she was a child, Kiva had overheard her parents talking about the ruthless northern royals and the rumors claiming that King Arakkis's wife was so afraid of him that she'd fled in the night, leaving behind their two children, Princess Serafine and Prince Navok.

But . . . why would a Mirraven prince be writing to Evalon's Royal Council?

Kiva scanned Navok's letter again, desperate for any hint of what it contained. Aside from the words Arakkis and Serafine, she also saw another name she recognized from long ago: Voshell. If she recalled correctly, that was Voshell Aravine, the crown prince of Caramor. But no other words stood out to her, making her sigh with frustration.

For a moment, Kiva entertained the idea of stealing the parchment and taking it to someone who could read Mirravish, but from the few names she'd gleaned, she knew it was valuable enough to be missed. The letter had to stay—she would just have to find out what it said some other way.

Shoulders drooping in resignation, Kiva inspected the rest of the cabinet's surface, finding nothing more interesting than a near-empty crystal decanter, the amber-colored spirits rippling as she pulled off the stopper, her eyes watering at the strength of the fumes. Quickly sealing it again, she noted a set of delicate tumblers stacked and ready for use, and deduced that the Royal Council must keep them on hand for celebrations — or perhaps commiserations.

Aware that every second she lingered was adding to the danger of being caught, Kiva swiftly tugged open the cabinet doors, only to find the inside bare except for some blank sheets of parchment and a few spare bottles of alcohol.

Disappointed, Kiva closed the cabinet again, her skin itching with desire to leave the room. She didn't know how long she'd have to wait for the council's arrival, but her anxiety was growing enough that she knew it was time to go.

Hurrying back around the mahogany table, Kiva's gaze trailed over the maps once more, a feeling of insignificance flooding her as she realized just how vast Wenderall was. There was so much she had yet to see even in her home kingdom of Evalon, and she'd never so much as set foot in another territory. Long ago, she'd dreamed of traveling to the pristine forests of Nerine, the salt mountains of Valorn, the desert kingdom of Hadris, and the sun-drenched lands of Jiirva. She'd imagined wandering through the harsh landscapes of Caramor and adventuring beyond Mirraven's renowned Darkwell Fortress into the Uninhabited North. She'd even entertained thoughts of chartering a ship and exploring the wilds of Odon, perhaps sailing all the way down to the abandoned Serpent Isles, or journeying to one of the near-mythical continents far across the ocean.

Her childhood fantasies had remained with her during her years at Zalindov, offering a mental escape on the darkest of days. Even now, Kiva still longed for the dreams of her youth, for the utter freedom of her imagination. Maybe one day she would have a chance to travel beyond Evalon, to experience the wonders of Wenderall for herself. Maybe one day she would be free to —

Kiva froze as a sound met her ears, yanking her viciously from her nostalgia. She stretched her senses as far as they would go, straining to hear beyond her panicked pulse.

There. In the distance.

Voices.

CHAPTER TEN

Ice flooded Kiva's veins as she stared at the open doorway, before she came to her senses and lunged forward to shut it. The voices seemed too far away for them to have reached the fork and noticed the light streaming into the tunnel, so her presence remained undiscovered, for now.

But the Royal Council was heading her way.

Jaren was heading her way.

And in closing the door, she had just trapped herself in the room.

For a single, heart-stopping second, all thoughts eddied from Kiva's mind as fear took hold, but then she snapped out of it and began searching desperately for a hiding place.

She looked at the bookcase overflowing with tomes, dismissing it immediately. She then considered whether she could remain unseen beneath the mahogany table, only to reject that idea just as fast. Gazing frantically around, her eyes came to rest on the ashwood cabinet, a gasp of hope leaving her as she bolted toward it, yanking open the doors and shoving aside the bottles of spirits and unused parchment. Her sore muscles burned in protest as she twisted her body into the cramped space, curling at the waist and wrapping her arms around her legs in order to fit. It took three tries before she was able to close the cabinet doors, but finally she managed to seal herself inside.

For a moment, Kiva could see nothing, the musty smell of wood overloading her senses, coupled with the more pungent scent of alcohol indicating that a bottle must have spilled at some point. The darkness was consuming, the walls closing in on her, hauling her back to her time in the Abyss when she'd been locked in the pitch-black cell for a fortnight.

Trapped.

Just as she was now.

Her breathing began to grow louder as her lungs constricted, recollected terror causing sweat to break out on her forehead.

She couldn't see.

She couldn't breathe.

She had to get out of there.

She had to get out of there.

But then her eyes began to adjust, a sliver of light trickling through a small gap between the cabinet doors offering Kiva a lifeline. She released a shaky breath and pressed her face against the wood, one eye able to peek out into the room beyond—

Just in time to watch the door open with the arrival of the Royal Council, Jaren at their head. Queen Ariana also accompanied them, having clearly abandoned her afternoon of paperwork.

Kiva reminded herself that she was no longer locked away in the Abyss, but she *would* be if they caught her. She had to stay calm, had to stay silent.

And she had to pay attention. Because inadvertently or not, she'd just found herself in the best position to spy on the Royal Council.

"—want you to acknowledge that it was reckless and dangerous," a middle-aged man with graying hair was saying, his beady eyes set in a frown. "Foolish, even. So much could have gone wrong. So much *did* go wrong."

"Horeth, if you intend to spend the afternoon scolding me like a child, let me know now," Jaren said with clear impatience. "I have better things to do."

Horeth—Kiva had heard that name earlier. He was the Grand Master of the Royal Council. And right now he was scowling at Jaren, as were the three other people who had trailed into the room behind him, two women and another man. All four of the council members wore red robes with glimmering circlets at their brows, Horeth's being gold, the other three silver.

Jaren and Ariana took their seats at the table, with the Grand Master and his three companions following their lead. Kiva had to crane her neck and squint through the gap in the cabinet to keep her eye on them all, but she was still able to see everyone reasonably well.

"I think what my son means to say is that he's aware his actions were . . . *rash*," Ariana said in a mollifying voice. "But when he heard news of Tilda Corentine's impending transfer to Zalindov, he saw an opportunity too great to resist."

Kiva's fingers twitched at the mention of her mother.

"And he nearly died because of it," a dark-skinned woman pointed out, her black hair pulled into a strict bun at the nape of her neck.

"Yisari's right," Horeth said with an imperious nod, his gaze spearing Jaren. "We've all read Naari Arell's reports, so we know Eidran Ridley volunteered to insinuate himself inside the prison for Tilda's arrival. We also know his ill-timed accident meant the plan should have been abandoned. What we *don't* know is why it wasn't — and why you, *the heir to our kingdom*, decided to risk your life by going into a hostile environment completely unprepared. For everworld's sake, look at your hand! You'll have that scar forever, and gods know how many others from your time in there."

Horeth had clearly never seen Jaren without his shirt on, or he'd know that a few new scars were the least of the prince's concerns. Even so, Kiva had to repress the shame she felt, since she was the one who had carved the Z into Jaren's hand. She wondered if Naari's reports had included *that* particular detail.

All eyes turned to the prince, but he only leaned back in his chair and crossed his arms. "Eidran's doing better, thanks for asking," he said pointedly. "His leg was damaged worse than we thought, so it's taking some time to heal, but he's staying with his family in Albree and they're helping with his rehabilitation. I'll be sure to pass along your regards."

Silence fell after Jaren's dry statement, and Kiva's lips curled up at the edges. This was a side of him she'd never seen before—princely, almost insolent.

"Perhaps we should move on," murmured the silver-circlet-wearing man, his head bald and skin milky white. "As we can all see, Prince Deverick is safely returned to us. Indeed, we were unaware he was even in Zalindov until after his escape. There's no point in dwelling on what has passed."

"Wise words, Feldor, as always," said the second councilwoman. She too was pale, though her visible skin was dusted with freckles and lined with age, her auburn hair streaked liberally with silver.

"Fine," Grand Master Horeth said, his features pinched with displeasure. "If we're not going to address His Highness's careless actions, then let's discuss his thoughtless decision in bringing not one, but *two* escaped criminals back to Vallenia with him—and right to the palace, no less."

Apprehension filled Kiva's body, but not because of Horeth's new line of discussion. It was the stormy look on Jaren's face that made her cramped muscles unconsciously tense.

"Tread carefully with what you say next, Grand Master," Jaren warned, his voice cold. He leaned forward, his eyes like shards of ice. "One of those *criminals* you're talking about is a young boy whose only crime was to love his mother too much—"

"His mother was a thief—"

"—and the other *criminal,* as you call her," Jaren continued over Horeth, a muscle fluttering in his jaw, "was barely seven years old when she arrived at Zalindov. I don't care what you say—there's something fundamentally wrong with our laws when *children* can be sent to a *death prison.*"

"But she—"

"Let's also remember that Kiva earned her freedom by triumphing over the Trial by Ordeal. If not for the riot, she would have been set free."

"We all know you helped her survive the Ord—"

"And ignoring all of that," Jaren said, refusing to let the Grand Master get a word in edgewise, "she spent every waking moment at Zalindov helping the other prisoners, often at great personal sacrifice. In my mind, that makes her a hero. Try to remember that the next time you think I'll sit back and smile as you call her a *criminal*."

Cheeks red and eyes blazing from having been interrupted so many times, Horeth spat, "Her father was suspected of—"

"I know all about her father."

With just six words from Jaren, the world fell out from beneath Kiva.

"Did you really think I wouldn't look into her?" he asked the table, incredulous. "The first thing I did when we arrived at the winter palace was ask Caldon to hunt down her prison records. But of course he was already three steps ahead of me. He'd started investigating her the day they met, all the way back at the first Trial. He briefed me straightaway, sharing everything I needed to know."

Kiva's shock transformed into a cold, horrified numbness.

"Then you know—" Horeth tried, but Jaren continued to cut him off.

"What I know is that Faran Meridan's alleged association with the rebels was exactly that—*alleged*." The prince's voice was as unyielding as his expression. "He was sentenced to Zalindov for suspected treason without proof of any crime on his part. Gods, the man spent his life *saving* people. And what did he get in return? A swift death, and the burden of leaving his daughter to suffer for a crime he may never have committed, all because she'd resisted his arrest."

"Exactly!" Horeth cried. "She *resisted his arrest!* That's a criminal offen—"

"She was *seven years old!*" Jaren all but yelled, his hands now fisted on the table. "She'd just watched her brother die in a senseless accident, and her father was being dragged away into the night. *Of course* she resisted his arrest. Anyone would have!"

Kiva didn't hear Horeth's reply over the ringing in her ears. She tried to calm her raging heartbeat, reminding herself that she'd told Jaren parts of her story months ago. He'd already known Kerrin had died — she'd just never told him *how,* or that she'd witnessed it. He'd also known about her father being in Zalindov, but she'd never revealed what Faran had been accused of. That was dangerous information, the kind that could make him question if she had ulterior motives, especially since she'd failed to divulge the full truth herself.

But . . . if Jaren had known everything since their first day at the winter palace, if Caldon had known for even longer . . .

The tightness in Kiva's chest eased as she realized that was *all* they knew. Caldon must not have dug any deeper after reading her prison records — not that he would have had a reason to. The charges against her father were unfounded and therefore led to a dead end. Furthermore, there was nothing in Warden Rooke's archives that could have linked her — or Faran — to Tilda, nor had she or her father ever been known as anything other than Meridan, with the name Corentine having been abandoned by her mother's great-something grandmother generations before Kiva had been born. Prior to Zalindov, her family had stayed clear of any rebel activity, so there was nothing incriminating in her history — and certainly nothing that was documented.

That meant she was still safe.

But she'd underestimated them. Both Jaren and Caldon. She couldn't afford to do so again.

"The only good thing out of this entire mess," Jaren said, running agitated fingers through his hair, "is that Kiva seems to have been too young to know it was the Royal Guard that ruined her life, or that Captain Veris himself was there that night." He was wrong on both counts, but Kiva wasn't about to pop out of the cabinet and correct him. "She hasn't shown any signs of recognition, but Veris remembers her like it was yesterday. *I'll never forget those eyes,* he told me." Jaren stared down at the table, his expression wretched as he whispered, "Gods, if she knew the truth, she'd never be able to look at me again."

He was wrong about that, too, even if Kiva wished he wasn't.

"What a tragedy that would be," Horeth said callously. He turned to the queen and said, "Your Majesty, you can't possibly want the Meridan girl running around the palace? The child, too — Tripper, or whatever his name is. They're a security threat. If nothing else, they should have guards on them at all times."

Jaren opened his mouth to argue, but Ariana placed her hand over his clenched fist, silencing him.

"I'll admit that when I first heard about my son's traveling companions, I was concerned," the queen said. "But I also knew he would never risk placing our family — or our kingdom — in any danger. Jaren trusts them, and I trust his judgment." She eyed each of the council members, her gaze lingering on Horeth as she finished, "You should, too."

"Trust is the first ingredient in a recipe for betrayal," the Grand Master returned, shaking his head — in disappointment or disgust, Kiva wasn't sure. But goose bumps prickled her flesh at his prophetic words.

"Horeth makes a good point," the bald-headed Feldor interjected. "What *is* the basis for your trust, Prince Deverick? An explanation might help us understand better."

"Kiva saved my life," Jaren said, his words simple, but every person in the room sat up straighter. "I'd be dead in a tunnel beneath Zalindov right now if not for her. I could barely stand without her help, let alone walk out of there on my own. She could have left me, and she didn't."

Queen Ariana's beautiful features had paled with each word Jaren spoke, though surely she already knew every detail of their escape.

Horeth, however, made a dismissive sound. "Naari would have found you eventually. And even if she hadn't, are we supposed to ignore your magic? You didn't need to *walk* out of there, Your Highness, and we all know it."

Kiva blinked into the darkness, realizing Horeth was right. If Jaren could hover above an underground river, he could have easily levitated himself to the tunnel exit and up the ladders. Hell, he could have just used his earth magic to crack open the ground, rising straight up to the surface.

"You're forgetting that I'd been tortured for a fortnight, and laboring for weeks before that on limited food and water," Jaren said, causing his mother to pale even more. "I'd also already expended a lot of my magic and had no energy for it to replenish properly. I was down to sparks and embers, nothing more."

He'd been down to sparks and embers because he'd used his magic protecting Kiva from the Ordeals. The little power he'd had left must have been what he'd used to light their path out of the tunnels—and then escape from Zalindov afterward.

"You truly expect us to believe that you're only alive today because of Kiva Meridan?" Horeth asked, scoffing.

"I don't care what you believe," Jaren stated. "But I *do* expect you to treat both her and Tipp with respect. They're here as my guests, and I won't hear another word against them."

He stared down each member of the council, daring them to argue further.

Only one of them did—but not in the same vein as before.

"Is that *all* they're here for?" the auburn-haired woman asked, a sly smile quirking her lips. "I've only seen Kiva from a distance, but I couldn't help noticing she's not difficult to look at, if you catch my meaning."

Jaren stilled. "Careful, Zerra."

The woman's smile deepened as she raised her hands in supplication. "Forgive an old crone her curiosity, but perhaps you might share with us your intentions for her. Do you plan to wed?"

Kiva experienced a full-body reaction to the suggestion. Her torso jolted, her eyes widened, her cheeks flushed, and a quiet gasp slipped perilously through her lips before she could clamp down on it.

"*Wed?*" Horeth spluttered. "Surely you jest, Zerra. The girl's a commoner. No, she's *less* than a commoner; she's a crim—"

"Do *not* finish that sentence," Jaren commanded, his voice like steel.

But he wasn't the only one at the table who was suddenly furious.

"My husband, your *king*, was once a commoner," Queen Ariana said, her tone enough to make Kiva shiver. "You're toeing a dangerous line, Grand Master. Have a care."

Horeth quickly backpedaled. "Forgive me, Your Majesty. I merely wished to express concern for your son—and for the future of our kingdom. If he intends to—"

"My intentions are none of this council's business," Jaren said in his firmest voice yet. "If the time comes when they *become* the council's business, then—and *only* then—will I make them known. Is that understood?" He waited until all four red-robed councillors nodded before he went on, "Kiva has spent over half her life locked in a nightmare. The last thing I want is to make her feel like she's trapped in another kind of cage, gilded though it might be. I have no idea what the future will bring for us, but right now she deserves the chance to live her life and follow her dreams. I can only hope she'll grant me the honor of being by her side on that journey, and if she does, you'll have to find a way to deal with it. I don't think I can be any clearer than that."

Kiva's chest constricted all over again at Jaren's heartfelt words. She couldn't allow herself to feel them so deeply, but despite her best efforts to resist, they burrowed in and held tight, warming her all over.

"The people will never accept her once they learn where she's come from."

Horeth's snide words made all the warmth within Kiva dissolve. But Jaren held the Grand Master's gaze, purposefully tracing the Z scar on the back of his hand as he said, "If they can accept me, they'll accept her. You do our people a disservice by assuming they judge as harshly as you."

The Grand Master frowned and opened his mouth to reply, but Ariana cut him off.

"I think we've spoken enough about my son's personal life today," she said, making it clear the subject was closed. "What other matters are on the agenda?"

Jaren took advantage of the council members' hesitation by jumping in and saying, "I'd like an update on the investigation into Warden Rooke's abuse of power. I've heard nothing since leaving the winter palace — has he been charged yet?"

Kiva jerked, her contorted joints barking in protest, but she couldn't help her reaction. Rooke was being investigated? Was he — Was he actually going to pay for what he'd done?

Feldor scratched his smooth scalp before answering, "We lodged your inquiry as requested, Highness, but Rooke isn't technically under our jurisdiction. He's not a citizen of Evalon — he answers to all eight kingdoms, and only Nerine and Valorn are backing your demand for justice. In this case, the majority rules, I'm afraid. Our hands are tied."

Kiva's hope faded all over again, before she reminded herself that she would just have to seek her own revenge against him. One day.

"So that's it?" Jaren asked, his frustration clear. "He's just allowed to keep on terrorizing the inmates? Poisoning them when he decides they need culling?"

"There's no proof he did that," Yisari said, a warning in her voice.

"I was there," Jaren shot back. "Naari, Kiva, Tipp — we all saw the prisoners dying, one after the other. We all wondered if we'd be next."

"And again, you have no proof that Rooke was behind it," Yisari repeated, spreading her hands in apology. "He's kept Zalindov's denizens under strict control for over a decade — that's longer than any other warden. It's his word against yours, and without tangible evidence, we won't sway the other kingdoms against him. They don't want to see him replaced when he's done such a fine job."

"He's a murderer," Jaren snarled.

"His victims were hardly innocents," Horeth said, before amending, "Most of them, at least."

Jaren glared at the Grand Master, before turning to his mother and stating, "We need to re-evaluate our sentencing laws. I can't speak for the other kingdoms, but I refuse to abide any citizen of this territory being arrested without a fair trial. There should be *no* innocents inside Zalindov. *None.* And the actual criminals who deserve to be locked away should still be afforded basic human rights." He addressed the whole table as he finished, "If we can't remove Rooke, then we should at least try to protect our own people inside those walls — and stop anyone who shouldn't be there from being arrested in the first place."

The council sat stunned after Jaren's declaration — as did Kiva — but Ariana nodded at his side, a small, proud smile on her lips.

"I agree," she said. Turning to Horeth, she ordered, "Meet with the Legal Guild and have them go through the Book of the Law to note what needs amending. Make this a priority."

The Grand Master blinked stupidly for a long moment, but not even he was foolish enough to refuse a direct command from his queen, so he nodded stiffly in agreement.

Little puffs of air left Kiva's lips as she realized how many lives might be saved if the laws were amended, but she couldn't dwell on what Jaren had instigated — and how it made her feel — because the council meeting was far from over.

"What's happening with the rebels?" Queen Ariana asked, moving the conversation along. "They've been quieter since Tilda's death, but last night they abducted Kiva—presumably to bait Jaren. Are they rallying again?"

"Our newest intelligence is frustratingly limited," Zerra said, her earlier smile gone, her freckled features now serious. "Ever since Rhune and Whitlock turned up dead, we've struggled to get our spies anywhere close to the inner circle, and not even they were able to infiltrate the main camp. It's like the Viper and the Jackal have a sixth sense when it comes to loyalty."

The Viper and the Jackal—Kiva didn't need to guess who *they* were, but she was curious how her siblings had come to be known by such names. She was also disturbed by the reference to the two dead men, her stomach turning over at the thought of Torell or Zuleeka being responsible.

"It's more likely that they have their own spies among us," Jaren said with a sigh. "They don't need a sixth sense if someone is telling them everything they need to know." He scrubbed a weary hand down his face. "Gods, I wish Eidran were here. He'd know exactly what we should do, and who we could trust."

"He trained Rhune and Whitlock, didn't he?" Feldor asked.

Jaren nodded. "Their deaths hit him really hard. That's why Naari and I made him come with us to the winter palace—to get him out of the city and keep him from doing anything rash. But even while we were gone, he was still brainstorming new ways to infiltrate the rebels." Jaren paused, as if suddenly remembering something. "Just before we left, he was certain he'd found a secret meeting place here in Vallenia. He'd planned to go in undercover once we got back."

Yisari's dark eyes were eager as she asked, "Did he tell you the location?"

A snort of amusement left Jaren. "In the last half hour alone, I've been called both reckless and foolish. Do you really think Eidran would have given me that information, knowing what I'd do with it?"

No one responded.

Queen Ariana turned to Zerra and said, "Send someone you trust to Albree. I want to know everything Eidran knows. Then prepare one of our newer spies to go in."

"He won't tell you," Jaren said. "After what happened with Rhune and Whitlock, he knows we have a leak somewhere, and he'll assume all our people have been compromised."

"He won't have a choice," Horeth stated. "Not if he wants to reclaim his esteemed position in the guard upon his return to full health."

Jaren had nothing to say to that, so the four councillors began suggesting names of who to send to Albree and who to sneak into an underground meeting. They then segued into a debate about how to weed out any rebel spies, with Ariana jumping in to offer her own opinions.

None of them were paying attention to Jaren, so they all missed the calculating look on his face. Similarly, no one had realized that he'd never answered Yisari's question, instead replying with his own.

Do you really think Eidran would have given me that information, knowing what I'd do with it?

Kiva was certain Jaren knew more than he was letting on. If Eidran *had* shared what he knew about a rebel meeting place, then it was almost a guarantee that Jaren would act on that information. Kiva would have to keep a closer eye on him, watching for him to make a move.

"—so we'll keep monitoring the rebel situation as best as we can, like we always have," Zerra was saying, prompting Kiva to tune back in. "But ultimately, we all know that while they're pests, they don't pose a real threat to Evalon."

Kiva's lips parted in indignation before she quickly snapped her mouth shut again.

"Try saying that to the people who have lost loved ones because of them," Jaren said, his face tight. "Or the ones who have lost their homes, sometimes their entire villages. I doubt *they'd* consider the rebels mere pests."

"None of us like the civil unrest they're causing, and especially not the resulting damages," Grand Master Horeth said, his tone placating for once. "But Zerra's right. As hard as they try, they'll never muster a force great enough to defeat our armies. And without the Royal Ternary, there's no other way for them to claim the throne."

Kiva's ears perked up at the strange words. The Royal Ternary— what was that? And what did it have to do with the throne? She made a mental note to ask her siblings the next time she saw them—just as she would be asking about the destruction caused by their uprising, praying they had a valid justification.

"For now, there's nothing more we can do about the rebels," Horeth continued. "Or rather, there's nothing more we *need* to do about them. We've already seen that they're growing quieter. With their queen gone, they'll eventually give up—we just have to wait them out."

"The Viper and the Jackal won't give up so easily," Jaren said, echoing Kiva's thoughts. "Eidran thinks one of them, perhaps both, could be directly related to Tilda. Her siblings, her cousins, her children—no one outside of their inner circle has seen their faces, so we can't guess their ages. But if Eidran's right, and if they've taken over leadership as we assume, then that means—"

"They could have Corentine blood," Ariana said, her sapphire eyes narrowing.

Kiva found herself grateful that Eidran was halfway up the coast, since his knowledge of the rebels seemed to be all that was keeping the Royal Council afloat.

"That's troubling, I'll admit," Horeth acknowledged, "but it still doesn't change anything. Corentine blood or not, they won't succeed.

We'll continue sending guards to protect our citizens in places of high rebel activity, but otherwise all we can do is wait for them to realize that their movement is doomed to fail."

Jaren frowned down at the table, clearly unhappy with the lack of initiative.

"In the meantime," Horeth went on, "we have a more pressing concern."

Jaren's gaze returned to the Grand Master, who pushed back from the table and stood, his robes cascading down his wiry body like a wave of blood.

And then he started walking across the room.

Directly toward Kiva.

She stopped breathing as he approached, terrified to make any sound that might give her away. He halted right in front of the cabinet, blocking her line of sight. All he had to do was bend down and open the doors, and she would be—

"We've received a letter from the King of Mirraven," Horeth said, and Kiva nearly whimpered with relief when she heard the rustle of parchment. Her view cleared when he strode back to his seat with the missive in his hands.

Groaning, Jaren asked, "What's Arakkis threatening this time? Let me guess: if we surrender Evalon to him, he won't kill us all? Maybe one day he'll find some creativity."

A wary silence fell, before Queen Ariana turned to her son and slowly said, "Arakkis is dead."

Jaren visibly jolted. "What?"

"I wrote to you," Ariana said, a crease in her brow. "Right after you left Vallenia for the winter palace."

Jaren was shaking his head. "The only notes I received were about Tilda being captured in Mirraven and you negotiating to have her sent to Zalindov."

"That happened after Arakkis was gone. Those negotiations were all with—"

"Don't say it," Jaren whispered, his face paling.

"Navok is king now," Ariana said quietly. Regretfully, even. "As you know, Mirraven laws state that if anyone of royal blood challenges the ruling monarch and defeats them in combat, they can claim the throne as their own. Navok challenged Arakkis. And he won."

"He killed his own father," Jaren said in a flat voice.

"Arakkis was no saint," the Grand Master pointed out.

"He was in comparison to his son."

The weight of Jaren's harsh declaration filled the room until Horeth cleared his throat and gestured to the parchment. "This arrived last night. Until now, Mirraven hasn't been responding to any of our recent missives. Nor has Caramor, for that matter."

Jaren reached for the letter and began scanning it immediately.

"As you can see," Horeth said, "unlike his father, Navok isn't threatening to attack."

"He's smarter than that," Jaren murmured, a look of concentration on his face as he translated the Mirravish words. His eyes narrowed at one point and his head jerked up. "Serafine is marrying Voshell?"

"One of Navok's first edicts as king was to betroth his sister to Caramor's crown prince," Horeth confirmed. Sourly, he added, "As if the two territories need to be any closer."

"They don't," Jaren said, his brow furrowed. "They're already joined at the hip—a marriage isn't going to strengthen them further, especially since we all know Serafine would rather die than wed Voshell. What's Navok playing at? This doesn't make any sense."

"Perhaps he's getting her out of the way so she doesn't think to challenge him?" Yisari suggested, brushing at a tendril of dark hair that had escaped her strict bun.

"Serafine Kildarion wouldn't hurt a fly," Jaren argued. "If she didn't look so much like her brother and father, I'd swear she was adopted. She's nothing like them."

"She must take after her mother in personality, then," Zerra mused.

"Let's just hope she doesn't meet the same end," Feldor said darkly.

Kiva's brows rose, wondering if perhaps the ex-queen hadn't fled in the night after all.

Or maybe she'd tried, and her cruel husband had caught up to her.

"Poor Serafine," Jaren said, his words genuine. "Navok is obviously using her for some kind of bargaining power. She doesn't deserve that — she was the only one of them who I could ever stand to be around during our northern diplomatic missions. Mirryn enjoyed her company as well — they became fast friends. And Caldon — well, obviously Cal liked her. Though she was always clever enough to spurn his advances."

Jaren rolled his eyes, prompting chuckles from around the table. But then they all sobered as he lowered the parchment and exhaled loudly.

"This letter doesn't really tell us anything, does it? Navok's just taunting us with pleasantries, wanting us on edge and worried about what he's planning." Jaren drummed his fingers on the table. "But regardless, send word to Ashlyn. If the armies of Mirraven and Caramor are stirring, we need our own to be ready."

"Our armies are always ready," Yisari said, with evident pride. "If those northern brutes think they can invade us so easily, they'll quickly learn why Evalon is the most powerful kingdom in Wenderall."

Jaren gave a distracted nod, his gaze scanning the missive again. "Something about this doesn't seem right to me. He's all but gloating about Serafine's impending nuptials. But *why?*" Looking at Yisari, he asked, "Do we have eyes inside Mirraven?"

"No one deep enough to provide anything useful," she answered.

"Get Ashlyn on it," Jaren commanded. "Tell her to send in her best, someone who can think quickly and adapt as needed. Navok is both cunning and perceptive—he'll smell a spy before they even set foot in Zadria, so whoever goes in needs to be crafty."

"I'll dispatch a messenger tonight," Yisari promised.

"Knowing Ash, she's probably already got someone on the inside who we don't know about," Jaren said, passing the letter to his mother. "But if she doesn't, she'll make it happen."

"And until then?" Horeth asked.

"We watch," Jaren said. "We listen. We wait."

"If they make a move, we'll stop them," Queen Ariana said in a hard voice. "No one threatens my family and my kingdom and gets away with it. *No one.*"

Kiva trembled at the fury in Ariana's voice, the words repeating in her ears long after the Royal Council moved on to talk about the other items on their agenda. Foreign trade negotiations, city maintenance updates, guild requests . . . all matters that were inconsequential to her. She soon grew bored, the discomfort of her physical condition becoming more obvious, her muscles aching and her backside numb.

Just when Kiva thought she wouldn't be able to survive another minute in the claustrophobic space, Jaren and Ariana rose to their feet, declaring the meeting over. She nearly wept with relief when the councillors followed them out into the dark passageway and the door sealed shut behind them.

Unwilling to risk discovery now, Kiva waited long enough for them to have returned aboveground before she finally opened the cabinet—and toppled straight out onto the hard stone ground. Lying there, she bit her lip against the pins and needles, waiting for the pain to ease.

It didn't.

She blamed Caldon and his torturous morning workout, though it was hardly his fault that she'd crammed herself into a cupboard for the better part of the afternoon.

It had been worth it, she reminded herself, gritting her teeth and standing to her feet. Not even Naari had been allowed in the room. Hell, not even *Mirryn* was privy to all the council's secrets—only the queen and her heir.

And today, Kiva.

Now she just had to find a way to communicate what she'd learned to Torell and Zuleeka.

An unpleasant feeling hit Kiva's stomach as she began her painstaking journey out of the room. She tried to convince herself that it was from hunger, and not because of how thoroughly she planned to betray the Vallentis family.

How thoroughly she planned to betray *Jaren.*

The last thing I want is to make her feel like she's trapped in another kind of cage.

His words echoed in her mind, her stomach twisting even more.

Right now she deserves the chance to live her life and follow her dreams.

If only it were that easy, Kiva thought. If only the last ten years had never happened. If only she weren't bound by duty, by love, by family.

I can only hope she'll grant me the honor of being by her side on that journey.

He would be by her side. Right up until the crown fell from his head.

Kiva had to stop in the middle of the darkened tunnel, the agony of that image almost too much for her to bear.

And then she continued on.

Because she had to.

But despite her best attempts to ignore it, the twisting pain stayed with her all the way up to the palace, lingering for what remained of the afternoon and long into the night, a steady ache that refused to fade.

CHAPTER ELEVEN

Kiva was burning.

Falling.

Drowning.

Water. So much water. She couldn't breathe.

Her skin was on fire. It burned. *It burned.*

Down she fell, the wind ripping her apart, the cold shredding her skin.

The *thwack* of a whip. A quiet, masculine moan.

Blood flowing into a drain.

Darkness — so much darkness.

She couldn't breathe.

SHE COULDN'T BREA —

"Wake *up!*"

Kiva gasped and shot up in bed to find a dark outline of a man hovering over her, gripping her shoulders. She shrieked and threw her fists at his naked chest, thrashing wildly to get free. He made an *oomph* sound but only held on to her tighter, trapping her arms. She opened her mouth to shriek again, but then —

"Kiva! *Kiva!* It's me!"

Jaren's voice finally penetrated, causing her to freeze.

"It was just a nightmare," he said, holding her firmly against his warm, strong body. "You're safe. I'm here." He stroked her sweaty hair away from her face and repeated, "I'm here."

"J-J-Jaren?" Kiva stuttered around her frantic, panting breaths. The room was dark, barely enough moonlight drifting in to make out his concerned features.

"I've got you," he told her, rubbing soothing patterns on her back.

Kiva was quaking so badly that she cuddled into Jaren's bare torso and burrowed her face in the crook of his neck, forgetting that she should be pushing him away and instead clinging to him like a child.

From the doorway to her bedroom came Tipp's hushed voice. "Is she a-all right?"

"She'll be fine," Jaren answered quietly. "You did the right thing, coming to get me. Why don't you go and wake Ori, have a sneaky hot cocoa, then go back to sleep. You can talk to her in the morning."

Kiva sensed Tipp's hesitation, but then she heard the door shut as he left her room.

Still clinging to Jaren, Kiva couldn't bring herself to let go, her body continuing to tremble. She didn't even care that they were alone, tangled together on her bed, with him only half dressed. All she knew was that she felt safe in his arms. They were all that was holding her together.

He was all that was holding her together.

"I have them too, you know," Jaren whispered, his fingers combing through her hair. "The dreams. Ever since Zalindov."

She burrowed deeper into him, recalling the sounds of distress she'd heard muted through the walls at the winter palace.

Against his neck she asked, barely a breath of sound, "What do you dream about?"

She knew she should put some distance between them.

But she didn't move.

Just this once, she told herself.

Just this once, she would allow herself to forget who he was—who *she* was—and rest in the comfort of his embrace.

"I dream of darkness, I dream of death," Jaren answered slowly. "I dream of you falling from that tower and me not catching you in time. I dream of you walking into the crematorium and never coming back out. I dream of—of—" He swallowed. "I dream of finding you at the bottom of the quarry, not breathing." He shuddered against her. "I dream of you dying, over and over, while I just stand there, watching."

His words prompted flashes of Kiva's own nightmare.

Falling.

Burning.

Drowning.

But also the soul-destroying darkness of the Abyss. And—

"I saw you getting whipped."

The words left her without her permission.

Jaren turned as still as a statue.

After the day she'd had, everything she'd heard, everything she'd felt—and was currently feeling—Kiva's guard was completely torn away. Because of that, she couldn't keep from continuing, "It was my fault. You—You saved me, and he—he *hurt* you." Her throat caught, making a jagged, painful sound.

"Sweetheart," Jaren murmured, kissing her temple.

She melted into him. She couldn't help it.

"I'm so sorry," she whispered, the apology coming from deep within her. "I never said it to you before. I should have said it to you before."

"You have nothing to be sorry about."

"I didn't say thank you, either," Kiva went on, not hearing him. She was still half asleep, her words tumbling from her lips without thought. "You saved my life, and I never said thank you. I—I was so angry that you'd lied to me, but you still—you still *saved* me. I'm alive because of you." Her voice became hoarse. "What kind of person doesn't say thank you?"

A comforting stroke of Jaren's fingers. "I'm sure you thanked me."

"I didn't," she argued, gripping him tighter. "I *didn't*."

"All right, then you're saying it now," Jaren said, his tone pacifying.

"I should have said it sooner."

"You're saying it now," Jaren repeated.

Kiva fell silent, emotion simmering within her. Her nightmare had left her raw. She was feeling so much — too much. Everything she'd been trying to bury for six weeks, for *ten years*, was rising to the surface.

"I'm sorry," she whispered again, the words breaking.

"You already said that, beautiful," Jaren whispered back, gathering her closer.

But this time, Kiva wasn't apologizing for what had already happened.

She was apologizing for what lay ahead.

And as Jaren continued to hold her, promising he would stay until she fell back to sleep, she knew she was in more danger than ever before.

Because she didn't want to let him go.

And she wasn't sure if she ever would.

When Kiva woke in the morning, there was a prince in her bedroom — but it wasn't the same prince who had stayed with her after her nightmare until she'd eventually dozed off in his arms.

"Training, Sunshine," Caldon said. "Up, up, up!"

Groggily, Kiva pulled back her covers, wondering when Jaren had left, but grateful that his cousin hadn't caught them in bed together.

A painful moan left her as she stood to her feet, her muscles protesting everything she'd put them through the previous day. But Caldon showed her no mercy once they reached the training yard, his second lesson turning into a replica of the first, just with extra box-stepping and an added running lap.

Kiva again vomited up the contents of her stomach, with Caldon unsympathetically pushing her to her limits — and beyond.

Sweating like a river and aching all over, Kiva wasn't sure how she made it back to her room afterward, but once she'd soaked in a long, hot bath and changed into clean clothes, she began to feel mildly human again. Embarrassment from the previous night tried to creep in, but she wouldn't let it take root. Jaren had been there for her when she'd needed him. Jaren was *always* there for her when she needed him. She just couldn't think about that, because when she did . . .

She'd seen him in the training yard that morning, facing off against Captain Veris again. He'd paused only long enough to look her way and send her a comforting smile before dodging the captain's next sword thrust, but that smile had been enough for her to know that whatever had happened between them in the night—and in the cavern yester-day—didn't require an explanation. Or a definition. They were what they were. Jaren and Kiva. Two people connected for better or worse. It wasn't something Kiva needed to dwell on. In fact, it was something she *couldn't* dwell on if she wanted to maintain any semblance of sanity. Her plans hadn't changed—even if her heart refused to listen.

A knock on her bedroom door startled her from her thoughts, and she assumed it must be Tipp coming to check on her after her night-mare. But when she opened it, she found an elderly servant woman, who bobbed into a quick curtsey.

"Begging your pardon, miss, but the healer who treated you the other night has sent word asking for you to meet her at Silverthorn."

"Rhessinda?" Kiva asked.

The woman nodded. "Yes, miss. I can have her return to the palace if you'd prefer?"

"No, no, that's fine," Kiva said. "It's a beautiful day. It'll be good for me to get out for a bit."

Staying active would help keep her sore muscles loose, too. Not to mention, it would give her an excuse to have some time away from Jaren. Distance, she reminded herself, was needed—even if she was failing spectacularly at following her own advice.

"Very good, miss," the servant said, curtseying again and departing.

Kiva had planned to spend her day snooping around the palace and mapping the grounds, but with everything she'd learned yesterday, she'd earned herself a break. It wasn't like she could offload the information yet anyway, still having no idea when her siblings intended to reappear.

After tugging on her boots, Kiva made her way down to the ground floor and stepped out into the spring sunshine. She'd been told upon arriving in Vallenia that she could come and go from the palace as she pleased, the guards having been ordered to give her free rein through the front gates. Because of that, she had no issue leaving the grounds, smiling politely to the Royal Guards and receiving respectful nods in return.

Kiva took her time meandering along the River Road toward Silverthorn, breathing in the fresh air and enjoying the sun on her skin. It was the last day of the River Festival, but the streets were nowhere near as crowded as the first night, with no pushing or shoving, just pockets of children dancing to upbeat tunes from wandering musicians.

It was almost a shame when Kiva reached the academy, her muscles burning anew as she ascended the steep hill atop which the campus rested. Moving stiffly to ease some of her agony, she headed in the direction of the main infirmary, having no idea if Rhessinda would be there but confident someone would be able to point her in the right direction.

Strolling down the arched stone pathway, Kiva admired the luscious green sanctuary between the buildings, again marveling at the serenity. She was so lost in her appreciation that she nearly collided with a woman walking in the opposite direction, and did a quick hop-step to the side just in time.

"I'm sorry, I wasn't looking—" Kiva broke off when she recognized the head of Silverthorn.

"Miss Meridan, what a nice surprise," Healer Maddis said warmly. "I was hoping to see you again."

"I, um, hello," Kiva said, uncomfortably aware that she'd nearly plowed down the elderly woman.

"Have you made a decision about your studies?" Maddis asked, pushing wire-framed spectacles up her nose.

"I—well—" It was on the tip of her tongue to say she wasn't interested, but she knew her lie would be unconvincing. "I'm still thinking about it," Kiva finally said.

Maddis smiled with understanding. "Take as long as you need. As I said the other day, the offer will remain open."

Kiva swallowed against the lump in her throat. "Thank you."

The matron removed her glasses and placed them in the pocket of her white healer's robe. "If you didn't come to speak with me, what brings you to Silverthorn?"

"Healer Rhessinda summoned me," Kiva said. She pointed to the bruise on the side of her face. "I'm guessing she wants to see how I'm feeling."

"Oh dear," Maddis said, gently turning Kiva's chin to the side. "That must have been a nasty bump."

"The swelling went down fast," Kiva said, "but it's still tender to the touch."

"Who did you say treated you? Healer Lucinda?"

"Rhessinda," Kiva corrected.

Maddis considered for a moment, before she offered an apologetic shrug. "I used to know all of our healers, but there are so many now, and I'm not as good with names as I once was. Lucinda, Rhessinda, Jacinda, Melinda—they all blur together, I'm afraid. It's a peril of growing older, but not the worst, I'll admit." Her dark face lit with self-deprecating humor as she waved a hand down her aging body. "Once everything decides to move south, it's all downhill from there. Something for you to look forward to."

Kiva couldn't help chuckling.

"Someone at reception will be able to help you find her," Maddis went on, gesturing to the infirmary Kiva had already been heading toward. The healer's attention was then snagged by a white-robed group lying on the grass, their faces tinged a sickly green. With a long-suffering sigh, she said, "If you'll excuse me, I need to have a word with some of the novices about their behavior at the festival last night."

With a pat on the shoulder, Maddis left Kiva standing on the path, but not before turning back to call, "I'll look forward to hearing once you've made your decision."

Kiva said nothing, not wanting to let the Matron Healer down. Not wanting to let *herself* down. But now wasn't the time—there were too many other things she needed to focus on. Her own desires would have to wait.

Right now she deserves the chance to live her life and follow her dreams.

Jaren's words to the Royal Council echoed in her mind, but Kiva closed her heart to them. Even if she made the selfish decision to put herself first, the scar on her hand would forever mark her as a criminal. No patient would ever trust her, no healing academy would ever accept her. One close look was all it would take for Maddis to rescind her offer.

And yet . . .

Kiva sighed, Jaren's words burrowing deep despite her best efforts to ignore them. Try as she might, she wasn't ready to give up on her dreams.

Because dreams were all she had.

Dreams where her family was safe and happy and living the life they deserved.

Dreams where she studied at Silverthorn and was able to help those who needed her, bringing comfort where there was suffering, light where there was darkness, and hope when all hope was lost.

Dreams where she and Jaren—

No.

She knew better than to dream about Jaren.

"Hey, over here!"

Kiva looked up to see that she'd been walking blindly along the path toward the infirmary, only to discover Rhessinda sitting on a bench in the sanctuary and waving at her.

Passing through one of the stone archways, Kiva approached the young healer, the grass soft underfoot, the smells of lilac and lavender from the nearby shrubbery tickling her nose.

"I got your message," Kiva said, taking a seat when Rhess patted the wood beside her.

While her white robes were spotless, the healer's ashy hair was again in a messy bun, a few tendrils hanging loose around her face. "How's the head?" she asked, her russet eyes examining the bruise much like Maddis had done.

"Much better," Kiva said. "The aloeweed gel brought the inflammation down faster than I expected."

"The poppymilk probably helped, too," Rhess said with a knowing wink.

Kiva grinned. "I slept like the dead that night. Not sure if that was wise after a head wound."

"If memory serves, I *did* tell you to wake regularly," Rhess said dryly. She then asked, "Other than the swelling, have you been feeling well enough? No slurring, numbness, coordination concerns? Drowsiness, vomiting, headaches? Anything like that?"

Admittedly, Kiva had experienced most of those things in the last two days, but all of them she attributed to training with Caldon, so she shook her head.

"You were limping when you walked over here," Rhess observed in a leading statement.

"I've recently started a new fitness regime," Kiva said, moderating her voice to keep from revealing how she felt about it. Judging by the mirth in Rhess's eyes, she wasn't successful.

"Ah," the healer said. "So just your standard muscle aches and pains?"

"If by 'standard,' you mean 'I'm dying,' then sure."

Rhess snickered. "I can give you something to help, if you want?"

"That would be appreciated."

Kiva expected the healer to say she'd have a muscle relaxant sent to the palace, but Rhess reached into her pocket and withdrew a small jar filled with a pale orange powder.

Seeing the look Kiva sent her, Rhess explained, "I keep what feels like a small infirmary on me at all times. Be ready for anything, I say." She handed over the jar. "Mix a pinch of that into your tea right before bed, and then again when you wake up. You'll feel better in no time."

Kiva removed the stopper and gave it a sniff. "Buttercress, ginger-weed, halo pods, and—" She took another sniff. "Lurmeric?"

"Well done," Rhess said approvingly. "I heard you have some healing experience."

"Nothing compared to what you do here," Kiva said, nervously fiddling with the sleeve of her sweater and making sure it covered her scar.

"Silverthorn is in a league of its own, I'll grant you that," Rhessinda agreed, glancing out across the grounds with an awe that Kiva understood deep in her soul. Rhess, however, was already living the dream that Kiva could only wish might one day find her.

"Thanks for coming all the way up here," the healer went on to say. "I wanted to check in after everything that happened the other night. Being abducted—that must have been frightening."

"I was unconscious for most of it," Kiva said, sticking to her lie. "Have you visited Caldon? His wound was worse than mine."

Rhess waited until two young healers walked past and continued deeper into the sanctuary before saying, "From what I hear, the prince has suffered much more grievous injuries in the past. He'll send for someone if he's worried."

Unable to help herself, Kiva said, "People usually jump at the chance to spend time with him." Pointedly, she added, "He's very handsome."

Rhess scrunched up her nose. "He certainly seems to think so."

Kiva laughed, surprised—and delighted—by the healer's candor. "Most women fall at his feet."

"I am not most women."

Kiva was beginning to realize that. And respect it. "So are you avoiding him on principle because he flirted with you?"

"I'm not avoiding him," Rhessinda stated. "I just don't want to see him." When Kiva's lips twitched, Rhess's eyes narrowed. "You can't judge—you're the one who stabbed him. If that doesn't send a message, I don't know what does."

Kiva winced. "In my defense, I thought he was someone else."

A beat of silence passed, and then suddenly Rhess was laughing. A moment later, Kiva joined her.

"I can't believe you stabbed a prince!" the healer exclaimed, holding her stomach.

"You're enjoying this way too much," Kiva said, though her voice rumbled with lingering humor. "You're a healer. Where's your sense of compassion?"

"You're not the first person to ask me that," Rhess said, still chuckling. "I must have missed the day they taught about bedside manner."

Kiva shook her head with amusement, feeling a growing connection to the healer. Their kinship seemed effortless—something that, if she'd still been at Zalindov, she would have avoided at all costs. But she wasn't at Zalindov now. She didn't have to push people away to save herself the pain that came with their death. That wasn't her life anymore.

With that in mind, when Rhess asked if she wanted to walk down to the river and grab some lunch, Kiva hesitated only a moment before agreeing.

It was all right, she told herself, to start building a life. To start making friends — *especially* outside of the palace, since everworld knew any relationships she built there were going to crumble soon enough.

"So what's your story?" Rhess asked as they left the academy and began strolling down the hill.

"I don't have a story," Kiva said, too quickly.

"Right," Rhess said with clear disbelief.

"I don't," Kiva argued. "I'm just your normal, everyday kind of girl."

"The scar on your left hand says otherwise."

Kiva nearly missed a step. But Rhess wasn't finished.

"Not to mention, you were abducted by rebels, you're living at the palace, and the crown prince looks at you like he would burn the world to keep you safe. But sure, you're just a normal, everyday kind of girl."

Kiva said nothing, unsure which of Rhess's observations was the most damning.

"Personally, I think normal is overrated," the healer said. She unfastened the band around her hair, her ashy locks catching in the breeze. "Normal is tedious, it's boring. The best people are the ones with stories, the ones who have lived through things others can only imagine in their wildest dreams — and their worst nightmares." She looked pointedly toward Kiva's hand. "People like you."

It was too late for Kiva to cover her scar, but Rhessinda didn't seem perturbed by it. There was no judgment in her tone, just curiosity.

"As for me," the healer went on, sidestepping a small child toddling away from his mother, the crowds growing thicker as they reached the River Road, "I have a story, too."

It was a taunting statement, begging for Kiva to ask more, but she knew that in order to receive answers, she had to be willing to give some.

Swallowing against her dry throat, she said, "I assume that story has something to do with how you ended up at Silverthorn?"

Rhess came to a stop beside the railing overlooking the river, her eyes turning dark. "It might."

Kiva took a minute to think before deciding that since Rhess had seen her scar and knew about her link to the royals, she might as well hear the rest.

So she told her.

She shared about her time at Zalindov and how she'd met Jaren. She shared about their escape and how they'd spent weeks recuperating in the mountains before venturing to the capital. She shared what she'd been doing with her days, training with Caldon and getting to know the royals, but then she stopped sharing, knowing better than to reveal anything about her family or the rebels to a near stranger. Even so, it was still more than she'd told anyone, ever.

When she was finished, Rhess whistled through her teeth. "I'd heard rumors that the Rebel Queen was at Zalindov and someone had volunteered to take her place in the Trial by Ordeal. You've got guts, I'll give you that."

Kiva's insides pitched. "There are rumors about me?"

She looked around the bustling River Road, half expecting to see families pointing and staring.

"People like to gossip," Rhess said. "But don't worry, everyone thinks you're dead."

Kiva jolted. "Excuse me?"

Shrugging, Rhessinda said, "No more news came after the fourth Ordeal, so the general consensus was that you'd failed." Thoughtfully, she added, "It probably wouldn't be too hard to get word out about your victory, if that's what you want. You'd get a lot of attention."

Kiva recoiled at the idea. "No, thanks. I'd rather be dead."

Rhess choked on a laugh, and, realizing how that had sounded, Kiva quickly amended, "You know what I mean—I'd rather they *think* I'm dead. The last thing I want is strangers coming up to me and asking questions."

"Oh no, *strangers*," Rhess said with a dramatic shudder. "They're the *worst*."

Kiva rolled her eyes. "Your turn. How did you become a healer?"

Rhessinda tugged at her white robe, her humor vanishing. "My parents were healers, so I guess you could say I followed in their footsteps."

"Do they live here in Vallenia?"

"No. They don't."

Something in Rhessinda's voice had Kiva bracing.

The healer sighed, as if reluctant to speak now that it was her turn, but nevertheless she shared, "When I was fourteen, a band of Mirraven mercenaries slipped past the border guards and raided our village—that's not uncommon that far in the north; they usually just take their spoils and leave. But those raiders were different. They weren't after coin. It was winter, they wanted bodies to warm them, and they didn't care how unwilling those bodies were. Our townspeople fought hard, but the mercenaries were ruthless. They—" Rhess turned to stare out at the water. "They made us pay. All of us."

Kiva swallowed, fearing what was to come.

"My parents did everything they could to keep me safe," Rhess said. Her voice wobbled slightly but then she took a deep breath, her tone deadening as she declared, "And then they were slaughtered before my eyes."

A small, devastated gasp left Kiva.

"The mercenaries took me and—" Rhessinda cut herself off, unable to finish, but Kiva didn't need her to. The haunted look she wore said it all.

Taking a moment to regain control, the healer continued, "I managed to escape. Timing, chance, luck. A combination of all three. Another family took me in, helped me heal."

Shadows grew in her eyes, spreading across her face. "There were some dark days. Days when I gave up. Days when I tried—really damn hard—not to feel anything. Days when I *didn't* feel anything." In a whisper, she admitted, "Those were the worst. Because when I didn't feel anything, I didn't have anything to hold me here."

Kiva's heart clenched.

With a sharp exhale, the shadows in Rhess's eyes began to clear. "My adopted family saved my life in more ways than one. It took time, but they helped remind me that life is too precious to throw away, no matter how hard it is, no matter how much it hurts. I wouldn't—" Her throat bobbed. "I wouldn't be here today without them."

Rhess's final statement was so implicit that Kiva had to blink away tears, realizing the choice the healer had nearly made.

But she hadn't.

She was here, she was alive, she had fought the darkness and won.

She had *survived*.

Just like Kiva.

"I told you," Rhess whispered, her gaze suddenly locking with Kiva's. "The best people have stories. Even if they wish they didn't."

Kiva blew out a shaky breath, unable to do anything but offer a solemn nod. She knew there was much more to Rhess's tale, just as there was more to her own, but they'd both revealed enough for now.

The healer seemed to think so too, because she quietly said, "I don't usually share about my family to people I hardly know, but you trusted me with your story, so it only seemed fair to trust you with mine. That said, I'd be grateful if you didn't tell anyone. I'm not after pity."

Shaking her head, Kiva promised, "I would never."

"And I'll keep your secrets, too," Rhess said. "I hope that goes without saying."

It didn't, normally. But there was no denying that Kiva felt a connection to the healer. They'd both suffered so much in their young lives that it was as if their souls recognized each other, the pain, the hurt . . . the healing.

"Come on," Rhess said, turning from the river and pointing to a cluster of market stalls set up further along the water's edge. "Feelings make me hungry. I need to stress-eat my weight in chocabuns."

And just like that, their heavy conversation passed.

"Chocabuns?" Kiva asked.

Rhess looked at her, aghast. "Don't tell me they didn't serve you chocabuns in prison?"

Kiva sent her a deadpan expression.

The healer grabbed Kiva's elbow and dragged her toward the stalls. "My friend, your life is about to change forever."

Rhessinda was right — and she was wrong.

The chocabuns turned out to be divine: smooth, velvety chocolate chunks mixed into a dough that melted in her mouth. But as good as they were, they didn't change Kiva's life. No, it was what happened after she and Rhess had ingested enough to warrant stomach aches, when they were walking back up the hill to the academy, moaning about never eating again.

It was just as they reached the entrance to Silverthorn and came to a stop, ready to part ways, that a man hobbled past them, heading toward the infirmary. He was holding his side, a look of pain on his face, but when Rhess asked if he needed assistance, he politely declined her offer.

He continued on, and Kiva put him from her mind — or she would have, if not for the tingling she felt in her hands, the glow that erupted at her fingertips.

Rhess sucked in a breath. "What the —"

Pure, unadulterated panic filled Kiva, and she shoved her magic away, harder than ever before. The golden light winked out like a candle, her skin normal once again, but the force of the suppression left her feeling nauseous, a headache stabbing at her temples.

Rhessinda's russet eyes were narrowed on Kiva's hands. "Did you just see —"

"I need to go to Oakhollow."

Kiva blurted out the words, partly in an effort to distract Rhess, but mostly because she couldn't ignore the facts any longer. Three times in three days her magic had risen to the surface against her will. She had no idea what was causing it, but she couldn't risk it happening again, not while she was living at the palace. If Jaren saw . . . if *anyone* saw . . .

Kiva needed to speak with her siblings. She couldn't keep waiting for them to come to her — they could take days before making contact again. Weeks, even.

Judging by what was happening with her magic, Kiva might not have that long. She had to risk seeking out Torell and Zuleeka herself, praying they'd be able to help. Neither of them had exhibited magic as children, but that could have changed. Even if it hadn't, their mother had once possessed healing magic, despite having chosen not to use it in order to keep them safe from discovery. Maybe Tilda had told them something that could explain what was happening to Kiva and how she could bring her magic back under control.

"Oakhollow?" Rhessinda repeated. "What's in Oakhollow?"

Offering a truth not even Jaren knew, Kiva swallowed and said, "My family." Swallowing again, she asked, "Do you know how I can get there?"

Rhess was looking at her closely, her gaze shifting from Kiva's face to her hands and back again. She then shook her head as if deciding that whatever she'd seen must have been a trick of the light, and Kiva nearly fainted with relief.

"It's fairly easy," the healer said, pushing windswept hair behind her ear. "You just follow the River Road and turn off it to leave the city through the South Watch, then head straight through the farmlands until you reach the first crossroads. After that, you take a left, then a right, then . . ."

Rhess continued giving instructions, which Kiva tried to memorize, but the healer soon paused at whatever she saw on Kiva's face.

"You know what? I'm due to head to Oakhollow for some house calls this week," she said. "Why don't I move my trip up to tomorrow, and you can tag along with me? I'll have to leave you alone for a few hours once we get there, but that'll give you time with your family, and at least you won't get lost."

Kiva was so grateful that she could have hugged the healer. "You don't mind?"

"I have to go at some point anyway. And you're not terrible company." Rhess's quick grin told Kiva that maybe she wasn't the only one to feel a growing friendship between them.

Because of that—and a myriad of other more desperate reasons— Kiva asked, "What time should I meet you?"

They quickly came up with a plan for their departure the next morning, with Kiva intending to leave the palace right after her training session with Caldon. If anyone asked, she would say she was spending the day with a Silverthorn healer—not a lie, even if it implied she'd be at the academy. It was the perfect cover, Kiva realized, somewhat bitterly. But she pushed away her guilty thoughts to focus on the positive.

Tomorrow she would see her brother and sister again. And while she had things to tell them—and more importantly, needed their help with her magical problem—she was also going to make the most of the opportunity.

She had questions, and it was about damn time they were answered.

CHAPTER TWELVE

As planned, Kiva started the next day with her early morning fitness training—another gruelling session, but on the plus side, she only vomited once.

The only hiccup came when Jaren called out just as she was leaving the training yard. For a moment, she feared he might have cleared his schedule to spend time with her, but he only apologized for not seeing her much the previous day, claiming to have been away from the city helping to rebuild a nearby village.

Before she could ask about it, he inquired about her visit to Silverthorn, and she launched into an account of her hours spent with Rhessinda. Jaren seemed delighted to hear about their budding friendship, making it easy for Kiva to share her false plans for the day, with him saying he was relieved because he had a full plate of meetings ahead anyway.

Hearing that, Kiva worried about missing an opportunity to eavesdrop, but when he mentioned the Merchants Guild, the Dockworkers Union, and the Minstrels Society—among others—she realized his appointments would be similar to the latter half of what the Royal Council meeting had covered, none of which would be relevant to her spying mission.

They parted ways when a message arrived from the minister of finance requesting Jaren's immediate presence, causing him to look at Kiva with woeful eyes, begging for her to save him. She only grinned and teased, "Poor baby prince," before telling him that the sooner he went to his meetings, the sooner he could be free.

Back in her room, Kiva bathed quickly and ate a light breakfast as she dressed for her outing, adding a hooded cloak to protect her from the coastal breeze she would encounter on her journey—and affording her discretion if needed.

Remembering to pinch a dose of muscle relaxant into her tea to help stave off the pain Caldon's session would later prompt, Kiva gulped it down and hurried from her room. She paused only twice on her way out of the palace: once when she passed Tipp and Oriel chasing Flox through the halls, the middle-aged Tutor Edna running after them and mumbling a prayer for patience, and the second time when Naari called her name, right as she was stepping out of the entrance hall.

"I hear you're heading to Silverthorn again," the guard stated.

Kiva was surprised that Naari wasn't shadowing Jaren's footsteps, but then she realized that many of his conversations must be confidential, just like the Royal Council meeting.

"I'm spending time with one of the healers," Kiva confirmed, keeping her expression open and honest.

Naari looked at her closely before sharing, "Jaren says it's important that you don't feel trapped here, that you've had ten years of being a prisoner and you deserve to remember what it means to be free."

The last thing I want is to make her feel like she's trapped in another kind of cage.

Jaren's words from two days earlier returned to Kiva, his thoughtfulness cutting her deep all over again.

"But you should know he's worried about your safety," Naari continued, "especially after what happened the other night. He won't take away your freedom—he'd never do that to you. So I'm asking you to have a care." Her amber eyes held Kiva's. "I've posted extra sentries along the River Road with orders to watch out for you, but there's a lot of foot traffic between here and Silverthorn, and even the most attentive of guards can miss things. Jaren won't say it at the risk of making you feel shackled, but I think you already know it would destroy him if something happened to you. So be smart."

Kiva's breath was trapped somewhere in her lungs, stopping her from responding, but she nodded her understanding—and her agreement.

"Caldon says you're useless with a blade," Naari went on, pulling a dagger from her cloak, "but I'd still feel better knowing you had one. Just in case."

Trying to hide the tremble in her hands, Kiva took the weapon and listened as Naari offered instructions on how to strap it to her calf, tucked beneath the leather of her boot but still within easy reach.

"Don't stab yourself," Naari warned.

"Why do people keep telling me that?" Kiva muttered.

Naari's lips twitched before she repeated her demand to be careful and vanished back into the palace.

Letting out a long breath, Kiva set off for Silverthorn, mulling over the guard's conversation. She didn't like the idea that Jaren was worried about her, but then she reminded herself that she shouldn't care *what* he felt.

The last thing I want is to make her feel like she's trapped in another kind of cage.

Everworld help her, why did he have to be so . . . *Jaren?* She knew it would be so much easier for him to order guards to follow her, or even request that she stay inside the palace grounds where it was safe. But he hadn't, instead putting her needs first, just as he always had.

On that thought, Kiva shook her head and imagined a mental door slamming shut, picking up her pace as she headed along the River Road. She was acutely aware of Naari's patrolling guards monitoring her from somewhere amongst the crowds, but instead of their hidden presence making her feel safer, her skin was crawling, like they would somehow be able to read her mind—and her guilt. The feeling only passed when she ascended the hill to Silverthorn and reached the campus grounds, finding Rhessinda waiting for her at the arched entrance.

"Perfect timing," the healer said with a bright smile. She had a large pack slung over her shoulder, likely filled with her medical supplies for the day. "Ready for an adventure?"

Kiva was more than ready, even if her stomach bubbled with nerves as she followed Rhess to the small stable complex situated just through the academy's front gates.

"I'm guessing you haven't ridden much in the last ten years?" Rhess asked, approaching a young stableboy who held the reins of two healthy-looking horses, one chestnut, one gray.

"That would be accurate," Kiva said, warily eyeing the horses. The last time she'd ridden on her own, it had been atop her family's docile old pony, a much, *much* smaller creature than those standing before her.

"We'll go easy," Rhess promised, before helping Kiva mount the gray mare who was charmingly named Bluebell.

Purposefully ignoring how far away the ground was, Kiva waited until Rhess was mounted on the chestnut before she casually asked, "Any chance we can avoid taking the River Road out of the city?"

A beat of silence passed before the healer observed, "It sounds suspiciously like you want to sneak out."

Thinking of the added guards monitoring the main thoroughfare, Kiva admitted, "I haven't told anyone where we're going, and I'd prefer to keep it that way. At least until—until—" She didn't have a way to finish her sentence, but Rhess's features softened.

"Hey, we all have our secrets," she said with understanding. "As long as they don't put either of us in danger, I don't mind keeping yours. I meant it when I said that yesterday—you can trust me."

Kiva blew out a breath. "Thanks."

Rhessinda considered for a moment before saying, "I know the backstreets pretty well. We can use them to get to the South Watch, but we'll have to jump back on the main road after we're through the city walls."

"That's fine," Kiva said. They were probably safe to take the River Road the entire way, since Naari had mentioned how the busy traffic meant the guards could miss things—and they wouldn't be expecting Kiva to be on horseback. But the backstreets would limit the risk significantly.

With the new route set, Rhess gave Kiva a brief reminder of the riding basics, and then they set off together from the academy.

Oakhollow was a half-hour ride from Vallenia, but that wasn't counting how long it took them to reach the edge of the city, their pace slower than it would have been had they taken the direct route along the river. Still, they eventually reached the South Watch and rode straight toward the wide open gates, passing travelers coming to and from the capital, many driving carts loaded with wares to trade, others wearing sigils marking them as messengers, and some just common city folk going about their days.

Kiva kept the hood up on her cloak and avoided eye contact with any of the watch guards, but she and Rhessinda encountered no problems, and were soon through the fortified city walls and riding swiftly along a well-worn dirt road. At first the crowds remained thick, but as they continued on, passing farms on either side until they turned off onto the coastal track, they eventually had the road to themselves.

"How's your confidence?" Rhess asked, gesturing toward Bluebell. "Ready to pick up the pace?"

"If I fall off and break my everything, you'll put me back together, right?" Kiva asked, only half joking.

The healer grinned and nudged her horse forward, prompting Kiva to do the same with Bluebell, the mare's long legs eating up the ground as they followed the track up a smooth rise and then along the cliffside path hugging the coastline. The sea breeze was crisp, but with the wind having pushed back her hood and her hair flying out behind her as they cantered high above the cerulean ocean, Kiva felt more invigorated than she had in a long time. She wanted to whoop and shout and laugh at the feeling, longing for it to last forever. But all too soon they had to leave the seaside and slow down, passing through numerous crossroads and into a heavily wooded forest.

"We're nearly there," Rhess said, tossing a water flask to Kiva. She indicated the trees surrounding them and continued, "This is the Emelda Forest. Oakhollow sits close to the edge, but the woods continue all the way down to Avila. It's easy to get lost in here, so make sure you don't wander too far from town today. You wouldn't be the first person to never come out again."

Kiva shuddered, the shadowy woodland seeming more sinister than before. But then the trees began to thin as the path opened up, a small, picturesque village quickly coming into view.

"If I leave you at the tavern, are you good to make your way to your family on your own?" Rhess asked as they rode out from the forest and into the bright sunshine.

Kiva nodded, even if she had no idea yet *where* in the village her family was. But the tavern would be the best place to ask after them.

Together Kiva and Rhess ventured deeper into the village, passing little wooden cottages with flowerpots in their windows, before finding a blacksmith, a small apothecary, a tailor's workshop, a bake house, and an outdoor market. In the center of it all was a larger establishment with a painted sign hanging over the door, curved script reading *The Tippled Boar* resting above a picture of a dancing pig that somehow managed to look highly inebriated.

"There's a stable out the back," Rhess said, when they halted near the entryway. Before she'd even finished, a young girl ran up to them, hay sticking to her messy clothes and the pungent scent of manure making it clear what her role was.

Rhessinda flicked her a silver coin and motioned for Kiva to dismount. She groaned when she landed on the ground, her legs stiff and backside aching despite the medicinal powder she'd taken that morning.

"Just wait until tonight," Rhess said, laughing.

The stablegirl hurried off with Bluebell, leaving Kiva to say, "I'll meet you back here in a few hours?"

"Let's aim for mid-afternoon," Rhess confirmed, gathering her reins. "We'll want to have you back in the city well before dark."

Kiva agreed, since the last thing she needed was for someone from the palace to start worrying enough to seek her out at Silverthorn.

"If you need help with any of your patients . . ." Kiva trailed off, realizing that she didn't know how to end her offer, since it wasn't as if she could say, *Come and find me.*

Thankfully, Rhess didn't notice her hesitation and just said, "Thanks, but you should enjoy your time with your family."

Kiva hoped that was possible, but considering their last encounter, she wasn't holding her breath.

Waving, Rhessinda nudged her horse away from the tavern. Kiva watched until she disappeared deeper into the village, then turned her attention back to the painted pig. She was careful to wipe the distaste from her expression before she stepped through the open doorway.

The interior of the Tippled Boar was much like any other inn she had encountered, both as a child with her parents and during the more recent weeks of travel from the winter palace to Vallenia. Low-lit luminium beacons chased away most of the shadows, and yet the grimy space still remained dark and gloomy, even with the sunshine trying to peek through the dirty windows—all of which were surrounded by numerous stuffed boar heads mounted to the walls.

An overpowering scent of ale tickled Kiva's nostrils as she walked deeper into the room, where a handful of patrons already sat at wooden tables and swayed on stools despite it being barely midmorning. She kept her head down as she passed them, moving straight to the oaken bar at the back of the room, behind which stood the middle-aged innkeeper wiping a soiled cloth along the wood.

"Hello," Kiva said.

The man flicked his dark eyes up to her but said nothing.

"I, um, I'm hoping you can help me find someone," she said.

"You orderin' a drink?" he asked in a gruff, gravelly voice.

"I—well—" Kiva stuttered, before pasting a friendly smile on her face. "It's a bit early for me. Perhaps later, after I've found who I'm looking for."

Again, the innkeeper said nothing.

Kiva took that as an invitation, and asked, "Do you know Zuleeka and Torell Meridan?" She didn't dare use the name Corentine, hoping her siblings weren't foolish enough to go about flaunting their bloodline. "They're a little older than me. Similar features."

"Who wants to know?" the innkeeper asked.

"Their sister," Kiva answered. "Kiva Meridan."

A *thunk* sounded from beside her when a full mug of ale slammed onto the bar, liquid sloshing over the sides as an older man toppled onto the nearest stool and leaned precariously toward her. "Keeeeeva," he slurred. "Tha's a purrrty name. I'm Grum—Grumed—Grumedon."

He looked pleased with himself when he finally shared his name, hiccupping between attempts and smiling a brown-toothed grin at her.

"How 'bout some bread, Grum?" the innkeeper asked, his gruff voice softening as he looked at the man. "Some stew? On the house."

Grumedon took a swig of his ale. "'S too early fer food. But keep these comin'." He waved the mug, more sloshing over the edges, some splashing down onto Kiva's boots.

"Grum—" the innkeeper started, but the drunken man spoke over him.

"Wha's a purty place like you doin' in a girl like this?" Grumedon asked Kiva.

"I'm looking for my family," she answered his mangled question. "Zuleeka and Torell Meridan."

"Ha!" Grum said, slamming his mug loudly, a wave of foam slopping over the top. "I knews it."

He said no more, so Kiva prompted, "You knews—erm, *knew*—what?"

Grumedon pointed a gnarled finger at her. "You 'ave yer mama's eyes."

Before Kiva could get over the shock of his statement, his body slumped and his head fell onto the bar, with loud, drunken snoring erupting from his wide open mouth.

The innkeeper sighed and took the mug away, wiping up the spilled liquid. "Every day, the same. He'll be out for hours." At whatever he saw on Kiva's face, he added, "Grum's lived a hard life, but he does all right. He's got people who care for him—they'll come and get him soon, make sure he's safe and warm. Don't worry, he'll be fine."

Unable to help herself, Kiva rasped, "Was my mother one of those people?"

The innkeeper said nothing, his standard response. But he surprised her when he pulled a piece of grubby parchment and a quill out from beneath the bar.

"Write a note. I'll see what I can do," he offered, albeit still gruffly.

Hope filled her, but Kiva was quick to say, "I need to see them today. As soon as possible. It's important."

The innkeeper made no promises, only repeated, "I'll see what I can do."

Realizing it was the best deal she would get, Kiva hurried to write her message.

$$\text{\#⅁ ～ⓞ ⓞⅯ☰ ⓞ\#⼚⼚》☰∧)(∥～ꙹ.}$$
$$\text{∴☰☰∧ ⓞ∥ ⼚⼚☰～⼂ ⼕\#ⓞⅯ ⼚∥◻.}$$
$$\text{◻ꙹ⌒☰∴ⓞ.}$$

I'm at the Tippled Boar. Need to speak with you. Urgent.

There was nothing secretive about what she wrote, but she still used the code only her siblings would understand, falling back into old habits.

"What's this?" the innkeeper asked, holding the note up to the light and frowning.

"Zuleeka and Torell Meridan," Kiva reminded him. "They'll be able to read it."

He made a grunting sound and placed it in his back pocket, but he made no move to do anything with it.

"When I said it's important, I meant life and death," Kiva told him. *Her* life or death, if she didn't get her magic under control. "Please, I only have a few hours."

His eyes came back to hers. "You orderin' a drink?"

Kiva gritted her teeth and shook her head.

He jerked his thumb to a doorway at the back of the tavern. "Then you can wait outside."

"Please," Kiva said again, this time in a whisper.

The man only pointed again, then turned and disappeared into the room behind the bar. A young woman took his place, pulling a face as she picked up his soiled cloth and swapped it for a fresh one.

With nothing left but to trust that the innkeeper would pass along her message, Kiva sighed and headed in the direction he'd pointed, stepping through the doorway to find a small open courtyard.

There were no other patrons outside, so she removed her cloak and sat at one of the wooden tables. Seconds later, the barmaid appeared and placed a steaming mug in front of Kiva, smiling and winking before she vanished back inside, calling over her shoulder, "Say hi to Tor for me."

Having no desire to read into the suggestive words, Kiva took a sip of the drink—spiced milk and honey—and tipped her face to the sunshine, willing her tight limbs to relax as she resigned herself to wait.

CHAPTER THIRTEEN

Kiva was pacing the courtyard after finishing her drink, time having slowed to a crawl. There was no sign of her siblings yet, but she couldn't sit around waiting all day. If the innkeeper wasn't going to come through for her, she would just have to find someone else to ask.

Decision made, Kiva threw her cloak back on, but just as she started toward the tavern doorway, heavy footsteps met her ears, and a tall figure hurried out from the darkness.

Kiva's shoulders slumped with relief at the sight of her brother, who wasted no time in closing the distance between them.

"Are you insane?" he asked, hugging her tightly. "What were you thinking, coming all the way here?"

"Nice to see you too, Tor," Kiva said, trying to keep the hurt from her voice.

He pulled back to look at her, his emerald eyes roaming her face, and then he renewed his embrace, sighing quietly beside her ear.

"I'm sorry," he said into her hair. "Of course I'm happy to see you. But it's so dangerous. How did you get away from the palace? Did anyone follow you? Have you—"

Kiva drew away, unable to keep from smiling. "You were never such a worrier when we were kids."

"I'm not a worrier now." Torell looked pointedly at her and amended, "Except for when it comes to my baby sister, who I love more than the world and want to make sure stays safe."

Throat tightening, Kiva noted, "I'm not much of a baby anymore."

"You'll always be my baby sister," Tor argued. "Whether you're seven or seventy, I'll never stop wanting to protect you." He moved a step backwards. "Now, why did you risk coming here, Mouse? Did something happen?"

Mouse.

Little mouse.

Her father's nickname for her.

Kiva had to blink back tears, having forgotten that Tor used to call her that as well. It took her a moment before she could respond, "Something's wrong with me. I need to talk to you and Zulee, somewhere private."

Torell held her gaze before he nodded and grabbed her hand, leading her back into the tavern. His skin was firm, his fingers callused, bringing Kiva's attention to the deadly array of weapons strapped to him, just like last time.

Her brother, the warrior.

So different from the young boy who had picked wildflowers with her and chased butterflies in the meadow beside their cottage, from the child who had nursed an injured fawn back to health and declared he would spend his life aiding sick animals. There was no trace of that gentle boy in the hard young man leading Kiva through the gloomy tavern, every part of him edged and lethal. At least physically. On the inside, she still saw traces of the brother she'd always felt closest to.

The first time Kiva had used magic, it was Tor whom she had gone to for comfort, her parents having never shared about Tilda's bloodline in the hope that none of their children would inherit her healing power. Kiva still remembered begging her mother for stories of the ancient royals Sarana Vallentis and Torvin Corentine, just as she remembered wishing for her own magic.

When the golden light had exploded out of her one day, it was Tor who had held her close as their mother finally shared her secret, warning that a target would be painted on Kiva's back if anyone learned the truth of what she could do; it was Tor who had wiped the tears from her eyes and promised he would keep her safe, that nothing would ever happen to her.

He hadn't been able to keep that promise. Not as a child.

But something told Kiva that the man he'd grown into would fight until his last breath if it meant protecting her from harm.

"Pull your hood up," Torell ordered quietly as they reached the tavern exit. He dipped his chin in farewell to the barmaid, but there was no sign of the innkeeper. Kiva would just have to thank him when she returned.

"I have a mare in the stable," she said as he led her toward a dark horse tethered to a wooden hitching post. "Should I—"

Before she could finish, Torell swung onto his mount, hauling her up behind him, her legs catching uncomfortably on his bulging saddlebags.

"Keep your face covered," he told her, "and hold on."

Kiva's hood flew back as they took off at a gallop, but she didn't dare loosen her grip on him, certain she'd fall straight off the rear of the horse.

Reaching the edge of the village, Tor steered them away from the main road and into the dense trees, dodging branches and splashing through creeks at an alarming pace. When they finally slowed, Kiva was breathing heavily and clinging to him with a white-knuckled grip.

"Are you trying to kill us?" she cried, slapping his shoulder.

Torell had the audacity to chuckle. "Olix knows these woods inside and out. We were perfectly safe."

"One misstep and we could have broken our necks!"

"You know I'd never let that happen," Tor said. "Is your hood still up?"

"No, my hood *isn't up*," she gritted out. "It hasn't been up since you tried to beat the land-speed record for fastest idiocy on horseback."

"That's not a thing," Tor said, humor threading his tone. "We're coming up to camp, and I don't want to risk anyone seeing your face, so pull it back up." He dug through one of his saddlebags and withdrew a silvery object, passing it back to her. "Put that on, too."

Kiva was vaguely aware of Tor withdrawing another silvery object, keeping that one for himself, but her focus was on what she held.

Between her fingers was a mask — one made almost entirely of coiled serpents.

Vipers, if she had to guess.

Leaning around Torell, she saw he also held a mask, his forged into a distinctly canine shape.

"The Viper and the Jackal," Kiva mused. "They really have no idea who you are, do they?"

"We don't trust easily," Torell said, affixing the mask to his face. "Not even among our own."

Kiva followed his lead, donning what must have been Zuleeka's mask and raising her cloak again.

"It's served us well," Torell went on as they picked their way through the now-thinning trees. "Only those in our inner circle know our identities, the rest of the time we wear masks, even doing day-to-day work around the camps. It was Mother's idea — *all royals wear masks,* she told us. But mostly she wanted Zulee and me to be able to move about the kingdom as freely as possible, not having to look over our shoulders all the time."

There was a sad, wistful note in his voice that had Kiva giving him a gentle squeeze around his middle. She opened her mouth to offer comfort, but the words dissolved when they reached the edge of the forest, the trees falling away to reveal an immense glade, the view beyond making her gasp quietly in amazement.

Tent after tent lined the clearing, too many for her to count, each one basic aside from some larger structures toward the center of the camp. It was in that direction Tor was steering them, with men and women of all ages calling out greetings as they rode by—addressing him as Jackal —and staring with clear adoration in their eyes.

He was their general, Kiva remembered. He'd fought with them, fought *for* them. Everything he did was for these people—these rebels.

Their rebels, Kiva reminded herself.

Because these were her people too, all of them devoting their lives to see her family reclaim what was stolen from their ancestor when he was nearly killed and forced into exile. For centuries, the rebel movement had slowly grown, dedicated to taking back the throne on Torvin's behalf, but never before had they allied with any of his heirs and stood a chance at legitimately removing the Vallentis family from power.

Kiva needed to know how it had happened—how Zuleeka had become the rebel commander, how Torell had become their general. She needed to know why their mother had forsaken her own warnings about the rebels, having always claimed they could never learn that the Corentine bloodline lived on. For so long Tilda had denied her own magic to keep their family from discovery, and yet here Kiva was, at the heart of the movement her parents never, *ever* intended for them to join.

"Zuleeka's in the command tent, just up ahead," Tor said, pulling Kiva from her thoughts. "The canvas is thick enough for privacy—we can talk freely in there."

Kiva's palms began to sweat as they came to a halt outside the largest tent. Tor helped her slide down to the ground, dismounting after her and giving Olix a hearty pat on the neck. At his low whistle, a young boy ran over, smiling fondly at Tor before leading the horse away.

"After you," Torell said, indicating the tent's entrance.

Straightening her shoulders, Kiva stepped inside, noting the open space that was mostly empty aside from a long wooden table laden with papers. A map of Wenderall was strung along the canvas wall, nearly identical to the one Kiva had seen in the Royal Council room. Movement caught her eye, and she turned to find Zuleeka sipping from a steaming mug, watching her closely. There was no sign of surprise in her blank features. No sign of warmth, either, especially when she said, "You're not supposed to be here."

Stung, Kiva unfastened her mask and shot back, "If you'd hit me much harder the other night, I wouldn't be anywhere."

Torell stopped beside her, removing his own mask to reveal his puzzled expression. "What's this about?"

Zuleeka didn't answer him, and despite still being upset about the head wound, Kiva didn't want to tattle on her sister. Only two days ago she'd decided to try harder at mending what had broken between them, and she was determined to follow through on that—even if they weren't off to a promising start.

"Nothing," she said. "I don't have a lot of time. I came from Vallenia with a friend, and she's meeting me back at the tavern in a few hours."

"A friend?" Zuleeka raised a dark eyebrow. "From the palace?"

"Of course not," Kiva said. "I'm not stupid."

She didn't appreciate the way her sister's mouth twitched into a smirk, so she ignored Zuleeka entirely and walked over to the table, resting the serpentine mask on its surface and taking a seat. Tor followed and sat beside her, with Zuleeka only doing the same after a firm look from him—but not without rolling her honey-gold eyes, as if she was horribly inconvenienced by Kiva's visit.

"What brings you to see us, little sister?" Zuleeka drawled. "Feeling homesick? Wanted a cuddle?"

Kiva's good intentions evaporated swiftly at her sister's passive aggression. "What's your problem with me? We're on the same side. You can cut the attitude."

"I don't know what you're talking about," Zuleeka said, swirling her tea. "I'm delighted to see you. You've made my week."

Torell sighed wearily and muttered something too low for Kiva to hear.

Taking a deep, calming breath, she reminded herself that she had no idea what Zuleeka had been through in the last ten years. While she couldn't imagine that it compared to being abandoned inside a death prison, there were many different kinds of hell a person could live through.

Focusing on her task, she considered why she was there, debating where—and how—to begin. There was so much she needed to tell them, but she couldn't keep her own curiosity contained a moment longer.

"I'd like to know about Mother," Kiva said. "How did she end up at Zalindov? How did *you* end up with the rebels? What happened after— that night?"

Zuleeka snorted. "Look at you, risking your life for a story. Figures."

"I'm not risking my life."

"No, just all *our* lives." Zuleeka's humor fled so fast that Kiva realized it had never been there to begin with. "Did you think of that before you tore off out of Vallenia? Did you give a damn about anyone but yourself? You were never this selfish when we were younger, but I guess ten years of putting yourself before everyone else leaves a mark."

"Zuleeka," Tor snapped. "That's enough."

Kiva tried not to show how much her sister's words hurt, how unfair they were. A lump lodged in her throat, but she spoke around it to say, "I came here because I'm having trouble controlling my magic, and I need your help to keep from getting caught." She swallowed. "But I'm also not leaving until you tell me about Mother. I deserve to know the truth." She didn't mention the Royal Council meeting, unwilling to reveal all her cards without first getting something in return.

"What's wrong with your magic?" Tor asked, concern flooding his face.

Kiva shook her head. "You first."

Seeing the serious set of her features, he yielded. "The night the soldiers came, we fled to a cottage in the mountains. There were people inside waiting for us. Rebels."

"But the rebels never knew about our family," Kiva argued. "Mama and Papa were so careful to —"

"They didn't know anything for sure, but they'd been chasing rumors for years, one of which eventually led them to us in Riverfell. Their leader at the time, a man named Galdric, had already approached our parents in the marketplace, but Mother and Father had laughed away his claims." The corded muscles in Tor's arms tightened. "The night that . . . everything happened . . . Mother took us straight to Galdric and offered to join the rebel cause in exchange for one thing."

"What thing?" Kiva whispered.

It was Zuleeka who answered, uttering one word. "Vengeance."

Unbidden, the memory of Kerrin being stabbed flooded Kiva's mind, followed by Faran being dragged away by the Royal Guard. She pushed the images away, even knowing they would never leave her completely.

"Over the next few years, we stayed with Galdric and his closest confidants, moving from safe house to safe house, with them plotting and planning and scheming with Mother," Tor went on. "We learned to fight, to protect ourselves. And Mother —" His voice caught. "Mother started using her magic publicly, no longer caring who might discover us."

"Skip ahead, Tor," Zuleeka said, still swishing her tea. "She doesn't need a history lesson."

"Feel free to jump in at any time," Torell shot back.

Zuleeka sent him a sickly sweet smile. "But you're doing such a good job."

Kiva looked closely at her siblings, noting the unmistakable tension between them. A decade ago, they'd been close — not as close as Kiva and Tor, but close enough to love each other dearly. This strain between them, this *anger* . . . Kiva had no idea what might have caused it.

"Eventually, they decided that it was time for Mother to take over leadership from Galdric," Torell told Kiva. "She had Corentine blood, she was their rightful ruler. Our rightful ruler," he corrected. "Galdric remained her closest adviser, but she had final say over everything the rebels did. Up until then, our numbers had been slowly growing as whispers spread about the return of Torvin's heir, but Mother was restless and wanted things to move faster. Once the reins were in her hands, she started a campaign for active recruitment, with rebels going from village to village, encouraging people to follow her cause. Our cause." Another quick correction.

Kiva caught on to his word choice and asked, "When you say 'encouraging' . . . ?"

Torell looked across the tent, not meeting her eyes. "She did what she had to do. *We* did what we had to do."

Their attacks grew bolder, to the point that they became openly hostile, causing damage to villages and loss of life to those who stood against them.

Kiva swallowed at the memory of Jaren's words from two days ago.

"You hurt people," she whispered. "Killed people."

"Only if they tried to hurt us first," Zuleeka said, inspecting her fingernails. "They got what they asked for." She met Kiva's stricken gaze, her own eyes cold. "Wars aren't won without sacrifice, little sister. Anyone who stands against us is our enemy—and enemies don't deserve mercy. Why should we care about them when they don't care about us?"

But Zuleeka was wrong. Kiva knew at least one person who did care—about *all* his people, *including* the rebels.

"Did Mother ever consider that maybe there was another way?" Kiva asked, her voice rough. "That innocent people didn't have to suffer in her quest for vengeance?"

"Innocent?" Zuleeka barked out a laugh. "You've been spending too much time with your handsome prince. It doesn't take much, does it?

Baby blue eyes and tousled golden hair, and you're ready to give up everything we've worked for."

"*You've* worked for," Kiva said tightly. "Everything *you've* worked for. Because in case you forgot, I was locked away that whole time, having no idea what was happening."

"Oh, I haven't forgotten," Zuleeka said darkly. "You got to sit back and relax for a decade while we gave every part of ourselves to the cause. Our blood, our sweat, our tears, all for you."

Kiva spluttered. *"Sit back and re— "* She broke off quickly. "What do you mean, 'all for me'?"

"Oh, please, as if you haven't figured it out," Zuleeka scoffed.

"Figured *what* out?"

"That Mother is dead because of you."

Kiva felt as if she'd been punched in the stomach. "What?" she breathed.

"Zu—"

"No, Tor," Zuleeka interrupted, slicing her eyes to him. "If she's so desperate for answers, then she can deal with the consequences."

A muscle feathered in Torell's cheek, but he didn't try to stop her again.

Turning back to the white-faced Kiva, Zuleeka said, "Mother was sick. A rotting illness, something we couldn't find a cure for. She could heal anyone else in seconds, but her magic never worked on herself. The infection spread slowly, over years, something none of us realized until it was too late."

Kiva closed her eyes, remembering how Tilda had arrived at Zalindov, a mere shell of a human.

"When the end was near, she became obsessed with freeing you. She was convinced that *you* should be the one to take over as Rebel Queen," Zuleeka went on, her features grim. "But Galdric and the other leaders knew Zalindov was too well fortified and the risk was too great. Once, they might have led the rescue themselves, since Mother spent years talking about how powerful you were, even as a child. All along, they'd intended for her to take the throne and you to be her heir—the Corentine blood in your veins was undeniable. But as Tor rose through the ranks to become general, and as I earned the respect of Galdric and his peers, they decided that we were enough to lead in Mother's place, even without your supposedly immeasurable magic. The rebel leaders knew we were Torvin's descendants, they didn't require anything more to see us on the throne. But Mother—" Zuleeka looked away. "The sicker she became, the more determined she was to see you one last time."

Kiva was having trouble breathing. "I was told she was captured in Mirraven."

"She was," Tor said, his voice thick.

"But only because she walked right into Zadria and knocked on the castle gates," Zuleeka said. "King Navok was more than happy to make a deal with the Rebel Queen, knowing how much it would piss off the Vallentis family—and how desperate they were to get their hands on her. In return, he only had to make it so the negotiations between kingdoms resolved with her heading to Zalindov. To *you*."

In a hoarse voice, Kiva shared, "But I didn't get to speak with her. Not really. She was so sick when she arrived. And she was—she was blind. You said she wanted to see me, but she—" Kiva sucked in a quick, painful breath and looked down at the table. "She didn't get to see me."

"No, she didn't," Zuleeka said. "And *you* didn't save her."

Kiva looked up again sharply. "I—"

"—healed some random child instead." Zuleeka sneered. "Well done, sis. Way to put your family first."

"No." Kiva shook her head. "No, that's not—Tipp isn't—It was too late. I wasn't there when she died. There was nothing I could do. I can't —I can't bring back the dead."

"And what about Father?" Zuleeka shot back. "Were you in the middle of an Ordeal when he died, too?"

Kiva turned to Torell, who looked like he was about to jump in and rescue her, but he hesitated, the grief on his face raw as he waited to hear what she would say.

"Papa made me promise," Kiva whispered. "I swore not to use my magic. Not even on him."

"And now both our parents are dead, and some boy—sorry, *Tipp*— is alive and well?" Zuleeka said. "Sounds fair."

"All right, that's enough," Tor finally stepped in, though his words were quiet.

Ignoring him, Zuleeka kept her burning gaze on Kiva and said, "One decision, that's all it would have taken. What's the point of having magic if you're too afraid to use it?"

Tears prickled Kiva's eyes, but she didn't let them fall. She *had* been afraid. She was *still* afraid. But even so, when the time had come to act, she'd put Tipp's life before her own, unable to watch as he—

"Wait, how do you know about Tipp?" Kiva asked, her voice thick. "No one else was in the infirmary." No one but Tilda, who was already dead.

Zuleeka drew a finger along the rim of her mug. "One of my rebel contacts inside Zalindov was under orders to protect Mother until we could rescue her. When the riot broke out, she hurried to the infirmary, but someone else beat her there. She saw the boy on the ground in a pool of blood, knew it was a mortal wound. But later she saw you running toward the front gate with him in your arms. She thought you were being sentimental, had no idea you were escaping with him in tow." Zuleeka paused. "My spies at the palace confirmed the appearance of the kid, but they said he was perfectly healthy. It was easy enough for me to put two and two together."

There was a lot to unpack there, but Kiva only asked, "Your contact inside—are you talking about Cresta Voss?"

Zuleeka nodded. "She's doing great things for our cause, even behind those walls."

"Pity she's stuck in there until she dies," Kiva muttered under her breath. She and Cresta had never seen eye to eye, despite her having saved the antagonistic quarrier's life shortly after her arrival at Zalindov. "You know she hates me, right?" Kiva said, louder. "She threatened Tipp's life, said she would kill him if I didn't keep Mother alive."

Zuleeka shrugged. "She didn't know who you were. And she was just following orders."

Kiva clenched her teeth. "I didn't need the extra motivation. I never would have let Mother—" She broke off at the triumphant look on her sister's face.

"Die?" Zuleeka offered. "You never would have let Mother *die?*"

"Let's move on," Tor interjected before Kiva could raise another defense. He looked to her and said, "You have your answers, Mouse. Now—"

"Wait," Kiva cut in. "The other night, you told me you came to rescue us."

Tor nodded slowly. "I tried, yes. Until we were called back."

"But what about this Galdric you mentioned? You said he wouldn't let Mother risk any rebels coming to free me, so what made him change his mind?"

"He didn't." Tor's face darkened with sorrow. "When Mother decided to go to Mirraven, she didn't tell anyone. She took off in the night, leaving only a short note explaining where she was going, and why. From what we've managed to piece together, Galdric was the first to realize she was gone, and he went after her, probably trying to stop her. But he—he never came back. All we found was his cloak, covered in blood." Tor's throat bobbed. "Too much blood."

Kiva sat back. "You think—she *killed* him?"

Tor looked down at his hands. "She wasn't in her right mind, toward the end."

That was all he said. But Kiva heard the heartache in every word, enough to know Galdric had meant a lot to her brother, and Tilda's actions, unwitting or not, had caused him deep pain.

She reached for his hand and wound their fingers together, offering the only comfort she could. And then she recalled what he'd said—that she had her answers now, even if she didn't like what she'd heard.

"Thank you," she said to them both, barely recognizing her own voice. "For telling me."

Zuleeka avoided her eyes, but at least Kiva now understood why her sister seemed to hate her so much.

She blamed Kiva for their mother's death.

It was unfair, but Kiva knew grief made people do, think, and say things they otherwise wouldn't. She also knew there was no point in trying to convince Zuleeka that she'd had no control over Tilda's actions—nor would she have endorsed them if given the choice.

"It's your turn now," Tor said, pulling Kiva from her dejected thoughts. "What's going on with your magic? Tell us everything."

CHAPTER FOURTEEN

Kiva took her time explaining about her uncontrolled magic bursts and her fears of it happening around the royals. When she was done, silence fell in the command tent as her siblings considered her troubles.

"Did Mother ever mention anything like this happening to her?" Kiva asked. "She spent years repressing her magic. If this is a side effect of that—"

"She didn't repress it," Tor said. When Kiva made to argue, he went on, "She just hid it from the rest of us. Even from Father."

"Little magics, she called it," Zuleeka said, her earlier antagonism having faded as she'd listened to Kiva, as if releasing her anger had eased something inside her. Now there was only a thoughtful expression on her face, no sneer in sight. "When she started strengthening her power to help our cause, she told us she'd been using it all along, just in small ways. A bruise here, a scratch there, always when we were asleep or distracted. She said she'd never been able to stop entirely, that the magic in her wouldn't allow itself to be silenced."

Kiva rubbed her forehead. "If that's true, how was I able to silence mine for a decade?"

"Perhaps your magic is weaker than hers was?" Tor suggested.

Zuleeka's eyes were calculating. "Or stronger. There was a reason she thought you should be her heir."

There was a bitter note in Zuleeka's voice that Kiva carefully ignored.

"You want to know what I think?" her sister continued. She didn't wait for Kiva to answer. "I think your magic is angry that you locked it away for so long, and these uncontrolled bursts are its way of demanding your attention. I think you need to listen to it, you need to *use* it."

Kiva leaned forward and hissed, "I'm sleeping three doors away from Jaren Vallentis. I can't *listen to it*. I need it to *stop*." As suddenly as it had arrived, the fight left her, and she slumped in her seat. "Please. If you know anything . . ." Whispering, she repeated, "I need it to stop."

Torell was looking at her with compassion, but Zuleeka still wore a calculating expression.

"There is one possibility," she said slowly. "Someone who might be able to help."

"Who?" Kiva croaked, willing to beg if needed.

Tor's face cleared with understanding. He shook his head firmly at Zuleeka. "Absolutely not. Are you crazy?"

Inexplicably, an amused smile stretched across her mouth. "*I'm* not."

"But *she* is — and then some." Tor shook his head again.

"If you have a better suggestion . . ." Zuleeka goaded, arching an eyebrow.

Kiva interrupted to ask, "Does someone want to fill me in?"

Tor pinched the bridge of his nose, but he waved a hand at Zuleeka, indicating for her to go ahead. She did, offering two nonsensical words.

"Nanna Delora."

Kiva blinked. "Nanna who?"

"Our grandmother," Zuleeka explained. "Mama's mother. Delora Corentine."

Kiva froze, having had no idea they even *had* any living relatives, let alone on the Corentine side.

"She has magic. *Had* magic," Zuleeka corrected. "If anyone knows how to repress it, it's her."

"She's also a raving lunatic," Torell stated. "Mother took us to see her once, right after we joined the rebels. She wanted to retrieve a family heirloom, but Nanna Delora took one look at us and screamed that we were interrupting her book club. She slammed the door in our faces, yelling that if she ever saw us again, she'd ride to Vallenia and turn us all in."

Kiva stared at him for a long moment, then asked, "What family heirloom?"

"A dagger," Zuleeka answered, frowning into her now-cold tea. "Torvin Corentine's dagger, passed down from generation to generation. It was known far and wide as a symbol of his reign. When Mother decided to lead the rebels, she knew having that dagger would help solidify her position, offering proof of her—*our*—bloodline. But Delora refused to part with it."

"She's an apothecary," Tor shared. "My guess is that she's spitting on our ancestors by using that dagger as her work blade. You know how apothecaries are—they bond with their blades and never let them go. Some even ask to be buried with them." He shook his head as if to clear his thoughts and said to Zuleeka, "This isn't a good idea. You and I may not have magic, but there has to be someone else who can help."

"Delora might be difficult, but she's Kiva's best bet," Zuleeka argued.

"Where do I find her?"

Both Torell and Zuleeka turned at her question. Seeing the serious look on her face, Tor said, "We won't be able to go with you. She made it very clear that we weren't welcome to return."

"I got that, what with her threatening you," Kiva said. "But I don't need a babysitter. Just directions."

"She might not help you," Tor warned. "She wanted nothing to do with—"

"Tor, *please*," Kiva interrupted quietly. "I have to try."

"She lives in a cottage at the edge of the Crewlling Swamplands, just beyond the Wildemeadow," Zuleeka said, ignoring Tor's disapproving look. "There's a small settlement nearby called Blackwater Bog—you can find it on any map. Head there and ask the first person you see about Murkwood Cottage. They'll point you straight to her."

"Thank you," Kiva said with deep gratitude.

"Kiva—"

"I'll keep my expectations low," she interrupted Tor. "But if there's even a *chance* that she can help me, I have to go to her."

She could see how much he hated this plan, but he finally offered a terse nod and said, "Just—be careful. Delora is unpredictable. And she has a very unusual guard dog. The kind you don't want biting you."

Hearing Zuleeka's snort, Kiva decided it was better not to ask.

"I need to go back to Oakhollow soon," she said. "Rhess knows I'm meeting you, but I still think I should be back before she returns to the tavern."

"Rhess?" Zuleeka asked, her eyes flitting to Tor in question. But he hadn't met her, having arrived at the Tippled Boar long after she'd left.

"Rhessinda Lorin," Kiva answered. "A healer from Silverthorn. She does house calls in the village, and when she heard I wanted to come here, she offered to be my guide."

"You're meeting all kinds of people lately, aren't you?" Zuleeka murmured.

"Not really," Kiva returned with a hint of attitude. "So far I've been too busy getting abducted by my own family, tortured by a prince, and befriended by a queen who unknowingly ruined my life. That doesn't leave me much time to socialize."

Tor leaned in close, his eyes suddenly blazing. "What do you mean, 'tortured by a prince'?"

Kiva quickly put him at ease. "Caldon has been teaching me to fight. Or that's the intention. For now, he's just making me regret my last ten years of malnutrition and inactivity."

Tor's tension dissolved. "You're training with Prince Caldon?"

"Being tortured," Kiva reminded him. "I'm *being tortured* by Caldon."

"What a waste of time," Zuleeka said with clear humor. "The only weapon you'll ever need is right at your fingertips."

Kiva looked down at her palms. "Magic isn't a weapon." She thought of what the Vallentis family could do, and added, "Mine isn't, at least."

"Magic is what you make it," Zuleeka argued. "It's a tool you bend to your will."

"Weapons hurt people," Kiva said. "My magic heals people."

"You said yourself that you've been repressing it for a decade. You have *no idea* what it can do. What *you* can do."

Before Kiva could say anything to that, Tor cut in.

"There's no point to this conversation," he said, with a firm look at Zuleeka. "If you want to be back at the tavern before Rhessinda, we should get going."

He started to rise, but Kiva pulled him back down.

"I didn't say that so we'd leave immediately," she said. "I have more to tell you."

Both Zuleeka and Torell straightened, giving her their full attention.

"I—" Kiva started, but for some reason, she had trouble continuing.

"Don't rush, we have all day," Zuleeka drawled.

Tor shot her a look, then said to Kiva, "Take your time. Gather your thoughts."

At his encouragement, Kiva decided to jump straight in. "The throne can't be taken by force."

"What makes you say that?" Zuleeka asked, her gaze sharp.

"I don't know how many rebels there are, but it won't make a difference—the palace is too defensible," Kiva said. She made a split second decision not to mention the secret tunnel entrance, since it wasn't as if they could sneak the entire rebel force through without gaining attention. Or that was what she tried to tell herself, if only to lessen her guilt. "Even if you managed to overcome the Royal Guard, the armies would be recalled, and they'd just take the throne right back again."

"I assume you meant to say 'we,'" Zuleeka said dryly.

Kiva ignored her and went on, "The only way to truly take and keep the crown is through legitimacy. The citizens of Evalon won't accept you—*us*—unless they're given a reason that can't be ignored. Something lawful, something just. Either that, or willful public abdication by the Vallentis family. But we all know that's never going to happen."

"Lawful and just," Zuleeka repeated thoughtfully. Dark amusement lit her features as she asked, "How do you feel about marrying a prince, little sister? Is that legitimate enough for you?"

Kiva jerked backwards in her seat, her reaction just as violent as when Councilwoman Zerra had asked Jaren about his intentions. But it wasn't the thought of marrying him that was so appalling—no, it was the thought of betraying him so thoroughly.

"Don't be ridiculous," Torell snapped at Zuleeka, to Kiva's relief. "We're not forcing our sister to marry anyone. That's not happening." When Zuleeka raised her hands in surrender, Tor told Kiva, "Our numbers are strong, but you're right—we'll never win the kingdom by a show of force. And frankly, I don't think we'd deserve it if we did."

Zuleeka tapped a fingernail against her mug. "It seems we have a new task for you, little sister. Find us a legitimate way to take the throne, something that will make Evalon accept us as their new rulers without contention."

"Oh, is that all?" Kiva asked with clear sarcasm.

"It's either that, or you find us a way to bring those royal bastards to their knees," Zuleeka stated. "I have to admit, it'd be satisfying to see them abdicate of their own volition."

"They're not all bad," Kiva said, the words slipping from her before she could stop them.

Tor didn't react, but Zuleeka's face turned stony.

"You need to choose, Kiva," she said in a low voice. "You can't claim to be on our side while staring longingly at your precious prince. It's him or us. *Them* or us. You can't have it both ways."

Kiva's insides twisted because Zuleeka was right: she couldn't keep going as she was, scheming with the rebels while sympathizing with the royals.

And yet . . . Zuleeka was also wrong. Because ten years ago, the decision had been made for her. The choice was no longer her own — it never had been.

She would put her family first.

Just as she always had.

"There's something else I need to tell you," Kiva said, shifting in her seat. "I managed to spy on a Royal Council meeting."

Torell stilled at her side, and the anger vanished from Zuleeka's face.

"They spoke for hours, mostly about day-to-day kingdom business, but there were a few things that seemed important." She paused. "Something's happening with Mirraven, and it's got them worried."

"Mirraven has been threatening to invade since before we were born," Torell said dismissively. "They've never managed it before, they won't now."

"Not without help," Zuleeka said.

"Caramor is with them," Kiva shared. "As allies, but soon by marriage, too."

"I heard about that — Princess Serafine and Prince Voshell." Zuleeka snickered. "What a match." Before Kiva could ask why that was funny, her sister went on, "How is any of this relevant to us?"

Gritting her teeth, Kiva said, "I mentioned it because the council is worried about Mirraven, but they're *not* worried about the rebels."

Zuleeka's eyes slitted. "Explain."

"The royals have spies among you — I assume you already know that, or you wouldn't be so cautious." Kiva tapped the silvery mask resting on the table. "They're not in deep enough to provide useful information, but there's a guard who seems to know more than anyone else, including that you—the Viper and the Jackal—have Corentine blood."

Torell swore, but Zuleeka didn't seem fazed.

"What guard?"

Kiva opened her mouth to share Eidran's name, but then she recalled what the council had said about the two spies he'd trained turning up dead. She didn't need something like that on her conscience, not when she was already battling so many other demons.

"They didn't say," Kiva lied. "But from the sounds of it, he's moved up north and is no longer a guard"—not until he'd fully recovered from his injury, at least—"so he's out of the picture now."

Zuleeka looked like she wanted to press for more details about Eidran's identity, so to distract her, Kiva quickly went on, "There's one more thing. Before that guard left, he heard about a secret rebel meeting place in the city. You might want to tell your Vallenian followers to keep a low profile, because I have a feeling he shared the location with Jaren."

"I'll warn them myself," Zuleeka said.

Kiva breathed a quiet sigh of relief. If Eidran had indeed told Jaren the address, then at least the prince wouldn't be walking into something dangerous.

At the thought, Kiva gave herself a mental slap, since what she *should* have worried about was that Jaren would learn rebel secrets. She needed to realign her priorities before she slipped up again and earned another verbal lashing from Zuleeka.

"Did the council mention anything else?" Torell asked.

Kiva answered by asking, "What's the Royal Ternary?"

Blank faces met her question.

"Ternary, as in three?" Zuleeka asked. "The Royal Three?" She frowned. "Three what?"

Kiva didn't know, so she shared, "I told you that the council isn't worried about the rebels. They think you'll—*we'll*—eventually give up, especially now that Mother is gone, and with her, the figurehead of the Rebel Queen."

"They'll soon learn how wrong they are," Zuleeka said coolly.

"That's not my point," Kiva said. "When they were talking about it, the Grand Master mentioned something called the Royal Ternary."

"In what context?" Torell asked, his head cocked in puzzlement.

Kiva tried to remember exactly what Horeth had said. "I think it was, 'without the Royal Ternary, there's no other way for them to claim the throne.'"

Both Torell and Zuleeka froze like marble.

Warily, Kiva asked, "Are you sure you've never heard of it?"

Zuleeka unfroze first, shaking her head in the negative. "I'll ask our palace spies to look into it." Tor opened his mouth, but Zuleeka went on, "Do you have more for us?"

Kiva held her sister's eyes, thinking of everything else she knew, including—and especially—the greatest secret of all.

Jaren's magic.

I trust them.

His words flitted across her mind, his steadfast faith in both Kiva and Tipp. It was a mere whisper of a thought, but it was enough.

"No," Kiva said, her voice catching slightly. "I've told you everything I know."

The lie tasted bitter on her tongue, but at the same time, a weight lifted from her shoulders. Revealing what she knew about Jaren's power wouldn't change anything—her brother and sister already believed him to have control over two elements, so what did it matter if he could wield all four?

Ignoring the churning of her stomach, Kiva kept her eyes locked with Zuleeka's, honey-gold connected to emerald green. Her sister looked away first, but only so she could turn to Torell and say, "Can you give us a minute?"

Tor hesitated, as if gauging Kiva's reaction to being alone with Zuleeka, but then he collected his jackal mask and stood.

"We should leave soon," he told Kiva. "I'll have Olix brought around and meet you outside in a few minutes."

Kiva nodded, her heart beginning to pick up speed as Torell left the tent.

"I haven't been treating you well."

At Zuleeka's words, Kiva jolted, her gaze swinging immediately back to her sister.

"After everything with Mother—" Zuleeka cut herself off, looking away and biting her lip. "It's been difficult for me. And I know I shouldn't blame you. I just—it's hard. When I look at you, I can't help thinking of how she went to find you. She left us, and she died. For you."

Kiva felt like there were knives in her throat.

"And it's not just that," Zuleeka went on, as if she now couldn't stop. "When I heard about the prince being in Zalindov with you, about the two of you growing close, I was so angry. I didn't understand how you could cozy up to him while Mama was dying before your eyes."

"I didn't know who he was," Kiva rasped out.

"But even after you found out, you still stayed close to him," Zuleeka returned. "Gods, from what I heard, you saved his life. A *Vallentis*. You could have left him to rot beneath that prison, but you *didn't*."

"He saved my life first," Kiva argued weakly. "Multiple times. And I wouldn't have escaped without him and Naari."

Zuleeka pulled a face. "His Golden Shield. I heard you're close with *her*, too."

Kiva was about to defend herself, but her sister raised a hand.

"Wait," Zuleeka said, blowing out a breath. "I'm not doing this right."

"Doing *what* right?"

"Apologizing."

One word, and Kiva stilled.

"I've treated you badly," Zuleeka said, semi-repeating her earlier words. "It's because of Mother, but it's also because I thought you'd turned your back on us. After what you've shared today, I can see I was wrong. Sneaking into a Royal Council meeting—even *I* wouldn't have asked you to take that kind of risk. I should have given you the benefit of the doubt from the beginning, and I'm sorry."

Kiva had no idea what to say, unsure if she even *could* speak around all that she was suddenly feeling.

"I can't promise that I won't still struggle with my behavior toward you," Zuleeka warned. "I—I need more time, especially to come to terms with what happened to Mother, and to try and not see her every time I look at you."

Kiva flinched.

"But if you're willing to give me that time, I'll try harder," Zuleeka went on. "I promise I will."

Once again, their eyes met and held. This time it was Kiva who looked away first, but as she did so, she whispered, "Of course I'll give you that time."

"Thank you, little sister," Zuleeka said, her voice just as quiet. She then cleared the emotion from her throat and added, "You should probably go before Tor starts to worry that we're killing each other in here."

Kiva couldn't believe it, but she actually chuckled. "He's a lot more anxious than he used to be."

"He's a lot more *everything* than he used to be," Zuleeka said with a comical roll of her eyes. "But no matter how much I want to wring his neck sometimes, he's a damn good general. Our forces would follow him to hell and back if only he asked. That kind of devotion . . ." She shook her head, wonder clear in her eyes. A hint of envy, too, but it was gone again in an instant.

As if unable to wait any longer, Tor peeked his head back into the tent and called to Kiva, "Are you coming?"

She sighed and rose to her feet, hiding a wince as she felt the movement in every part of her.

"Until next time," Zuleeka said.

There was enough warmth in her words that Kiva's heart filled with hope, the feeling remaining with her long after she refastened the silver mask, bid her sister farewell, and left the tent.

Zuleeka's private conversation repeated in Kiva's mind as she and Torell rode back to Oakhollow, their pace much more sedate than earlier.

Deep in his own thoughts, it was only when the trees began to clear in the distance that Tor broke the silence to say, "She wasn't always so difficult."

Kiva's arms tightened reflexively around him. She hadn't shared that their sister had apologized, and she didn't do so now, curious to hear what Torell would say.

"She and Mother were really close, especially toward the end," he explained. "They spent every minute together—they'd take off into the woods for hours, then return laughing as if they didn't have a care in the world. There was such a sense of contentment between them, so much hope, so much love."

Kiva's heart gave a pang of longing.

"And then Mother left," Tor continued, steering Olix around a fallen tree trunk. "Something changed in Zulee after that. A darkness came over her, a deep anger brimming just under the surface. At first, I thought it was just grief mixed with the pressure of being the commander, especially with Galdric gone, but it's been months now, and it's only grown worse." His voice lowered. "She's keeping secrets, sneaking out of camp at all hours. She won't share her plans, won't even say where she's getting most of her information. The palace spies she mentioned? I have no idea who they are; all I can figure is that they're in deep enough for privileged information."

"You're worried about her," Kiva observed quietly.

"I don't know who she is anymore," he replied. "I don't know the person leading the rebels. That doesn't worry me—it *terrifies* me."

Kiva pressed closer, trying to offer comfort. "I thought you were co-leading them?"

Tor snorted. "That's what Mother wanted. Galdric, too. But it's like when I tried to free you from Zalindov—if I make a call Zuleeka disagrees with, we can't risk division by arguing. I care about our people too much to put them through that, even if I—" He broke off quickly.

"Even if you what, Tor?"

It took several moments before he whispered, "I'm tired, Mouse. I'm tired of seeing good people suffer for a cause I'm not even sure I believe in. A cause I'm not sure I've *ever* believed in."

Kiva stilled at his back.

As if the admission had loosened his tongue, Tor went on, stronger, "Zuleeka told you today to choose, but I was never given that option. Nine years old, and I became a rebel by default, shaped and molded to become their weapon. Their *general*." His distaste at the title was clear, but then he released a long breath and acknowledged, "I'm who I am today because of what they taught me. I'm strong, I'm capable. I'm a leader. A warrior. I'll always be grateful for that. But this life isn't one I ever would have chosen for myself."

"Tor," Kiva whispered, holding him tight.

He sighed and pushed away a low-hanging branch. "It is what it is. And I'm lucky, compared to many." A pause. "Compared to you."

Kiva's brow furrowed. "Me?"

"I would give anything, *everything*, to have kept you out of Zalindov," Tor said, every word filled with pain. "I would have traded my life in an instant if I'd known they would let you go. I hate—" His voice broke. "I *hate* that you were alone in there for so long. I can't imagine what you went through to survive. I don't even know *how* you survived."

"I'm not sure, either," Kiva admitted, shadows of memory filling her mind. "But I did, and we're together again now—that's all that matters."

Tor took a hand off the reins to squeeze her fingers at his waist. "If anything happens to you—"

"It won't," Kiva told him firmly, ignoring that she had unpredictable magic and was attempting to overthrow a kingdom, committing treason by merely breathing. "But what are we going to do about you? It sounds like you're having second thoughts."

"How I feel doesn't matter. I've committed my life to this cause."

"A cause you just admitted you don't believe in," she pointed out.

"And yet, I'll do what it takes to see it through."

His words were unyielding but completely without passion, as if he'd resigned himself to his fate.

Kiva's heart ached for the little boy she'd once known, his dreams having been stolen the same night she'd forfeited hers.

Quietly, she asked, "Why are the rebels fighting for us? I know why *we're* on this path, but why does anyone else care enough to risk their lives?"

"To them, we're royalty," Tor answered, his voice now carefully devoid of emotion. "For hundreds of years, all they've wanted was a Corentine back on the throne. Or at least, that's the case for the most fanatical of Torvin worshipers, the ones whose families have stayed dedicated from generation to generation."

"But what about the newer recruits who don't care about bloodlines?" Kiva pressed. "Is it because they don't like the Vallentis family?"

"There will always be people who disapprove of how a kingdom is run, regardless of who sits on the throne, so that's true for some," Tor confirmed. "Others just want anarchy for the sake of anarchy. But the rest . . . Never underestimate the power of hope, Mouse."

Kiva frowned into the thinning trees. "Sorry?"

"The rebels weren't always so destructive," he said. "Back when we first started to actively recruit, people joined us because Mother offered them something they desperately wanted—she healed them of their injuries and illnesses, just like Torvin did before he was exiled. But then—"

Tor stopped suddenly, but Kiva nudged him. "Then what?"

He waited until they'd splashed through a shallow creek before answering, "At first, Mother didn't ask for anything in return for her magic. Whenever we traveled to a new village, she healed everyone who came to her. But then one day she began to say they needed to *earn* their healing by proving themselves loyal. People were so desperate to help their loved ones—and themselves—that they joined our cause, waiting for the day Tilda Corentine would reward their devotion. As the time passed, she stopped healing people altogether, and started thriving on the chaos caused whenever the village guards were provoked, almost like she thought the bloodshed would turn more people to us. In some cases it did—but at what cost?" Tor shook his head. "To this day, I've never understood her strategy, but despite the unrest, people keep joining us in the hope that they'll be healed."

"But . . . Mother is dead," Kiva said carefully. "And neither you nor Zulee have magic." Her eyes widened. "They're not expecting *me* to—"

"No, no." Tor halted her growing panic. "Most of them haven't heard about Mother yet. And like I said, she hadn't healed anyone in a long time—long enough that the rebel leaders endorsed Zulee and me taking over despite us having no magic. It's enough that the people *think* we do, as Corentine heirs."

His voice was bitter, revealing exactly how he felt about the deceit.

Kiva closed her eyes, now having a better understanding of the rebels but almost wishing she'd stayed oblivious. In her quietest voice yet, she breathed, "What happens if we succeed?"

It was a question she hadn't allowed herself to consider before, partly for fear of how it made her feel. For so long she'd wanted vengeance, wanted *justice,* and yet she couldn't envision what the future might look like if her family *did* manage to take the throne.

"Honestly, I don't know," Tor said, with another loud sigh. "In theory, you, me, and Zuleeka would rule together." He sounded as if he was swallowing nails, and Kiva couldn't help feeling the same. The idea of ruling the kingdom, even if it was her birthright . . .

An image of Silverthorn crept into her mind, a reminder of everything she'd be giving up. Her hopes, her dreams, her ambitions.

Her future.

But then more images came to her.

Kerrin with a sword through his chest.

Faran being dragged off by the Royal Guard.

Tilda covered in blood, blind eyes staring at nothing forevermore.

Three lives, all gone.

Kiva could no longer deny that, like Tor, she was having second thoughts. But she also couldn't forget the atrocities that had been committed against her family, the heartache she would never heal from. The Vallentis family had done that to her.

And that was why, even if her heart was divided, she had no choice but to do the same to them.

Even if it cost her everything.

CHAPTER FIFTEEN

Torell left Kiva at the Tippled Boar after making her promise not to return to Oakhollow, claiming the risk of discovery was too great. In return, Kiva handed back Zuleeka's mask and agreed to send any messages through the innkeeper, before giving her brother a warm hug goodbye.

Rhessinda found her in the tavern's courtyard shortly afterward and maintained a mostly one-sided conversation on the ride back to Vallenia. By the time they dismounted outside Silverthorn's stables, the sun was dropping below the horizon.

Sensing Kiva's anxiety, Rhess shooed her away. "I'm here every day for the morning shift—come find me if you want a break from palace life," the healer invited. "We can go get chocabuns."

"Sounds perfect," Kiva said, before taking off down the hill and hurrying along the River Road, reaching the palace in record time.

She'd barely unfastened her cloak when an angry knock sounded at the door to her room.

Kiva froze, a million fears hitting her all at once.

What if someone had seen her leave the city?

What if they'd followed her to Oakhollow?

What if she'd been spotted in the rebel camp?

What if the mask hadn't fooled them?

What if—

"K-Kiva, I know you're in there! I heard you c-c-come back!"

The breath whooshed out of her as she opened the door to find Tipp standing there, his freckled face set in a frown.

"You've been g-g-gone *all day*."

There was no denying the accusation in his tone, but Kiva was unsure why it was there.

"I went to Silverthorn."

Not a lie. And yet, she still hated herself for the half-truth.

"I w-w-wanted to show you what Ori and I d-did in art class today, and you weren't here!" Tipp cried. "I always know where t-to find you, and I c-couldn't!"

Kiva suddenly understood why he was so upset.

For three years, Tipp had been able to seek her out anytime he'd needed her. At Zalindov, she'd always been in the infirmary. At the winter palace, they'd barely left each other's sides as they'd acclimatized to their new freedom. Even when they'd reached Vallenia, Kiva had never disappeared for as many hours in a row as she had today.

Tipp had missed her.

Tears touched the back of her eyes as she took in his fiery distress, but she didn't want to embarrass him, so she blinked them away and said, "I'm sorry, I lost track of time. Would you like to show me now?"

His anger was immediately replaced by eagerness as he tugged her into the sitting room. On an easel near the window was a canvas covered by a sheet, and Tipp quickly whipped it off, revealing what lay beneath.

"It's u-us!" he declared proudly, pointing to the portrait.

The tears Kiva had swallowed back returned with a vengeance at the sight of what the young boy had created.

The brush strokes were imperfect and the colors were eccentric, but Kiva could easily recognize herself in the painting, her dark hair floating in the breeze, her emerald eyes comically wide. One of her hands held a redheaded, freckle-faced boy who was beaming widely, and her other hand—

"That's me, you, and Jaren," Tipp said. He then shared a long-winded story about how the art tutor had asked him to paint how he saw his future, and Kiva had to tune him out, her heart *aching* as she took in the rest of the portrait's details.

Kiva's other hand was entwined with Jaren's, the two of them smiling at each other, the River Palace in the background, and—

Crowns on their heads.

Both of their heads.

In the distance were the blurred figures of Oriel, Mirryn, Caldon, Naari, Queen Ariana, and a man Kiva assumed was King Stellan. Even Flox was in the painting, curled up on Jaren's feet.

It was a family portrait.

Created by an eleven-year-old.

Who had been asked to paint his future.

"... and then she said the g-grass shouldn't be purple, but I reminded h-her that she said t-to use my imagination, and w-what's more imaginative than p-purple grass?"

Tipp finally paused to take a breath, before looking at Kiva and waiting for her verdict.

She felt as if pins were stabbing into her tongue, but she somehow managed to force out the words, "It's perfect."

The gap-toothed grin he sent her lit up the room. She couldn't resist wrapping her arms around him, partly to keep him from seeing the devastation on her face, and partly just so she could feel him in her arms, safe and alive.

He would never have the future he envisioned, but she was damned well going to make sure he had *a* future, and that no matter what happened in the coming days, he wouldn't be left on his own. Tipp would always have a home at the palace, regardless of who it was with—she would make sure of it.

"Sorry, am I interrupting? I can come back."

Kiva glanced up to find Jaren standing in their doorway, his hair messy enough to indicate he'd been running his hands through it all day, his clothes rumpled. He looked like he hadn't slept in weeks, but instead of making him less attractive, those flaws only made him more real, more human, more —

Giving herself a firm mental slap, Kiva released Tipp and, when the young boy ran over to greet Jaren, quickly covered the painting.

"J-Jaren!" Tipp yelled, crash-tackling him on approach. "Do you want to c-come and see —"

"How were your meetings?" Kiva quickly interrupted.

"Long," Jaren said, sighing when Flox ran into the room and collapsed on top of his feet. "How was Silverthorn?"

"She was g-gone *all day*," Tipp shared, repeating his earlier accusation. There was no anger in his voice this time, his attention wholly focused on unlatching Flox's claws from Jaren's leather boots so he could pull the fluffy creature into his arms.

Jaren's golden brows rose. "All day? You must be tired."

"Pot, kettle," Kiva said, gesturing to his disheveled appearance.

"Today was . . . challenging," Jaren said. He looked as if he were about to say more, but then changed his mind and shared, "If you two don't have any other plans, everyone is free tonight for the first time since we returned home. Are you up for a family dinner?"

Kiva's stomach tightened, but Tipp offered an excited, "Y-Yeah!"

"Go wash up, kiddo," Jaren said, tipping his chin toward Tipp's bedroom. "We'll wait for you."

Tipp handed the disgruntled Flox to Jaren — the creature's mood brightening the instant he was in the prince's hands — and took off into his room.

"Should I, um . . ." Kiva waved to her outfit, fearing her clothes were too casual for dinner with the royal family.

Jaren's eyes didn't wander from her face, his tone soft as he said, "You're perfect, just as you are."

His implication was impossible to miss. Kiva's breath caught, but she was saved from having to respond when Tipp skipped back and declared, "R-Ready!"

If Kiva had been asked to recall anything about their walk across to the western palace, she wouldn't have been able to answer. Not with Jaren's words repeating in her mind, like a feather stroking her skin.

You're perfect, just as you are.

Part of her was furious with him as they stepped into the small, intimate dining room where his family waited. How dare he be so kind, so loving, so *Jaren?* Why couldn't he act like the haughty prince he should have been — more like his sister? Hell, even more like the flirtatious Caldon, who Kiva felt a growing fondness toward, but whose personality acted like a romantic repellent.

You're perfect, just as you are.

Kiva wanted to cry. Instead, she straightened her shoulders and ignored how good it felt to have Jaren's hand resting against her back, guiding her into the room.

A quick glance revealed that an ornate ashwood table lay at the center of the space, already set and brimming with food — carved meats and roasted vegetables, saucers of gravy, cheese platters, thick, luscious breads, and a whole host of other delicacies that made Kiva's mouth water just looking at them. Interspersed between the golden plates was a trail of dainty luminium drops, the speckles of light making the buffet look almost magical, especially when combined with the crystal vases full of snowblossoms. In the background, the floor-to-ceiling windows looked straight out to the manicured gardens, a sight that was beautiful at night and would be even more spectacular during the day.

As phenomenal as the display was, Kiva couldn't appreciate it as much as it deserved. Not when the royal family turned as one to look at her, Jaren, and Tipp upon their entry into the room.

Anxiety swept over Kiva, but Tipp was immune to the attention, bounding straight over to the spare seat beside the grinning Oriel. The two boys immediately bent their heads together and began whispering in a way that would have alarmed Kiva at any other time, but she was too focused on staying calm as Jaren nudged her toward the head of the table.

"I don't believe you've met my father yet," he said as the middle-aged, well-dressed man rose from his seat on their approach.

The King of Vallenia stood up—*for Kiva*.

"I've heard so much about you," King Stellan said, reaching for her hand. Her fingers felt numb, but his grip was gentle as he closed both of his hands around hers and smiled warmly.

He had Jaren's smile.

And that wasn't all they shared.

The king's hair was darker than the rest of his family, like a rich caramel, which explained the browner shades that blended through Jaren's golden locks. Stellan's eyes were also different, being a coppery color unlike the blue that his wife and children shared, with a gold rim that had been inherited only by Jaren.

Tall, broad shoulders, honeyed skin—aside from the hair and eyes, he was what Kiva envisioned Jaren would look like in twenty years.

It wasn't a bad image.

At all.

And yet . . . there was something Kiva couldn't quite put her finger on: a wanness to his face, a strain about his features, a dullness in his eyes. She wouldn't have given it any further thought, except that as his hand held hers, she felt it.

The king was sick.

Kiva knew it in every part of her. *Her magic* knew it, her fingers, no longer numb, starting to tingle.

NO! she screamed inwardly.

If ever there was a place she absolutely *could not* lose control of her power, it was in a room filled with almost the entire Vallentis family.

So she shoved it down, deeper and deeper, just as she had with Rhessinda, praying with everything inside her that the golden glow wouldn't burst forth.

Because if it did, she was dead.

Her head ached from the effort, her stomach knotted painfully, her bones felt like they were *melting*, but when the king finally released her hand—

Her skin looked exactly as it should.

Kiva's relief was so intense that her knees wobbled, but she made herself return Stellan's smile and say, "It's an honor to meet you, Your Majesty."

The king waved a hand in the air. "Please, we don't stand on ceremony in this family." He leaned in, a twinkle in his eyes. "Especially among . . . *friends.*"

His gaze flicked from Kiva to Jaren, his emphasis prompting warmth to touch her cheeks. Gods, she hoped the Royal Council hadn't spoken with Stellan, especially Councilwoman Zerra. Or Queen Ariana, since she'd also heard every word down in the tunnels. If one of them began another conversation about *intentions* at dinner, Kiva might very well die of embarrassment.

"Why don't you sit by me," Stellan said, pulling the chair out for her. "I want to hear all about the extraordinary young woman who survived a decade in—"

"I was thinking we could tell Kiva and Tipp more about our family," Jaren cut in smoothly. "Share some stories, let them get to know us a little better."

Kiva sent him a grateful look, knowing he'd sensed her growing tension and had swiftly intervened.

"Family stories?" Caldon spoke up from where he sat next to Mirryn, a devious grin stretching across his face. He raised his goblet and tipped it toward Kiva. "You're in for a treat, Sunshine. I have dirt on everyone at this table. Prepare to be entertained."

"Caldon, dearest, I don't think—" Ariana started, but was interrupted by the arrival of Naari and Captain Veris.

Kiva's heart gave a panicked *thump* as she again feared that someone had discovered her true outing that day, but then she saw that the guard and captain were in casual clothes, their stances relaxed.

"Sorry we're late," Naari said, taking the empty seat beside Caldon. "We were working drills with some of the new recruits."

"How're they looking?" Stellan asked.

Jaren nudged the stiff Kiva into the seat the king was still holding out for her. Once she was settled, he sat to her right, his father reclaimed the spot angled at the head of the table to her left, and—

Captain Veris took the seat directly opposite her.

Nerves prickled Kiva as the captain gave a quick nod—of greeting? Respect? She wasn't sure. She made herself take a deep breath, calling to mind everything Jaren had said during the council meeting, how Veris remembered her from ten years ago, but Caldon hadn't discovered anything incriminating in his investigation. To them she was only Kiva Meridan—her true identity remained safe.

"It's a cocky lot this year," the captain answered the king. "They're good, and they know it. But we'll whip them into shape."

Kiva must have made an alarmed sound, because as everyone started to fill their plates, Jaren leaned in and said, "He's talking figuratively. We don't whip our guards."

"No, we just make them run training drills over and over until their eyes bleed from sheer boredom," Caldon said dryly, buttering a slice of bread.

"What are the three qualities that make a good Royal Guard?"

Veris asked, looking around Naari at Caldon, his salt-and-pepper hair shining under the luminium chandelier.

"Oh, dear gods," the rakish prince murmured, reaching for his wine. "I'm going to need something much stronger than this."

"Discipline," Veris said, ticking off his fingers. "Discipline. And discipline."

"That's only one thing," Caldon said. "As I keep telling you. *Every time you say it.*"

"Maybe one day you'll remember what it means," Veris shot back.

"At least I can count to three," Caldon mumbled, refilling his drink and gulping more down.

"All right, children, no fighting on family night," Queen Ariana chided, though her eyes danced as she looked between Caldon and Veris, the latter of whom was older than she and therefore hardly considered a child.

But Kiva was stuck on the words she'd used.

Family night.

Feeling queasy, she reached for her own goblet, a light sniff revealing it to be mulled apple juice. She took a large sip just as Oriel bounced in his seat and turned to the captain.

"Uncle Veris—"

Kiva nearly spat out her juice.

"—Mother says I can start training with you when I turn twelve. Can Tipp join us?"

"I don't see why not," Veris answered, spearing some beans with his fork. "As long as you both take it seriously."

"We will," Oriel said, with Tipp nodding eagerly beside him.

Kiva, however, couldn't keep from looking at Veris and wheezing out, *"Uncle?"*

The captain's brown eyes lit with humor, making it clear he hadn't missed her shocked reaction. "Not by blood."

"Veris and I grew up together," King Stellan told Kiva, passing her a bowl of roasted potatoes. "My parents died from river fever when I was young, so Veris and his family took me in. When he became a recruit with the Royal Guard, he invited me to his graduation ceremony, and that's where I met the love of my life."

The queen blushed—*blushed!*—at the way Stellan looked at her, before taking up the story, "My parents weren't thrilled that I was being courted by a young man without title or rank. And an orphan, no less. Veris had to get creative in helping us sneak out to see each other. If not for him, who knows where we might all be today?"

"Ari's parents eventually realized what a catch I was," Stellan told Kiva with a satisfied smile. "And we lived happily ever after."

The words settled heavily in the room. Tipp and Oriel were oblivious, stuffing their faces and giggling as they snuck scraps to Flox beneath the table. But everyone else . . .

They knew the king was sick, that his happily ever after was coming to an end.

Clearing her throat, Kiva acted as if she couldn't feel the sadness that had come over the table. "That's a lovely story," she said.

"It is, isn't it?" Caldon said with mock disgust. He speared some glazed pork and pointed it at Kiva. "But I promised you entertainment. So it's my turn to share a tale now, and I know just the one."

Caldon, Kiva was quickly realizing, wasn't just a pain in the ass. He was a *smart* pain in the ass. He'd read the room, sensed the mood, and understood that something was needed to lighten the atmosphere. She wondered how often he did it, his attention-seeking used as a means to distract his family when they needed it most.

She considered it further as she ate her meal, listening to him recount the details of a diplomatic trip he and Jaren had taken to the desert kingdom of Hadris in the far west of Wenderall. The moment he'd begun his story, Jaren had groaned quietly and begun shoveling food into his mouth, avoiding Kiva's eyes. She knew why when Caldon came to the end of his wild tale.

". . . and of course he had no idea I'd spiked his drink, but if anyone needed to get sloshed after fourteen straight hours of fending off arranged marriages, it was our Jaren. How was *I* supposed to know he wouldn't sleep it off like a normal person, but instead he'd go running into the Midnight Markets and dance until dawn?"

"It didn't happen *quite* like that," Jaren said dryly. "And as I recall, I wasn't the only one who went to those markets."

Caldon didn't seem to hear him. "They still call you the Pantsless Prince to this very day," he said, grinning widely.

"It's better than what they call you, cousin," Mirryn cut in, a smirk on her face.

Kiva looked at Caldon. "What do they—"

"Nothing!" he said quickly. Stuffing his mouth with carrots, he repeated, "Absolutely nothing!" Only it came out more as, "Abforooty nuffingk!"

The look he shot both Jaren and Mirryn made it clear there would be consequences if they dared to answer.

Deciding to play nice, the princess launched into a new story, one from when she, Jaren, and Caldon were children. The three of them had snuck out of the palace one night, having overheard a diplomat from Nerine talking about visiting a Red House before traveling back to his kingdom. In their innocence, they'd assumed he'd meant a literal red-colored house, and so they'd followed him to the docks. What they'd seen—

"We were grounded for a month," Mirryn shared. "But not because we snuck out—because of how embarrassed Nerine's royal ambassador was when he found us in all our wide-eyed horror and had to return us to our parents. I'll never forget how red his cheeks were when he stammered about how important it was for him to experience all the hidden depths of our culture."

"He definitely wanted to explore *hidden depths,* but we all know he didn't give a damn about culture," Caldon murmured into his goblet.

"Caldon," Ariana scolded.

"As if you weren't thinking it, Aunt."

The queen didn't comment, instead breaking off some bread and dipping it in oil. "Who has another story? Perhaps one that *doesn't* involve humiliation?"

"Humiliating stories are the best, though," Caldon said, reclining in his chair.

Mirryn seemed to agree, since she returned his devious look and asked, "Do you remember Jaren being accosted by those courtiers when we stayed at the palace in Lyras?"

Jaren made a distressed sound. "Someone kill me. Right now."

The princess grinned wickedly and went on to share about a fanatic group of men and women who refused to so much as let Jaren feed himself while he was in their kingdom.

"It's an offense to say no to Valornian hospitality," Mirryn told Kiva with clear mirth. "Poor Jaren is adored just a little *too* much by our western allies."

Kiva snickered along with everyone else, even as she heard Jaren's quiet sigh. When she glanced at him, his eyes were lit with self-deprecating humor, telling her that no matter how embarrassed he might be, he wasn't going to ruin his family's fun.

However, after everyone else started jumping in with their own memories, he finally reached a breaking point.

"How did I not know about that one?" Caldon asked, roaring with laughter at the tale Oriel had just shared, involving a seaside vacation and a kindly old woman who had been convinced Jaren was her long-lost grandchild.

"Maybe it's so I could avoid delightful moments like this," Jaren returned. He looked around the table. "Please, for the love of the gods, someone share something that *doesn't* involve me."

"I have a story," Captain Veris said, pushing his empty plate away. "It's about a tenacious teenager who escaped from a Jiirvan arena, crossed the Forsaken Lands with nothing but the swords on her back, navigated the deadly underground streets of Ersa, then finally stowed away on an Evalonian vessel returning to Vallenia." He sent a fatherly wink to Naari. "All of that, you already know. But I've never shared what happened immediately after I found this one"—he jerked his thumb at the guard—"spewing over the side of the ship."

Veris launched into a boisterous tale about how he'd first met Naari, and how she'd convinced him to take her under his wing rather than toss her to the sharks.

His detailed account had the royals laughing and Naari rolling her eyes, but Kiva only half-listened, unable to shake what Veris had said in his introduction.

Naari had fought in one of Jiirva's notorious arenas.

Kiva had heard rumors about them, enough to know that while they weren't always a death sentence like Zalindov, anyone sent to an arena came out as one of two types of people: a warrior . . . or a corpse.

Not only that, but Naari had *escaped*—and then crossed the Forsaken Lands alone.

Kiva had already respected the guard for all that she'd overcome in her short life—not the least of which was losing her hand after protecting Jaren from an attack—but now Kiva's esteem for the young woman grew considerably.

As did her concern.

Naari would die before she let anything happen to Jaren. Not just because it was her job to protect him, but also because her being there tonight—at a *family dinner*—meant she wasn't just a guard to the royals, Golden Shield or not. If she sensed even a hint of betrayal, Kiva knew Naari wouldn't hesitate to end her, no matter what bond had grown between them.

Her food settling uncomfortably in her stomach, Kiva tuned back in to the conversation just as Naari took over from Veris, sharing a part of the story that left him chuckling with embarrassment and denying every word. The king piped up with gleeful confirmation, adding his own details, causing the table to laugh anew.

And from there, they continued. Each of them sharing moments from their lives, sometimes joyous, sometimes humiliating, sometimes simply revealing parts of their histories, doing exactly what Jaren had requested upon their arrival in the room—letting Kiva and Tipp get to know them.

With each new story, Kiva died a little more on the inside. Outwardly, she smiled along with everyone else, but inwardly, she couldn't stand what was happening.

The Vallentis family was just so *normal*.

But not just normal—they loved each other, so deeply. It was evident in every word they spoke, in every glance they shared, in every comedic insult and every soothing compliment.

And it wasn't just the royals. They behaved the same toward Veris and Naari—hell, even toward Kiva and Tipp. Everything about them promoted inclusivity, acceptance, and such a tender affection that Kiva felt as if a vise were squeezing her chest.

I'm tired of seeing good people suffer for a cause I'm not even sure I believe in.

Torell's weary voice returned to Kiva, his statement resonating so strongly in her.

And then she heard Jaren's voice.

You're perfect, just as you are.

She wasn't, though.

She was so far from perfect, and one day soon, he would know.

And he would hate her.

The thought left Kiva struggling to draw air into her lungs, but she made herself continue to smile as he and his family went out of their way to make sure she and Tipp felt included.

Kiva had never hated herself more than she did that night—and she knew the feeling wasn't going to leave her anytime soon.

Perhaps never.

CHAPTER SIXTEEN

Unsurprisingly, Kiva couldn't sleep that night.

After dinner ended, she tossed and turned in bed, guilt and shame keeping her awake until she finally donned a silk robe and left her room.

Given that it was the dead of the night, Kiva didn't see anyone as she ventured along the gold-and-white corridors, and she didn't expect that to change when she reached her destination. But upon entering the River Room, she found she wasn't alone.

Jaren stood beside the window-wall, looking out over the Serin River, blissfully unaware of her presence.

Wearing only loose-fitting long pants, the low light revealed the scars marring his back, all of which Kiva had seen before, many times. Only two nights earlier she'd felt them beneath her hands as he'd comforted her in bed. But looking at them now, pain lanced through her, the thought of anyone hurting Jaren — the Butcher, his mother, *anyone* — causing her both physical and emotional distress.

Wars aren't won without sacrifice, little sister.

Zuleeka's harsh words blazed across Kiva's memory.

It's him or us. Them *or us. You can't have it both ways.*

Kiva closed her eyes, certain of only one thing: she was going to hurt Jaren. She would be the reason something horrible happened to him. And she — And she —

She couldn't let that happen.

But she also couldn't stop it.

Staring at him, Kiva felt like she was being ripped in two. On one side was her dedication to her family and their cause. And on the other —

Was Jaren.

But also Caldon.

And Naari.

Young Oriel and Flox.

Even Princess Mirryn and Queen Ariana and King Stellan.

The whole Vallentis family.

Captain Veris, Kiva wasn't yet sure about, but despite him being there the night her family was destroyed, it wasn't his sword that had killed her brother. She still remembered his growled words: *This wasn't meant to happen. This* never *should have happened.*

Without her permission, these people had worked their way into her heart, forcing her to see them not as royals and guards, but as human beings. As a *family.*

For ten years, all she'd wanted was to ruin the family that had ruined hers. But now that she knew them . . .

I'm tired of seeing good people suffer for a cause I'm not even sure I believe in.

Torell's words were going to haunt her, she was sure of it.

Unable to withstand her troubled heart, Kiva backed away silently, not wanting to disturb Jaren and risk whatever new kindness he would offer, her very own form of torture. But some sixth sense made him look over his shoulder, his body stilling as he caught sight of her, before relaxing again.

"Couldn't sleep?" he asked, leaving the window-wall and walking her way.

"Looks like I'm not the only one," Kiva returned, her voice hoarse with all she was feeling.

"Come sit with me for a bit?" Jaren asked, nodding to the plush lounge. "I could use the company."

Peering at him closely, Kiva could see he wasn't lying. The earlier strain had returned to his features, a deep weariness mixed liberally with unease.

You can get to him in a way no one else can, learn things about him, about his plans, about where he's most vulnerable.

Zuleeka's words from days ago returned to Kiva, her inner turmoil growing because she knew what she needed to do.

Moving slowly over to him, she sat on the far edge of the couch and prompted, "You look like you have the weight of the world on your shoulders."

She'd left him plenty of room, but when Jaren sighed loudly and took a seat beside her, he was close enough for their arms to brush.

"Want to tell me about it?" Kiva offered, part of her wishing he would say no.

But he didn't.

Because he was Jaren.

And he trusted her.

So he shared, "The Royal Council is concerned about a threat to the kingdom."

"The rebels?" Kiva asked, playing dumb.

"No," Jaren said. "Well, yes, but also no."

Kiva waited for him to go on, even if, thanks to her eavesdropping, she already knew what he would say.

"The rebels have been quiet since Tilda's death," he said with a quick, apologetic look, knowing how much Tilda had meant to her as a patient. "They're still causing some trouble, but nothing like before the winter—aside from their attempt to abduct you, which we can only assume was to remind us that they're out there."

He paused, then shared, "There are rumors Tilda left behind an heir old enough to take over, maybe more than one. We won't know for sure until they restart their attacks." He blew out a long, frustrated breath, before rolling the tension from his neck. "So until that happens, for the first time in years, they're not my main concern."

"But something is troubling you," Kiva observed, still acting oblivious. "It has been since we arrived here, with you locked in meetings and looking more and more miserable after each one."

"Miserable?" Jaren repeated, a hint of humor touching his eyes.

An easy comparison came to Kiva. "Like how Flox looks when he can't follow you somewhere. That kind of miserable."

Instead of adding to his mirth, Jaren's hand quickly covered her mouth. "Shhh. Don't say his name or you'll wake the clingy devil."

A tilt of his chin over to the window revealed the fluffy creature asleep on the ground, right where Jaren had been standing. As they watched, Flox's eyes fluttered open, his head popping up fast once he realized he was alone, a *mew*ing sound of distress leaving his mouth. But then he turned and looked their way, his little silver face brightening as he bounded over to them.

Jaren groaned as Flox leapt straight onto his lap, curled up again, and was snoring softly a moment later.

Slicing his eyes to Kiva, Jaren said, "I blame you for this."

Biting back a laugh, she combed her fingers through Flox's soft fur. "It's not my fault you're so irresistible."

At first, Kiva didn't realize what she'd said, but then she noticed Jaren had gone still beside her, and she mentally replayed the words.

"Irresistible, huh?" he teased, his eyes dancing.

Kiva tried to rally. It was either that or jump out the window and drown herself in the Serin. "You know—to, um, a fox thing."

If anything, Jaren's amusement only grew. "A fox thing?"

"Ferret? Racoon? I have no idea what he is."

Jaren chuckled. "He's a silverbear."

Squinting at the dozing creature, Kiva observed, "He looks nothing like a bear."

"I didn't come up with the name," Jaren said, still grinning. "They're rare, only found in the wilds of Odon's northern mountains. Flox was a gift from their king and queen."

"To Oriel?"

"To me." Sheepishly, he added, "More a bribe than anything else."

"Let me guess," Kiva said dryly. "They have an heir of marriageable age?"

Jaren didn't meet her eyes, which was confirmation enough. "Ori was lonely at the time. There weren't many kids around the palace, and Mirry, Cal, Ash, and I were all so busy with politics and training. When Flox arrived, I gave him to my brother, and they became fast friends."

"And yet, he's much more obsessed with you," she noted.

"I hear it's because I'm irresistible."

The look Jaren sent Kiva made her want to jump out the window all over again.

Clearing her throat, she returned to their earlier topic. "Before we were interrupted"—she stroked Flox's spine—"you were talking about a threat to the kingdom."

Jaren was silent for a long time, long enough for Kiva to wonder if he'd changed his mind about sharing, but then he said, "Do you remember what I told you in Zalindov about the other kingdoms fearing the rebel movement will spread into their lands? How in some cases it already has?"

Kiva bit her cheek and nodded.

"Do you remember what else I said?" Jaren asked. "About Mirraven and Caramor waiting for any sign of weakness?"

"You think they're going to invade?" she asked, feigning concern —not that she *wasn't* concerned.

"Something is stirring up north," Jaren said, not quite answering. "There have always been warnings, threats, the usual. But something has changed recently, from around the time we started negotiating with Mirraven for Tilda's transfer into our custody. They were so difficult, refusing to accept any of our terms, no matter how generous."

That last part was news to Kiva, and she straightened beside him.

"I've only learned about most of this since leaving Zalindov," he went on, "and it doesn't make sense to me. We offered them some things they've wanted for a long time, including greater access to our luminium stores and looser restrictions for border crossings, both of which would hurt our economy while boosting theirs. But they weren't interested."

A strange feeling came over Kiva, and she flattened her free hand against her suddenly churning stomach, recalling her sister's words from earlier that day.

King Navok was more than happy to make a deal with the Rebel Queen. In return, he only had to make it so the negotiations between kingdoms resolved with her heading to Zalindov.

Kiva had been so caught up in everything else that she hadn't thought to question the deal Tilda had proposed in return for Mirraven turning down Evalon's request for an extradition agreement. But now Kiva couldn't help wondering—what had her mother offered? What had she *done?*

"The council fears what their lack of cooperation means, especially since they're no longer answering any of our missives," Jaren said. "The same goes for Caramor. Both kingdoms have always envied Evalon —our lands are rich and prosperous while theirs are largely barren. They've never hidden their desire to invade us, but with the Tanestra Mountains in their path, and our armies prepared to meet any attacking force, they've always been too smart to try. Now, though . . . I can't help thinking they've decided it's worth the risk, especially while we're distracted by our internal troubles with the rebels."

Throat dry, Kiva asked, "Then isn't it good that the rebels are quiet right now? Because you're *not* distracted?"

Jaren nodded, but he didn't seem convinced.

"Why do you still look so concerned?" Kiva asked.

"It's just—" Jaren ran a hand through his hair, the golden ends sticking out all over the place. "I love my people too much not to worry about them. It's an intrinsic part of who I am—wanting to keep them safe. So I don't like the idea of any threat looming over us, even if I'm confident of our own defenses."

Kiva couldn't keep from raising an eyebrow. "You're the heir to the richest land in Wenderall. You're *always* going to have threats looming over you."

Jaren made a sound that was part laugh, part groan. "Believe me, I know." He then straightened his shoulders and said, "Even if Mirraven and Caramor decide to try, they won't make it very far into Evalon. We have too many defenses blocking them. It's a fool's errand, and that's the only reason I'm able to sleep at night."

When Kiva turned skeptically toward the darkened windows, Jaren amended, "Well, most nights."

"So you're worried in general, but not about anything specific," she summarized.

"I'm worried about plenty of specific things." Jaren looked at Flox and added, somewhat dryly, "Like whether I'll ever be able to leave this couch."

"Such a conundrum," Kiva teased.

Jaren smiled, but then he quickly sobered. "Speaking of leaving, I meant to tell you earlier, but we got distracted by the most humiliating dinner of my existence."

Kiva snickered in memory.

"I'm leaving for Fellarion in the morning," he continued. "The city leaders want to discuss infrastructure and farming and a number of other things that need overseeing. I'll be gone for at least four days, possibly more."

"Oh," Kiva said, secretly delighted. If Jaren was gone, he wouldn't notice if she went missing for a few hours—and after another near miss with her magic tonight, she was more desperate than ever to find her grandmother. "Well, uh, thanks for telling me."

"I was going to invite you along," he said. "But I'd rather not be responsible for you dying of boredom."

"I appreciate that," Kiva said, shuddering inwardly as she recalled the second half of the Royal Council meeting.

"I also heard you've been offered a position at Silverthorn," Jaren added, "and I didn't want to risk pulling you away from your dream." He leaned closer, his expression filling with pride. "Congratulations, Kiva."

Right now she deserves the chance to live her life and follow her dreams.

Her chest tightened at the remembered words. "I haven't accepted yet."

"I heard that, too." Jaren cocked his head to the side. "I'm just not sure why."

"I—" Kiva swallowed. "I just want to make sure I'm ready first."

"Healer Maddis says you are."

That wasn't what Kiva had meant by ready. "She only says that because of my father."

"She knew him?" he asked, surprised. "You told me he was a healer —did he study at Silverthorn?"

"Sort of," Kiva hedged. "Maddis said he was one of her best students." She knew better than to give Jaren more of her family history —he already knew too much for comfort. And yet . . . he'd still defended Faran to the Royal Council. Kiva, too, by association.

"Like father, like daughter," Jaren said, looking at her warmly and sliding a comforting arm behind her shoulders.

Kiva couldn't speak for a long moment, his words resonating deeply.

It was true—she *was* like her father. She had his healer's heart, his compassion for people, and, long ago, she'd also had his eternal optimism.

But then Zalindov had happened.

And Faran had been taken from her.

In all the time since then, she'd become so obsessed with vengeance that she hadn't stopped to think about what *he* would have wanted. For her. For their family.

Or perhaps she hadn't considered it because she already knew the answer.

Faran would have wanted them to forgive, and to move on. He would have wanted them to chase their dreams, to be happy, to *live*.

He wouldn't have wanted them bent on revenge.

He would have just wanted them safe.

And deep down, Kiva knew he would be turning in his grave if he knew what his children were up to.

"Speaking of fathers," Kiva said, croaking slightly and needing to not think about her own. She settled deeper into the lounge, unintentionally leaning into Jaren. "King Stellan, is he—um—"

"Is he what?"

In a whisper, Kiva asked, "Is he sick?"

Jaren froze beside her. But then his arm curled tighter, either to comfort himself or to comfort her as he breathed out a quiet, "Yeah."

"Is it terminal?" Kiva kept whispering.

Jaren nodded. "It's in his blood." His free hand smoothed Flox's ears as he shared, "There's been more bad days than good lately. That's why you didn't meet him before tonight—he's been in bed all week."

Softly, Kiva asked, "How long does he have?"

"We don't know," Jaren admitted, just as softly. "It could be years, but most likely months. Possibly weeks."

"There's nothing you can do?"

Shaking his head, Jaren said, "We've tried everything. Now we just keep him as comfortable as possible."

Seeing the raw pain on his face, Kiva erased the last of the distance between them, resting her head on his shoulder and wrapping her arm around his stomach, being careful not to dislodge Flox. She knew it wasn't wise, that she should keep her distance, physically and emotionally.

She knew—but she didn't care.

Not when Jaren was upset.

Not when he needed her.

"I'm sorry," she whispered.

In response, he placed a soft kiss on her temple.

Silence fell between them, long enough for Kiva to decide it was time to return to her room. But just as she was about to do so, her eyes drifted shut and she descended into sleep.

CHAPTER SEVENTEEN

When Kiva woke the next morning, she was in her bed, the blankets snug around her. She cast her mind back and realized Jaren must have carried her to her room and tucked her into bed.

A mortified groan left her, but then a hard knock on her door had her shooting upward, with Caldon calling through the wood a moment later to say it was time for training. The last thing she wanted to do that morning was work on her fitness — not when she was so anxious to find Nanna Delora — but knowing the prince would hunt her down if she tried to skip their session, Kiva hurried to change into her training clothes.

"I hate dawn," she said upon meeting him in her sitting room.

"Good morning to you too, Sunshine," Caldon returned, tweaking her nose.

She pulled a face and followed him outside, whinging all the way. As if to punish her sour attitude, he made her do double the amount of box steps and added an extra two running laps, leaving her in agony but also feeling proud of herself when she only vomited once.

"I think I'm getting better at this," Kiva panted after they finished their final lap.

"We're not done yet, Sweet Cheeks," Caldon said, his breathing perfectly steady.

Kiva was about to object, partly because she was exhausted, and partly because she wanted to get to Blackwater Bog, find her grandmother, and return to the palace before anyone realized she'd been gone.

But then Caldon revealed two wooden swords, and her excitement at holding a weapon, childproof or not, made her swallow her complaint.

"You're not ready for real steel," the prince told her, "but we can start practicing some basic forms, getting you used to the feel of it in your hands and building on your core strength."

Kiva tossed the blade from hand to hand. "It's a bit light, isn't it?"

Mirth filled Caldon's expression. "Let's see if you're still saying that when we finish."

Kiva was naively confident when he guided her through some introductory moves, reminding her to retain the correct posture he'd been drilling into her for days. He kept his own wooden blade sheathed, making her slice into the air, her abdominal muscles squeezing as she turned her hips at his command, thrusting and parrying with snail speed.

"It's all about control, about balance," Caldon told her. "With a heckuva lot of repetition."

Within minutes, Kiva's muscles were burning—*all* of them. At any one time, she had to be in complete control of her body, while still listening carefully to Caldon's merciless corrections: "Look up!" "Back straight!" "Watch your feet!" "Slow down!" "Tighten your core!"

Toward the end, he ordered her to speed up, forcing her into a set of quick steps, lunges, and constant footwork that demanded perfect balance and concentration. When he finally said she could stop, she wasn't only physically shattered, but mentally, too.

"That wasn't terrible," Caldon said, looking down at Kiva, who had collapsed spread-eagled on the ground. "But we have a lot of work to do."

Kiva whimpered. "Would you care if I told you the only part of me that doesn't hurt is my hair?"

"I'd care," Caldon answered. He grinned and added, "Because as long as any part of you doesn't hurt, that means I need to push you harder tomorrow."

Kiva didn't have the energy to reply. Or cry, which was what she really felt like doing. Never before had she been more grateful for Rhessinda's quick-acting muscle relaxant powder that was waiting in her room —if only she could summon the strength to get there.

"All right, Sweet Cheeks, I'll help you out, just this once," Caldon said, hauling her up to her feet.

"You're too kind," Kiva groused—or she tried to, but her words ended in a pain-filled groan as she sought to keep her legs from crumpling beneath her.

"Usually, yes," Caldon agreed. "But today it's also for self-serving reasons."

"With you, it usually is."

"Be nice," Caldon said, "or I won't play tour guide."

It took Kiva a second to realize what he'd said. "I'm sorry, what?"

"Your boyfriend felt bad about leaving you," Caldon informed her, wiping a speck of dirt off his training shirt, "so he asked me to entertain you while he's gone. Show you the city, introduce you to the best of Vallenia, that kind of thing."

The pain fled Kiva as dread took hold. "That's really not necessary." Quickly, she added, "And he's not my boyfriend."

Caldon waved a hand. "Semantics."

"Seriously," Kiva said, "I'm fine keeping my own company."

"Be that as it may, I made my cousin a promise," Caldon said, collecting her wooden sword and nudging her toward the training yard exit. "Until Jaren returns, you and I will be spending some quality time together. Lots and lots of quality time." With another easy grin and a quick wink, he finished, "Consider me your new best friend, Sunshine. Where you go, I go. Doesn't that sound fun?"

For the next few days, Kiva couldn't sneeze without Caldon being close enough to offer her a handkerchief.

Each morning, they continued their training, with Kiva only surviving the new sword practice thanks to heavy doses of Rhess's pain-killing muscle relaxant. As soon as Caldon declared their sessions over, he barely gave her enough time to clean up and change before he was upholding his promise to Jaren by whisking her off into the city.

Kiva didn't have a spare second to even *try* to sneak away, and while she'd experienced no further magic bursts in that time, she was increasingly aware of the power lurking beneath her skin, like a whispered reminder that it was there — and it wanted out. Recalling how her mother had apparently used "little magics," Kiva wondered if doing the same might help keep hers from bursting free. But the fear of discovery kept her from any such attempt, and she cast the thought from her mind.

When Saturday morning arrived — five days since Jaren's departure — Kiva was desperate enough to hatch a drastic plan. Jaren had said he'd be away for four days, possibly more, and that meant he could return at any time. When he did — along with Naari and Captain Veris — it would be so much harder for her to leave the city undiscovered.

During her brainstorming, she'd considered using Silverthorn as an excuse again, just like when she'd snuck away to Oakhollow. But with Caldon shadowing her steps, she knew he would only follow her. Even so, Kiva had decided that the academy would still help her evade the prince, if in another, more extreme way.

The first part of her plan began when she finished her morning training and Caldon revealed the places he planned to take her that day, starting with the Temple of the Forgotten Gods, then heading over to the Singing Gardens. After that, they would take a dip in Sarana's Baths, and finish with a hike up the Warrior's Steps to catch the sun setting over the city.

Kiva felt tired just thinking about it all, and she used that emotion to turn pleading eyes on him and say, "Do you mind if we stop at Silverthorn on our way? I want to pick something up."

"Are you being vague on purpose?" Caldon asked, running his fingers along his wooden sword.

Kiva placed her hands on her hips and shamelessly lied, "I was trying to spare you the details, but since you're such a busybody, I have cramps and want to grab some moonflower."

Caldon frowned. "You should have told me earlier. I would have gone easier on you if I'd known you were in pain."

"I'm in pain *every* morning with you," Kiva returned, feeling a sliver of guilt at his unanticipated compassion. "You've never cared before."

"That's different," he said. "And you know it."

If Kiva *had* been suffering from her monthly cycle, she might have been emotional enough to hug him. Instead, she swallowed her gratitude and agreed to meet him after she'd bathed.

The second part of her plan took place when they arrived at Silverthorn, with Kiva loosing a relieved breath at seeing Rhessinda sitting on the same bench as the first time she'd sought the healer out.

"Do you mind giving me a moment with her?" Kiva asked Caldon, gesturing toward Rhess. "I, um, just want to talk to her about some of my, uh, symptoms."

The prince seemed surprised by her fake embarrassment, and she swore inwardly, realizing that, as a healer, she should have been perfectly at ease talking about all bodily functions. Thankfully, Caldon let it go and halted on the path, leaning against one of the stone arches to wait.

Kiva hurried straight over to Rhessinda, who stood upon her approach.

"What's with the royal bodyguard?" she asked, tossing her ashy braid over her shoulder.

"Not a bodyguard. More a well-meaning but frustratingly clingy babysitter." Kiva shook her head. "Never mind about that, I need your help. Can you take me to the apothecaries' garden?"

Rhessinda didn't waste time asking questions. "Sure. It looks like you're in a rush — we can cut straight across the sanctuary."

Kiva turned to Caldon, miming that she would be back in a few minutes. Part of her was surprised he didn't follow when she and Rhess set out across the grass, but then she reminded herself that she wasn't a prisoner—Caldon was spending the day with her to keep her company, something that he thought she would want. That *Jaren* thought she would want. At any other time, she would have been humbled by their thoughtfulness, and for the hours Caldon was sacrificing to show her the beautiful city.

"Want to tell me what's going on?" Rhess asked casually as they crossed a narrow brook and passed through a small grove of citrus trees, hints of orange, lime, and lemon scenting the air.

"I need to ask a favor, but I don't want you to get in trouble," Kiva answered.

Rhess snorted. "Please. Do I seem like the kind of person who worries about trouble?"

No, she didn't. And that was why Kiva had come to her for help. "I need to get away from Vallenia for the day."

"Back to Oakhollow?" Rhess asked as they headed toward an impressive greenhouse. It hadn't been part of Kiva's tour the first day, when she'd seen only the apothecaries' workroom where the medicines were made and readied for collection.

"Not Oakhollow. Somewhere else."

As much as Kiva was growing to value Rhess's friendship, she still had many secrets that couldn't be shared. But the healer didn't press, and only asked, "What do you need?"

Kiva quickly explained about Caldon dogging her steps and how she needed to take him out of the equation, finishing with, "I'm thinking a sleeping remedy. Perhaps a combination of moradine and rosaron." Normally she would only use moradine—like what the queen had given Tipp the night of Kiva's abduction—but the addition of rosaron would ensure a deeper sleep for a fully grown adult like Caldon.

"That should definitely work," Rhess said without a hint of judgment.

They reached the outer edge of the apothecaries' garden, a small picket fence hedging in numerous rows of medicinal plants. Had she the time, Kiva would have spent hours wandering the aisles and exploring the greenhouse at their center, but today wasn't the day for sightseeing.

"Where to?" Kiva asked Rhess, indicating the large garden.

The healer hesitated, and Kiva wondered if she was having second thoughts about helping her steal from the academy. But then Rhess stepped over the small fence, striding with purpose toward a mounted signpost. Seeing it, Kiva realized she could have left Rhess out of her plan entirely, since the sign offered a detailed map of every bed in the garden.

"Moradine and rosaron, right?" Rhessinda asked.

"Right," Kiva confirmed.

Rhess searched the map, found them both listed in the same garden bed, and led the way in their direction.

"So you plan to drug Prince Caldon and then sneak away from the palace to some unknown place?" the healer said as they wandered along the path. "Sounds wise."

"I'm visiting family," Kiva said.

"I thought you already did that."

"*Different* family."

"As long as my aiding and abetting doesn't result in you getting hurt," Rhess said. "Or lost. Where are you headed?"

Kiva bit her lip as they approached the desired garden bed, realizing that she'd forgotten to consult a map. "Blackwater Bog. Do you know it?"

"Oh, sure, that's just up north a bit," Rhess said as they came to a halt on the path.

"Where the Wildemeadow meets the Crewlling Swamplands," Kiva recited.

The healer turned to look at her, squinting. "You have no idea where you're going, do you?"

Kiva sighed and shook her head.

Rhess chuckled. "Don't worry, it's really easy to find. Just head north out of Vallenia and follow the signposts. You only have to skate the eastern edge of the Wildemeadow, not travel through the middle of it, so it's a fast journey." Quickly, she warned, "But don't go beyond Blackwater Bog. The swamp will swallow you alive."

Kiva shuddered at the thought. "Thanks," she said, fully aware that she owed Rhessinda big time.

The healer shrugged away her gratitude and pointed to the flower bed. "Here we are."

Kiva crouched and plucked a few bright red moradine petals along with some yellow-streaked leaves from the rosaron shrub. "Perfect."

Aware that Caldon could come looking for her at any time—which was also why she didn't try to take off without him, since there would be hell to pay if he discovered her gone—Kiva hurried with Rhessinda out of the garden and across the sanctuary again. When they reached the prince, he sent a flirtatious smile to Rhess—which she ignored—and asked Kiva if she was ready to go.

"Can we head back to the palace quickly first?" she replied after they said goodbye to Rhess, following the next phase of her plan. "I'm wearing new boots and they're rubbing. I don't want to end up with blisters."

The prince showed no signs of impatience, instead agreeing that she needed appropriate footwear given how much walking their day would require.

Nerves skittered in Kiva's stomach when they arrived at her sitting room, the most challenging task now before her.

"Why don't you take a seat," Kiva said, motioning to an armchair near the window. "I may be a few minutes."

Caldon followed her suggestion, clearly not in a rush, though he did say, "Just grab your first comfortable pair."

Instead of heading straight to her bedroom, Kiva drifted over to a tea tray the palace servants kept warm at all hours of the day. With shaking hands, she poured two cups, carefully slipping the moradine petals and rosaron leaves out of her pocket and dunking them into Caldon's tea, pushing them to the bottom.

After spending weeks with him at the winter palace, one of the few things she knew was that he was very fond of his morning tea. Praying that today would be no different, she turned with a bright smile and walked over to hand him the teacup.

"We could have gotten something while we were out," Caldon said, accepting the steaming offering. "I was planning to show you this cute little teahouse on the way to the temple. It's owned by an ex-apothecary, and it looks like half a forest has relocated into her store. I figured you might like to see it, but I guess we can always stop there on the way back."

He raised the teacup to his lips, and Kiva had to stop herself from knocking it out of his hands. Jaren may have asked Caldon to show her around the city, but it was Caldon who had spent time carefully deciding where to take her based on her interests. She hated repaying his kindness by drugging him, even if she'd been left with little choice.

Caldon smacked his lips after his first sip. "This tastes different." Kiva's heart skipped a beat, until he gave it a deep sniff and asked, "Did you add cinnamon?"

He took another large gulp as he waited for her answer, but the potent sleeping mixture took effect before she could reply.

Kiva had never worked with moradine or rosaron before, neither having been part of her mediocre garden at Zalindov, though her father had taught her how to administer both. She'd given Caldon a large enough dose to knock him out for hours, confident there would be no ill effects aside from grogginess and disorientation upon his waking—which would only work in her favor.

She hadn't, however, expected the drugs to kick in so fast, and she had to lunge forward to grab him when he nearly toppled out of the armchair. Both his teacup and hers crashed to the ground, spilling brown liquid everywhere.

But Caldon was out. And that was what mattered.

He would be safe in her sitting room. Tipp would be in the western palace studying with Oriel until early evening, and any servants who entered would just assume the prince was taking a nap. When Caldon awoke, Kiva *hoped* he'd think the same, but if he had doubts, she would be back long before the drugs left his system, giving her plenty of time to convince him that he'd dozed off while waiting for her to change her boots.

Making sure the prince was comfortable, Kiva quickly cleaned up the mess, then hurried to grab her travel cloak. Just as she was about to leave, the door to the hallway opened—

And Tipp skipped through it.

His face brightened at the sight of Kiva, but then he saw Caldon passed out in the armchair, the spilled tea slowly drying on the floor.

Tipp wasn't a fool. It took him less than two seconds to take in everything—including Kiva's travel clothes and the startled look on her face—and turn to her with accusing eyes.

"What d-d-did you *do?*"

Kiva raised her hands. "It's not what it looks like."

"It looks like y-you drugged C-Caldon."

Wincing, Kiva admitted, "I didn't think you'd be back until later."

"I n-needed a sweater. We're h-heading out into the gardens, and it's g-g-going to rain soon."

Kiva had noticed the clouds while walking back from Silverthorn, but she wasn't about to let poor weather disrupt her day.

"Now, t-tell me what you're doing," Tipp demanded, his hands on his hips.

Aware that he'd worked in Zalindov's infirmary long enough to recognize that Caldon's state wasn't natural, Kiva settled on a half-truth. "He's been watching me like a hawk since Jaren left. I just needed some space."

"So y-you *drugged* him? He's been n-nothing but kind to us — *all* of his family have b-b-been nothing but kind. And now you g-go and do *this?*" His voice rose. "*Why*, K-Kiva?"

Kiva used the guilt she was feeling in an attempt to sway Tipp, sharing another partial truth. "There's someone I need to visit, and I didn't want him coming with me."

"*Who?*"

It was a risk, Kiva knew, but she trusted the young boy to keep her secrets — if she asked him.

Some secrets, at least. Not all of them.

And so she said, in a whisper, "My family."

Tipp's anger vanished. "Your *w-what?*"

"I have a brother and sister living just out of the city," Kiva answered, thinking it safer to share about Zuleeka and Tor rather than offer any mention of Delora. Her siblings were well hidden and desired to stay that way, whereas her grandmother was a wildcard. "I want to go see them."

Tipp's freckled brow furrowed. "Caldon could have t-taken you."

"I haven't seen them in ten years," Kiva said, lying now. She made her lip wobble — not difficult, considering how dreadful she felt. "I don't know if they'll want to see me after . . . everything. And if they turn me away, I'd like to lick my wounds in private. That's why I want to go alone." Quietly she finished, "He's only sleeping."

Tipp was looking between her and Caldon, deep in thought. "This is important t-to you, isn't it?"

Kiva nodded. "More than I can say."

That, at least, was the truth.

The young boy remained silent for another minute, before finally nodding. "I'll c-cover for you."

Kiva blinked with surprise, but Tipp wasn't finished. He headed toward his bedroom, talking to her the whole time.

"Everyone thinks h-he's with you today anyway, so I'll k-keep Ori out of here, and if anyone a-asks, I'll say Cal was out late last n-night and is sleeping it off."

Tipp returned to the sitting room carrying a pillow and blanket, carefully draping the latter over the prince, and lifting his head for the former.

"If he w-wakes up before you return—"

"He won't," Kiva said. "I'll be quick."

"If h-he *does,*" Tipp continued, "I'll tell him you thought he m-might be sick and you left him to r-rest."

Kiva's eyes welled with gratitude. "You won't say anything? About where I'm going?"

"I get the f-feeling you'd like it kept secret."

Kiva was too choked to do anything other than nod.

"If it's important t-to you, it's important to m-me," Tipp said quietly, walking over to wrap his arms around her waist. "We're in this t-together, Kiva. Always."

She pulled him close and only released him when he started to squirm, after which he sent her a gap-toothed grin and pushed her toward the door.

Needing no further encouragement, Kiva hurried outside and headed directly to the stables. Caldon had taken her out on horseback for two of the last three days, so the royal grooms didn't ask questions when she politely requested they saddle her a mount. Within minutes, she was trotting along the path, waving to the guards as she passed through the front gates, and riding out into the city.

Only then did she breathe a sigh of relief, turning north to finally, *finally* seek out her grandmother.

CHAPTER EIGHTEEN

The ride to Blackwater Bog was quicker than Kiva had anticipated, perhaps twenty minutes once she left the city's walls and nudged her horse into an easy canter, with them skirting the Wildemeadow's rolling hills until the land flattened and turned marshy, heralding the swamp up ahead.

Given how swift her travels were, Kiva remained confident she would return to Caldon long before he woke—and that she'd beat the looming rain clouds that were moving steadily closer. Her certainty only grew when she passed an elderly man walking his dog in the sleepy little village, and he happily provided directions to Murkwood Cottage, along with a warning that Delora valued her privacy. Because of that, Kiva had to travel much deeper into the Crewlling Swamplands than she'd hoped, but at least the path, while narrow and soggy, seemed safe enough.

"Easy, boy," she told her nervous mount, patting his neck. "We're nearly there."

Rounding one final bend, she finally saw Murkwood Cottage up ahead, surrounded by thick vegetation and nestled beside a murky body of water. Made of stone with a thatched roof and a smoking chimney, the dwelling was quaint—in a creepy, swampish way.

When Kiva came to a halt, she'd barely dismounted before the front door burst open and a white-haired woman hobbled out, a cane in her hand that she lifted into the air and brandished like a weapon.

"Private property!" she screeched from her porch. "This is private property! Can't you read?"

She pointed to a sign on the path so covered in moss that Kiva could barely make out the two capitalized *P*s, let alone the rest.

"I'm looking for Delora," Kiva said, not leaving her horse's side in case she needed to make a quick getaway. "Is that you?"

The elderly woman squinted at Kiva for a long minute, then thumped her cane on the ground, moving an angry step forward. "I told you never to come back here, girl! I won't give you what you want—not now, not ever!"

Kiva stilled. Zuleeka and Torell had said they'd visited with their mother, but that had been *years* ago. Did Delora think Kiva was Tilda? Her *daughter?*

"I'm sorry," Kiva said, her throat tight. "But we've never actually met. I'm Kiva."

Delora's squint deepened, her familiar emerald eyes—Corentine eyes—mere slits, before she finally leaned back on her haunches. "Ah, so you're not the she-devil." Brandishing her cane again, she said, "But I'm guessing she sent you here. I won't give it to you, either, so go back to where you came from. Shoo!"

"Please," Kiva said, raising her hands. "I'm not here for anything." She quickly corrected, "I mean, I *am*, but not—"

"*I won't give it to you!*" Delora repeated, yelling now.

Kiva was at a loss, so she blurted, "I need your help controlling my magic."

Delora's mouth snapped shut. She pressed her lips together, looking Kiva over from head to toe. "You're the one she left to rot in that prison, aren't you? The one she said was better off there?"

Kiva's face paled, but she reminded herself that Delora hadn't seen her mother in nearly a decade, and there was no way Tilda would have thought Kiva was "better off" inside Zalindov.

"I was locked away for ten years," Kiva said in answer. "I kept my magic hidden that whole time and didn't use it until a few weeks ago when I healed someone who was dying. Now it's bursting out of me at random."

"So?" Delora said, raising two bushy white eyebrows.

"So," Kiva said through gritted teeth, "I'm living at the royal palace. With the Vallentis family."

Delora threw back her head and laughed. Something in the murky water—something *large*—moved quickly at the sound, ducking beneath the surface before Kiva could see what it was.

She has a very unusual guard dog, Torell had warned.

Shuddering, Kiva waited for her grandmother's humor to fade. Finally, she tapped her foot on the ground and said, "I'm glad you find this funny."

"Give me a minute," Delora said, still chuckling. "I'm just trying to imagine it. I assume they have no idea who you are?"

"No. And I'd like to keep it that way."

"Let me guess," the old woman drawled, leaning more of her weight onto her cane. "You plan to follow blindly in your family's ill-fated footsteps, seeking to steal a throne that you believe is yours for no other reason than a diluted bloodline. Am I right?"

Kiva said nothing.

Delora snorted, then turned to hobble back through her front door. "I can't help you, girl."

"Can't, or won't?" Kiva asked, tying her reins around a low-hanging branch and hurrying up the porch steps.

"Won't." Looking over her shoulder, Delora added, "Go back to your palace and your vengeance, and leave me alone."

"Please," Kiva said, begging now. "I just want it to stop. That's all I want. A way to control it. It just—It needs to stop."

Delora paused at the threshold and turned back to look at Kiva. Her perusal lasted for a long moment, before she finally observed, "You really did only come here for that, didn't you?"

Quietly, Kiva said, "They'll kill me if they find out who I am."

"Isn't that what you plan to do to them?" Delora said without mercy.

Kiva flinched. "No. No I—" Her voice broke. "I don't want them dead."

Delora snorted again. "So you just want them destroyed, then."

It wasn't a question.

"Will you help me or not?" Kiva asked.

Another long moment passed, long enough for hope to well within Kiva, but then—

"Can't," Delora said.

Kiva deflated, but before she could try begging again, Delora nonsensically continued, "I've got book club."

"You've—what?" Kiva stumbled over her words.

"Today's Saturday," Delora said, as if that should mean something to Kiva. "Book club is on Saturday. The ladies will be here any minute." She pointed her cane toward the side of her cottage. "There's a shelter around back. Settle your horse, then come inside. We should have just enough time to make scones. You're whipping the cream."

Before Kiva could respond, the old woman hobbled through the doorway and slammed it behind her.

"What just happened?" she whispered to no one, uncertain if her grandmother had agreed to help or not. But since Delora hadn't sent her packing, Kiva quickly followed her instructions, praying book club would wrap up quickly.

Hours—and *hours*—later, Kiva sat surrounded by overflowing bookcases in Delora's cozy living room, a crackling fireplace battling the chill of the storm that had unleashed outside, its intensity only slightly more ferocious than the five elderly women sitting in a circle and shouting at each other.

"I just think there's a redemption arc in his future," Clovis said, jabbing her page and nearly upsetting her tea.

Bretwalda, who was clumsy enough to have already spilled numerous cups, argued, "But we're talking about *this* book. Gavon is *much* more swoonworthy."

"I don't care if Killian finds redemption," Yinn stated around a mouth full of scone, the fourth batch of which had just come out of the oven. "He's sexier as a villain."

Merrilee nodded fervently, the rosy-cheeked woman having whispered barely five words since arriving. She was, for that reason, Kiva's favorite, with the other four — including her grandmother — so passionate in their commentary about the bodice-ripping romance that Kiva feared her face would never return to its normal color.

For the thousandth time, she looked out Delora's boxy windows, seeing the streaks of lightning and the pouring rain, along with the swift approach of twilight. She wouldn't be leaving soon, even if book club did miraculously come to an end.

Anxiety slithered like a snake inside Kiva with every minute that passed. Caldon would be awake by now, and even if he believed Tipp's lie about her leaving him to rest, she would still have to explain where she'd been — the one thing she'd wanted to avoid. Her plan had failed, and upon returning to the palace, she would have to face the consequences.

The very thought made Kiva feel ill.

Another hour — and another batch of scones — later, the storm began to pass, the rain a mere drizzle outside, but night had well and truly fallen.

As desperate as Kiva was to return to Vallenia, she still needed her grandmother's aid, so she waited impatiently as Delora's four friends *finally* began to pack up their things.

"I say you give her what she wants, Delly," Clovis declared out of the blue, rising slowly with the aid of her wooden walking frame. "She seems like a good egg."

Delora sniffed. "What she wants and what she needs are two different things."

Kiva stilled, realizing they were talking about her.

Over the course of the day, she'd left the room only a handful of times, mostly to whip up more scones at her grandmother's command. Delora must have used one of those opportunities to fill her friends in — and given how they were all now peering at Kiva, they clearly knew she had magic and wanted to stop it.

Did that mean they knew who she was? Who Delora was? Whose bloodline they both shared?

"Being Torvin's descendant doesn't automatically make her evil. You turned out all right," Bretwalda said kindly, patting Delora's wrinkly hand.

Well, that answered *that* question.

Though . . . Kiva didn't understand why she'd associated Torvin with evil. He'd spent his life healing people. They'd loved him so much that Sarana had grown jealous enough to try and kill him — her own *husband* — forcing him to abandon the throne and flee to safety. If anyone was evil, it was Sarana, not Torvin.

"*I* turned out all right because I put all that behind me," Delora told her friends. "*She* is related to the she-devil who wants only one thing."

The present tense pulled at Kiva's heart, reminding her that she still had to tell her grandmother that Tilda was dead.

"But she's *not* her," Yinn said, transferring the leftover scones into her fabric bag. "All she wants is help controlling her magic, not using it to hurt people."

"So she says," Delora said gruffly, spearing an angry look at Kiva. "But she wouldn't be the first Corentine to lie. We've made an art out of it."

"I swear," Kiva jumped in to defend herself. "That's all I came here for. Nothing else."

Delora waved a disbelieving hand. "Bah."

Kiva opened her mouth to argue again, but at that moment, Bretwalda stood and swung her purse around, the solid weight of it smacking into Merrilee's face, splitting her cheek open and sending her tumbling back into her chair.

At the sight of gushing blood, Kiva moved to inspect the cut. But her magic, simmering all day along with her impatience, had finally had enough of being stifled. It exploded out of her, stronger and brighter than ever before, and this time she didn't try to repress it. These women already knew her secret, so she might as well help the stunned Merrilee, even if it would leave her feeling drained for her ride home.

Focusing on the power at her fingertips, Kiva urged her magic to seal the wound, gently coaxing it as she'd started to learn as a child.

Magic is your friend, her father had shared when her mother refused to teach her. *Treat it kindly, and it will return the favor.*

Kiva hadn't been treating her magic kindly, stuffing it away for so long. No wonder it was angry.

Silence fell in the cottage when Kiva stepped back, the cut gone as if it had never existed.

"Did you mean to heal her? Was that deliberate?" Delora demanded after Merrilee whispered her quiet gratitude.

Kiva shook her head.

Her grandmother sighed and scrubbed her weathered face, before she set her features and turned to her friends. "Take care on the path. Mr. Chomps likes to poke about on land after a storm. And you know he startles easily."

An image of the large creature that had ducked beneath the water returned to Kiva's mind, and she shuddered all over again.

"That beastie's already taken a chunk out of me," Clovis said, pulling up her skirt to reveal an aged scar. "He's not getting another taste."

"He's friendly enough if you leave him alone," Delora said without sympathy. "Now, go home before it starts raining again."

Kiva didn't know what alarmed her more: that four *very old* women, one who had a walker, were about to make their way through the swamp in the dark while there was a carnivorous beast "poking about," or that she herself would be making the same trek soon. The four friends, however, were unconcerned, and merely said their goodbyes, disappearing into the night.

Delora turned to Kiva and loosed a long, resigned breath, before approaching the nearest bookcase and pulling out a black-spined book entitled *1,001 Pies and Pastries.* The cover opened to reveal a hollowed middle, inside which rested a single dagger. Aside from the clear gemstone embedded into the hilt, it was unremarkable, and yet Delora watched Kiva with intense focus as she removed the weapon from its hiding place.

Kiva could only assume the blade was Torvin's famed dagger, the family heirloom Tilda had tried to retrieve without success. Since Kiva didn't want the door slammed in *her* face, she was careful to act as if she didn't know what it was and simply asked, "Are you planning on stabbing me? Because that's what it's going to take to get me to leave without your help."

The tension left Delora's shoulders, as if she'd feared Kiva would leap forward and wrest the blade from her. But the dagger held no value to Kiva, and she was careful to keep from looking at it for too long lest Delora think any differently.

"Come with me," the old woman ordered, hobbling from the room.

Warily, Kiva followed her grandmother into her cramped kitchen. Splashes of flour dusted the bench from her last baking attempt, but Delora ignored the mess and shuffled toward a set of mounted shelves that contained an array of rare plant cuttings, including fresh specimens in jars of water.

Struggling not to ask questions, Kiva watched Delora pull leaves, stems, and flowers from her collection, laying them out on a chopping board before lining up the dagger's edge. Just before she made her first cut, she slitted her eyes at Kiva and demanded, "Turn around."

Kiva balked, not wanting her back toward someone holding a lethal weapon. "Sorry?"

"Turn around," Delora repeated, making a circling motion with the blade. "It's a secret recipe."

"But I—" Kiva clenched her teeth against her protest, seeing the unyielding look on the woman's face.

"If you want my help, turn around. Otherwise you're on your own."

With that ultimatum, Kiva spun away from her grandmother, calling her every foul name she could think of under her breath.

"I'm old, but I'm not deaf," Delora said. Remarkably, there was a hint of humor in her voice.

Kiva listened as the steady chopping sounds began, recalling what her brother had said about Delora being an apothecary.

My guess is that she's spitting on our ancestors by using that dagger as her work blade.

Torell had been right. Instead of using any of her standard kitchen knives, Delora had chosen Torvin's blade as her apothecary dagger, the weapon that was a symbol of his reign—of *their* reign, as his heirs.

Kiva shook her head, marveling at the woman's nerve.

"All done," Delora declared a few minutes later, and Kiva whirled to find the chopping board empty and a small stoppered vial resting beside the dagger.

Delora plucked up the offering, rolling it between her fingers. "You said you want your magic gone. Did you mean forever?"

My magic is a part of me. Like an arm or a leg.

Jaren's words came back to Kiva as she considered her grandmother's question. While her present circumstances meant her power was more a burden than a blessing, the idea of never being able to access her

LYNETTE NONI

magic again made her feel cold all over. Even if she'd forced it away for a decade, it had always been there, ready to come forth at her command. If it disappeared *forever* . . .

"No," she replied. "I just want to be able to control it. To stop these magic bursts from happening. I just need *time*."

When she no longer had to hide her magic, there was so much good she could do with it. So many people she could help, following in Torvin's footsteps.

Delora didn't look pleased with Kiva's answer, but she still handed over the vial.

"This will dampen your magic, lulling it to sleep. Take one mouthful now, and then one every morning with breakfast."

Kiva unstoppered the vial and gave it a whiff, recognizing hints of tilliflower, silverwheat, garrow, and mirkmoss. She'd also seen tumumin and hogweed on the bench before her grandmother had made her turn around. She didn't, however, reveal her rudimentary knowledge of potions, instead saying, "There's barely enough here for three days."

"That's because it's not a permanent solution," Delora said. "And even if it was, I don't have enough ingredients on hand for more."

Kiva looked at her in panic. "Then what am I supposed to—"

"Come back on Tuesday, and I'll try to have some more waiting for you," Delora said. "You have enough to last you until that night. You'll be fine."

Kiva wasn't as confident, especially given what she would face upon her return to the palace. She might never be allowed out again.

Though . . . there was always the secret tunnel exit, if she had no other option. But finding a horse would be a problem.

"I'm not sure if I can," Kiva hedged. "It's difficult for me to—"

"Come back, don't come back, I don't care," Delora stated, wiping a cloth over her dagger.

With three days to figure it out, Kiva set it from her mind and raised the vial to her lips, grimacing at the bitter aftertaste. An uncomfortable sensation prickled beneath her skin within seconds, but just as she grew concerned, it vanished, replaced by a sudden coldness that made her gasp aloud. Before she could get used to the feeling, it turned into a burning so intense that she nearly cried out. A moment later, ice flooded her veins all over again, and then —

Nothing.

Absolutely nothing.

Kiva *felt* the change, like part of her had simply disappeared. Her hand trembled as she held it out and called her magic to the surface, waiting for the tingling and the golden glow to appear. But there was nothing to summon.

My magic is a part of me. Like an arm or a leg.

Jaren's words replayed again, and Kiva realized how right he was. This feeling of something missing, of something so vital to who she was now gone . . . It was enough to make her want to smash the rest of Delora's vial on the ground.

But she didn't.

It wasn't forever, Kiva reminded herself, almost desperately. She could put up with it for now, a small sacrifice for a larger goal.

Breathing deeply as she adjusted to the strange, hollow feeling inside her, Kiva looked to her grandmother and asked, "Is this what you take? To stop your magic?"

"I told you, it's not a permanent solution," Delora said. "You need to learn how to control your magic, not repress it. That's the only way you'll stop your outbursts."

"How did you do that?" Kiva asked.

"I didn't."

Kiva waited for Delora to expand, but she said no more.

"So . . . you *do* still practice?" Kiva said, recalling her siblings' claim that Tilda hadn't suffered because she'd never stopped using her power.

"No, I don't."

Kiva's brow furrowed. "If you don't take this"—she indicated the vial—"and you don't use your magic, then how do you keep it from—"

"Question time is over," Delora interrupted firmly enough that Kiva knew not to press.

Hobbling back into the living room, the old woman returned her dagger to its book and repeated, "Come back in three days." Upon seeing the fear creep into Kiva's expression, she sighed and added, "I'll have a think about other ways that might help you. But I can't make any promises."

If Kiva hadn't thought she'd end up with a cane slamming into her stomach, she might have hugged her crotchety grandmother.

"Thank you for this," she said quietly, pocketing the vial and reaching for her travel cloak. She didn't like how the potion made her feel, but there was no denying that her anxiety levels were already much improved.

Delora waved away her thanks. "Go on, get out of here. And keep your eyes open on the path back into town."

The last thing Kiva wanted was a reminder about the unknown Mr. Chomps being out on the prowl, so she nodded her agreement—while repressing a shiver. With a quiet but grateful goodbye, she left the cottage, eager to leave the swamp far, far behind her.

In three days, she would be back again.

She would find a way.

She always did.

CHAPTER NINETEEN

The skies opened up again when Kiva was halfway back to Vallenia, leaving her a shivering, sopping mess by the time she rode through the palace gates.

With an affectionate pat to her mud-flecked horse, she left him in the hands of the royal grooms, before sloshing her way up the darkened gravel toward the palace.

Painfully aware of how late it was, Kiva braced as she dripped water up the red-carpeted staircases, certain she'd find Caldon waiting in her suite, ready to unleash his fury.

What she *hadn't* anticipated was that Jaren would have returned in time to witness it.

Kiva repressed a groan as his gaze sliced to her upon entry, his face uncharacteristically blank.

Caldon, however, was staring at her with unbridled rage, his arms crossed, his cobalt eyes blazing.

Both princes were standing, as was Naari, who frowned at Kiva with clear disappointment. Mirryn alone reclined on the couch, appearing entertained.

Kiva paid the princess no mind, nor did she worry about anyone else for the moment, because her eyes landed on the final person in the room. Tipp was huddled on the armchair she'd left Caldon in, his arms around his knees, his face pale, looking anywhere but at her.

Alarmed by his posture, Kiva hurried over and crouched by his side, her clothes sloshing with the movement.

"Tipp?"

He didn't respond, and her concern only grew, until finally he looked at her, his lip wobbling as he whispered, "I'm s-s-sorry. You were g-gone for so long, and everyone was s-so worried. I had t-to tell them."

Kiva closed her eyes with resignation, all the excuses she'd come up with on her ride back now useless. Even so, she cupped his cheek with her ice-cold hand and said, "It's all right. I don't blame you."

Rising again, she turned to face the others. No one spoke, as if waiting for her to make the first move. But when she continued to just look at them, Caldon finally snapped, pointing a finger at her face and demanding, "Where the *hell* have you been?"

"I—"

"You were abducted barely a week ago!" he interrupted loudly. "You don't go wandering off on your own, and you *certainly* don't leave the city for any reason, least of all to see your siblings who haven't cared a whit about you for a decade. Gods, Kiva, I thought you were smarter than that."

"But I—"

He cut her off with another finger jab. "And you do not, under *any* circumstances, *gods-damned drug me.*" Yelling now, he finished, *"What the hell were you thinking?"*

Kiva curled her arms around her middle, unable to defend herself in the face of his—admittedly justified—anger.

"Cal," Jaren said quietly, lowering his cousin's hand. "Let her speak."

"This ought to be good," Mirryn said gleefully from her position on the couch, a goblet of wine in her hand.

Kiva didn't look at the princess, her focus torn between Jaren and Caldon, one who was vibrating with rage, the other who was eerily calm.

Swallowing, she drew her wet cloak tighter and asked, "What did Tipp tell you?"

"No," Caldon snapped. "You don't get to repeat what we already know. We've been worried—*for hours.* We were just about to call the guards to launch a search party. *Another* search party. So you need to start talking. Right now."

Through all of this, Jaren remained silent, his face still alarmingly blank. Caldon's anger she could handle. But Jaren's remoteness?

That was too much for Kiva to bear.

"I'm sorry," she whispered—to them both. "I didn't mean to scare you. I just—" She drew on everything she was feeling, repeating the performance she'd given Tipp earlier that day. "I just wanted to see my family. To see if they—if they—" She made her throat bob, allowed tears to pool in her eyes. "To see if they wanted anything to do with me. After Zalindov."

Caldon's anger didn't fade, but Jaren's eyes flickered with compassion, his expression thawing. He reached for the blanket Tipp had left out and moved forward to wrap it around her shoulders, reminding her of how soaked she was.

"You were gone a long time," Jaren said quietly.

"I got caught in the storm," Kiva said, a partial truth. "I decided it was safer to wait it out." She indicated her drenched clothes and offered a small, self-deprecating smile. "I didn't realize the rain wasn't finished."

"The storm didn't hit until late this afternoon," Caldon stated, ignoring her attempt at levity. "You had plenty of time to return before then."

"We had ten years of catching up to do," Kiva lied. "I didn't realize how quickly the day was passing."

"You still haven't said *where* you were," Caldon said. "All Tipp could tell us was that it was 'just out of the city'—we had no idea where to look for you."

"I didn't ask you to look for me." The words left Kiva before she could stop them.

"What part of this aren't you understanding?" Caldon growled, his ire rising anew. "We *care* about you, Kiva. Ignoring that you deliberately kept me from coming with you—which I would have done in a *heart-*

beat, as you damned well know—when you didn't return, we thought something had happened to you. Do you have any idea how that feels, to know someone you care about is missing, possibly in danger, and you don't know how to find them?"

The tears welling in Kiva's eyes weren't fake this time.

Caldon had lost both his parents after a storm had hit. He'd had no way to find them, or to know if they were still alive.

There were too many parallels with what Kiva had put him through that afternoon, unintentionally making him relive the worst moments of his life.

"I'm sorry," she whispered again, her voice breaking on the words.

Her emotion didn't sway Caldon. "Saying sorry doesn't change what you did. I can't even stand to look at you right now." True to his word, he turned his fiery glare to Jaren and demanded, "Come find me later."

He didn't wait for his cousin to agree before storming out of the room.

Kiva stared after him, feeling numb.

"He'll come around. Give him time."

Turning slowly, Kiva faced Jaren again, the breath leaving her when she found his expression no longer closed, but flooded with everything he'd felt while she'd been gone. Fear, dread, desperation. And relief—so much relief that she was safe.

Her knees wobbled at the knowledge of how much power she held over him.

. . . And at the knowledge of how much, with a single look, he held over her.

Unable to continue holding his gaze, Kiva couldn't resist—didn't *want* to resist—when he drew her into his embrace.

"I won't tell you not to do it again," he whispered. "I won't trap you here. But please, it would mean a lot if you could tell someone where you're going next time."

Kiva nodded against his chest, unable to lie to his face, his generous understanding prompting a sharp pain within her.

This was the Jaren that she hated.

Because *this* was the Jaren that she — that she —

Kiva didn't finish the thought, refusing to admit how deeply she'd come to care for him.

And it wasn't only Jaren. If her continued numbness was any indication, Caldon had also clawed his way into her heart, if in a more platonic way. Try as she might, she couldn't stop replaying his parting glare and his quick, angry departure.

Clearing her throat, Kiva stepped back from Jaren, longing to escape into her room and be done with the day.

"Is that it?" Mirryn asked incredulously from the couch. "Aren't we all curious about how her reunion went?"

"Mirry," Jaren said, quietly but firmly. "If Kiva doesn't want to tell us, then she doesn't have to."

"I'd like to know."

The words came from Naari, who until now had remained silent. One look revealed that she was still upset, having explicitly told Kiva to be smart, to be safe — neither of which she'd been that day.

"K-Kiva?" came Tipp's hesitant voice. "Will you t-tell us? Please? What happened with y-your family?"

Jaren's open expression said the choice was hers, but after what she'd put them through, Kiva felt compelled to answer.

"It went . . . well," she said. "We ate scones and drank tea and talked for hours."

Now she was mixing her stories. If she wasn't careful, she would be caught in one of her many tangled lies.

"Your brother and sister, right?" Jaren probed. "That's what Tipp told us."

"Yes. Zuleeka and Torell." Kiva only felt safe sharing their names because the Royal Council hadn't yet been able to identify the Viper and the Jackal, and Tor had confirmed they'd kept their identities secret so they could move freely around the kingdom.

"And where, pray tell, did you meet these siblings of yours?" Mirryn asked, peering at Kiva over her wine.

Since Torell and Zuleeka were safely hidden deep in the forest, she offered another partial truth by saying, "Oakhollow."

Naari made a startled sound. "You rode to *Oakhollow* on your own? Do you know how many people get lost in those woods?"

"I didn't go into the woods," Kiva said, continuing to lie. She almost wished she'd admitted to visiting her grandmother in Blackwater Bog right from the beginning, but then she recalled that at least four elderly residents now knew her secret. If someone were to travel to the swamp and ask questions . . . No, it was safer for Kiva to continue talking about her siblings, both of whom would be much harder to locate.

Or that was what Kiva thought, until Mirryn said, "I think you should invite them here for lunch. Tomorrow."

Kiva's eyes unconsciously widened. "Pardon?"

"It seems only fair," the princess said. "You've gotten to know our family—we should get to know yours."

"I—um—" Kiva tried to think up an excuse, but her mind was blanking.

"That's settled, then," Mirryn said, rising elegantly. "Send them a missive. I'll have the kitchen staff prepare something delicious. We'll make an event of it."

"No, please, I don't—" Kiva tried.

Mirryn waved her now empty goblet. "I'm kidding. We'll keep it informal. No need to look so panicked, Kiva. It'll be fun."

Fun was the last word Kiva thought it would be, but Mirryn sashayed out the door before she could protest.

"They might not be able to make it on such short notice," Kiva said weakly to Jaren and Naari. Tipp alone looked excited by the idea of meeting her siblings, his vibrancy returning now that he knew she wasn't in any serious trouble.

"All you can do is ask," Naari said, gesturing to the small desk in the corner of the sitting room. "Write your note, and I'll have the royal courier deliver it tonight."

Feeling pressured, Kiva moved toward the desk, her mind screaming that this was a bad idea. But with no valid reason to object, she reluctantly took her seat and pulled out a fresh sheet of parchment, frustratingly aware of Naari moving closer as she began to write.

Dearest brother and sister,

It was so wonderful being reunited with you today. Thank you for welcoming me into your home in Oakhollow, and for offering comfort when I struggled to control everything I was feeling. I'm confident the coming days will be better.

In return for your kindness, I wish to invite you to lunch at the River Palace tomorrow. Please reply at your earliest convenience, but I understand if you are unable to attend.

With love,

Kiva

"All done?" Naari asked, shamelessly reading over her shoulder.

Kiva nodded, hoping the near-rambling words were innocent enough to avoid suspicion—but also that her siblings would note the hidden details she'd offered, including that she'd found a way to repress her magic and how they needed to turn down her invitation.

Jaren approached, and Kiva braced herself for his perusal of her message, but he only gave it a passing glance before saying, "You're not using your code?"

Kiva stilled. "Sorry?"

"The note you sent your family when we left Zalindov was written in a code," Jaren said. "I figured it was a sibling thing."

"You're right," Kiva said, her voice rough. "I'll, uh, add something at the bottom, just so they know it's definitely from me."

Dipping her quill again, Kiva barely kept her hand from shaking as she finished her message.

Got stuck at Bog today. Told royals I was with you. They want to meet. Don't come.

Kiva almost underlined the final two words, but she feared that might be overkill.

"What does it say?" Naari asked, squinting at the scribbles.

"That I'm looking forward to seeing them again," Kiva lied, folding the message and writing *Torell and Zuleeka Meridan* on the front, before addressing it to *The Tippled Boar, Oakhollow.*

Naari plucked the finished note from her hand, a hint of suspicion in her amber eyes, but since that was the guard's natural expression, Kiva tried not to let it faze her.

"I can't w-wait to meet your family," Tipp said. "Mirry's r-r-right—lunch is going to b-be fun!"

Kiva forced a smile, hoping she didn't look as sick as she felt.

Surely Tor and Zuleeka would know better than to come.

And yet . . . as everyone slowly dispersed from her sitting room, Kiva couldn't help fearing that curiosity alone might draw her siblings to the palace, her gut churning at the thought of what the following day would bring.

CHAPTER TWENTY

That night when Kiva settled into bed, numerous worries battled for her attention. More than anything else, she couldn't get Caldon's furious face out of her mind. She'd never seen him that angry, not even when she'd stabbed him.

She had to go to him, she realized, pushing back her blankets. She had to at least *try* to make things better. It was the only way she'd be able to soothe her twisting insides.

The problem was, Caldon didn't sleep in the palace—he slept in the barracks.

Unable to just don a dressing gown and wander down the hall to his room, Kiva had to find a dry cloak and fasten it over her pajamas, tucking her long silk pants inside a fresh pair of boots. Her dark nightclothes were barely visible beneath her cloak, but she was careful to clasp the front tightly as she left her room and ventured downstairs and out into the night.

With the storm having cleared, there was a bite to the air that had Kiva moving swiftly along the path toward the brightly lit barracks. It was late enough that Caldon should be somewhere in the sleeping quarters, which, if she recalled correctly, were located between the mess hall and the private infirmary.

Upon arriving at the entrance, Kiva reached the doors as two guards were walking out, a man and a woman wearing polished armor and clearly on their way to begin the night shift. They looked at her with curiosity, but neither stopped her as she brushed past. Because of that, she turned and asked, "Excuse me, can you tell me where I can find Cal—er, Prince Caldon?"

The female guard arched an eyebrow, and Kiva cursed inwardly, realizing how her presence there—*in the middle of the night*—could be construed. She tightened her fingers around her cloak and kept her head high, willing the blush away from her cheeks.

The male guard—someone Kiva recognized from the training yard—didn't bat an eyelash, so she hoped that meant he'd keep his companion from spreading any uncomfortable rumors.

"The prince has a private room," the man answered, before offering quick directions.

Kiva thanked him and continued inside the building. While curious, she didn't pause to tour the infirmary, nor did she linger at the multiple doorways she passed, many of which she assumed led to private quarters and meeting rooms, and others to dormitories where the lower-ranked guards bunked together.

As Kiva approached Caldon's room, nerves fluttered within her. She halted outside his door, staring at the wood and summoning her courage before knocking quietly. When no answer came, she frowned and knocked again, louder.

For one embarrassing moment, Kiva wondered if Caldon had company—the kind he wouldn't want interrupted. Grimacing, she started backing away, but then the door opened, revealing the prince in sleep trousers and a rumpled, unbuttoned shirt. His hair was tousled and his eyes were squinting into the brighter light of the hallway, indicating he'd just been rudely awoken.

Kiva bit her lip, fearing he'd now have another reason to be angry at her—not that he needed it. As it was, he already appeared to be debating whether or not to close the door on her.

"Please," she rasped. "I'd really like to talk."

Caldon's lips pressed into a thin line, but he moved to the side, allowing her entry.

Slipping past him, Kiva looked around his quarters with unveiled interest. Aside from the bed, desk, bookcase, and wardrobe, the room was bare, the space practical and functional. There was no art on the walls, no clutter on the floor, everything perfectly in its place—with no personality whatsoever. It was so antithetical to everything Caldon was that Kiva felt a thread of alarm, enough that, instead of opening with a repeat of her earlier apology, the first thing she blurted was, "Why don't you live in the palace?"

Caldon closed the door and leaned against it, crossing his arms over his semi-bare chest. "Why are you here, Kiva?"

He didn't answer her question. But worse, he'd called her by her real name. Not Sunshine, not Sweet Cheeks. She loathed them both—or so she told herself—and yet she would have given anything to hear either of them from him right now.

"May I sit?" Kiva gestured to the chair behind the desk.

Caldon didn't move from the door. "No."

Kiva had known this would be difficult, but he wasn't even *trying* to make it easier for her.

"I know you're upset with me," she said in a placating tone. "You have every right to be."

"How generous of you," he said flatly, his face hard.

Wincing, Kiva reminded herself of *why* he was so angry—and that it wasn't just because she'd drugged him.

Do you have any idea how that feels, to know someone you care about is missing, possibly in danger, and you don't know how to find them?

Unable to hold his angry gaze, Kiva looked away, her eyes landing on his desk and seeing something she'd missed during her initial scan, the only hint of color in the otherwise utilitarian space.

It was a small, framed portrait—a boy and girl, both grinning widely with their arms around each other, behind whom stood a man and woman smiling adoringly down at them.

Kiva's heart gave a painful throb as she shifted closer, her fingers itching to take hold of the frame, but she made herself resist. Even so, she knew exactly what she was looking at: Caldon and his family, before tragedy had ripped them apart.

"I screwed up," she whispered.

Caldon straightened in surprise.

"I made a mess of things today. I should have just told you I needed some alone time. I hate—" Her voice broke. "I hate that I put you through that."

She reached for the portrait then, trailing her fingers gently along the edge.

"I know what it's like to have your family taken from you," Kiva said hoarsely. "To feel that emptiness—that *pain*—and fear it's never going to leave you."

Caldon's throat bobbed.

"I know how it feels to be left with nothing but darkness," Kiva went on, before offering a quiet, dangerous admission. "I know what it's like to *become* that darkness, how consuming it is. It's so much easier to hide in the night than to fight for the light."

Gods, did she know that.

"I also know how tempting it is not to feel any of those things," Kiva whispered. "To shut everyone out so you never have to experience that kind of agony again. I know, Cal. *I know.*"

He uncrossed his arms, his eyes shining with the hint of tears.

"My family was taken from me ten years ago," Kiva continued to whisper. "What I did today was wrong, but can you really tell me that if you were given the choice, you wouldn't do whatever it took to be re-united with your parents again?"

It was a low blow, using his own heartache against him, but nothing Kiva had said was a lie—not this time.

"I truly am sorry," Kiva said quietly. "More than you'll ever know."

Caldon's jaw was clenched tight, but as he looked at Kiva and saw the genuine remorse on her face, he finally loosened it and sighed loudly, before ordering, "Get over here."

Kiva hesitated, worried that he was about to throw her out.

But then Caldon was moving toward her, his strides long and swift, until suddenly he was drawing her startled body into his arms.

"Don't ever scare me like that again, do you hear me?" he whispered into her ear. He pulled back to hold her eyes, adding much more firmly, "And if you ever—*ever*—drug me again, I'll throw your ass in the dungeon for a week. Maybe more. Is that clear?"

Kiva nodded, stunned by his embrace, by his forgiveness.

"You're right—you screwed up today," Caldon went on. "But you're also right that, if ever there was a reason to act as foolishly as you did, then at least it should be for family." He stepped back, putting some space between them, while still remaining close. "Jaren came and told me everything I missed. I hope your siblings come tomorrow, if only so we can see if they're worth all the fuss you caused today."

Kiva's insides tumbled at the reminder.

"Are they?"

She blinked at the two almost snapped words. "Are they what?"

"Are they worth it?" Caldon asked, his face serious. "You risked a lot to reunite with them. But despite that, you came back to us afterward. You're staying with us, not them—that says something."

As Zuleeka had said over a week earlier, Kiva could hardly spy on the royals from inside the rebel camp. And yet . . . She considered Caldon's words, wondering where she would choose to live if it were up to her.

She knew the answer immediately, panic hitting her as she realized how comfortable she was at the palace—not because of how lavish it was, but because of who she shared it with.

Everworld help her.

Needing to regain a sense of control, Kiva forced a wry grin to her face and asked, "Are you kicking me out?"

Caldon rolled his eyes. "It's becoming a full-time job to look after you, so no." His head angled to the side. "Not unless you give me a reason to."

"I'm not *that* much trouble," Kiva argued, if only to keep from admitting that there were *multiple* reasons why he should keep her away from his family.

"I beg to differ," he said. "Kidnapped by rebels, attacked by Mirravens, disappearing to places unknown in misguided attempts to visit—"

"Wait," Kiva cut in. "What do you mean, attacked by Mirravens?"

Caldon leaned a hip against his desk. "I think there was more to your abduction than we understand. Jaren, Naari, Veris—they weren't there. But after I cleared the building of rebels and came to get you, that next group that ambushed us . . . I don't think they were connected to the first. I think they wanted something different. *That's* why I was so worried about you today—I thought Mirraven had captured you."

Kiva blanched, recalling that Caldon had already aired his suspicions after the incident and he'd been ignored. But if what he said was true—.

"Why would Mirraven want me?"

Caldon sent her a sharp look and countered, "Why would the rebels want you?"

Kiva couldn't answer that, since she couldn't admit to their fake abduction.

"So you see," Caldon went on when she didn't reply, "keeping an eye on you is much easier when I know where you are. Or at least where you *should* be." His pointed gaze caught hers. "Stunts like today don't help."

Kiva looked guiltily at the ground. She wasn't sure if she believed Caldon's claim about Mirraven—the rebels *had* been recruiting further north, and Zuleeka could have easily left more people behind than she'd implied. That was much more likely than Kiva being targeted by a second, unknown group on the very same night. The coincidence was too great, and she resolved to put it from her mind, having enough to worry about without adding hypothetical concerns to the list.

Yawning loudly, Caldon pushed off from his desk and moved toward the door. "As much as I've enjoyed this midnight chat, I need my beauty sleep. Let's get you back to your bed. Big day tomorrow."

"It's all right, I can make it on my own," Kiva said, butterflies swarming anew at his reminder.

"Move your ass, Sunshine," Caldon said, opening the door and giving a jerk of his chin, apparently not taking no for an answer.

Kiva was just relieved that he'd called her Sunshine again, her butterflies fading as warmth crept back in.

Shuffling past him and out into the slumbering hallways of the barracks, she couldn't resist repeating, "Why don't you live in the palace?"

This time, Caldon answered. "I do have rooms up there. Have you seen my wardrobe? Where do you think I keep most of my clothes?" He raised a comical brow, and Kiva stifled a grin. But then she sobered as he went on, "I prefer it down here. I grew up moving from barracks to barracks, so it reminds me of that. Of a different time, of things I—" His voice caught. "Of things I don't want to forget."

Kiva's chest tightened at his admission. Jaren had been wrong when he'd said Caldon was avoiding anything that might remind him of his parents. It was the opposite—Caldon was doing everything he could to remember them. Except, perhaps, the things that hurt too much. Like seeing his sister. And visiting the army camps. And taking up the mantle of leadership that he'd been born into, that he'd worked hard for, that he'd *wanted*.

It didn't take a genius to figure out that Caldon was punishing himself. That even three years on, his grief remained raw enough to dictate his decisions.

Kiva could empathize with that, more than anyone. She also knew he wouldn't want her pity, so she mustered a wry smile and said, "Yeah, I can see why you like it down here. It's so private. Peaceful, too. And there's so much space. It's like your own little haven of solitude."

She'd timed her comment perfectly for when they walked past an open doorway into one of the larger guard dormitories, the bunks cramped together, the loud sounds of snoring—and other bodily functions—echoing out to them.

Caldon's lips twitched. "I'm sure we could find you a spare room, if you'd like to move down here."

Kiva pulled a face, and Caldon's lip twitch became a full grin.

"It's cold outside," Kiva said, not rising to his bait—but that only amused him more. "You should button up your shirt or you'll catch a chill."

Caldon laughed quietly but made no move to fix his outfit. "Abs like these deserve to be seen."

Kiva shook her head, unable to keep from snorting in response.

With the mood considerably lighter between them, they made their way out of the barracks and up the path to the palace. Upon reaching the front entrance, Kiva insisted that she didn't need an escort all the way to her bedroom, and quietly bid Caldon a good night.

Just as she was turning away, he called out to her.

"You say you became the darkness, that it consumed you," he said, his cobalt eyes soft on hers, "but I call bull on that. I've never met anyone who shines as brightly as you do."

And with that unexpected—and profound—compliment, he walked away, leaving her fighting back tears as she stood there in stunned, heartfelt silence.

CHAPTER TWENTY-ONE

Kiva was still reeling from Caldon's parting words as she made her way through the palace toward her bedroom.

Everything that had happened that day had finally caught up with her, making her feel tired enough to sleep, but her plans of falling swiftly into bed vanished when she spotted a shadowy figure dressed all in black and moving quickly, disappearing around the next corner.

She knew those shoulders. She would recognize them anywhere.

The figure was Jaren. But . . . why was he sneaking around his own palace?

Do you really think Eidran would have given me that information, knowing what I'd do with it?

Kiva groaned. *Of course* Jaren would choose tonight of all nights to investigate the secret rebel meeting place—if that was indeed what he was doing. Either way, Kiva's curiosity was too great to ignore.

Wishing she'd changed out of her pajamas before visiting Caldon, Kiva pulled her cloak tighter and hurried after the prince, careful to keep a generous distance between them.

Down he traveled, floor after floor, until he reached the ground— and then went lower.

Into the tunnels.

Jaren wasn't taking any chances, Kiva realized, as she followed him under the river and toward the western palace, both of them diligently keeping to the shadows. He didn't intend for anyone to see him leaving the grounds—because he was heading to the hidden escape passage.

Kiva's pulse sped up when he disappeared through the door leading off the main thoroughfare. She couldn't trail directly after him; if she didn't give him time to move further down the tunnel, she'd be discovered.

It was agony. She felt exposed, shifting nervously from foot to foot. But it was the middle of the night, and the underground network was eerily deserted. No one knew she was there. No one knew *Jaren* was there.

Naari was going to kill him when she found out.

If she found out, Kiva mentally corrected.

When she judged enough time had passed, Kiva opened the door— *quietly*—and slipped through. She rushed down the numerous steps in the low-lit passage, only stopping once she reached the fork in the path.

Listening intently, she tried to hear how far ahead Jaren might be. If he'd slowed down, she could collide with him in the pitch-black tunnel, but if he'd sped up, she might lose him. She had to be able to see where he went upon leaving through the grate; if he disappeared into the city, she'd never be able to find him.

Kiva decided against waiting too long and tore off down the right tunnel, the darkness stealing her sight. In the distance, she heard the telltale sign of scraping metal, her heart pounding as she realized Jaren was nearly aboveground—and she was too far away.

Throwing caution to the wind, she sprinted blindly forward until the barest hint of moonlight touched her vision, coloring the tunnel a midnight blue. She skidded to a halt and approached more carefully, finding the staircase only a few steps ahead.

Kiva dashed up it as fast as she dared and reached the top to see the iron grate back in place. She pushed the metal upward and slid it aside, wincing at the gods-awful screeching sound. But there was no need to worry about Jaren—or *anyone*—having heard, because when she peeked her head out, all she could hear was the lapping of the river; the grate was much closer to the bank than she'd thought.

Kiva took a second to get her bearings, noting the fortified palace walls behind her and the Serin to her right, with nothing but a slice of darkened parkland between her and the nearest city streets. There were no gilded fences, indicating she was at the rear of the palace, but she must have been around the corner from the guarded gate she and Caldon had used the night of her abduction. Not a single person was in sight — except for Jaren, blending into the shadows as he hurried through the trees across the park.

Hauling herself out of the grate, Kiva sprinted after him, diligently following as he sped along a street that hugged the river, past luxurious waterfront apartments and guild halls, commerce chambers and merchant warehouses. The buildings were lit merrily from within, but the path was dark enough to keep them hidden from any wandering eyes.

On and on they continued, soon reaching one of the more run-down neighborhoods that bled into the docks, the area as close to slums as Vallenia had. They were only at the edge of it, though, still near enough to the wealthier inner-city streets that Kiva didn't feel like she was going to be mugged and left for dead.

As she trailed after Jaren, she began to wonder if she'd made a mistake in leaving the palace. Even if he *was* chasing Eidran's lead, Zuleeka had promised to forewarn the city-based rebels. Jaren wouldn't find anything — or anyone — that he shouldn't. That meant there was no point in following him.

But still, Kiva couldn't help herself.

Especially when she saw him turn down an alley and pause in front of a shadowy building, looking quickly over his shoulder before ducking through a doorway.

Kiva's eyebrows shot toward her hairline as she approached the scarlet door, the sounds of loud music and raucous laughter coming from within, echoing out into the otherwise silent alley. But it wasn't only music and laughter she heard — there were also the low sounds that would only come from a Red House, one of Vallenia's renowned brothels.

Heat touched Kiva's cheeks as she wondered if she'd been wrong about Jaren's purpose in leaving the palace. But—no. *Caldon,* perhaps, might have visited a Red House, but Jaren didn't strike Kiva as the kind to seek pleasure from strangers. This had to be the address Eidran had given him.

Bracing for what she was about to walk into, Kiva raised her hood before opening the door and stepping inside. The pungent scent of incense burned her nose as her eyes adjusted to the crimson-hued interior, the luminium lights covered in scarlet cloths and casting red shadows across every visible surface.

The parlor was crowded with people, some cloaked and disguised, others already in various states of undress. Some were standing, some reclined on lush wine-colored furniture, others were dancing to the loud, sensual music. Wispy sheets fell from the ceiling as if to offer a sense of privacy, but the fabric was sheer enough to see through, straight out of a voyeur's dream.

Kiva made her way deeper into the room, keeping her face hidden as she searched for Jaren. There were enough patrons that it took her two full scans before she spotted him talking to a heavyset woman who was pointing toward the corner of the crimson parlor. His cloaked head dipped in thanks before he set out in that direction.

Kiva tried to see what was over there, but there were too many writhing bodies and wispy sheets distorting her view. She edged closer, ignoring the arms reaching out to her as she passed by, the whispered invitations that she quietly declined. Glazed eyes and too-relaxed smiles flooded her vision everywhere she looked, sweat dotting skin despite the coolness of the air, glittery golden powder on lips, noses, fingers.

Angeldust.

Other drugs too, perhaps even a Red House cocktail available only to its patrons.

Kiva shook her head and waded through the crowd, her view finally clearing enough to watch Jaren approach the far corner. Seated there was a small group of people, none of whom seemed the slightest bit interested in what was happening all around them.

No, Kiva thought, her breath catching. Zuleeka was meant to have told the city rebels to find a new meeting place, to not meet at all, *anything* that would keep them from discovery.

Jaren was no fool. If he'd infiltrated Zalindov, he could surely convince a small group of rebels that he was one of them. Kiva had to warn them.

Or . . . maybe warn *him.*

Because as another dancing couple shifted out of her way, and another wispy sheet rippled with movement, Kiva could see what she'd missed upon her first perusal: one of the figures was wearing a silver mask made of coiled serpents.

The Viper was here.

Zuleeka was here.

And from one breath to the next, she was on her feet, her sword slicing through the air toward the crown prince of Evalon.

CHAPTER TWENTY-TWO

All the air expelled from Kiva's lungs as she watched the blade slash toward Jaren.

"*NO!*" she screamed, but only those nearest to her heard, the music too loud, the crowd too thick. She was too far away to do anything other than stare in horror at what was about to happen.

Zuleeka was fast, her sword streaming through the air.

But Jaren was faster.

Kiva didn't even see him draw his weapon, but instead of Zuleeka slicing open his torso, there was a shriek of steel as their blades met, the sound loud enough to gather significantly more attention than Kiva's shout.

Hazy-eyed patrons turned to watch as the rest of the rebels leapt to their feet, all of them unsheathing swords and rushing at Jaren.

He was vastly outnumbered —

And then he wasn't.

Because suddenly Naari was there, her hood flying back to reveal her ferocious expression as she appeared out of the shadows, her two swords blurring through the air.

The Viper — *Zuleeka* — immediately switched her focus to Naari, as if seeing the Golden Shield as the greater threat. The two of them spun violently around each other while Jaren fought the other rebels, defending not only himself but also the nearest civilians who had begun to realize the danger and were scrambling away. Screams met Kiva's ears as they panicked, tripping over each other in their haste to get to safety — and those screams only grew when the front door crashed open and a contingent of silver-armored Royal Guards burst into the Red House, led by Captain Veris.

Even the most drug-addled of patrons sobered at the sight, those who were scantily clad reaching for their clothes, and those who were still disguised lowering their hoods further—Kiva included.

She needed to leave, *right now.*

But before she could blend into the flow of bodies, she saw her sister notice the guards streaming her way. Zuleeka gave a quick signal to someone out of sight, and in the space of a blink, all the lights went out.

The screams of the patrons became earsplitting, elbows and shoulders smacking into Kiva as they blindly rushed by her. It was only seconds before the luminium was reignited, the room returned to its crimson shade, but Kiva already knew what she would see.

Zuleeka and the rebels were gone.

Kiva used the pandemonium inside the Red House to her advantage, hurrying out with the panicked patrons and dissolving into the darkness of the alley before anyone could recognize her. She cringed at the thought of how much trouble Jaren must be in, certain Naari had to be apoplectic.

Tonight had been close—too close. If Naari hadn't appeared when she had, Jaren would have been left to face the entire rebel group, including Zuleeka, on his own. And if the Royal Guard hadn't stormed in, then the rebels might not have fled. Someone could have been hurt. Someone could have been killed.

And it would have been Kiva's fault—because she'd been played.

Walking slowly back along the river, Kiva realized Zuleeka had never intended to warn the rebels that their meeting place had been compromised. She'd instead used them to set up a trap.

It was clever, Kiva had to give her that. And if it had worked—

She didn't finish her train of thought, unable to stomach where it led.

The entire journey back to the palace, Kiva couldn't figure out who she was angrier with: Zuleeka, Jaren, or herself. Zuleeka had taken a risk by coming to the city tonight, and she'd taken a greater risk by orchestrating an attack on the crown prince. But Jaren had fallen right into her hands by acting impulsively, following a dangerous lead without any backup.

As for herself, Kiva was more frustrated than ever by her dual mentality, unsure who she'd been fearing for most during the fight: Zuleeka or Jaren. If her sister had been hurt—or *caught*—then Kiva didn't know what she would have done. But the same was also true for Jaren, who had been in just as much peril, perhaps more.

She couldn't continue on like this, feeling as if she were constantly being split in two. It was exhausting—and it was driving her insane.

Kiva was rubbing her temples by the time she reached the iron grate and lowered herself into the tunnels. Tired and cold, all she wanted was to get to her suite and fall into bed.

But when she finally made it back to her room in the eastern palace, she realized her night wasn't over yet.

Because Naari was sitting on her bed in the dark, her voice low and lethal as she uttered just two words:

"Nice walk?"

Kiva froze just inside the doorway, her mind blanking at the sight of the guard's glittering amber eyes.

"You're lucky the storm cleared," Naari said, her tone now deceptively courteous. "That would have been an unpleasant journey in the rain."

"I wasn't—" Kiva started, deciding to play dumb, but she was interrupted.

"I would think very carefully about your next words if I were you," Naari warned, rising in one fluid motion, her leather-clad body rippling with fury.

Kiva bit her cheek and stepped further into the room. The moon streamed in from the balcony, the sight peaceful—but not enough to fill her with any sense of calm.

Sighing with resignation, she said, "If you're going to yell at me, just yell at me."

Naari's eyes narrowed. "And why would I yell at you, Kiva? What part of tonight would I be angry about?"

Wisdom told Kiva to hold her tongue.

"Do you have any idea how badly things could have gone?" the guard demanded. "If I hadn't seen you and Jaren sneaking out of the palace—"

Kiva winced, realizing *that* was how she'd been discovered, right from the very beginning.

"—and if I hadn't raised the alarm with Veris and told him where I assumed you were heading—" Naari paused her tirade to snap, "Don't look at me like that, do you really think the person who gave Jaren that lead didn't know he'd act on it, and therefore made sure I had the details, too? Please."

Kiva swore quietly, realizing that of course Eidran would have told Naari. The two guards had planned the Zalindov mission with Jaren —they were as close as anyone could be.

"I honestly don't know if I'm more furious at Jaren for being a reckless, obstinate fool, or at you for following him instead of stopping him," Naari stated, scowling fiercely. "Why in the name of the gods did you sneak after him, Kiva? *That's* the part I can't figure out."

Kiva rubbed her arms in an attempt to stall, her mind scrambling for a believable excuse.

"Well?" Naari demanded.

"If you saw the crown prince slinking around like he wanted to avoid notice, wouldn't you be curious?" Kiva asked, turning the question around on her.

"I wouldn't follow him halfway across the city."

Kiva decided not to point out that Naari had done exactly that. Instead, she drew emotion into her voice and said, "He hasn't been sleeping well, ever since Zalindov. I was worried about him."

"Which one is it?" Naari asked, evidently not buying it. "You were worried, or you were curious?"

"Both," Kiva said, cursing her slow, tired mind. "I followed him because I wanted to be there for him, if he needed me. I had no idea what we'd be walking into."

"And when you figured it out—you know, when there were *swords* and *screaming*," Naari said with clear sarcasm, "you didn't think to reveal yourself and return to the palace with us?"

Kiva forced a contrite expression onto her face. "I didn't want Jaren knowing I'd followed him. How would I explain that?"

"How, indeed."

At that point, Kiva asked, with genuine trepidation, "Did you tell him?"

Naari stared at Kiva for a long moment, as if trying to gauge whether or not she was truly innocent. Finally, she exhaled loudly and said, "No. After he and I had strong words about his actions, I returned him to his quarters and came straight here to wait for you. He has no idea you were at the Red House or that you saw what happened."

"What *did* I see?" Kiva asked, adopting a guileless look. "Who were those people that attacked him?"

Naari moved back to Kiva's bed, patting the blanket beside her. Warily, Kiva perched on the edge, trying to hide how much tension she still felt.

"The lead Jaren was given suggested that the rebels have a secret meeting place in the city," Naari said. "That's who he went looking for tonight."

Kiva adopted a stunned look. "Those were *rebels?* But—wait. If Jaren knew, why did he risk going on his own?"

She should get a medal for her acting.

"Why does Jaren do anything?" Naari said, running an aggravated gloved hand through her cropped hair. "He's trying to protect his people. The rebels have been quiet lately—he wanted to know why, and if they plan to stay that way. He didn't think he'd get answers by storming in with reinforcements."

"By the looks of it, he didn't get answers anyway," Kiva noted, still playing along.

"It was almost like they knew to expect him," Naari murmured, frowning. "The Viper is never in the city—she shouldn't have been here at all, and yet, she didn't seem surprised to see Jaren. She jumped him before he'd uttered a single word."

Kiva had to be careful now. "The Viper?" she asked, trying to make her voice sound normal. "Was that the one in the mask?"

Naari nodded, her face darkening. "She's a rebel leader—perhaps *the* leader, now that their queen is gone." The guard looked down at her hand, flexing her fingers. "She and I go way back."

A horrible feeling suddenly twisted within Kiva as she watched Naari staring at her hand.

At her *prosthetic* hand.

"Is she—Did she—" Kiva couldn't even get the question out.

"It happened three years ago, around when the rebels started to become a real problem," Naari said, still looking down at her fingers, unaware of the dread now filling Kiva. "I was eighteen and had only recently arrived in Evalon after sneaking onto Veris's ship. By that time, he believed in me—more than anyone—but I had a lot to prove, mostly to myself. I wasn't Jaren's personal guard then, but I was part of a group who traveled with him to visit some of the inland villages hit the hardest by the rebels. He wanted to see for himself, to check on his people and assist with the rebuilding."

Naari's gaze turned inward as she continued her story. "At one of those villages, Jaren heard about a family living just up the road whose young son had been injured in a rebel skirmish, and he wanted to see how the boy was faring. There had been no rebel activity in the area for a long time—Jaren should have been safe to walk the short distance on his own, but I erred on the side of caution and accompanied him."

There was a long pause, as if Naari was living out her memory all over again.

"I've thought about that day too many times to count in the last three years," she said in a quiet, musing voice. "I don't think they knew we were there—that Jaren was there. I think it was just a matter of bad timing."

Kiva was barely breathing. "What happened?"

Naari clenched her prosthetic fingers into a fist. "There were only two of them—the Rebel Queen and the Viper. They stumbled out of the forest onto the road right in front of us, mid-conversation. My guess is they were heading to the village for supplies, but the moment they realized it was Jaren standing before them, the masked Viper drew her sword and lunged straight at him."

Kiva could see it play out in her mind: Zuleeka's shock at Jaren's appearance, the opportunity to take him down too great to resist.

"I—I froze."

Naari's stuttered admission came from somewhere deep within her, a dark place full of regret.

"Years of fighting in Jiirvan arenas, and I'd never frozen before, not once," she whispered. "I still don't know what happened. Darkness swirled in my vision, and my limbs just wouldn't obey me. Classic signs of a panic attack, I know. It was—" She shook her head. "I've never felt anything like it before. It was terrible, not being able to control myself. Not being able to *do* anything."

She drew in a shuddering breath. "It felt like everything happened in slow motion. I saw the Viper lunging at Jaren, and I saw him reaching for his own blade just in time to meet hers, much like tonight. Tilda screamed out 'No!' and raised her hand as if to stop me, but I was no threat—I was so frozen I could barely *breathe*. But then it was like my adrenaline finally kicked in and suddenly the darkness vanished in a blaze of light, just as Jaren stumbled backwards and the Viper bore down on him." Naari's throat bobbed. "I jumped in her path as she slashed out with her sword, but I didn't have time to draw my own weapon, so I stretched my arm out to protect him and—"

Naari didn't finish. She didn't *need* to finish.

Kiva already knew what had happened.

She was going to be sick. Right there on her lush carpet. What her sister had *done*—

Naari cleared her throat and unfisted her hand. "Everything after that is a bit hazy. Veris and the other guards had realized something was wrong and were running toward us. Tilda dragged the Viper away and disappeared into the forest. Jaren made sure the best healers worked on me while he hunted down the most advanced prosthetic available. He then made me his Golden Shield, an honor no other Royal Guard has received in over fifty years." Naari offered a self-deprecating shrug. "I guess I haven't done too badly."

Kiva battled back all she was feeling to croak out, "Was—Was tonight the first time you've seen the Viper since then?"

"I've crossed blades with her a few times in the last three years," Naari answered. "But like tonight, she always manages to get away, usually just as I've got her cornered. She should have been named the Rat or the Weasel, but I suppose she's slippery like a snake."

And venomous like a viper, Kiva thought.

"But anyway," Naari said, tugging at the hem of her leather gloves. "You can see how she and I have unfinished business. One day we'll finish what we started, and believe me, that day can't come soon enough."

It took everything in Kiva to keep from flinching at Naari's hard declaration. The idea of the two of them facing each other again, of what might happen to either of them . . .

Gods, Kiva needed to figure out the mess in her head.

It's him or us. Them *or us. You can't have it both ways.*

She closed her eyes against Zuleeka's words, exhaustion overwhelming her.

"It's been a long day," Naari said, rising to her feet. "I won't tell Jaren you followed him tonight, but if it happens again—if *either* of you try to sneak out again—"

"I won't," Kiva said quickly. "I promise."

She was careful not to think about her return to Murkwood Cottage in three days, lest Naari read the lie on her face.

"Get some sleep, Kiva," Naari said, her voice gentling. "And don't worry about the Viper and the rebels. I spent most of my life in a kingdom oppressed by corrupt rulers and full of desolate and hateful citizens. I escaped that for good reason, and I'll never allow it to happen here. The rebels won't win—ever. You're safe with us. You always will be."

With those words, the guard offered a small smile before leaving the room, oblivious to the devastation she left in her wake.

CHAPTER TWENTY-THREE

When dawn arrived the next morning, Kiva nearly wept at the sound of Caldon's familiar knock on her door. But her lingering fatigue vanished when he greeted her with a tight smile and the unpleasant news that her siblings had replied, accepting her invitation to lunch.

While Kiva had half expected the news, she was still furious that they'd ignored her warnings — Zuleeka especially, after last night. If discovered, all three of them would be charged with treason, the punishment for which was public execution — if the Vallentis family was feeling merciful — or a one-way trip to Zalindov. Both possibilities left Kiva clammy despite the crisp morning air that greeted her as she followed Caldon outside.

Unaware of her inner turmoil, the prince pushed her harder than ever in their training session, making her realize that perhaps he hadn't *completely* forgiven her for yesterday, even if he was back to his normal bantering self. By the time they were done, Kiva could only hobble up to the palace, where she gifted herself a long, hot soak in her bathtub.

Too nervous to eat much for breakfast, Kiva did make sure to swallow her prescribed mouthful of Delora's bitter potion, shuddering at the skin-crawling feeling of it taking effect. It was a means to an end, she reminded herself, and the day would come when she wouldn't need it. She might even start to cherish her magic, as Jaren did his, training and strengthening it and using it for good without thinking of it as a burden. But with her siblings coming to the palace today, it was more important than ever that she have her power under control — or at least out of the way.

"Knock, knock!" came Mirryn's voice, prompting Kiva to hide the stoppered vial in her bedside drawer just as the princess burst into her bedroom.

Mirryn smirked as she eyed Kiva from head to toe. "I know I said lunch would be informal, but you might want to reconsider your outfit. We don't want dear Jaren having a heart attack at the table."

Kiva tightened the towel she'd wrapped around herself upon leaving her bath. "Please, let yourself in," she invited dryly. "It's not like I'd want my privacy or anything."

"You haven't had privacy in a decade," Mirryn said without a hint of compassion, taking a seat on Kiva's bed. "You can deal with a few more minutes."

Those few minutes became considerably longer when Mirryn declared herself Kiva's stylist for the day, demanding she try on outfit after outfit until she found the perfect combination to wear to lunch.

At any other time, Kiva would have asked the princess to leave, but with butterflies somersaulting in her stomach and the familiar comfort of her magic gone — something Kiva hadn't appreciated until it was no longer there — she was oddly grateful for Mirryn's ceaseless prattle.

The princess was in one of her better moods, reclining on Kiva's bed and sharing how the plans for her birthday masquerade were coming together, with it now only three days away. All too soon she cut herself off by declaring it was time for lunch, asking Kiva if she wanted to meet her siblings out in front of the palace or wait for them in the River Room, where a table had been set up.

Kiva didn't like *either* option, but Mirryn chose for her, dragging her outside so they could wait alongside Jaren, Caldon, Tipp, and Naari.

If there was one good thing about that morning, it was that the king and queen had been called away to celebrate the opening of a bridge deeper in the city. Prince Oriel had gone with them, begging for Tipp to join them, but the redheaded boy had chosen to stay and meet Kiva's family.

"You look like you're going to throw up," Caldon commented from Kiva's side. "Or pass out. I can't tell which."

"Could be either," Kiva muttered, causing him to chuckle. "Maybe both."

"It's going to be fine," he told her in an uncommon show of comfort, nudging her in the ribs. "And if it's not, then it's not. What's the worst that could happen?"

Kiva nearly started hyperventilating at the thought. She looked across to Jaren, longing for his steadying presence, but he'd been distant all day—not cold, but more like he was stuck in his own head. She wondered if it was because he'd been caught—and likely yelled at—by Naari last night, but she had a feeling it was more than that. He was normally so attuned to her, but today he didn't sense her need for reassurance. Instead, his eyes were glued to the front gates, his face almost hard as he watched two figures approaching on horseback.

Oh, gods, Kiva thought, clenching her hands. *Here we go.*

In what felt like seconds, Torell and Zuleeka came to a halt before them, dismounting and handing their reins to the waiting grooms. Both siblings were dressed in simple clothes, Tor wearing dark pants and a forest green shirt with the sleeves rolled to his elbows, Zuleeka in leggings and a modest tunic dress, no sign of a weapon on either of them. Or a mask.

They weren't the Viper and the Jackal today.

But they also very much were.

Kiva walked forward on quaking legs, forced a welcoming grin onto her face, and channelled Tipp's over-the-top excitement to exclaim, "I'm so glad you could make it!"

Tor returned her grin, his eyes sparkling with barely suppressed humor as he pulled her into a hug.

"It's going to be fine," he whispered, unknowingly repeating Caldon's words. "Take a breath and calm down."

She followed his order, feeling only marginally better when she stepped back.

"Hello again, little sister," Zuleeka said, her expression filled with so much warmth that Kiva blinked in shock, a feeling that only grew when she was drawn into a deep embrace.

Zuleeka was hugging her.

For the first time in ten years.

Startled as she was, Kiva wrapped her arms around her sister, tears prickling her eyes as she recalled what Zuleeka had said when they'd last parted.

I'll try harder. I promise I will.

Kiva wasn't oblivious — she knew Zuleeka was playing a role for the royals, acting like the doting sister. But the warmth on her face, the tightness of her hug — that felt genuine. Zuleeka *was* trying, just as she'd promised. They would both need time to heal from their rocky start, but there was suddenly so much hope inside Kiva that her queasy sense of dread began to fade.

Even so, that didn't stop her from whispering into her sister's ear, "I was there last night. You have a *lot* of explaining to do later."

Pulling away just in time to catch the flash of surprise on Zuleeka's face, Kiva linked arms with both of her siblings and led them over to where the others stood. "I'd like you to meet my brother and sister, Torell and Zuleeka. Tor, Zulee, this is, um . . ."

Words fled her as she realized she had no idea how to introduce the royals to their greatest enemies.

"I'm Caldon," the prince said smoothly, stepping forward to save Kiva, shaking Tor's hand and kissing the back of Zuleeka's. Surprisingly, he didn't attempt any flirtation, as if he knew the last thing Kiva needed was for him to be propositioning her sister.

"I'm Mirryn," the princess said, continuing the introductions. She pointed to the rest of the group. "That's Naari, Tipp, and —"

"Prince Deverick," Jaren cut in, crossing his arms in a decidedly unwelcoming way.

Kiva rocked back on her heels, startled not only by the formal name, but also by the coldness in his tone. His eyes were like blue ice, the gold rims like blazing flames.

"It's an honor, Your Highness," Zuleeka said, curtseying deeply and looking at Jaren from under her lashes. "Thank you for taking such good care of our sister. We can't tell you how much she means to us — and how grateful we are."

Kiva felt a twinge of discomfort at the simpering words.

"Now that she's back, we can be a family again. Just like we've always wanted," Zuleeka said with a bright smile, looking fondly at Kiva.

Jaren said nothing, but his face remained like stone.

Something was very, *very* wrong.

Had he figured out that it was Zuleeka he'd crossed blades with last night? Did he know the Viper and the Jackal stood before him? Why else would he be so *angry?*

And yet he didn't call for the guards, but simply said, "Lunch awaits us," before turning on his heel and striding into the palace.

"Someone's got a prickle in his pants," Caldon murmured to Kiva, but she was too busy trying not to panic to reply.

He couldn't know. Surely Jaren *couldn't* know. Zuleeka and Torell never would have come if they'd thought there was even a *chance* of being outed. But if not that, then why was Jaren so upset?

And then there was Naari, who was hurrying after Jaren — Naari who had no idea she was about to dine with her nemesis, the person who had cut off her *hand*.

The guard might not realize, but Zuleeka had to know who she had inflicted so much damage upon three years ago — and who she had crossed blades with multiple times since then, including just last night.

Gods, Kiva didn't think she could do this.

But she had to. So she took a steadying breath and followed her siblings into the palace, listening with half an ear as Mirryn played the courteous tour guide and Tipp offered his own boisterous commentary.

"Why didn't you tell me your brother looked like *that?*" Caldon asked quietly, bringing up the rear of the group with Kiva.

"Like what?" she murmured distractedly.

"What do you mean, 'like what'?" Caldon said, exasperated. "Like *that.*" He waved a hand toward Tor's strong back. "He's delicious."

That was enough to shock Kiva from her fears, and she whipped her head toward the prince. "I thought you were into girls?"

Caldon pulled a face. "Firstly," he said, "*women*. I'm into *women* — not *girls*. There's a difference."

Kiva raised her hands in apology. "All right, sorry."

"And secondly," Caldon said with strained patience, "I'm attracted to who I'm attracted to. And right now, there is nothing about *that*" — he dipped his chin toward Torell — "that isn't attractive." Somewhat woefully, he added, "I can't believe you kept him a secret."

"In my defense, I didn't see him until yesterday," Kiva said, sticking with her lie.

Caldon had nothing to say to that, but there was something in his silence, some hidden depth to it that Kiva couldn't identify. It vanished, however, when they approached the River Room and he leaned in to whisper, "Listen, I don't know what's going on with Jaren, but I can make a pretty good guess. I'll help as much as I can, but if I'm right, this lunch is going to be uncomfortable. Whatever happens, just remember that he cares for you, and because of that, he's angry. *Very* angry." Caldon paused. "To be honest, I'm right there with him. But one of us has to keep things civil, and given his feelings for you, I doubt he's going to be putting on his princely airs today. So just . . . be gentle with him."

"What are you talking about?" Kiva whispered back, gripping his elbow to slow his steps.

"Think about it, Sweet Cheeks," Caldon said, holding her gaze. "How would you feel if someone you were falling hard for was locked away for more than half their life, and then their siblings swooped in like nothing had happened, wanting to be a family again after ten years of abandonment?" Caldon shook his head. "That's not right, Sunshine, and you know it."

Kiva gaped at Caldon. "Jaren's angry at my family because I was sent to Zalindov? But — But —" She flailed, before hissing, "That doesn't make sense! It's not like *they* sent me there!"

She was walking on thin ice, but Caldon didn't seem to notice her inflection.

"They left you in there, though," the prince said. At her incredulous face, his voice dropped to a stunned whisper. "You have no idea what I'm talking about, do you?"

Kiva didn't get a chance to reply before Mirryn called to them from inside the room.

"Do you two plan on joining us today?"

Caldon covered Kiva's hand that was still gripping his elbow, her fingers now cold, and guided her into the River Room.

"Sorry, lover's spat," he said with a winning smile.

Kiva shot him a look and tried to tug her hand free, but he only held on tighter, walking her over to the table that was similar in style to the dinner she'd shared with the Vallentis family. Instead of a roasted meal, there were mountains of salads and cheeses and breads, along with cold meats and raw vegetables, all plated beside crystal goblets full of sparkling juice and vases bursting with snowblossoms. In the background, the Serin River glittered through the windows, the spring sunshine touching the surface like liquid gold.

At any other time, Kiva would have marveled at the display. Today she had to stop herself from running out of the room.

Everyone had already taken their seats as she and Caldon approached, with him pushing her into the space beside Jaren before taking the empty chair at her other side.

Kiva's hands trembled at the seating arrangements. Naari and Tipp were fine, but Zuleeka was next to the princess—a disaster waiting to happen—and Torell was directly opposite Jaren, with the prince glaring between both of Kiva's siblings, but his wrath focused most intently on her brother.

"This looks delicious," she made herself say, barely recognizing her own voice.

"It's much better than what we're used to, that's for sure," Torell said amiably, waiting for the royals to start helping themselves before following their lead.

"Kiva tells us you live in Oakhollow," Jaren said. He was the only person at the table not filling his plate. "How do you spend your time?"

"I'm a blacksmith," Torell answered, layering slices of ham inside a fresh bread roll, his thick arm muscles validating his lie. "Zulee's a seamstress."

Kiva was glad she wasn't eating or drinking anything, because she would have spat it all over the table.

"A seamstress?" Mirryn repeated, turning to Zuleeka with an arched eyebrow as she looked, somewhat judgingly, at her simple outfit.

"A modest trade," Zuleeka said, ducking her head in a contrived show of humility. "But my mother always encouraged me to follow my dreams."

The words hit Kiva right in the chest.

"And you dream of being a seamstress?" This time there was no missing the derision in Mirryn's tone.

Jaren must have heard it too, and despite his frosty demeanor, he saved Zuleeka from answering by asking another question. "We haven't heard much about your mother—does she live with you in Oakhollow?"

Kiva wished he'd left Zuleeka to face Mirryn's disdain. As far as she could recall, she'd never shared anything about her mother—for good reason—and whatever prison records Caldon had unearthed would have only had information on her father. She scrambled to think of a way to redirect the conversation.

Zuleeka, however, didn't blink an eyelash before responding, "She did. But unfortunately she passed while Kiva was at Zalindov. They say it was natural causes, but if you ask me, Mother was heartsick for her daughter. It was a terrible loss for us all."

When I look at you, I can't help thinking of how she went to find you. She left us, and she died. For you.

Kiva's grip on her fork turned painful at the memory of Zuleeka's words.

"I'm so sorry to hear that," Jaren said softly, and Kiva knew the sentiment was for her.

"It's tragic, both our parents dying while she was gone," Zuleeka said, nibbling on some cheese. "But at least she still has us."

Jaren reached for his crystal goblet, his body so tense that Kiva feared the dainty stem would snap in his hand.

"Can you t-t-tell us some stories from when K-Kiva was younger?" Tipp asked eagerly.

Kiva could have launched across the table and kissed the boy for his attempt at lightening the atmosphere, unwitting as it was.

"The more embarrassing, the better," Caldon put in. "We need something to use against her next family night."

"Family night?" Zuleeka repeated, her brows raised in perfect imitation of how Mirryn had looked at her. "How . . . quaint."

"We used to have family night," Torell said quickly, with a warning look at their sister. "Of course, ours was almost every night, since our parents weren't busy running a kingdom." He forced out a short laugh before turning to answer Tipp. "Young Kiva was a menace. A real wild child."

"Was she really?" Caldon asked, leaning forward with delight. Kiva couldn't tell if it was genuine or if he was just doing his part to help bring some levity to the meal.

"She was always running off and getting lost in the woods, swimming so deep in the river that she'd get caught in the current, rolling through fields of wildflowers and returning home covered in mud—the list of trouble she got up to was endless."

"Don't act like you weren't right there beside me," Kiva said, pointing her fork at him.

Tor ignored her and went on, "But there was this other side to her, too. This serious side that came out whenever she helped our father treat his patients. Her compassion, her empathy, her patience—we knew years ago that she would follow in his footsteps. Our sister, the healer." He met her eyes across the table, his voice gentle as he finished, "This world is lucky to have her."

A lump rose in Kiva's throat at the affectionate look on his face.

"Kiva's the b-best healer *ever*," Tipp declared around a mouthful of food. "She saved m-my life at Zalindov. I wouldn't be h-here without her."

Every part of Kiva froze at his words.

Did he—Did he *remember?*

An image of his bloodied torso assailed her mind, of her hands flooding him with golden light, her magic healing his fatal wound until it was barely a scratch. If he knew what she'd *done*—

"I got r-really sick," Tipp went on, his face solemn. "Lots of people were d-dying. But Kiva stayed b-by my bedside and looked after me until I w-was better." He looked at her with such love in his eyes that Kiva nearly cried—partly from that look, but mostly from relief at the story he was recounting.

He didn't remember.

Her secret was safe.

"She saved lots of people there, kiddo," Jaren said. "Over many years." Quieter, he finished, "Too many years."

At the sorrow in his tone, Kiva couldn't keep from reaching under the table and placing her hand on his leg. He instantly lowered his own and entwined their fingers, his thumb making soothing circles as if thinking she needed his comfort, rather than the other way around.

"It's funny," Zuleeka mused, "but Kiva probably saved more lives locked up in Zalindov than she would have if she'd stayed in our little village. I guess this is one of those times where we can say everything worked out for the best."

Jaren's grip tightened enough that Kiva feared what he was about to say, about to *do*, but before he had a chance to decide, Torell got in first.

"Zuleeka," he snapped. He said no more, but that coupled with his stern frown was enough.

Their sister looked around the table, noting the strained expressions, and her mouth fell open. "Oh gods, that didn't come out right, did it?" She shook her head quickly. "All I meant was that some very dangerous people now owe their lives to Kiva. That can only be to her benefit, right?"

When no one responded—though Jaren *did* look like he wanted to throw his goblet at her face—Zuleeka grimaced apologetically, before plucking an olive off Mirryn's plate. Kiva gaped at her in horror, but the princess seemed amused by her gall. Either that, or Mirryn was considering spearing Zuleeka's hand with her fork.

"Careful, Zuleeka," Caldon said dryly, noting the move as well. "My cousin isn't known for her generosity. Do that again, and you may well lose a finger."

Zuleeka sent him a flash of teeth and plucked another olive off Mirryn's plate. "I don't scare easily."

This time it was Kiva who had to keep from throwing anything at her sister. In a warning voice, she hissed, "Zulee—"

"I h-have an idea!" Tipp cried over her, bouncing in his seat. His mouth was so full that it had sounded like, "Ih-haffndeer," but then he swallowed and looked at Mirryn before saying, "They should c-come on Wednesday!"

Kiva tensed. "Tipp—"

"What's on Wednesday?" Zuleeka asked.

"It's Mirry's b-birthday," Tipp answered, and not for the first time did Kiva wish he would stop speaking. "She's having a b-big party to celebrate. A m-masquerade."

"Sounds fun," Zuleeka said, a dangerous light entering her eyes.

"It w-will be!" Tipp exclaimed. "Can they c-come, Mirry?"

Quickly enacting damage control, Kiva interjected, "Tipp, we don't invite people to parties that aren't ours. It's rude."

"But I've n-never had a party to invite a-anyone to," he said, making Kiva's throat burn.

"It's fine," Mirryn said, with an imperious wave of her hand. She turned to Zuleeka and Tor. "You're more than welcome to join us. In fact, since you're Kiva's family, I insist."

"No," Kiva said before anyone else could. "That's very kind, but I'm sure they have other plans."

She looked firmly at her siblings, begging them to agree.

"Kiva's right," Torell said, sensing her distress. "It's a very kind offer, but we couldn't possibly—"

"—say no to a royal invitation," Zuleeka cut in smoothly. She looked at Mirryn, a bright smile gracing her lips. "We'd be delighted to join you, Princess. Thank you for the invitation."

"Zulee—" Tor tried, but the look on her face halted his words.

"Mother taught us not to turn our noses up at unexpected blessings, brother," she said, the words innocent enough but causing a vise to press in on Kiva's lungs—a feeling that only worsened when Jaren changed the topic, leaning forward to address Torell across the table.

"You said you're a blacksmith," the prince observed, eyeing Torell's muscular build. "Does that mean you know your way around a blade?"

"I've had some experience," Tor answered carefully. "Mostly from volunteering as a village guard a few years back."

"Fancy a quick sparring match?" Jaren patted his perfectly flat stomach. "We can work off our lunch."

Having watched him eat even less than her, Kiva didn't believe his reasoning. Tor, too, must have noticed Jaren's lack of appetite, but he still pushed his plate away and stood.

"I'd be honored to cross swords with you, Your Highness," he said, before offering a wry grin. "But you'll have to forgive my sloppy footwork."

No, no, no, no, no.

What the hell was Torell *thinking?* He couldn't spar with Jaren—and *especially* not when the prince was in such a foul mood.

"I'm sure it'll come back to you quickly enough," Jaren said, unlinking his hand from Kiva's suddenly numb fingers and standing as well.

"Jaren, mate," Caldon murmured, seeing Kiva's rapidly paling face, "maybe you should—"

"It's just a friendly match," Jaren said, but despite his words, his eyes were glacial. To Torell, he waved a hand toward the doors. "Shall we?"

Kiva silently pleaded with her brother, but Tor only sent her the smallest of reassuring smiles that did absolutely nothing to calm her.

"Boys and their swords," Mirryn said, sighing as she too rose, along with everyone else around the table. She turned to Zuleeka and rolled her eyes in a distinctly unprincess-like manner. "Thank the gods that we women have much more sophisticated methods of working through our feelings."

"While I agree with you on principle, I'm sure you and I have very different coping techniques," Zuleeka said. Quickly, but with an undeniable hint of mockery, she tacked on, "Your Highness."

Mirryn's eyes narrowed, not missing the scorn in those final two words.

Afraid she'd have to pull both her siblings out of the royal dungeons if they didn't start showing some gods-damned respect, Kiva shot a warning look at Zuleeka before hurrying after her brother and Jaren.

Naari kept pace beside her, the guard having remained silent during lunch, watching for any sign of a threat from Kiva's family. But now she offered a comforting glance and murmured, "Don't worry. Jaren knows what he's doing."

Kiva wasn't so sure.

"He won't hurt your brother," Naari promised. "You know he'd never let any harm come to someone you care about."

The statement pierced Kiva, since she knew it was true. Jaren wouldn't hurt Tor—but what if *Tor* hurt *Jaren?* Her brother had spent the last decade training to be a warrior, a *general.* What if—

"Breathe, Sunshine," Caldon said, stepping up on her other side. "Everything will be fine."

That was easy for him to say. Two of the people he cared most for in the world weren't about to go head-to-head in a "friendly" sparring match.

Trying to remain calm, Kiva stepped outside with Tipp skipping along beside them, and Mirryn and Zuleeka trailing behind. All too soon they were in the training yard, where Torell was already holding a sword and facing Jaren, both of their blades raised into attack positions.

"Can't you stop this?" Kiva begged Naari, begged Caldon, begged anyone who would listen.

"I think it's best if he gets this out of his system, Sweet Cheeks," Caldon said, circling an arm around her shoulders.

"Truly, Kiva," Naari said. "I wouldn't let this go ahead if I was worried—about either of them."

Kiva appreciated the guard's confidence, but Naari didn't know how skilled Torell was. Hell, *Kiva* didn't know, having never seen him in action. She had, however, seen Jaren sparring with Caldon and Captain Veris, sometimes both at once, with Naari jumping in as well. She'd also seen how fast he'd reacted to Zuleeka's attack at the Red House, and how capably he'd fended off the rebels. Recalling all of that helped ease some of the suffocating fear in her chest.

And then it returned with a vengeance when their swords began flying through the air, a blur of parries and lunges, overhead strikes and underarmed thrusts.

An appreciative whistle came from Caldon. "Just when I thought your brother couldn't be more attractive." There was a dry edge to his voice as he added, "Who'd have thought being a blacksmith would result in *that?*"

Kiva didn't respond, too busy watching the match. Her brother's moves were as faultless as Jaren's, something that made Naari shift uneasily, but the guard didn't intervene. That was likely because she'd noticed what Kiva was beginning to suspect: Jaren and Torell were sparring with fervor, but they were also holding back.

"I'm curious," Jaren said casually between strikes, his voice carrying over to where Kiva and the others stood, "how you felt knowing your sister was in prison for so long." He deflected Torell's blade without effort. "Was it easier just to forget about her? To act like she'd never existed?"

Stomach clenching, Kiva stepped forward, but Caldon's arm tightened around her.

"Wait," he said quietly.

"I thought about her every day," Tor replied, feinting to the left. "I *missed* her every day."

Jaren saw through the feint and swung his sword in an arc, Tor hurrying to meet his blade in a clash of steel that left Kiva's ears ringing.

"And yet, you did nothing," Jaren said, panting slightly from everything he was feeling. "You just left her there. On her own. A *child.*"

"You make it sound like we had a choice," Torell snapped, his emerald eyes fierce as he launched into a series of lightning-fast strikes.

"She was *seven years old,*" Jaren all but yelled as he ducked, jumped, and dodged Tor's attacks, before returning his own set of counter-strikes in quick succession. "She lost over *half her life* to that miserable place, and you, her *beloved brother*"—a quick thrust forward that Tor barely managed to deflect—"left her in there to *rot.*"

"Jaren, *stop,*" Kiva croaked, but he didn't hear her over the clanging steel.

"What were we supposed to do?" Torell demanded, feinting again, this time to the right. "Storm the gates? Tear down the walls? Take on the guards? Please tell me, *Your Highness,* how was I supposed to save my baby sister from a decade of hell—in *your* prison?"

"She was a *child,*" Jaren repeated through gritted teeth, as if that was supposed to mean something. "A *minor.*"

With those two words, sudden dizziness overcame Kiva as she began to realize why Jaren was so upset—so *angry.* Warden Rooke's voice whispered in her ears, a conversation they'd had when she'd tried to get him to free Tipp:

As long as he has no guardian to claim him, Rooke had said, *he's considered a ward of Zalindov. He can go free, but only if someone comes to collect him.*

Tipp hadn't had anyone left to come for him. But Kiva . . .

She swayed on her feet, Caldon's arm being all that kept her standing.

Jaren lowered his sword, stepping right into Torell's space and glaring at him eye to eye. "Evalonian law states that children under the age of twelve are exempt from any punishment that results in a life sentence. Kiva became a ward of Zalindov the moment she arrived, but the only thing *you*"—he jabbed a finger into Tor's chest—"had to do was claim guardianship, and she would have been released. That means you had *five years* to get her out. All you had to do was *ask*—and you *gods-damned know it.*"

Kiva couldn't breathe.

Her throat was too tight, her airway too blocked.

. . . Her devastation too real.

"Sunshine, I need you to take a breath."

Kiva could barely hear Caldon's frantic whispering, but when blackness started dotting the edges of her vision, she managed to suck in a pain-filled gasp.

"Good girl," Caldon murmured.

She didn't hear him.

Because as Kiva somehow moved out of her own cloud of agony, her eyes landed on Torell's pale, horror-struck face.

I would give anything, everything, *to have kept you out of Zalindov,* he'd told her nearly a week ago. *I would have traded my life in an instant if I'd known they would let you go.*

Jaren was wrong—Torell *hadn't* known about the law, that he could have freed Kiva anytime before her twelfth birthday. He'd only been a boy himself, just two years older than her—how was he supposed to have known? But despite that, his torment was splashed across his face, enough that even Jaren could see, the anger bleeding right out of him.

"Torell, I—" Jaren started to apologize, but Tor raised a hand to cut him off.

His emerald eyes shimmered with tears as he looked at Kiva, but then he turned to Zuleeka, his voice rough as he asked, "Did you know?"

"Of course not," she said quickly.

Kiva's heart cracked, hearing the lie. Given Torell's tortured expression, he'd heard it, too.

Zuleeka had known.

For five years, Kiva could have been freed. All it would have taken was for someone to claim her. Someone to come for her. Someone to *want* her.

And if Zuleeka had known —

"Did Mother know?" Tor rasped.

Zuleeka met his gaze and repeated, "Of course not."

Lie.

Lie, lie, *lie.*

Torell closed his eyes, tears leaking from them as he handed his sword back to Jaren. "I think it's time for my sister and me to leave."

"Torell —" Jaren tried again, but again Tor interrupted him.

"Thank you for doing what I couldn't," he whispered, as if he couldn't manage anything louder. "Thank you for protecting her, for freeing her. I wish —" His voice broke. "I wish I'd known. I would have — I would have —"

Jaren placed a hand on Tor's shoulder. "I know that now. I'm sorry."

Torell only nodded, wiping his face and murmuring quiet goodbyes to the silent Mirryn, Caldon, Tipp, and Naari, unable to even glance at Kiva before spearing a look at Zuleeka and storming off in the direction of the stables.

"You'll have to forgive my brother," Zuleeka said after a long pause. "He can be emotional sometimes." She sent them all a smile that no one returned, not even Tipp, and finished, "I'd best follow him. We'll look forward to seeing you at the masquerade."

And then she dipped into a quick, almost mocking curtsey, and hurried after Torell.

Without looking at anyone, Kiva croaked out, "Excuse me."

She took off toward the stables, catching up with her siblings just as they reached the entrance and called for their horses to be brought out.

"What the hell was that, Tor?" Zuleeka demanded. "You —"

"Do *not* talk to me right now," Torell cut her off, his expression livid.

Kiva moved closer and took his white-knuckled hand, opening his clenched fist and lacing their fingers together.

"Tor, it's all right," she said quietly, her throat thick with unshed tears.

"It is absolutely not all right," he returned, quick as a whip. But then his features softened, and he whispered, "I'm so sorry, Mouse. I had no idea that—"

"I know," she interrupted. "I know you didn't." She made herself turn to Zuleeka and say, "But you did. You and Mother."

This time, without their royal audience, Zuleeka didn't deny it.

Swallowing thickly, Kiva said, "You could have gotten me out. You wouldn't have even needed to use force—they would have let me go."

Zuleeka didn't meet her eyes, instead looking out toward the manicured palace gardens. "I know you'll have trouble believing this, but you were safer in there than out here."

An incredulous sound left Kiva. "I was *what?*"

"You were saf—"

"Have you *been* to Zalindov?" Kiva demanded. "Every day I had to fight for my life. Every *minute* sometimes. And that's not even counting the Trial by Ordeal that would have killed me if not for Jaren's intervention in *every single task*. It's a miracle I survived at all, let alone as long as I did."

Zuleeka chewed on her lip and looked down at the ground.

"Why, Zuleeka?" Kiva said, her voice breaking. "Why did you and Mother leave me in there? You have to tell me," she begged. "You owe me that much."

Zuleeka exhaled loudly. "This isn't something we should talk about here." She glanced pointedly at all those inside the bustling stable complex.

"Figure out a way," Torell said in a hard voice. "Kiva deserves the truth. And I want to know, too."

Shooting him an annoyed look, Zuleeka's features gentled again as she turned back to Kiva and relented. "That problem you have, the one you're working to control," she said carefully, "*that's* why Mother thought it best you stay in there. She said you were protected behind those walls, safe from discovery. If anything happened, word wouldn't get out about it and cause problems for our family or our . . . *friends*." She went on to say, "And even if you'd slipped up and someone *had* learned the truth, you were already locked away. Nothing worse could happen to you." A pause. "But if it makes you feel any better, Mother always intended to free you one day. When the timing was right."

Silence fell in the wake of her words, until Torell grated out, "That's worse than I thought. Why didn't I know about this?"

"Because you would have ignored Mother and gone to get Kiva out," said Zuleeka.

"You're damned right I would have," Tor snarled. "As *you* should have. I can't *believe*—"

"What's done is done," Zuleeka interrupted, losing patience. "We can't change the past, so there's no point in regretting it. Kiva's fine, she's here, she's safe, she survived. That's what matters."

Kiva couldn't process how betrayed she felt—by her own family. Her own sister. Her own *mother*.

You're the one she left to rot in that prison, aren't you? The one she said was better off there?

Delora had spoken true yesterday, repeating what she'd heard. But how—*how*—could Tilda have imagined that Kiva was safer in a place like Zalindov? *Why* had she thought it best that her daughter be locked away, her magic hidden, when she herself had begun practicing again out in the world? Was she so afraid of discovery, of all her plans for vengeance being ruined, that she'd allowed her daughter to suffer needlessly for ten years?

Kiva couldn't fathom the possibility. But she did know that she was hurting. *So damned much.* And she needed to be alone to work through that.

"I want you to leave," she whispered, not looking at either of her siblings. "I need some time. On my own."

Zuleeka reached for her, but Kiva shifted out of the way.

"Please, you have to understand," Zuleeka implored. "I told you that wars aren't won without sacrifice—"

Kiva flinched so violently that her head snapped back, realizing that in this instance, *she* was the sacrifice.

"—and as hard as it was for her, Mother had to weigh the risks, deciding that we were all safer if you remained in there until—"

"Stop talking," Torell finally snapped. "Kiva doesn't want to see you right now. *I* don't want to see you right now. Just—Just go check if our horses are nearly ready."

Zuleeka's eyes held Kiva's, the honey-gold begging for her to understand.

I'll try harder. I promise I will.

Kiva looked away.

Sighing quietly, Zuleeka murmured, "I'll see you at Mirryn's birthday," before striding off into the stable complex.

Kiva waited until she was out of sight, then turned to her brother. "Can you stop her from coming to the party? It's not safe. Not smart. And I don't—I don't want her here."

No matter how much she wanted her sister back, right now Kiva didn't want to be anywhere near her.

Torell blew out a loud breath. "I'll do what I can. But you know what she's like."

He winced suddenly, realizing what he'd said—how Kiva *didn't* know what Zuleeka was like because she was nothing at all like the child she'd once been.

"I'm so sorry, Mouse," he repeated his earlier words, just as quietly. "Ten years . . . I don't even know what to say."

"I don't want to talk about it anymore," she told him hoarsely. "But I—I don't blame you. You know that, right?"

"You should," he said, with bitter self-loathing. "I do."

Kiva gripped his hand tighter. "Don't, Tor. If I have to worry about how you're feeling on top of everything else . . . it's too much."

He blew out another loud breath and drew her into his arms. "I can't promise not to be upset—I love you too much not to hate what you went through, especially now that I know you could have been freed years ago."

"Just don't hate yourself for what you had no control over," Kiva said. "Promise me that much."

A long moment passed before he finally said, "I'll try."

Knowing it was as good as she was going to get, Kiva pulled back and wiped under her eyes, giving him a gentle push in the direction of where Zuleeka had disappeared inside the stables. "Go," she said. "And feel free to give her the silent treatment on the ride back."

"I plan on giving her the silent treatment for much longer than that," Tor muttered angrily, before leaning in to kiss Kiva's forehead and striding away, leaving her alone but for the company of her tormented thoughts . . . and her shattered heart.

CHAPTER TWENTY-FOUR

Kiva avoided everyone for the rest of the day, sneaking from the stables to her room and burrowing into her bed. She didn't care that she'd wasted the afternoon, needing to wallow in all that she'd learned, needing to *grieve*.

She had multiple visitors as the hours passed, their quiet knocks and even quieter voices identifying them as Jaren, Tipp, Caldon, Naari, and even Mirryn, each coming at different times to see if she'd allow them entry. But none invaded her privacy when she failed to answer, giving her the space she so desperately wanted.

Night fell outside her windows, and despite her growling stomach, she didn't move from her bed to seek out dinner, remaining curled around herself until she finally felt like she could breathe again. It eventually happened, mostly thanks to Zuleeka's reminder that they couldn't change the past. For whatever inexcusable reason, her mother had left her in Zalindov. It was done; there was no changing it. Now Kiva needed to let it go and move forward.

It was soon after she came to her decision that another knock rattled on the door, and this time she rose from her bed to answer it. She was surprised to find not one of her friends, but an elderly servant standing on the other side.

"Miss Kiva," he said, bowing slightly, "Her Majesty the Queen apologizes for missing lunch and invites you to enjoy a nightcap with her before turning in for the evening. She specifically told me to mention that she's ordered hot cocoa, with extra cocoa."

Kiva's stomach rumbled so violently that the servant looked at her in alarm, but he only finished, "She's awaiting you in her personal sitting room and requested that I escort you at your earliest convenience."

It would have been easy for Kiva to decline the offer. She'd grown close enough to the queen to know there was no pressure on her to attend. That wasn't what Ariana would even *want*—she'd be one of the first to encourage Kiva to take whatever time she needed to get over the pain of her day.

It was, perhaps, for that very reason that Kiva finger-combed her hair and followed the man from her room. She'd never have admitted it aloud, but while she was hungry and tempted by the hot cocoa, what she wanted more than anything else was a mother's comfort—even if that mother was Ariana Vallentis.

Not seeing Tipp or anyone else as she left her suite, Kiva walked silently behind her escort, wondering if any of the servants dotting the hallways were rebel spies who would report where she was going and why. But then she decided that she didn't care. She wouldn't think about her mission, her family's cause, *anything*. Tonight was hers to enjoy, to recover, to heal.

After a quick walk across the golden bridge to the western palace, the queen's personal chambers came into view, being almost a straight shot over the river from where Kiva had started. Her escort ushered her directly into the room, before backing out and closing the gilded doors behind him.

Kiva paused at the entrance, spinning around to take in the sheer opulence surrounding her.

The queen's sitting room had high ceilings, lush carpet, and windows that looked out at both the Serin and the gardens, the latter dotted with luminium beacons like fireflies stretching into the distance. An elegant chandelier hung like a collection of teardrops, the walls were mounted with framed artwork, and an assortment of fresh flowers and leafy potted plants brought a dash of color to the otherwise gold-and-white décor. As Kiva continued turning, she saw a crackling fireplace nestled into one wall, the flames warm and inviting, and opposite it was—

Kiva gasped and was unable to resist moving toward the grand piano. She'd never seen anything like it before, the legs, cover, and sides made entirely out of transparent, sparkling crystal.

"'S lovely, isn't it?"

Kiva was admiring the black and white keys, the only part that was ordinary—and yet still beautiful—when the voice reached her. She whirled around to see the queen reclining on a red velvet chaise, watching her over the rim of a wine goblet.

"Do you play?" Ariana asked, her voice slurring slightly.

"Uh, no," Kiva answered, looking closely at the queen, and wondering just how much she'd had to drink.

"Jaren used to play all the time," Ariana said, her gaze turning distant. "He doesn't now."

Kiva walked slowly forward, an inner sense warning that something wasn't quite right. But her trepidation eased when she saw the tray of hot cocoa and an assortment of mini cakes, her insides warming as she noted the effort the queen had gone to.

"He doesn't?" Kiva asked. The thought of Jaren playing the piano was too beautiful for her poor brain, so she pushed it away before it could take hold. "Why not?"

Ariana took a large gulp of her wine. "He won't come here anymore."

The five slurred words had Kiva freezing to the spot—but it wasn't only them, it was also that she'd moved close enough to note what she hadn't seen from further away.

Ariana's glazed eyes, waxy skin, trembling hands . . .

. . . and the golden powder smeared around her mouth, beneath her nose, inside her nostrils.

Angeldust.

The queen was high.

And when the queen was high —

He won't come here anymore.

Kiva backed away, seeing the glorious room with new eyes.

This was where the queen had hurt Jaren. For years.

This was where she succumbed to her addiction, lost control, inflicted untold amounts of pain.

And Kiva was alone with her, no one but the male servant even knowing she was there.

"Have some cocoa, Kiva," the queen slurred, elongating Kiva's name into three syllables. "I had it made 'specially for you."

Kiva's heart raced as she considered her options. She could flee, risking an overreaction but ensuring her own safety, or she could sit where Ariana was patting the chaise beside her and have a drink as planned. While her hunger had vanished at the sight of the golden powder, Kiva knew choosing the latter would limit the probability of offending the monarch. But she also knew that angeldust users, especially functioning addicts, were unpredictable, prone to mood swings and violence, often forgetting their actions once the drug passed through their systems. The danger was simply too great for her to chance.

Decision made, Kiva took another step backwards and said, "I'm suddenly not feeling very well, Your Majesty. Please excuse me — I think it's best if I retire."

Kiva dipped into a respectful curtsey. Sober Ariana might not expect her to stand on ceremony, but there was no telling how the drug affected the queen's memory. Rising swiftly again, Kiva offered a shaky smile and turned toward the door.

"Not so fast."

The three words held no trace of Ariana's usual warmth and kindness. Instead, they were as cold as ice, imperious and demanding all at once. They stopped Kiva in her tracks — but not because she thought it wise to listen. She was more desperate than ever to flee the room, consequences be damned.

Only, she couldn't move.

It wasn't just the queen's words that had been filled with ice — water had risen from the floor beneath Kiva's feet and then frozen, trapping her in place.

Panic overwhelmed her as she tried to break free, her efforts futile as the ice block spun slowly at Ariana's command, turning Kiva to face her once more.

"Are you trying to leave me?" Ariana slurred. "We haven't had our cocoa yet."

"No, I, um —" Kiva stuttered with fear.

Suddenly, the queen let out an earsplitting shriek. With a quick, overarm throw, she hurled her goblet at the supper tray, wine and cocoa and cake flying everywhere. Rising, she staggered toward Kiva, her hand slicing the air, the gleam of a golden ring catching in the light.

"Look what you did! *Look at this mess!*" the queen yelled. "I wanted us to have a nice time together, and you ruined it! *Why did you have to ruin it?*"

At the savage look on her face, Kiva tried harder than ever to dislodge her feet, but the ice remained fixed, its grip unyielding.

"Your Majesty, *please,*" Kiva begged, knowing she might as well be talking to a wild animal. "I didn't mean to. I'm sorry. It was an accident." The words spilled from her, anything she thought might mollify the queen.

Her relief was nearly crippling when the anger disappeared from Ariana's features, the ice underfoot cracking before turning back to water and then evaporating entirely.

Despite being free, Kiva didn't dare move a step.

"Why do you look scared?" Ariana demanded, stumbling through the spilled food and drink toward Kiva. "We're friends, aren't we? Don't you like me?"

"Of course I do," Kiva answered quickly.

The queen heard the fear in her voice, and her sapphire eyes narrowed. "LIAR!" she screamed. "YOU'RE LYING TO ME! EVERYONE ALWAYS LIES TO ME!"

At her enraged look, Kiva scurried backwards, but she barely made it three steps before the queen stabbed her finger in a sharp motion, bringing Kiva to a halt once more.

Not because her feet were iced.

But because she couldn't breathe.

Kiva's hand flew to her throat as she tried to suck in air, but instead, she bent double and coughed out a mouthful of water. And then another. Coughing and coughing, she tried to clear her lungs of the fluid that was suddenly filling them, *flooding* them.

Pure terror hit Kiva as more and more water streamed out of her. She searched desperately for something she could use as a weapon, seeing only the upset supper tray. Hacking and spitting, she collapsed to her knees and crawled toward the queen's shattered wine goblet. She wrapped her fingers around a broken shard of crystal, but a vicious tug on her hair had the makeshift blade slipping from her hand as she was dragged through the spoiled food and away from any chance of defending herself.

"Why did you have to lie to me?" Queen Ariana asked woefully. "I wanted so much for you to like me."

"Please!" Kiva tried, but all that came out was a watery gurgle.

Burning—her lungs were *burning.*

Darkness began to press in at the edges of her vision, and she realized this was it. She had no defense against Ariana's magic. The water was flooding every part of her, drowning her on dry land.

And then, suddenly, it wasn't.

With a loud *BANG!* the doors to the queen's sitting room slammed open as Jaren sprinted through them. A quick, horrified glance had him waving his hand toward Kiva, her lungs clearing in an instant. A second wave sent his furious mother flying through the air across the room.

"Kiva," he gasped, running to her side. She was still coughing violently, tears spilling from her eyes as she fought the pain and sucked in heaving gulps of oxygen.

"Hold on to me," Jaren said. Heedless of the sopping, dirty mess covering her, he pulled her up into his arms and strode out of the room, his face like granite.

"Jaren, my love!" Ariana called, stumbling after them. "My sweet baby boy!"

The doors slammed shut on an invisible wind the moment they were through. Around her continued coughing, Kiva could hear the queen banging on them from the inside, but Jaren's magic kept her sealed away.

"J-J-J—"

"Don't try to talk," he said, his voice tight. He looked down at her, his tone softening as he instructed, "Just focus on your breathing, sweetheart."

Kiva spent the whole trip back to the eastern palace inhaling and exhaling, until finally she was able to breathe somewhat normally again. Still shaking, she was reluctant to loosen her grip on Jaren, so she didn't resist when he led her not back to her room, but to his.

Kiva had never been inside Jaren's private rooms before, but after what had just happened, she barely summoned a passing interest. She did note that his sitting room was nowhere near as opulent as the queen's chambers, closer in style to what Tipp and Kiva shared, but that was all she saw before he strode into his bedroom, sitting down on his bed with her resting in his lap.

The room was dark, moonlight shining in through windows that, like Kiva's, opened to a balcony over the Serin River. The space was considerably larger than her own guest quarters, with masculine shades of gray and navy intermingling amongst the standard gold and pearl of the palace. Even his bedding was darker, his large four-poster bed nothing short of luxurious.

"Kiva," he said hoarsely, gently cupping her face. "I am so, *so* sorry."

Kiva felt the devastation of his words deep inside her.

"I don't know how I'll ever—"

"Shhh," she interrupted, unclenching his jacket and placing a finger against his lips. "It wasn't your fault."

Her voice rasped slightly, but it was a minor inconvenience compared to the alternative.

Jaren had saved her life.

Again.

Unable to bear up under the weight of that, Kiva leaned forward until her head rested in the crook of his neck, whispering, "Thank you."

A pained sound left Jaren, and he wrapped his arms around her once again, uncaring about the mess she was transferring onto him. "Please don't thank me." In a quiet, agonized voice, he added, "I thought she'd stopped. She *told me* she'd stopped."

Kiva clutched him even tighter, feeling his anguish as if it were her own. Weak and vulnerable, she couldn't stop herself from pressing the softest of kisses to the underside of his jaw, offering the only comfort she could.

Jaren froze beneath her, but then he released a long breath and buried his face in her hair, drawing her closer.

"I don't know what I'd do if anything happened to you," he whispered.

Kiva's throat tightened as she whispered back her own horrible truth, something she wished was a lie—but it wasn't. "Same."

At her single, tremulous word, Jaren tilted her head back so she was staring straight at him.

The air fled her lungs all over again at the look on his face, at everything he was allowing her to see, everything he *wanted* her to see.

Her skin began to tingle at the heat in his eyes, warmth flooding her veins and chasing away any lingering cold from the queen's attack. She was still shivering, but no longer from fear—it was a different kind of shivering now.

Anticipation flooded her, *yearning* flooded her, and despite her mind screaming that this was a bad idea, that it would only end in heartache, she didn't stop Jaren as he slowly inched closer.

Kiva sucked in a swift breath—

But at the last second, Jaren shifted, his lips coming to press against her forehead, before he whispered against her skin. "Stay with me tonight."

It wasn't an order, and despite the heat that had been in his eyes just moments ago, Kiva knew he didn't intend for anything more intimate to happen between them.

Disappointment filled her, but at the same time, so did an acute sense of relief.

"I'm not sure—" she started, her voice wobbling from the intense feelings still simmering within her.

"Please," Jaren begged.

The crown prince. Begging.

"After what just happened, I need to know that you're safe," he said, still quietly.

He was still shaken, Kiva realized, perhaps more than she was. Because of that, she slowly nodded her agreement.

Jaren breathed a grateful sigh and kissed her forehead again, before pulling back. "I'll get you something to change into."

And then he was lifting her off him and onto his bed, the back of his hand stroking her cheek before he strode across the dark room to his wardrobe.

Kiva managed to pull herself somewhat together before he returned and handed over one of his clean long-sleeved shirts, after which she quickly ducked into his bathroom to rid herself of her soiled clothing.

When she stepped back into Jaren's room, he'd changed into a pair of sleep pants—and nothing else.

Kiva's mouth dried and she forced her eyes away from his bare chest just in time to see him still at the sight of her in his shirt, the hem of which barely skimmed her mid-thigh.

What am I doing? Kiva's panicked mind screamed. She couldn't do this. She definitely *shouldn't* do this.

Preparing to offer an excuse to leave—*any* excuse—Kiva opened her mouth just as Jaren cleared his throat and said, "I want to give you something."

Kiva snapped her mouth shut.

Instead of continuing, he angled his head and asked, "Is there a reason you're not leaving the bathroom doorway?"

A shaky breath left Kiva but she started toward him, determined not to show how nervous she was. When she reached him, he motioned to his bed, and they both shuffled in and reclined against the headboard, side by side.

"I should have given this to you sooner," Jaren said, turning a small box between his fingers. "I didn't even think about it. But that was stupid of me—I should have known better."

Bitterness filled his voice toward the end, enough that Kiva placed her hand over his, stopping his fidgeting.

He blew out a breath and opened the box, revealing a shiny amulet resting on a bed of velvet.

Kiva had seen it before. She'd *worn* it before. It had saved her life from the Trial by Fire, after which it had ended up in Naari's hands, and Kiva had forgotten all about it.

At the end of a glittering chain sat the Vallentis crest, the four elemental quadrants — made of ruby, emerald, topaz, and sapphire — divided by a golden sword and an arrow, then topped with a crown.

It was beautiful, Kiva could admit, albeit grudgingly. And that beauty only grew when Jaren pressed a finger to it, his eyes focusing intently, and the gemstones began to *glow*.

Red, green, white, and blue, the colors grew brighter and brighter until Jaren finally removed his hand and they faded back to normal.

"What just happened?" Kiva asked, squinting at the amulet.

Jaren held it up and said, "May I?"

At the open, patient look on his face, Kiva shrugged and turned her body away from him. A moment later his hands came around her neck, the amulet dropping against her breastbone before he clasped it into place.

"This will protect you from any magical attack," Jaren said when she was facing him again. "I've pushed my power into it — not just fire, like with your Ordeal, but earth, water, and air, too. If anyone tries to use magic to hurt you, it'll act like a shield, keeping you safe."

Kiva stared at Jaren.

"You don't believe me," he said, misreading her expression. He reached for her hand. "Look."

Fire burst from his fingertips and Kiva tried to jerk away, but Jaren held firm.

"Look," he repeated, indicating where the flames shifted from his flesh to hers. She couldn't feel anything — no pain, no burning — just like when she'd been in the crematorium.

"How long will it last?" Kiva croaked, unable to process the value of his gift.

And what it meant.

Jaren was protecting her—from his own family.

From *himself.*

"Long enough for you to get away next time," he said, clearly still upset. He then shook it off and added, "You shouldn't have problems from anyone else here, but there *are* anomalies out there—people with magic outside of the royal line. This will keep you safe from them, too."

Kiva looked down at the amulet. "I don't know what to say."

"Say you'll keep it. Say you'll wear it."

"I will," Kiva agreed. "I promise."

The amulet had saved her life once before. Regardless of whose crest it was, she would be foolish to reject such a powerful gift. Especially given what was coming.

Don't think about that, Kiva told herself. *Not tonight.*

"It's been a long day," Jaren said, pulling the blankets over them. "We should sleep."

Kiva nodded, burrowing into his impossibly lush bedding. With both of them on their sides facing each other in the dark, she couldn't keep from saying, "Your bed is better than mine."

A startled laugh left Jaren. "I'm glad you think so."

She burrowed even deeper, marveling at how natural it felt to be lying so close to him without any shred of discomfort.

"How did you know about—" Kiva couldn't finish her whispered question, but Jaren knew what she was asking.

He tucked a tendril of hair behind her ear, the action raising goose bumps on her skin. "I went to your room to check in on you, but Tipp said you'd left. He'd overheard Oswald delivering Mother's invitation, and the moment he told me, I just—I knew something was wrong." In a quiet voice, he finished, "I'm sorry I didn't get there sooner."

"I'm just grateful you came at all," Kiva said. She then repeated her earlier words. "Thank you, Jaren. You always seem to be saving me."

"And I always will," he returned. The depth of emotion in his response would have shaken Kiva, if he hadn't quickly—and *awkwardly*—added, "You know, if I have to. Which hopefully I won't. Ever again. But if I do, then I will. Of course. Obviously."

Laughing at how flustered he was, Kiva placed her finger over his lips for the second time that night.

"Good night, Jaren."

He sighed against her finger. "Good night, Kiva."

She snuggled deeper and was just beginning to drift off when Jaren's voice came to her again, whisper soft. "Kiva?"

"Mmm?" she murmured.

"I'm sorry about today. With your family."

Even if she'd decided to move past it, Kiva still felt the ache of betrayal all over again.

"And I'm sorry I was so angry," Jaren continued. "I just—"

"I know," she interrupted in her own whisper.

Half asleep and entirely unable to keep her guard up, Kiva shifted forward until she was pressed against him. He automatically rolled onto his back and pulled her closer, her head coming to rest on his bare chest. Without thinking, she laid her hand over his heart and curled her leg around his knee, the two of them perfectly entwined.

He didn't say anything else, but just as Kiva succumbed to sleep, she whispered one last time, "I know."

CHAPTER TWENTY-FIVE

When Kiva woke the next morning, her entire torso was plastered to Jaren's, their legs tangled in an impressive feat of flexibility.

Panic hit her, but she told herself to remain calm. She just had to slip away before he stirred. If she could extricate herself without jostling him too much, then —

"Morning."

Kiva froze, barely having managed to remove her arm, let alone anything else.

"You're not trying to sneak off, are you?" Jaren asked, his voice husky and yet still bubbling with humor.

"Erm . . ."

Moving impossibly fast, Jaren flipped them both over, the breath *whoosh*ing out of Kiva as she found herself on her back and looking up into his highly amused face.

"Let's try that again, shall we?" he murmured, kissing the hinge of her jaw. "Good morning, Kiva."

A garbled sound left her, her stomach pooling with heat as his lips moved boldly to her neck and kissed the sensitive spot right beneath her ear.

"Did you sleep well?" he whispered there, his mouth brushing her skin with each word, prompting a delicious shiver to travel down her spine. Another unintelligible sound left her, causing him to chuckle quietly and say, "I did, too."

Kiva gripped his bare waist, unsure whether to push him away or pull him closer. Before she could decide, he drew back and looked down at her with a soft expression. "Spend the day with me."

Her mind was so addled by his touch that it took her a moment to respond. "Pardon?"

The word was breathy enough that she would have been mortified if Jaren's eyes hadn't softened even further, with him instantly ducking down and placing a feather-light kiss on the corner of her mouth, as if he couldn't help himself. It happened so fast that Kiva would have wondered if she'd imagined it, if not for the tingling that remained in its wake.

"Spend the day with me," he repeated.

This time, Kiva ignored everything he was making her feel in an attempt to focus. "Don't you have meetings?"

"I'll reschedule." He leaned in until his face was all she could see. "Please. I need a day off. And I want to spend it with you."

It would have taken a much stronger person than Kiva to say no, especially when he was looking at her like . . . like . . . like *that*.

"All right," she surrendered. "But if you mean the *whole* day, then you're telling Caldon."

Another quiet chuckle from Jaren. "I think you can survive missing one training session." He tilted his head toward his balcony. "And besides, it's already well past dawn."

Kiva followed his gaze and gasped at the bright sunlight, having no idea how she'd slept so late. "He's going to kill me tomorrow," she moaned, already fearing the punishing workout.

"Then we'd better make sure today is worth your inevitable demise."

With those mirth-filled words, Jaren lifted his weight off Kiva and pulled her out of bed, his arms remaining loosely wrapped around her.

"How's this for a plan," he said. "You go get dressed while I rearrange a few things, and I'll meet you at your suite in twenty minutes. I know a great breakfast place right on the river that makes the best egg and bacon rolls in all of Wenderall, so we'll grab something to eat, and then—" He grinned. "Well, then you'll see."

"You're being very mysterious," Kiva told him.

His grin widened. "You're one to talk."

Kiva had no defense to that, so she rolled her eyes and pushed away from him, walking toward the door. She'd just opened it and was about to step through when Jaren called her name, making her pause and turn back to him.

"Best sleep I've ever had," he said quietly.

Kiva swallowed at the look that had returned to his eyes. She wanted to lie, but what came out was the absolute, undeniable truth. "Me too."

Jaren was right about the egg and bacon rolls. One bite and Kiva nearly inhaled the rest, having eaten so little the previous day. The taste also helped wash away the bitterness of Delora's potion, which Kiva had downed the moment she'd returned to her room. With only one mouthful now left in the vial, she would have to find her way back to her grandmother tomorrow as agreed, but that, she decided, was something she could worry about later.

"I told you," Jaren said as they meandered along the river, noting how quickly she finished her roll and graciously handing over what remained of his.

Kiva thought about objecting, but she didn't have the willpower—like most things when it came to Jaren. It was only after she was done and licking her fingers that both rolls reached her stomach, making her regret her poor life choices.

"You're looking a bit uncomfortable there," Jaren said, lips twitching as he watched her holding her belly and moaning. "Do you think you can walk up the hill, or should I carry you?"

He gestured toward a familiar road, one Kiva had traveled numerous times since arriving in the city.

"You're taking me to Silverthorn?" she asked, tilting her head in puzzlement. The amulet shifted around her neck, a reminder that it was resting beneath her sweater, protecting her from harm. "I'm not *that* unwell. I just ate too much."

Jaren chuckled and wound an arm around her waist, leading her off the crowded River Road and onto the quieter side street toward the academy. "We're not going there for you."

Alarm filled Kiva. "Are you all right?"

"I'm fine," he answered quickly. "We're not going there for me, either." He paused. "Well, I guess we kind of are. But not in a way that—" He broke off. "Never mind. You'll see when we get there."

Her curiosity piqued, Kiva followed him up the hill, expecting to walk right through the front gates. But before they reached the campus, Jaren guided her between two narrow apartment buildings, moving deeper into the shadows until he was certain they were out of sight.

"This isn't creepy at all," Kiva stated, looking around.

"If you think this is bad, never accept Caldon's offer for a night out on the town," Jaren returned, reaching into his pocket and withdrawing two small golden objects. "*Especially* if he mentions chasing the spirits of our ancestors or hunting the ghosts of the gods."

Kiva blinked for a long moment, before slowly saying, "There's so much there that I don't even know what to ask."

Jaren chuckled. "It's a story that can wait for our next family night." He held out one of the golden items. "Here."

Kiva took it, turning it over in her hands. An uneasy feeling hit her at the sight of the simple but elegant mask, but this one wasn't silver and there were no coiled serpents, so she swallowed her trepidation and asked, "What's this for?"

Jaren peeled back his mask and affixed it to his face. "For what we're about to do, I have to be Prince Deverick." He pointed to his masked features, a self-conscious look coming over him as he indicated what she held and added, "If you don't mind, I think you should wear one, too."

Kiva frowned. "But I'm not royal. No one cares who I am."

The reason for his unexpected look became clear when he said, "Humor me. I'm . . . thinking ahead."

The breath left Kiva at his implication, Tipp's family portrait flitting across her mind, the image of her and Jaren holding hands and wearing crowns impossible to forget.

Perhaps you might share with us your intentions for her.

Councilwoman Zerra's words returned to Kiva, an odd swooping sensation hitting her, the feeling not entirely unpleasant.

Jaren didn't seem to expect a response, and after waiting for her nod of consent, he plucked the mask from her numb fingers, gently sticking it to her face.

"It suits you," he murmured, smoothing down the edges.

Kiva was having trouble drawing air into her lungs, but she managed to wheeze out, "Erm, thank you."

Jaren grinned, his mask ending at the tip of his nose, leaving his mouth visible. His eyes were like twin pools of sunlit ocean staring out from behind the golden filigree, impossibly beautiful and frustratingly distracting.

Kiva cleared her throat and looked away, touching the cool metal on her face. "All right, Prince Deverick," she said, his official name feeling strange on her tongue. "I think it's time you explained why we're heading to Silverthorn."

Jaren didn't respond other than to grin wider and lead her onto the campus. She tried to keep an eye out for Rhessinda as they traveled the stone pathways, but was distracted when they started up a fork in the path toward the infirmary for long-term patient care and rehabilitation.

As soon as they stepped into the large building, it became clear that Jaren knew his way around the sterile hallways, with healers and residents waving as they passed, none surprised to see him. They did, however, send curious glances toward Kiva, making her grateful that the mask shielded her from their prying looks.

"Nearly there," Jaren said as they ascended a wide, spiraling ramp up to the higher levels.

"Nearly *where?*"

Once again, he didn't answer, but he did halt when they reached the top of the ramp, turning to her and asking, "Would you mind if I borrowed your amulet? I have to wear it when I'm here because—well, you'll understand in a minute."

Kiva squinted at him in question, but when he just waited patiently, she huffed out a breath and fished the amulet from beneath her sweater, handing it over. He immediately placed it around his own neck, making sure the crest was resting over his clothes, clear for all to see. Only then did he continue guiding her along a white corridor until they reached a closed door at the end.

Frustrated by the lack of answers, Kiva started to say, "Jaren—" just as he opened the door. Before she could finish, multiple shrieks of *"PRINCE DEVERICK!"* pierced her ears, and she abruptly swallowed her complaint.

Kiva stood in the doorway, stunned, as the beaming Jaren strode into the room, waving to all the delighted faces around him.

Children, Kiva mentally corrected—waving to all the delighted *children* around him.

One quick glance at the small beds lined up beside each other, the mishmashed art plastered to the walls, and the colorful toys strewn haphazardly across the floor told Kiva that they were in the children's ward of the long-term patient infirmary.

And at the center of it all was the crown prince, his arms stretched wide as the children scrambled from their beds—some much slower and weaker than others—and hurried over to him.

"He's always so good with them."

Kiva turned to find a white-robed Silverthorn healer having crept up beside her, the middle-aged, dark-skinned woman watching the prince with clear adoration—not for who he was, but for what he was doing. Because as Kiva watched, Jaren raised his hands . . . and the children started flying.

Squeals of joy left them as they zoomed around the ward, with Jaren seeming to know who needed to be more careful and treating them accordingly. Parents and visitors looked on, all smiling at the prince with love and appreciation, as if they'd seen this before. Numerous times.

It was enough for Kiva to turn to the healer and ask, "Does he come here often?"

"Every week," the woman replied, motioning for Kiva to step further into the room. "Well, at least when he's here in the city. He was gone for most of the winter—the children were devastated—but he came again as soon as he returned. He's so generous with his time, especially since he divides his hours evenly amongst the other places, too."

Kiva watched as Jaren waved his hand and flowers appeared around the room, joined by blossoming vines that crept across the ceiling and up the walls, the ward coming alive with natural beauty. And with it, Kiva suddenly understood why he'd needed the amulet.

It was a cover.

The public knew Prince Deverick controlled both wind and fire magic, but nothing more. If he'd been here and done this before, he must have come up with a story about the amulet, making them believe his family had imbued it with power for him to manipulate—when really, he wasn't using it at all.

Kiva's throat grew tight and she rasped out, "Other places?"

The healer nodded. "Oh, yes. He gets around, our Prince Deverick. He visits all the orphanages, the elderly respites, even helps feed and clothe the homeless down near the docks. Whatever he can do to ease the suffering of others."

Tears prickled the back of Kiva's eyes, her throat tightening even more, keeping her from forming a response.

The healer noted her reaction and stepped closer to quietly say, "Queen Ariana is respected well enough, but Prince Deverick? He's the people's prince. He's *our* prince. The day he inherits the throne will be the best day in Evalon's history." She shifted her gaze to Jaren, who had returned all the children to the ground and was now juggling fire balls to their shrieks and laughter. "That young man is destined for greatness. He's going to be the best king we've ever seen. I'm certain of it."

Kiva couldn't take any more.

Because as Jaren summoned water droplets and made them sparkle like beads of light, wowing the children anew, she couldn't help looking at him and knowing down to her bones that the healer was right. He *would* be a wonderful king — the *best* king.

And her family was planning to take that from him.

She was planning to take that from him.

"Goodness, Healer Tura, what did you say to our visitor? She looks like she's about to be ill."

Kiva forced her eyes from Jaren to see the Matron Healer entering the ward, evidently recognizing her despite the mask.

"We were just talking about how wonderful the prince is, Matron," Tura said. Her eyes turned alert as she looked at her charges. "If you'll excuse me, it looks like young Katra is about to cause some mischief."

She headed quickly toward a little girl who was tying one of Jaren's still-growing vines around her own feet, clearly hoping it might rise enough to dangle her in the air now that he'd set all the flying children back down.

"I was hoping to see you again, Miss Meridan," Healer Maddis said once they were alone. "When I heard Prince Deverick was here with a companion, I hurried over to see if it was you."

"I'm sorry, Matron Healer," Kiva said, "but if this is about me attending —"

Maddis waved her hand. "I said you could take your time deciding, and I meant that." She pulled a jar from her robes, a pale ointment contained within, and held it out. "I came to bring you this."

Kiva unstoppered the lid, noting familiar scents but unable to identify every ingredient. "What is it?"

"It's for your hand."

It took Kiva a moment to process the words, but when she did, her eyes shot up to meet Maddis's.

Unaware of her sudden distress—or perhaps ignoring it—the Matron Healer went on, "It won't erase the scarring completely, but it will promote regeneration of the cells, helping it to fade over time." She tilted her chin toward Jaren. "Our prince might like to use some, too."

And then, revealing she could sense everything churning within Kiva, Maddis gently took her left hand, pulling back the sleeve to expose the Z scar—the same scar Kiva had been certain would doom her if the Matron Healer learned about it.

"Our scars define us," Maddis said quietly, the tip of her finger tracing the three slashed lines. "They tell a story of courage and survival. They tell of who we are at our deepest being, of the challenges we've faced and overcome." Whispering now, she patted Kiva's hand and finished, "Not all scars are as visible as this. I daresay you have many more on the inside. But never forget that every scar is beautiful. And you should never, *ever*, be ashamed of them."

With the kindest of smiles, Maddis released Kiva and turned back toward the doors, leaving without another word.

Overwhelmed, Kiva just stood there, breathing deeply.

Maddis knew she'd been in Zalindov.

Knew, and *didn't care.*

She hadn't rescinded her offer and told Kiva she could no longer be a student, hadn't crushed her dreams.

No—only Kiva was doing that. Kiva and her commitment to her family and their mission and everything that was keeping her from the life she wanted, including Silverthorn. Even now, after the betrayal she'd learned of yesterday, after everything she could no longer deny feeling for Jaren, *even now* she was still faithful to her brother and sister and their plans for vengeance.

Because after ten years, she didn't know how *not* to be.

Even if she wished—so desperately *wished*—she could let it all go.

Her heart and mind at war, Kiva glanced up and caught Jaren's content gaze. Seeing that she was now alone, he held out a hand, beckoning her over.

And so, with a tight smile, she pocketed the jar and strode toward him, beaming genuinely at the children who squealed with renewed delight at having another visitor to play with.

"What do you say we have some fun?" Jaren asked her.

Looking at him, Kiva's smile grew even as her heart broke, and she answered, "Let's do it."

Kiva and Jaren spent almost the entire day at Silverthorn, moving from ward to ward and bringing joy to children and adults alike. It didn't matter that she had no elemental magic, because Jaren was more than eager to follow any requests she made. With a wave of his hand, he had entire rooms filling with bubbles that refused to pop, fire animals frolicking around water fountains, and tropical forests springing up out of nothing.

Over the course of the day, so many healers spoke with Kiva, sharing how much Jaren's generosity meant to the children and their families, claiming it was the highlight of their weeks.

The people's prince, Healer Tura had called him.

She wasn't wrong.

With each new child's laugh and each new thrill of Jaren's magic, Kiva was forced to acknowledge that she was in more trouble than she'd thought.

Because every time Jaren looked at her, smiled at her, touched her, she knew deep down what she would do if they ever had another night like last night, another morning like that morning.

She wouldn't push him away.

She would hold on to him, for as long as she could, for as long as he'd let her.

Because she was in—

"You're very quiet," Jaren said, bringing her thoughts to a screeching halt.

Her dangerous, *dangerous* thoughts.

"Hmm?" Kiva replied, praying her face didn't betray her and wishing they hadn't removed their masks upon leaving the academy grounds.

"I didn't mean to tire you out," he continued as they walked slowly along the River Road back toward the palace, the sun setting in the distance. "I just wanted to show you that my life isn't always filled with council meetings and dreary politics. And I thought—" He ran a hand through his hair and looked at the amulet that was once more around her neck. "I guess I wanted to share something with you that I've never shared with anyone else. I thought you might appreciate it. Enjoy it, even."

Kiva saw every expression shifting across his features, the doubt, the self-consciousness, the uncertainty. All there because of how much he felt for her, and how much her opinion meant to him.

Her voice was rough with emotion when she replied, "I did appreciate it. And I did enjoy it. More than I can say."

He sent her a relieved grin, but it faded quickly at whatever he saw on her face.

Tugging her to the side and halting them next to the railing, he asked, "Do you want to tell me what's wrong? All day, it's like there's been a . . . sadness about you." He eyed her carefully. "Is it because of the children? I thought you'd be all right with it, as a healer." Quickly, he added, "Not that you'd be fine with them being sick, I just meant—"

"I know what you meant," Kiva said, cutting him off. She'd thought she'd hid her misery well, but as always, he was able to read her better than most.

Use it, came a voice that sounded suspiciously like Zuleeka. *Use this opportunity. He's giving you the perfect opening.*

"I—" Kiva started, and then stopped. The amulet shifted, as if it were begging her not to do this. Or perhaps that was merely her own heart.

There are things he doesn't even share with the Royal Council, with his family . . . But you have his ear.

That was definitely Zuleeka's voice—and it kept coming.

Find us a legitimate way to take the throne, something that will make Evalon accept us as their new rulers without contention.

Feeling sick to her stomach, Kiva turned to lean on the rail, unable to look at Jaren as she said, "It was hard, seeing you with them today. How much you love them. How much they love you."

Jaren leaned beside her, his arm resting against hers. "Why was that hard?"

"Because—"

Do it, sister.

"Because—"

It's him or us. Them *or us. You can't have it both ways.*

Kiva closed her eyes at the memory. She had made her choice then. And she had to stick with it.

"Because I couldn't help worrying about something happening to you. To your family." She pushed the words out fast, as if doing so would make it easier.

A startled sound of humor left Jaren. "What?"

Committed now, Kiva explained, "I know you're not worried about the rebels at the moment. But—" She made herself look at him with fear in her eyes. "But they abducted me, Jaren. And that means they're still conspiring. What if they've found a way to hurt you?"

Eyebrows rising, Jaren asked, with clear incredulity, "You're worried about the *rebels?*"

His sentiment was genuine, despite having been attacked by rebels himself only two nights earlier.

"If they try to take the throne—" Kiva said, but she was cut off when another startled laugh left him.

"Let me stop you there." He cupped her face, his voice gentling. "You have *absolutely* nothing to worry about, Kiva. I promise you. As much of an annoyance as they are, they'll never have the numbers required to take the kingdom by force. And even if they did, our citizens would never accept a ruler who spilled so much innocent blood."

"But what if they've found another way?" Kiva asked, keeping an anxious furrow on her brow. "What if they know of something lawful that forces you to abdicate and the people to accept them?" Swallowing back bile, she made herself add, "If they have a Corentine heir among them, they'd have a valid claim, wouldn't they?"

"Firstly, that's unconfirmed," Jaren said.

"But you believe it's true," Kiva pressed.

He acknowledged her point and continued, "And secondly, you're right. There is a way they could, theoretically, be willfully accepted by the people."

Kiva's heart stopped in her chest.

"But when I say 'theoretically,'" he went on, "the chance of it happening is so slim—impossible, really—that it's not even worth thinking about."

Barely able to push sound through her lips, Kiva asked, "How can you be sure?"

Jaren was silent for a long minute, just looking at her. She didn't have to try to school her face, dread filling it without any effort at all.

"You really are concerned about this, aren't you?" Jaren finally murmured, his hand shifting around to the back of her neck, his thumb stroking her skin in comfort.

"You have no idea how much," Kiva answered, speaking true.

He gave her one more comforting stroke before trailing his hand down her arm until their fingers tangled once more.

"Come with me," he told her quietly. "I want to show you something."

CHAPTER TWENTY-SIX

Jaren led Kiva to the less familiar western palace, guiding her through the halls until they came to a set of large gilded doors that opened into a library so magnificent that Kiva spent a full minute turning in a circle with her mouth open.

As with the rest of the palace, the library was colored gold and white, but here the walls were made of bookshelves that rose at least three floors high, with spiraling ladders between them and balconies on each level, all looking down to the open floor that was sparse but for the numerous comfortable reading chairs. In the center of it all and stretching up to the muraled ceiling sat a massive, twisting trunk of a pale oak tree, like an ancient guardian watching over the tomes.

"I take it you haven't been in here before?" Jaren said, mirth filling his tone at Kiva's reaction.

She could only shake her head, awed into silence.

Jaren chuckled softly, then led her deeper into the open space, toward the base of the leafless oak tree. "At the risk of you never leaving, there's an entire section on the second floor dedicated to herbal lore and the healing arts. Silverthorn residents often make requests if their own library falls short on a specific subject."

Kiva longed to run straight up the nearest spiraling staircase and bury herself in what could only be the rarest of books, but she shook off her wondrous daze and asked, "Why did you bring me here?"

"To show you this." Jaren stopped before the tree trunk and indicated a small shelf that had been cut into the wood. On it lay a single book, the leather aged, the pages discolored and frail, and yet given how old it was — and *what* it was — it was remarkably well preserved. By magic, no doubt.

"Is this what I think it is?" Kiva whispered reverently as she read the title.

"The Book of the Law," Jaren confirmed, opening the cover and flipping through the ancient pages. His serious eyes locked with Kiva's. "No one other than my mother and the Royal Council knows what I'm about to tell you. The ruling monarch, their chosen heir, and Evalon's supreme governors — that's how it's been since Sarana Vallentis sat on the throne and created the laws which we uphold to this day." He tapped a finger against the book. "My father doesn't even know, nor do Mirry or Cal or Ori or anyone else. Just Mother, the council, and me. I need you to understand what I'm saying."

Kiva understood. He was trusting her. With his life — and with his kingdom.

In a wobbling voice, she said, "Maybe you shouldn't tell me."

Part of her prayed that he wouldn't.

Because that same part feared that whatever he was about to share could spell his doom.

It's him or us. Them *or us. You can't have it both ways.*

Kiva shoved her sister's voice away.

"It's important to me that you feel safe here," Jaren said quietly, "that you're not worried about a future that will never happen. It goes without saying that this is my greatest secret — *Evalon's* greatest secret — but if it's going to help you sleep better at night, then I want you to know it. I trust you, Kiva. You have to know that by now."

Please stop, Kiva wanted to say. *Please don't.*

But she held her tongue as Jaren flipped more pages, before pausing and pointing at the aged ink.

The scrolling calligraphy was written in ancient Evalonian, a language only the most educated of scholars still understood. At the very bottom was an addendum in minuscule print, the lettering so small that Kiva had to squint to make out the individual words.

It was to this addendum that Jaren was pointing as he said, "I told you that there's a way the rebels could, theoretically, take over leadership of the kingdom in a legitimate manner, and the means to do so is written right here."

Kiva's heart sped up to unhealthy levels.

"It's a clause buried in the fine print of our very own laws, one that reveals the only instance in which the citizens of Evalon must yield— peacefully—to a new monarch. Similarly, any current rulers must also surrender to the new leadership without contention."

Kiva wondered if she was about to pass out.

"The clause states that the person or persons who possess the Royal Ternary in its entirety have an automatic right to the throne, above and beyond all blood ties, political powers, and royal lineages," Jaren recited. His brow crinkled in thought. "So really, I suppose it doesn't matter if the rebels have a Corentine heir or not. But since their entire movement is founded on the misguided premise of avenging Torvin for something he deserved in the first place, then I assume they'd flail without one of his descendants to lead them."

Kiva's head was spinning. The Royal Ternary—the words she'd heard the Royal Council speak during their meeting, the same words she'd asked her siblings about, none of them knowing just how secretive the answer might be.

Despite her internal struggle, Kiva ignored what Jaren had said about Torvin in favor of asking the only acceptable question, her voice hardly more than a croak: "What's the Royal Ternary?"

"It's three objects," Jaren answered, flipping through the pages again. "The first is this—" He tapped a finger against the Book of the Law. "The second is the Royal Signet—a golden ring worn by the current ruler of Evalon. My family's crest was fashioned to imitate it, so it's basically a much smaller version of the amulet you're wearing, just without the power to channel magic."

Thinking of the ring she'd seen on Ariana's finger last night—and countless times before—Kiva asked, "Your mother wears it?"

Jaren nodded. "When I inherit the throne, it'll pass to me."

Kiva couldn't meet his eyes. "And the third object?"

Jaren pointed to the new page he'd opened. On it was a drawing of two outstretched hands holding a simple jewel, spherical and without color, like a shining diamond or the purest of crystals.

"The Eye of the Gods," Jaren said. "It's the reason why you don't have to worry about anyone taking the kingdom from us."

Peering at the jewel, Kiva asked, "The Eye of the what?"

"Let's sit," he said, guiding her to the nearest reading lounge. Once comfortable, he answered, "You already know the tale of Torvin and Sarana—or, *one* of the tales. The story you shared in Zalindov is one I've heard before, but it's not the only one. And it's not the one I believe." He shook his head. "That doesn't matter. All the tales start out the same, with them falling in love. Can we agree on that?"

Kiva nodded, curious about the other stories he'd heard, but not enough to interrupt him.

"Legend claims that when they ruled together, some of the ancient gods still lingered in this world, not yet having left to watch over the everworld," Jaren said. "Upon the union of Sarana and Torvin, those gods decided they were no longer needed, believing our people safe and our lands protected by the powerful magic the two rulers possessed. As a parting gift, they bestowed a precious jewel—the Eye of the Gods— upon the newlyweds, a blessing to mark their worthiness as leaders. To this day, it's said that whoever holds the Eye has the gods' approval to rule in their stead."

"You told me the Eye is the reason I don't have to worry," Kiva managed through numb lips. "Nothing you've just said makes me feel any better."

Jaren chuckled. He actually *chuckled.* "Breathe, Kiva," he said, giving her hand a comforting squeeze. "The reason you don't have to worry is because the Eye is almost impossible for anyone to steal. We keep it—"

"Don't tell me," Kiva blurted.

Jaren shook his head indulgently at her, even more amused, and said, "I told you I trust you. And besides, my sharing where it is won't cause any harm. You'd literally have to get through an entire *army* to steal it."

Kiva blinked, not following.

"The Eye travels with the current general of Evalon's armies," Jaren revealed. "Right now, Ashlyn has it, hundreds of miles north of here. Not only does she have powerful wind *and* earth magic protecting it, but any thieves would need a force large enough to overcome our significant military numbers—and therefore, they'd already have a force large enough to conquer Evalon without needing the Ternary at all." He paused, making sure she was paying close attention, as he finished, "The rebels don't have that kind of force. And if they ever came close, we'd take other precautions."

Slowly, the tightness within Kiva began to ease.

"Mirraven and Caramor, on the other hand," Jaren said, his tone conversational but his face hardening, "their alliance *is* a concern, since they *do* have those kinds of numbers, collectively. But even if they knew the true value of the Eye—which they *don't*—they wouldn't care. They're not after a legitimate means to take Evalon. They wouldn't bother with the Royal Ternary—they'd just use their armies to take over." He squeezed her hand again, perhaps feeling the return of her tension. "But that's not going to happen. We're watching the mountain passes closely, and we have all the advantages on our side. They can't beat us. Mirraven, Caramor—and definitely not the rebels. None of them pose a true threat to Evalon, and Royal Ternary or not, they never will."

Kiva didn't know whether to laugh or cry.

Jaren had just told her how to take his throne—and also revealed that it was all but impossible.

Relief and devastation warred within her.

. . . But relief won.

Releasing a long, shaky breath, Kiva said, "So this clause says someone has to have all three objects? Not one or two, but all of them? And that's the *only* way they can be considered true rulers?"

"All three," Jaren confirmed, smiling at whatever he saw on her face. "So you can relax. The Eye is well protected and the Book and the Signet are kept safe here at the palace. The Royal Ternary clause can't be enacted without all three."

"And there's no other way for someone to take power, outside of bloodshed?" Kiva pressed.

Jaren laughed quietly. "Careful, or I'll start to think you're planning to overthrow me yourself."

Kiva forced out her own breathy laugh, aware of how desperate she was sounding. "Sorry," she said. "I just—"

"I understand," he cut in gently. "You're worried. But I hope you now realize you don't have to be."

She did realize that, just as she realized that ten years of her life had been dedicated to a cause that had no chance of succeeding. Even if the rebels one day outmanned the royal armies, the Evalonian people wouldn't abide a bloody transfer of power. Unless the rebels survived the warfare and were then able to steal the Eye from the magic-wielding general—doubtful, if Ashlyn Vallentis was anything like her family—then without the Royal Ternary clause making them stand down, the citizens of Evalon would fight back.

Kiva, however, had a feeling that the rebels might not care about that, especially with Zuleeka as their commander. As their future queen.

Wars aren't won without sacrifice, little sister.

"Come on," Jaren said, breaking into her uneasy thoughts. "While we're here, let me give you a proper tour."

And so Kiva followed the crown prince around the magnificent library, mulling over everything he had shared . . . and having no idea how to feel about it.

When Kiva returned to her room later that night, there was a note waiting on her bed. Her muscles clenched when she recognized her sister's familiar handwriting, the coded words offering an address and a time, after which was a roughly drawn map with clear directions—the latter two hastily added in Torell's penmanship.

Uneasy at the thought of a rebel spy slipping the message into her room, Kiva considered ignoring the summons, especially since she was still upset about the disastrous lunch. But as painful as the betrayal was, she'd already resolved to let it go. If she wanted to have any kind of positive relationship with her sister—which, frustratingly, she still did—then she should at least hear what Zuleeka had to say.

Kiva looked at the address again, noting that it was down at the docks, a reasonable walk away. The meeting time was quickly approaching, so without second-guessing herself, she grabbed a cloak and strapped Naari's dagger beneath her boot before sneaking out.

While Kiva wasn't doing anything wrong in meeting up with her siblings—ignoring who they really were, of course—she decided to be cautious and use the secret iron grate exit, not wanting to risk anyone seeing her leave through the front gates.

Once she was aboveground again, Kiva jogged across the parkland to the luminium-lit city streets. She then ventured northeast, keeping

Tor's map in mind while also relying on her memories from when Caldon had given her a tour of the docks last week.

Located beside the harbor, where the Serin River flooded out to meet the Tetran Sea, the docks were the first port of call for any ships traveling to and from Vallenia. Largely made up of warehouses and other storage buildings, they bustled with activity during the day as crewmen loaded and unloaded vessels of all sizes, and pop-up street markets sold local seafood alongside rare silks, spices, soaps, perfumes, and numerous other goods from across the ocean, all peddled by incessant vendors.

At night, however, the docks were nearly deserted—as Kiva soon discovered upon her arrival. She cursed her siblings for choosing such an isolated meeting point, even if she understood the necessity.

Pulling her cloak tighter, Kiva hurried along the darkened streets until she reached the address she'd been given, finding a small warehouse tucked between two much larger ones. She was just about to search for the entrance when she heard her name called from the claustrophobic alleyway between the buildings, and she squinted into the blackness to see Tor and Zuleeka waving her over.

"Couldn't we have done this in the daytime?" Kiva complained as soon as she reached them, the space so tight that they were nearly standing on top of each other. "You two might have had a decade of learning how to defend yourselves, but I can barely swing a wooden sword. If anyone is murdered tonight, we all know who it'll be."

Tor grinned at her grumbled rant, but Zuleeka's lips didn't so much as twitch.

Kiva looked warily at her sister, noting her uncomfortable expression.

"Thank you for coming," Zuleeka said, shifting from foot to foot and avoiding Kiva's gaze. "I—We—I—" She blew out a frustrated breath and tried again. "I called you here so I could say sorry. For yesterday. For what you learned, but more, for how you learned it. I didn't handle that well. Any of it. Including my behavior during lunch. And I know it's no excuse, but it was just—it was hard to be there, at the palace. With them. I let that cloud my judgment, when I shouldn't have."

A startled breath left Kiva. She hadn't known why she'd been summoned, but she certainly hadn't expected a stammered apology. Especially not one that sounded genuine.

"Zulee has thought long and hard about everything that happened," Tor said, his crossed arms and hard features making it clear that he'd pushed her to do so. "She knows what she did was wrong—not just yesterday, but also not freeing you from Zalindov."

"It was Mother," Zuleeka defended quickly. "She really did tell me you were safer there, especially with your magic. That *we* were safer, too. And I was young, Kiva. Young and scared. So I listened to her. Her reasons made sense—that if you were discovered, we'd all be discovered. It could have ruined everything. But with you in Zalindov and us moving from place to place, if something had happened while you were locked away, no one would have been able to find us. And—" She stopped, as if catching herself.

Kiva had already heard Zuleeka's argument, and despite there being some logic to it, there wasn't enough to justify leaving a child in hell. Regardless, she still pressed, "And what?"

Hesitantly, Zuleeka said, "This will sound awful, but—" She took a breath and admitted in a whisper, "I didn't want to end up at Zalindov, too. The very idea haunted my nightmares."

Kiva closed her eyes, unable to look at her sister. She knew all about Zalindov haunting her nightmares—but she'd also had to *live* in that nightmare. Alone. For ten years.

"I'm sorry," Zuleeka whispered. "I shouldn't have listened to Mother, I know that now. I should have told Tor, and we should have come for you. We failed you. *I* failed you."

Feeling raw, Kiva took a moment to gather her thoughts. She'd lost ten years of her life needlessly, so she wasn't capable of just forgiving Zu-leeka like that had never happened. But her sister had made a good point about how she'd also been young. If their positions had been reversed and Tilda had told Kiva that everyone was safer if Zuleeka remained locked away, wouldn't she have trusted that their mother knew what she was talking about?

Sighing deeply, Kiva said, "Let's just—Let's try to forget about it. As you said yesterday, what's done is done."

Zuleeka looked startled. So did Torell.

"You'd be . . . all right with that?" Zuleeka asked slowly.

"I'm not *all right* with any of this." Kiva's voice rose in the dark alleyway, before she lowered it again to add, "I'm also not *all right* with how you tried to kill Jaren two nights ago, and how you're the reason Naari lost her hand. But I can't change any of those things either, can I? So for my sanity's sake, we need to—"

"Hold on, back up," Torell interrupted, his brow furrowed. To Zu-leeka he asked, "I know about Naari, but what's this about Jaren?"

Zuleeka didn't answer, instead looking at Kiva and saying, "If I'd wanted to kill the prince, he'd be dead. That wasn't my intention. I'd just hoped to rattle him a little. Remind him we're not going anywhere."

Kiva marveled at Zuleeka's overconfidence, but only said, "He knows you're not going anywhere. But he also doesn't see you as a real threat in the grand scheme of things. And with good reason, given what I learned today."

Both of her siblings turned alert, and Kiva scrambled to think of how to downplay her statement, before realizing she didn't have to. The information Jaren had shared couldn't hurt him or his family. Not when one piece of their guaranteed demise was hundreds of miles away and protected not only by magic, but also an entire army.

"What did you learn, Kiva?" Torell asked, morphing from her lov-ing brother into the commanding general of the rebels.

Warring with herself, Kiva debated what to say. On one hand, she was still dismayed that her family would have no swift means to lawfully take the kingdom. But on the other hand . . .

That young man is destined for greatness. He's going to be the best king we've ever seen.

Healer Tura's voice came to Kiva again, the words ringing true. Having witnessed Jaren amongst his people today and seeing how much he cared for them not just in speech, but in actions, Kiva had known.

The kingdom was better off in his hands.

She felt like a traitor to her own family, but try as she might, she couldn't imagine Evalon with Zuleeka as its queen, not even with Tor as its king. And she certainly didn't want to rule it herself, having no idea how to juggle politics and diplomacy. She'd been bored to tears just *listening* to the Royal Council discuss mundane kingdom matters — the idea of having to take part in such conversations made something inside her shrivel up and die.

Jaren, however, had spent a lifetime being groomed for the role, loving every second of it.

He truly was the people's prince.

And so, while Kiva knew she should be more upset, there was no denying the relief she felt knowing that, at least for now, the Vallentis family was safe, their throne secure.

"Kiva?" Tor called when she remained silent for too long. "Did you discover something?"

Licking her lips, she said, "Yes. I did. And you're not going to like it."

An unpleasant feeling twisted inside her as she told her siblings about her visit to the library and her viewing of the Book of the Law, sharing everything she'd learned about the Royal Ternary clause — Jaren's greatest secret, something only he, his mother, and the council knew. And now his blood-sworn enemies, too. Kiva hated betraying his trust, but she consoled herself with the knowledge that no harm would come to him; it was an unactionable secret, one he would never even know she'd shared.

When she finally finished speaking, the only sounds in the alley were a light dripping noise and the distant hiss of a tomcat.

And then Tor cursed loudly, slamming his fist into the wall of the nearest building. *"Gods dammit!"* he cried, punching it again.

Alarmed, Kiva grabbed his arm, wincing at the blood covering his knuckles. She reached for her magic, longing to take away his pain. But then—

Nothing.

Delora's potion—Kiva had forgotten.

She couldn't access her magic while under its effects, not even by choice.

"Calm down, brother," Zuleeka said, placing her hand on his shoulder. "There was never any guarantee Kiva would learn something to help us—this doesn't change our plans."

"Exactly!" Tor yelled, throwing out his arms. *"It doesn't change anything!* We have to keep doing what we've been doing!"

Zuleeka's eyes narrowed. "And what's so wrong with that?"

I'm tired of seeing good people suffer for a cause I'm not even sure I believe in.

Torell's words returned to Kiva, words she instinctively knew Zuleeka wouldn't understand. Jumping in to save him, she quickly said, "It's my fault—you asked me to find a lawful way to take the throne, and I didn't. I'm sorry."

"You did what you could, little sister," Zuleeka said. She was much calmer than Kiva had anticipated, but then again, she had a lot of making up to do from the previous day—the previous *ten years.*

"You're sure, though?" Zuleeka continued. "That it's impossible to steal the Ternary? The Eye sounds like the trickiest part—is it really so well protected?"

"Jaren said it goes wherever the current general goes," Kiva said. "So it's with Ashlyn and the armies—and shielded by her magic, too."

Zuleeka sighed. "Well, it's a blow, but we won't give up. We knew claiming the throne would take time, we just need to be patient."

Kiva snuck a quick look at Torell, finding him staring furiously out into the darkness.

This life isn't one I ever would have chosen for myself.

A lump formed in Kiva's throat at the remembered words, and she pressed into his side, offering comfort in a way that, hopefully, Zuleeka wouldn't question.

Tor exhaled loudly and wrapped an arm around her shoulders, pulling her closer. But then he stilled, his gaze focusing on her neck.

"What's this?" he asked, lifting the golden chain.

"A gift from Jaren," Kiva answered, pulling the amulet out from beneath her clothes. "I had a run-in with his mother last night, and he gave me this afterward to protect me from any future magical attacks."

Both Torell and Zuleeka froze at her words.

"The queen *attacked* you?" Tor exclaimed.

"Are you all right?" Zuleeka asked, her concern warming Kiva so much more than her earlier apology.

Kiva didn't share how close she'd come to drowning in the queen's sitting room—she'd already given them plenty to worry about tonight. "I'm fine," she said. "Jaren used his magic to save me."

"Fire magic against the queen's water magic?" Zuleeka asked, arching an eyebrow. "How did *that* work?"

Kiva quickly covered, "He has wind magic too, remember? He used it to throw Ariana across the room." That wasn't a lie. They just didn't need to know he must have also used his water affinity to counteract Ariana's power.

"He did *what?*" Torell asked, gaping.

"And then he used it again to slam the doors shut behind us, locking her in her rooms," Kiva shared.

"Whoa," Torell said, with clear admiration.

"It was pretty impressive," Kiva admitted. "The things they can all do with their magic . . ." She shook her head in amazement.

"No one should have that much power," Zuleeka said, a dark edge to her voice. But then it lightened as she added, "At least they're all limited in some way. Imagine if we had another Sarana Vallentis among us, with all four elements? Now, *that* would be a concern."

It took every scrap of acting skill within Kiva not to react. She should tell them. They were her family. But—

I trust you, Kiva. You have to know that by now.

Kiva had betrayed Jaren in so many ways—she couldn't betray him in this.

"So this amulet," Tor said, squinting at it in the dark. "It protects you from elemental magic?"

When Kiva nodded, her siblings leaned in for a closer look, with Zuleeka touching each of the colored gems as Kiva explained how it worked.

"You're lucky the prince cares so much for you," Zuleeka mused. "This is some gift."

"Hopefully I'll never need it again," Kiva said.

Tor cocked his head. "I thought you said Jaren gave it to you *after* the attack?"

"He did," Kiva confirmed. "But he also gave it to me in Zalindov —well, technically it was Mirryn who gave it to me—and it saved me from the fire Ordeal. Without it, I would have been turned to ash."

Her brother's face paled, but Zuleeka just continued staring pensively at the amulet until Kiva tucked it back beneath her sweater. Only then did Zuleeka shake off her thoughts and say, "We shouldn't linger here for much longer. But with everything else that happened yesterday, we didn't get to ask—how did you go with Nanna Delora? Your note implied she helped you?"

"You're right about her—she doesn't like us very much," Kiva said. "I'm pretty sure she thought I was there to steal Torvin's dagger—at least until I convinced her otherwise." She turned to her brother and added, "She's using it as her apothecary's blade, just like you guessed."

Tor snorted. "Figures."

"She showed it to you?" Zuleeka asked, stunned. "I thought it was hidden."

"It *is* hidden," Kiva confirmed. "She keeps it in a hollowed black book called *1,001 Pies and Pastries.* And she didn't show it to me in the sense of gloating about it—she used it to make a potion, something to suppress my magic."

"So she *was* able to help?" Torell said, relief filling his features. Zuleeka's, too. "That's great, Mouse."

"It's not permanent," Kiva warned. "She only gave me enough to last until tomorrow. I have to go back to get some more."

"You're seeing Delora again tomorrow?" Zuleeka asked.

Since Kiva had just said that, she only nodded in confirmation.

"I know this is a big ask," Zuleeka said, "but I've been thinking about this since we last talked about it and, well . . ." She took a breath. "Do you think you can try to bring the dagger back with you?"

A short, incredulous laugh left Kiva. "Uh, *no.* If I show even a hint of interest in that blade, Delora will toss me from her cottage."

Probably into the swamp.

With Mr. Chomps.

Kiva shuddered.

"It's just . . ." Zuleeka brushed a strand of dark hair behind her ear. "I told you that the rebels recognize it as a symbol of Torvin's reign, and we all know how powerful symbols are. With Mother now gone"—her words caught slightly—"having it in our possession will help boost their confidence in us as their new leaders. The Corentine Dagger returned to its rightful heirs."

Kiva saw the validity of what Zuleeka was saying, but she still argued, "If Delora refused to give it to Mother, why would she give it to me?"

"She's a cranky old bat who's holding on to that blade out of spite because she hates our bloodline, and yet, for some reason she's helping you," Zuleeka said. "That must mean she likes you, at least a little." She then begged, "It couldn't hurt to ask, could it?"

Kiva thought of Mr. Chomps again and winced. But then she relented, "I can't promise anything, but if Delora's in a good mood, I'll see what I can do."

Zuleeka smiled. "Thank you."

Looking at the brightness radiating from her, Kiva found herself wishing Zuleeka would act like this more often. *This* was the sister she remembered from her childhood, the girl who had feelings and cared about things, not the hardened commander of the rebels. Perhaps there really was hope for them yet.

"We need to go," Torell said, peering in the direction of the water. "The dockworkers change shifts soon, and someone might see us if we wait around too long."

Zuleeka glanced at Kiva. "Do you feel safe getting back to the palace on your own?"

Despite having grumbled earlier about the likelihood of being murdered, Kiva answered, "I'll be fine."

Zuleeka nodded, then informed her, "We'll set up a meeting with the other rebel leaders to talk about our next steps. It might take some time —the camps are scattered all across the kingdom, and this is the kind of conversation we'll need to have in person."

"You have more than one camp?" Kiva asked, surprised.

Zuleeka looked amused. "We've been growing our numbers for years
—you didn't think we'd all fit outside of Oakhollow, did you?"

Kiva felt a sliver of unease, but she was comforted by knowing there
was no plan in motion, no action the rebels could carry out—not yet.

"We'll be in touch again soon," Tor told Kiva. His features were
again stoic, as if he'd returned to his decade of resigned acceptance.

"I'll let you know if I learn anything else in the meantime," Kiva
said, though she wasn't sure she was telling the truth. The lines had
blurred, good and bad no longer seeming so black and white.

"For now, just focus on keeping your cover and suppressing your
magic," Zuleeka said, before quickly adding, "And please do try convincing Delora to hand over the dagger. The value of it . . ." She trailed
off, her longing expression saying more than words.

"I will," Kiva promised.

After quick goodbyes, Zuleeka and Torell took off deeper into the
narrow alleyway, disappearing into the blackness, while Kiva turned
and headed out the same way she'd arrived. Walking swiftly, she'd barely
made it one building along when a cloaked figure stepped out from the
shadows, the large male form causing her pulse to skyrocket.

Without thinking, she reached down and yanked Naari's dagger
from its holster.

But then the figure lowered his hood, revealing the familiar face of
Caldon.

"Gods, you scared me." Kiva forced a laugh and lowered her blade.
"I thought I was in real trouble."

"You *are* in real trouble," Caldon said, his voice as hard as his face.

"I . . . am?" Kiva asked. Outwardly, she made herself remain com-
posed, but on the inside, adrenaline was tearing through her as panic set
in. While she was confident he couldn't have heard anything she and her
siblings had said down in the alley—it was too narrow for them not to

have noticed him slipping in to eavesdrop—he could have easily seen the three of them meeting. And he obviously knew Kiva had snuck out of the palace. Caldon wasn't an idiot—he'd clearly followed her for a reason.

"Let's cut the bull and get straight to it, Sunshine," Caldon said, prowling toward her. "What did your brother and sister want?"

"Zuleeka wanted to apologize for what happened yesterday," Kiva answered quickly, truthfully. A partial truth, at least.

Caldon came to a stop right in front of her. "Let me rephrase." He leaned in, his eyes like cobalt fire as he asked in a lethal voice, "What did your brother and sister—the Viper and the Jackal—want?"

CHAPTER TWENTY-SEVEN

With Caldon's words, the world stopped.

Pure terror flooded Kiva's veins, prompting her to raise her blade again, the reaction automatic. But Caldon moved like lightning, grabbing her wrist and spinning her so her back slammed up against his front, his hand closing over the dagger and pressing it to her throat.

"You seriously thought that was a smart idea?" he growled into her ear.

Kiva's pulse thundered with the knowledge that she'd been discovered, certain she was about to die.

But then Caldon released her.

One second, her life was flashing before her eyes. The next, she was stumbling as he spun her to face him once more.

"A few things worth noting," he said conversationally as he slid Naari's blade into his belt, meeting Kiva's panic-stricken gaze. "The first is that I know exactly who you are, *Kiva Corentine,* and I have almost since the day we met."

Kiva swayed on her feet.

"Captain Veris recognized you during your first Trial," Caldon explained, which Kiva already knew from overhearing Jaren tell the Royal Council. "Before I visited you in the infirmary, he told me about the night you and your father were arrested. *He,* however, only remembers you as Kiva Meridan." Caldon's tone was full of wry disbelief. "You're lucky he wasn't curious enough about the girl who would risk her life for the Rebel Queen to fill in the gaps like I did, scrounging for records of you and your father that eventually led me to the rest of your family. 'Meridan,' my ass." He snorted ruefully.

Everworld help her, the prison records. But—there shouldn't have been anything incriminating in there, and certainly no way to tie Kiva to the rest of her family and their true bloodline. Just how deep had Caldon dug to figure out who she was?

Full body trembles racked her frame, until—

"I just told you I've known for months, so you can stop looking like you're about to piss your pants."

Months.

Caldon had known about her *for months.*

And yet—

He'd still saved her.

He'd still trained her.

He'd still befriended her.

What part of this aren't you understanding? he'd demanded after she'd returned from her grandmother's. *We* care *about you, Kiva.*

All that time, he'd known exactly who she was.

"Why?" she breathed, incapable of anything louder. "Your family means everything to you—why didn't you turn me in, knowing how dangerous I could be to them? To *you?*"

Without hesitating, Caldon said, "Because I was planning to use you."

Kiva jolted.

"We've had trouble getting spies into the rebels' inner circle, and I thought you might be our way in. All I needed was to keep you close and gain your trust. And if that didn't work, I would've blackmailed you—I certainly had enough leverage."

Despite her being the guilty party, Kiva couldn't help feeling hurt by his admission.

"But then I started getting to know you," he went on, "and I realized you weren't the hateful little rebel I'd expected. By the time we left the winter palace, I knew you cared enough about Jaren that you had to be struggling with whatever plans you had. So I decided to wait and see what you'd do—who you'd choose."

You need to choose. It's him or us. Them *or us. You can't have it both ways.*

Kiva pushed her sister's voice away and, through dry lips, asked, "Choose?"

Caldon ignored her contrived uncertainty. "I'll admit, your staged abduction came as a surprise—though I'm guessing we have your sister to thank for that special reunion." He frowned and added, "I still don't know why Mirraven attacked us after I dealt with your rebel friends. That day you drugged me and took off, I *was* genuinely worried that they'd captured you—Mirraven, not the rebels. I knew you were safe from *them*." He rolled his eyes.

"You let me drug you," Kiva wheezed.

"I didn't *let* you drug me," Caldon argued. "I'm still mad at you for that. It's embarrassing—you knocked me out using herbal tea."

"And Torell," Kiva went on, spiraling, "you told me you're attracted to him. If you already knew who he was—"

"Have you *seen* him?" Caldon interrupted. "Corentine or not, any-one with functioning eyes would be attracted to him."

Kiva rubbed her temples, but then she stopped as belated realization hit her. "You didn't tell Jaren."

"Everworld help me, of course that's the only part you care about," Caldon muttered, looking up to the heavens.

"It's not all I care about," Kiva defended. "But it's pretty damn im-portant."

"Why's that?" Caldon asked without mercy. "Because you know how much the truth would break his heart?"

Kiva looked away. "It was never meant to happen like this. Any of it."

"Oh, so you *didn't* intend to make us all love you enough that we wouldn't notice when you stabbed us in the back? That wasn't part of your plan?"

"That's not—I didn't—I haven't—"

But she had. She'd left Zalindov with that very intention, to infiltrate the palace, to get to know the Vallentis family, to find their vulnerabilities, and to use what she discovered against them.

All along, that had been her task.

Her *choice*.

But not anymore.

Kiva was done.

She couldn't hold on to the pain of her last ten years any longer, couldn't justify usurping a kingdom whose heir would willingly give his life to keep his people safe. *That* was the kind of leader Evalon needed.

She finally understood now. Her mother's vengeance was not her own. She could choose to forgive, to let go of old grudges and ancient betrayals and just—

And just be Kiva Meridan.

Her mother's daughter—but her father's, too.

Faran Meridan, the healer who inspired her dreams.

Dreams she could follow, as soon as she let go of her past.

As soon as she let go of Kiva Corentine.

At the revelation, a weight lifted from her shoulders, sudden enough that she staggered on her feet.

"I'm all right," she whispered when Caldon reached out to steady her.

"You were thinking pretty deeply," he said. "What's on your mind?"

Kiva looked up at him, seeing his solemn gaze, recalling everything he'd said, how he'd known about her and kept her secret, giving her the benefit of the doubt. Her most unexpected ally—and her most unanticipated friend.

"I'm sorry," she whispered. "You were right, I *have* been helping my family. But—I stopped. Even tonight, I only told them useless information, something they can't act on, not now. They have to come up with new plans, which will take time. Weeks, months, years, I don't know. All I know is that I—" She swallowed. "I'm done." Quickly, she added, "I still love them; of course I do. But I also love—" She choked on the name, and changed course to say, "I also care for your family. And if I'm honest with myself, I've known for a while now that I can't be a part of anything bad happening to you. Any of you. Not anymore."

A moment passed. Then another. All the while, Kiva looked at the ground, fully aware that she'd just admitted to the highest form of treason. In one move, Caldon could plunge Naari's dagger into her heart, and be justified in his actions. Her life was in his hands.

As it had been, apparently, for months.

The unbearable silence continued, until finally—*finally*—he put her out of her misery.

"That wasn't so hard, was it?"

Caldon's humor-filled tone had Kiva's eyes shooting upward, and then they widened like saucers when he tugged her into his arms for a rough hug.

"You're a pain in my ass, Sunshine," he told her gruffly. "But you sure keep things interesting around here."

Kiva released a half laugh, half sob, and held on to him tightly. "Aren't you angry?"

"Are you kidding me?" he asked, drawing back. "You've been conspiring to bring down my entire family. Our entire *kingdom*. Just because I've known all along doesn't mean I'm not furious." Kiva bit her lip until he relented, "But if anyone can understand how important family is, it's me. And while I think your sister is a nasty piece of work, your brother—"

"Please don't start telling me how attractive he is again."

"*Your brother,*" he repeated, "doesn't really have his heart in it, does he?"

Kiva rocked back, startled. "How do you know that?"

Shrugging, Caldon said, "Despite my performance yesterday, that wasn't the first time I've seen him."

Gaping now, Kiva asked, "You've met him before?"

The prince shook his head. "We didn't meet. Last time my sister came to Vallenia to report on the status of the armies, I left for a while and—" He broke off, frowning. "I know Jaren told you about my tragic past—you basically told me as much when you came to my room the other night, so you can quit the confused act."

Kiva tried to school her face.

"How you've managed to trick everyone for so long is a mystery to me," he murmured incredulously. But then he continued, "When Ashlyn came, I traveled inland and stopped at a village that happened to be the rebels' most recent target. When the local guards grew fed up with their propaganda, things turned violent."

Kiva grimaced and looked out at the water.

"It was a mess," Caldon said. "The townsfolk joined in, some helping the guards, some helping the rebels; men, women, even children, all fighting." His voice changed as he went on, "And then I saw your brother. He was like an avenging god among men, his jackal mask alone making people tremble at the sight of him. But the thing I'll never forget is that he wasn't attacking anyone. He was *protecting* them. All of them. Even the guards."

"What?" Kiva breathed.

"He was careful to make sure no one noticed," Caldon said, "but I was on the roof and had a bird's-eye view, so I saw him sneak behind a building and remove his mask. No longer the Jackal, he began to save the very people his fellow rebels were trying to hurt, knocking out the most dangerous assailants from both sides but never inflicting more harm than that. It was so incredible that I couldn't bring myself to tell anyone about it afterward—or reveal his identity. Your brother has some impressive skills, Sunshine. Like, *seriously* impress—"

"Go back," Kiva interrupted. "Did you say you were on the *roof?*"

He scratched his cheek and looked past her shoulder. "I'm still not sure how I got up there, but I *may* have been drowning my sorrows at the tavern for so long that I could hardly stand up straight, let alone join in the fight." He wrinkled his nose. "Poor timing on my part, but I sure had the best view in town."

At the thought of a drunken, useless Caldon watching the battle while lusting after her rebel-leader brother, Kiva burst out laughing.

"I'm glad *you're* amused," the prince huffed. "I was hungover for three days."

"Sounds like you deserved it," Kiva replied, still snickering.

He made a *harrumph* noise but didn't disagree.

"Anyway," he said, "from what I saw that day, your brother doesn't seem as committed as I'm guessing most people assume."

"He's not," Kiva admitted. "He never chose this life. He's just . . ."

"Trapped," Caldon said, understanding.

"Exactly," Kiva agreed.

The prince released a sigh. "Well, maybe that'll change after to-night. You said their plans have been delayed, right? That might give him the chance to break free somehow."

Given the resignation Kiva had seen come over Torell, she had her doubts. But she also wouldn't give up hope. She'd do everything she could to encourage him to make the same decision she'd made.

The same decision, she realized, that their grandmother had made. And, prior to the events of ten years ago, the same decision their mother had made—and held on to for most of her life.

It wasn't impossible to walk away from the rebels' mission. Hard, but not impossible. *Harder,* of course, when the current Vallentis family had caused so much personal heartache, but again, if Kiva could forgive them, then maybe . . .

"What are you thinking?" Caldon asked, using the tip of his finger to smooth the wrinkle between her brow.

"That you might be right—with a little help, Tor could break free," Kiva said. "He could get his life back, just like I did."

"Forgive me for pointing this out, but you're still a work in progress," Caldon said dryly, indicating the alleyway where she'd met her siblings.

"We're all a work in progress at something," Kiva returned, reminded all over again of how close she'd come to disaster tonight. If someone else had followed her . . . If they'd done the same research as Caldon . . . If Caldon himself had cared less about her or decided she wasn't worth the risk of keeping alive . . .

"You need to stop this," he said, smoothing her forehead again. "Keep frowning, and you'll age thirty years in no time. Maybe forty."

She batted away his hand and deliberately deepened her frown.

"That's lovely," he said. "Real charming."

"Have you always been this annoying?" Kiva asked.

"You bring out the best in me, Sweet Cheeks."

Kiva sent him a deadpan look.

He chuckled, before sobering again. "It's late—we need to get back to the palace. But before we go, I have one last question."

"I thought you already knew everything about me?" Kiva shot back.

"Do you have healing magic?"

The breath left Kiva. But then, slowly, she nodded. "I do. But Zuleeka and Tor don't."

Caldon pulled Naari's blade from his belt, causing Kiva's heart to stutter. But he only waved it and said, "So, if I stabbed myself with this right now—"

"*Don't!*" Kiva cried, lunging for it. Only when it was safely back beneath her leather boot did she realize he hadn't put up a fight and was looking at her with raised eyebrows. She cleared her throat and explained, "I can't use my power right now."

His questioning look only grew, so Kiva gave in and told him the real reason why she'd drugged him, candidly sharing about her magic bursts and her grandmother's suppressant potion. The only thing she left out was that she'd have to return to Blackwater Bog the next day, fearing he'd try to stop her—or worse, insist on accompanying her. She very much doubted Delora would appreciate the royal company.

When she was finished, Caldon stared at her for a long moment, before finally grinning. "Doesn't it feel good to get all that off your chest? No more secrets between us, Sunshine." His face turned serious as he warned, "I mean it. As much as I love you, if I get so much as a *hint* that you've lied to me and you're planning to hurt my family, I'll slit your throat myself. Understood?"

Kiva gulped. That seemed to be answer enough for Caldon, since he slung his arm around her shoulders and began leading her out of the docks, whistling merrily the entire way back to the palace.

CHAPTER TWENTY-EIGHT

The next morning, Kiva awoke to an anxious feeling that she couldn't shake. Part of it, she knew, was from being confronted by Caldon last night, even if he'd given no indication that he planned to reveal her secret. The very thought knotted her stomach, making it difficult to swallow the final mouthful of Delora's potion.

After a strenuous training session, she returned to the palace, her anxiety growing at the sight of so many people flooding the halls. With Mirryn's masquerade only a day away, preparations were in full swing, countless servants, caterers, and entertainers rushing about, enough to keep Kiva firmly on edge, even if she couldn't pinpoint why.

Unable to handle her growing distress, Kiva intended to slip out after her breakfast, not only for some peace and quiet, but also to sneak in her trip to Blackwater Bog. But just as she was preparing to leave, Mirryn fluttered into her room, followed closely by two maidservants wheeling a rack of dresses, and an elderly man with a tape measure around his neck.

"Good, you're here," Mirryn said to Kiva.

"What's, uh, going on?" she asked, eyes wide.

"You need an outfit for tomorrow night," the princess answered, and with no further warning, she began giving orders to the maidservants as the tailor approached Kiva to take her measurements. He then forced her into gown after gown, with both him and Mirryn providing a running—and critical—commentary.

"Too puffy!"

"Needs more sparkle!"

"Not enough bosom!"

"Far too much bosom!"

"Why are there so many ruffles? Less ruffles! *No* ruffles!"

And on it went.

For *hours*.

By the time they finally settled on the perfect dress, it took all of Kiva's remaining patience to keep from screaming when the tailor, Nevard, stated that they now needed to choose a mask.

Ready to pull out Naari's dagger and threaten violence, Kiva turned pleading eyes to Mirryn, only to find the princess looking back at her with clear amusement. She did, however, recognize that Kiva was at her wits' end, and calmly said to Nevard, "Why don't we pick one for her, and send it along later. It can be a surprise."

The tailor looked horrified by the thought, but he bobbed his head. "As you wish, Your Highness."

He and his entourage swiftly packed up, leaving only the gown and a pair of matching slippers before disappearing out the door.

Mirryn, however, remained behind, reaching out to take Kiva's hands.

"I heard you had an . . . incident . . . with Mother the other night," she said. "Are you all right?"

Having not expected this conversation, and certainly not with Mirryn, Kiva haltingly admitted, "It . . . surprised me. She's always been so lovely to me. So *motherly*. The change in behavior was, um, a little shocking." And it had nearly killed her, but Kiva left that part unsaid.

Mirryn nodded solemnly. "I'm not defending her actions, but just so you know, she'd had a bad day. Father nearly fainted when they were celebrating the bridge opening, and it's not public knowledge that he's sick, so Mother feared rumors might start spreading. After they returned and he'd gone to bed, the angeldust helped her take the edge off. She only ever uses it when she's feeling overwhelmed." Quickly, she added, "But again, I'm not defending her. What she did to you—" Mirryn shook her head, then touched the amulet around Kiva's neck. "I'm really glad Jaren gave you this."

Kiva had no idea how to reconcile this new, concerned side of the princess, so she settled on nodding her agreement.

"You should also know, she doesn't remember," Mirryn said. "Mother, I mean. She was asking about you yesterday, wondering where you and Jaren were and wanting to make sure you were all right after reuniting with your family." Mirryn's blue eyes held hers as she went on, "She's come to care for you, Kiva. Very much. Just like we all have. And I know it might be hard for you to believe right now, but when Mother loves, she loves hard. *Especially* those she considers family."

A squeeze of Mirryn's fingers made Kiva realize, with some shock, that she was being included in that statement.

"There isn't anything she wouldn't do for us," the princess went on. "I know she'd bring down entire kingdoms if anything ever happened to Jaren or Ori or me. She wouldn't hesitate to do whatever it took to make sure we were safe. Just as I know the same would be true for you."

Kiva was breathing heavily, unsure why Mirryn was saying all this.

With a final hand squeeze, the princess released her and finished, "I know it's hard, but if you can find it in your heart to forgive her, to remember that it's the drug and not the user . . ." She trailed off, seemingly unable to finish.

But Kiva didn't need her to say more, already aware of how addictions worked, and more familiar with angeldust than she would have liked. Too many of Zalindov's inmates had relied on the drug, especially those who were assigned to the harder work allocations, like the tunnellers and quarriers. But their dependence only caused more problems in the long run, their addictions hard to shake, the withdrawal almost impossible to survive, especially in a prison environment. And the risk of overdose . . . So many of them had chosen a numbing death over a pain-filled life, a decision that had never failed to devastate Kiva, each and every time it happened.

"Anyway," Mirryn said when Kiva remained silent for too long. "That's enough seriousness. I just wanted you to be aware that she has no memory of what happened, and it's best if we keep it that way."

Kiva wondered how much of Jaren's abuse had been kept hidden from the queen, whether she was even aware of what she'd done to him before he'd learned how to protect himself. Kiva was willing to bet Ariana had no idea, just as she was willing to bet that Jaren had taken all of her drug-addled cruelty in order that his siblings might be spared.

I thought she'd stopped, he'd said after his mother's attack. *She told me she'd stopped.*

Would Ariana have stopped for real if she'd known about the damage she'd caused him? Or was she too reliant on the drug to give it up? It was difficult to know for sure—and that was perhaps why her children had kept the truth from her. Kiva wasn't convinced she would have made the same decision, not if someone she loved was being hurt, but nevertheless she felt great compassion for the impossible situation they were in.

"I'll make sure we choose the perfect mask to go with your dress," Mirryn went on, acting as if their heavy conversation had never happened. "You're going to look absolutely stunning—I can't wait to see Jaren's reaction."

Heat flooded Kiva's cheeks, and she quickly deflected, "What about you? Have you chosen your dress?"

"I have," the princess confirmed, but instead of looking pleased, sadness touched her eyes. "It was a gift from my girlfriend, something she gave me before—" Mirryn broke off and looked away, quietly correcting, "*Ex*-girlfriend, now."

"I'm sorry, Mirry," Kiva said softly.

Just as softly, the princess said, "I really thought she was the one, you know?"

There was so much pain in her voice that Kiva nearly hugged her, but she resisted, unsure how it would be received. "Did she ever write back and explain why she wanted to break up?"

The princess nodded and shared, somewhat bitterly, "Her family got involved. They didn't think we were a good match."

Kiva stared. "Don't they know who you are?"

"It's *because* of who I am that they don't approve," Mirryn said. "Apparently they don't want a princess in the family. Go figure." Before Kiva could utter her shocked disbelief, Mirryn went on, her tone forcefully brighter, "There's nothing to be done about it, but at least I *did* get a gorgeous gown to wear to my party. My ex always had such brilliant taste in clothes—wait until you see it, Kiva. Your dress is beautiful, but mine is spectacular."

There was a desperate look in Mirryn's eyes, as if she were begging Kiva not to ask anything else that might make her hurt more. But Kiva had no intention of doing so, not when the princess had shown her a rare kindness that day. Instead, she held her tongue as Mirryn went on to describe her dress, and then eventually bid her farewell.

Releasing an exhausted sigh as soon as she was alone, Kiva checked the time, and was dismayed to see that it was already well past noon. She immediately began panicking about everything she still had to do, before realizing she was fretting over nothing. Her trip out to Blackwater Bog shouldn't take much time—assuming her grandmother didn't have a midweek book club meeting—so she could allow herself a few minutes to relax.

But with Mirryn gone, Kiva's earlier unease began to creep in again. What she really needed, she decided, was some normalcy. Too much of her time lately had been spent with royals; she desperately wanted to see another friendly face, someone who didn't live in a palace.

A plan quickly formed in Kiva's mind: she would seek out Rhessinda at Silverthorn and, if she was free, enjoy a nice lunch with her, after which she would borrow one of the academy's horses and ride to Murkwood Cottage. If all went as intended, she would be gone and back long before nightfall, with no one even knowing she'd left the city.

Pleased with herself, Kiva tucked her amulet beneath her sweater and left her room. Eager to avoid the masquerade chaos, she hurried to the front gates, nearly breaking her neck when she tripped over one of the many gardeners scattering luminium drops along the hedges in preparation for the party.

After an easy walk along the river, Kiva felt considerably more relaxed by the time she reached Silverthorn. Failing to spot Rhessinda in the sanctuary, Kiva entered the largest of the infirmaries, the one for treating illnesses and injuries, and approached the reception area.

"Excuse me," Kiva said to the registrar, a young man with square glasses. "I'm looking for Rhessinda Lorin."

"What's she in for?"

"Pardon?"

"Is she sick? Hurt? Tell me why she's here, and I'll direct you to the correct ward. They'll be able to give you her room number."

Kiva shook her head. "No, she's a healer."

"Oh." The man straightened his glasses. "Sorry, I'm new."

He said nothing else, so Kiva asked, "Can you tell me where to find her?"

Sending her a bland look, he replied, "Do you know how many healers work here?"

He then lowered his head and returned to his work.

Torn between amusement and incredulity at his rudeness, Kiva turned and left the infirmary. Seeing a small group of young healers eating lunch together on the grass, she headed in their direction.

"Sorry to bother you," she said to them, "but can you point me in the direction of Healer Rhessinda?"

Blank stares and head shakes met her question, with one saying, "We're novices. The only healers we know are our teachers."

Sighing, Kiva thanked them, then returned to the path. As she debated her next steps, she passed three older healers, but none were able to offer any insight into her friend's location. She was just about to try the remaining infirmaries when she belatedly remembered what Rhess had said about working the morning shifts — and it was no longer morning.

With her lunch plans foiled, Kiva decided to cut her losses and treat herself regardless, leaving the academy and wandering back down to the river where she indulged in a chocabun — or three — and a serving of roasted vegetables flooded in gravy. Fully satisfied, she returned to Silverthorn and headed to the stables, pleased to be met by the same stableboy as last time.

Smiling at him, Kiva politely requested that he prepare her a mount. He squinted at her clothes, clearly noting that she wasn't wearing a healer's robe — nor was she accompanied by Rhess this time — but he seemed to remember her and, with a shrug, took off into the small barn. Minutes later, he returned leading Bluebell by the reins.

"You have a good memory," Kiva said, handing him a silver coin for his troubles — courtesy of Jaren and his royal coffers.

"She liked you," the boy said shyly. "I thought you'd want to ride her again."

"The feeling is mutual," Kiva said, stroking the mare's dappled neck. "I'll have her back to you in no time."

He didn't seem at all concerned by her plans, turning the silver coin in his fingers and pocketing it with great delight as she mounted and left the academy.

That, Kiva thought as she rode away, had been much too easy. But as she turned north and began her journey to Blackwater Bog, a smile spread across her face, because it was about damned time that something finally went her way.

CHAPTER TWENTY-NINE

The ride to Murkwood Cottage was uneventful, the weather perfect, the road clear, her horse calm, and by the time Kiva dismounted at her grandmother's doorstep, any lingering unease had completely faded away.

It returned in an instant when Delora hobbled out onto the porch, her cane in hand, her weathered face set into a frown.

"You came back."

"You told me to," Kiva said slowly, gauging her grandmother's mood. "It's been three days. Your potion has been working perfectly, thank you. I can't feel my magic at all."

"Hmmph," Delora huffed. "I suppose this is where you try to convince me that you came back for more of it and not for the dagger that made it?"

Kiva eyed the old woman warily. She'd thought they'd made progress the other day, but now she felt like they were back to square one. "I *did* come back for more of it." She hesitated, recalling her promise to Zuleeka, and admitted, "Though, if you're willing, I'd like to talk to you about the dagger while I'm here."

Delora raised her cane and pointed it at Kiva, repeating her actions from their first meeting. "I knew it! You're just like the rest of your rotten family! I bet the she-devil sent you here to do her dirty work, didn't she? *Didn't she?*"

Kiva crossed her arms, looping her horse's reins through the crook of her elbow. In her coldest voice, she said, "If you're talking about my mother, then no. She didn't send me here. Because she's dead."

Without missing a beat, Delora said, "Good riddance!"

Kiva rocked backwards. "That's your daughter you're talking about. How can you say that?"

"Your mama was a poisonous snake, and this world is better off without her," Delora answered heartlessly, without a single fleck of grief in her emerald gaze. "But I wasn't talking about her — I meant your sister. She's been pestering me for years, turning up every few months, trying to get her claws on that blade. Says she only wants to see it, that's all. Bah! What lies. She's as hateful as your mama was. As dangerous, too. I can smell it all over her — don't act like you can't."

It was true that Zuleeka was more resentful than she'd ever been as a child, and certainly demanding, but she had her reasons, Kiva knew. What she *didn't* know was why her sister had lied to her, or at the very least implied that she hadn't seen Delora in years.

Before Kiva could consider a justifiable explanation, her grandmother continued, "I won't give you the dagger, not now, not ever. And I won't give you any more potion either, so you can go on and get out of here."

Kiva paled and took a step forward, nearly slipping on the wet, swampy path. "Please, I don't care about the dagger. Truly — that's between you and Zuleeka. But I need that potion. It's stopping me from —"

"All it's doing is delaying the inevitable," Delora cut in. "I told you it wasn't a permanent solution. You keep using it, and there's no telling what'll happen when you finally let your magic loose. My guess is, you'll become just like your mama, everything good and pure in you turning dark, your power leaving nothing but death and destruction in its wake."

The croaking of frogs and distant birdsong met Kiva's ears, but it was drowned out by the ringing that started, growing louder as she whispered, "What are you talking about? My mother's magic — *my* magic — it's healing magic. It *helps* people. There's nothing dark about it."

Delora scoffed. "Oh, please. Your mama used her magic to kill people. Just like Torvin Corentine did all those centuries ago."

The ringing stopped.

The croaking stopped.

The birdsong stopped.

For one moment, Kiva heard nothing, every noise, every *thought*, eddying from her mind as she stumbled backwards, kept from falling only by bumping into the solid weight of her horse. "What?" she mouthed, unable to infuse any sound into the word.

Delora stared at Kiva through narrowed eyes. "She didn't tell you, did she? That sister of yours?"

Kiva could barely breathe, let alone form a response.

"Let me guess — she said your mama died of a rotting illness? Something there was no cure for?" Delora snorted. "I'll bet she did. But I'll also bet she didn't share that it was Tilda's own magic that rotted her from the inside out. The moment she started using it for evil, it turned on her, spreading like an infection, straight to her very soul. There's a price for that kind of power. To master death, one must be willing to die."

Mother was sick. A rotting illness, something we couldn't find a cure for . . . The infection spread slowly, over years, something none of us realized until it was too late.

At the memory of Zuleeka's words, Kiva swallowed. "I don't understand. Our magic — Corentine magic — it's *good*. It *heals* people."

"And how does it do that?" Delora asked, leaning more heavily on her cane. "You manipulate the human body. Your magic promotes the accelerated regrowth of cells, the banishment of toxins, making changes to blood and tissue and organs and gods know what else. But that manipulation works both ways. With a single thought, you can stop a heart. Burst an artery. Cause a brain bleed. Collapse a lung. The list is endless, the power of life and death in your very hands. Your mother knew that. And ten years ago, when she came out of hiding, she was angry enough to use it that way. She grew in power and strength, reaching a point where she didn't even have to be touching someone to hurt them, to kill them. Last I heard, she could walk by a group of people and wave her hand, snapping all the bones in their necks. Just like that, they were dead."

Bile rose in Kiva's throat. "You're lying."

"Why would I lie? That's my daughter—you think I'm proud of what she became?" Delora looked away, staring out at the brown, murky swamp water. "There is good news, though. That kind of magic takes a toll, which means the damage she caused was limited, even with dedicated practice. That, and she wasn't nearly as strong as Torvin. She could harm a few people at time, but him? He could lay waste to entire villages. Why do you think Sarana Vallentis tried to kill him? Once his power turned corrupt, he was a danger to the entire kingdom. To the entire *world*. Husband or not, she had to put her people first."

"No," Kiva said, raising her hand in a stop motion. "That's not— *That's not*—"

"I'm guessing your mama told you a different history, didn't she? One where poor little Torvin was the victim of mean old Sarana's jealousy?" A mocking sound left Delora. "Of course she did. Make no mistake, girl, Torvin might have started out good and kind and a healer of the people, but he became the worst kind of evil there is. And every Corentine since him, at least the ones born with magic in our blood, have had to decide whether or not to follow in his footsteps." She held Kiva's horrified gaze. "Your mother chose wrong. And you—" She shook her head. "With how long you've repressed your power, I fear it's only a matter of time before you head down the same dark path. There's no potion in the world that can stop you from your own bad choices."

Trembling all over, Kiva didn't know what to say, what to *think*.

If Torvin's magic had corrupted him, if he'd been killing people— *villages*, as Delora had claimed—then Sarana had been justified in trying to end him. But that meant . . . the entire rebel movement was founded on a lie. Their whole purpose was to reclaim the throne of Evalon for its supposedly rightful ruler, someone who had been unfairly exiled and stripped of his title. But if Delora was to be believed, then Torvin had lost all rights to his crown when he'd stopped serving his people, when he'd started *hurting* them.

Kiva felt sick.

She was related to a monster.

And her mother—

Her mother had turned into him.

Unable to stomach such damning revelations, Kiva pushed away from Bluebell and ran straight to the water's edge, vomiting up a foul mix of chocabuns, vegetables, and gravy.

"You're a good little actress, I'll give you that much," Delora called, not moving from her porch.

Kiva wiped her hand across her mouth and staggered back toward her grandmother, tripping over creeping vines and sidestepping a snake that slithered right past her into the swamp. "I didn't know," she rasped. "None of this—*I didn't know.*"

"Well, now you do," Delora said in a no-nonsense voice, indifferent to Kiva's inner turmoil. "And you can consider it a warning. It's what awaits you if you're not careful."

"I would *never*—"

"You can't tell the future, girl," Delora interrupted. "Tilda hid her magic for most of her life, determined never to use it for evil. And then—" Delora snapped her gnarled fingers. "One day she just didn't care anymore. One day she *wanted* to hurt people. You can't tell me with absolute certainty that you'd never do the same."

"But that's the thing—I *can*," Kiva said, strength returning to her voice. She moved closer, stopping at the foot of the porch steps. "I've spent my life helping people, learning to heal them not with magic, but with medicine. My father—" Her voice broke. "My father taught me to love people, to feel what they feel, to care for them, even the worst of them. And I did. For ten years, I helped the worst people in this world. Not once did I consider wanting to harm them. Even those I hated. I just—" She shook her head. "I don't have it in me. I know I don't."

Delora eyed her for a long moment. Kiva held her gaze, unwavering in her self-confidence. She wouldn't become like Torvin, like her mother. She was her own person, and she decided her own path. And while, yes, she'd done awful things in her life, she wasn't like them.

She wasn't a monster.

"I can see you believe that," Delora finally relented. "And I hope you're right, girl, I really do."

Kiva took a step up the porch. "Then will you help me? That potion is all that's keeping my magic in check. If you can give me just a little more—"

Delora's face was set. "I told you, it's not a permanent solution. You need to learn to control your magic. That's the only way you can be sure to use it in the right way, by actively choosing to do so. You can't keep on repressing it—that's just a disaster waiting to happen."

"But—" Kiva flailed, desperate. "You've repressed yours. You told me so when we first met."

"I said nothing of the sort."

"You said you don't take the potion, but you don't practice, either. So there must be *some* way you keep from—"

Delora laughed, a harsh, grating sound. "You really don't know, do you?"

Kiva threw out her arms, wincing when one went straight through a large spiderweb. "Know *what?*"

Delora laughed again, but there was no humor in it. "If she didn't tell you, I'm certainly not going to." She jabbed her cane toward Kiva's horse. "You need to leave. There's nothing for you here."

Turning on her heel, she began hobbling slowly toward her open door.

"Wait!" Kiva cried, causing her grandmother to pause and look back over her shoulder. In a hoarse, defeated voice, she continued, "At least give me the stupid dagger. You clearly have no desire to be associated with our bloodline, and if what you've shared is true, I don't blame you. But Torvin's dagger is important to the rebels, and Zuleeka would like—"

Kiva cut off when Delora threw back her head and howled. "Torvin's dagger? Is that what the she-devil calls it?"

Uncertain now, Kiva said, "She said it's a family heirloom."

"Well, she's not wrong about *that*," Delora said dryly, before laughing all over again. But then she sobered, her voice unyielding as she stated, "I'd rather die than see that dagger in your sister's hands. You can tell her that from me."

And then Delora stepped through her door, slamming it behind her without another word.

Tears sprang to Kiva's eyes, but she didn't let them fall. There was no point—they wouldn't convince her grandmother to make more potion. But that didn't mean Kiva was out of options. She'd seen some of the ingredients on Delora's bench, and she still had a few drops left in her vial, enough to confirm the others by scent alone. She would figure out how to make the damned stuff herself.

Stomping with determination back to her horse, she remounted and tore off along the swampy path. She refused to think about everything Delora had said, their supposed family history too awful for her to dwell on. Right now, her focus had to be on making sure she stayed in control of her magic. Silverthorn would help her—she knew her way to the apothecaries' garden now. All she needed to do was snatch her vial from the palace and then get to work.

Lost in her righteous anger—and trying desperately to suppress her growing despair—Kiva nearly rode straight to the palace stables, having forgotten that her mount belonged to the academy and she still had a cover to maintain. Changing directions, she quickly returned her horse, giving the mare a grateful pat and handing her reins to the stableboy.

"That was quick," he said.

"As promised." Kiva summoned a smile she didn't feel, thanked him for his help, and turned to leave.

She made it back to the palace in record time, intending to duck straight back out again with the vial. But the moment she stepped into her sitting room, she came to a jarring halt at the sight of who awaited her.

The entire Vallentis family, minus Oriel but including the sickly looking king, stood in the room, along with Naari and Captain Veris, all of whom, upon Kiva's entry, turned to her, their tension palpable.

The blood drained from Kiva's face.

Did they know?

Did they know?

But a quick glance at Caldon revealed him offering the slightest of head shakes, indicating her secret was still safe.

She felt little relief, since something was clearly wrong, and she swallowed against her suddenly dry throat to ask, "Has something happened?"

"Where were you today, Kiva?" King Stellan asked. His features were pallid, but his voice was full of steel.

Wondering if they knew she'd snuck out of the city again, Kiva hedged, "I—I went to see my friend at Silverthorn. The healer who came to the palace that night to treat me after—after—"

"It's all right, Kiva, please be at ease," Ariana said, walking over and taking Kiva's hands. Despite her kind words, there was still a strained air about her. But rather than question it, Kiva focused on compartmentalizing her memories of the last time she'd seen the queen — when Ariana had attacked her — in order to keep from ripping her hands away.

"So you've been gone from the palace all day?" Captain Veris asked, watching her closely.

"Just since lunch," Kiva said.

"But you were here before that?" he probed. "This morning?"

Kiva nodded, her stomach flipping when the tension in the room thickened.

"Did you visit the western palace at all? The Royal Library?"

At the captain's question, Kiva looked to Jaren. His face was completely shuttered, causing her more alarm than anything else. "Not since yesterday," she answered slowly. "That was my first time there."

"But you didn't return today?" Veris pressed.

"No, why would I have?" Kiva's forehead crinkled. "What's going on?"

Naari stepped forward and declared, "The Book of the Law was stolen this morning."

The only thing Kiva could hear for a moment was her own pulse in her ears. But then she looked around the room, at all the hard faces — at *Jaren's* hard face — and she gasped, "You think it was me?"

The queen's voice was soothing as she said, "We're just trying to ascertain who might have had access to it. With so many workers here to prepare for tomorrow's masquerade, it's been a challenge tracking everyone down. But since no one could find you . . . Kiva, darling, we just want to hear your side of the story."

"There *is* no story," Kiva exclaimed, pulling her hands away and backing up a step. Turning to Jaren, she asked him directly, "Why would I—"

She broke off suddenly, remembering why Jaren had taken her to the library, why he'd shown her the Book of the Law in the first place.

The Royal Ternary.

The Book was one of three items that could cause his family's ruin.

And last night —

Kiva had told Zuleeka and Torell about it.

She'd told them *everything.*

But she'd also told them that without all three items — one of which was hundreds of miles away — it could do nothing.

Surely they wouldn't have risked stealing it for no reason? Not when doing so would endanger Kiva's life, the coincidence of the timing too glaring to be ignored?

No wonder Jaren was looking at her like that. He had every reason to be suspicious of her. *She* would have been suspicious, had their roles been reversed.

"I didn't do it. I *swear,* I —" Kiva broke off quickly and turned to Naari. "Did you say it happened this morning?"

The guard nodded. "Sometime between ten and noon."

The breath left Kiva in a rush of relief. "I was here," she told them, her words desperate. "Right here, in my room. Trying gowns on. We didn't leave all morning."

"We?" Naari asked.

Kiva turned pleading eyes to Mirryn.

"Silly me, I forgot to mention that, didn't I?" the princess said, her tone more entertained than apologetic. "Kiva was with me and Nevard until lunch." She sent a wink to Jaren. "Just wait until you see what she's wearing tomorrow, brother. You're welcome in advance."

"Mirryn," Ariana said in a stern, incredulous voice, "why didn't you say something?"

"I forgot," the princess repeated, defensive. "I have a lot on my mind lately, Mother."

Immediately, the tension in the room dissolved, replaced by a combination of remorse—directed toward Kiva—with lashings of frustration—directed toward Mirryn.

But Kiva didn't care what anyone else thought aside from Jaren, and she returned her attention to him, only to find that he was moving toward her, his face no longer shuttered, but flooded with emotion.

Barely stopping before he collided with her, he drew her close, whispering into her ear, "I was sure it couldn't be you, but after yesterday, the timing—"

"I understand. I would have questioned it, too," Kiva said, inwardly screaming at her siblings. If they'd had *anything* to do with this, she would never forgive them. It was just pure luck that she had an alibi—from the princess herself no less.

"Well!" Caldon said, clapping his hands. "I'm glad our favorite little criminal didn't steal a priceless Evalonian relic, but we *do* still need to figure out who took it. Are there any other leads?"

Kiva pulled back from Jaren to scowl at Caldon for the felonious title, but he only smirked in response. There was, however, a hint of suspicion lurking in his cobalt gaze, enough that Kiva knew to expect a confrontation later if he found any evidence that she—or her family—had anything to do with the theft.

"We'll go through the list again," Veris said. "With the masquerade being on this side of the river, there weren't too many itinerant workers who had access to the western palace today, but a small number of caterers and entertainers did request tours. We'll question them all again, along with the servants, until we get to the bottom of it."

Kiva knew that if anyone could find the perpetrator, it was Veris, and she again prayed that her siblings had nothing to do with it.

She should have prayed harder.

Or rather, she should have added another name to her prayers, a different name, because just as everyone began to leave, a small, scared voice called out, "I n-need to tell you s-something."

All eyes turned toward Tipp's doorway, the young boy clearly having been eavesdropping. His freckled face was pale, his expression racked by guilt.

"It w-was me. I stole the B-B-Book of the Law."

CHAPTER THIRTY

The next few minutes were some of the longest of Kiva's life as she help-lessly watched Veris, Naari, and the royals interrogate Tipp.

It turned out that while he *had* stolen the Book of the Law, he'd done so unknowingly.

They were still trying to understand what, exactly, had happened.

"Tell us again, buddy," Jaren said, seated on one side of Tipp, with Kiva on the other. She was holding the young boy's hand tightly, his skin clammy, his small body trembling, and it took everything in her not to grab him and run from the room.

"P-Peri asked me to get it, said she wasn't allowed in the library, b-but that I wouldn't get in any trouble."

"Peri?" Jaren asked.

"Perita B-Brown, one of the s-servants," Tipp answered. "She works in the w-western palace k-kitchens. She always slips m-me and Ori sweetcakes whenever we m-manage to sneak away from T-Tutor Edna."

He looked guiltily toward the king and queen, but they had larger concerns than the two mischievous children.

"Did she say why she wanted it?" Jaren asked.

"She s-said Mirry asked for it."

All eyes turned to the princess, whose only reaction was to arch her elegant golden brows.

"Peri was afraid of d-disappointing Mirry," Tipp continued, "but she also d-didn't want to lose her job if anyone s-saw her where she shouldn't be. She knew Ori and I s-spend so much time in the library f-for our studies, so she just — she just asked me to h-help." He looked around the room, his eyes wide with apology. "I didn't know I was d-doing anything wrong. I thought it was for M-Mirry."

"Princess, do you have anything to say about this?" Captain Veris asked her.

She sent him a bland look. "Why would I want to steal something that already belongs to me?"

"Technically, the Book of the Law doesn't belong to us," Caldon said. "It belongs to the people."

Before Mirryn could reply, Jaren interjected, "I know all of the palace staff, but I don't recognize the name Perita Brown."

"I can't recall her, either," Ariana agreed. "It's possible she gave Tipp a fake name."

"Or us," Jaren said.

"*Or* she's not really a servant at all and found a way to sneak in, all so she could steal our precious Book," Mirryn said.

"How long have you known her, Tipp?" Caldon asked.

"Since we first a-arrived here. Two w-weeks."

"So she's been planning this awhile, then, if Mirryn's right," King Stellan stated, rubbing a hand over his weary face. He didn't look as if he'd be standing for much longer. Had things been different, Kiva might have considered trying to heal him once her magic returned, but *that*, she knew, was out of the question.

"I don't know," Jaren said, "something about this doesn't feel right."

"You think?" Caldon said, with clear sarcasm.

Jaren ignored him, returning his attention to Tipp. "Can you describe her for us?"

Sudden nerves hit Kiva, a horrible thought coming to her: what if Peri was *Zuleeka?* What if she'd worn a disguise and acted like a servant to earn Tipp's favor, all so he could steal the Book for her?

But . . . no. There were too many flaws in that plan, not the least of which were that Tipp had met Zuleeka, and Kiva had only shared about the Royal Ternary last night, not two weeks ago.

When Tipp began to describe the servant, Kiva's chest loosened even further, because the middle-aged woman had no features in common with her sister. Veris and Naari paid close attention, asking more pointed questions to glean as many details as possible, before telling the royals they would start searching for her immediately.

The two guards left the room shortly afterward, with the rest of the Vallentis family following in their wake. Jaren lingered the longest, but he too left when Tipp turned to Kiva and clung tightly enough to bruise, the prince recognizing that the young boy needed to be alone with the person who made him feel safest.

Kiva could have kissed Jaren for his understanding, but instead she just sent him a small smile, which deepened in gratitude when he promised to update them as soon as there was any news.

Aware that her plans for the rest of the afternoon had been foiled, Kiva forced her own needs aside and spent the next few hours trying to comfort Tipp, who was inconsolable with guilt.

That guilt only grew when Jaren returned later that night with grim news.

They'd found Perita Brown.

But she was dead.

He didn't say how, but he did share that the Book of the Law hadn't been with her — and they now had no leads. But the Royal Guard would continue their search, Jaren said. They wouldn't give up until the Book was safely returned.

Kiva had her doubts — even without anyone knowing it was part of the Ternary, the ancient text had to be worth a fortune. It was surely long gone by now.

Before leaving for the second time, Jaren crouched down in front of Tipp, looked straight into his tear-swollen eyes, and said, "We don't blame you, kiddo. It was an honest mistake."

Tipp didn't seem to hear Jaren, more distraught than ever by what he thought was his role in Perita's death, unwitting or not.

The young boy started crying all over again, and Jaren shot an alarmed look at Kiva, but she just shook her head, knowing it wasn't his fault.

"Can you help get him to my room?" she asked quietly.

Together, they coaxed Tipp into releasing his death grip on Kiva long enough to be relocated to her bed, where he curled up against her once more, sniffling into her already drenched sweater.

"Can I do anything? Get you anything?" Jaren asked. "Help in any way?"

He was clearly at a loss as to how he might offer comfort, and Kiva could relate. She'd only seen Tipp like this once before, the day his mother had died. That night, she'd held him for hours, and she intended to do the same tonight until he was ready to face the world again.

"We're all right, thanks," Kiva replied. Running her fingers through Tipp's silky red hair, she added, "He just needs a little time."

Jaren nodded, but he still seemed reluctant to leave.

"Go," Kiva encouraged. "I'll take care of him."

"I know you will," Jaren said quietly. And with those confident words, he kissed her brow, gave a shoulder squeeze to Tipp, and left the room.

Kiva barely slept a wink that night, and not just because Tipp took a long time to finally cry himself to sleep. So many worries were crowding her mind, from the royal theft to everything her grandmother had revealed, and then of course her anxiety over not having had the chance to replicate Delora's potion. Come morning, her magic would be back, and gods knew what might happen then.

But it wasn't only fears that kept her awake.

It was also Tipp's nightmares.

More than once, he woke up with a startled cry, clutching at his stomach and gasping about a golden light, before falling straight back to sleep again.

Every time it happened, Kiva's heart stopped, certain he must have remembered what she'd done. But when morning finally arrived and she carefully broached the topic, he only looked at her in puzzlement, having no recollection of any dreams, to her great relief.

No longer crying and clinging to her, Tipp was still subdued as Kiva readied herself for her training with Caldon, and when it was time to leave, he shyly asked if he could come watch.

And so, while Kiva sweated and ached her way through her work-out, Tipp sat at the side of the training yard, as if he couldn't bear to be separated from her. Part of it, she thought, was due to a particularly heart-wrenching moment during the night, when he'd asked if he would be sent back to Zalindov. Feeling his fear as if it were her own, Kiva had promised that wouldn't happen, but she knew for herself how that dread lingered, and if Tipp felt safer when he was near her, then she would let him stay as close as he needed.

That became more of a problem when they returned to their suite after her training ended. Normally Tipp would be heading to tutoring with Oriel, but he showed no signs of leaving, and Kiva was more aware than ever of the empty vial sitting on her dresser.

But then she realized there was no reason why Tipp couldn't go with her to Silverthorn. She didn't have to tell him what the potion did, and he was used to her concocting all kinds of remedies from their years to-gether in Zalindov's infirmary. He might even be able to help.

Decision made, she left him alone long enough to wash and change, after which they both ate a quick breakfast before she informed him that she needed to leave the palace. Panic flooded his face, vanishing only when she said he could come, at which point some of the brightness she was used to flitted back in, his excitement at visiting Silverthorn clear, even muted as it was.

Together they left the palace, the hustle and bustle of the previous day magnified now that the masquerade was mere hours away. Kiva was grateful to be escaping the madness, and she sensed that Tipp was, too, with his spirits lifting further as they walked along the River Road, the empty vial tucked safely in Kiva's pocket. Her magic was back—she could feel it again, humming just beneath her skin—but so far it hadn't caused any problems that morning. And she *certainly* didn't have any nefarious desires to use her power to hurt anyone. Whatever had happened to Torvin, whatever dark footsteps Tilda had followed in, Kiva maintained that she wouldn't succumb to the same temptation. Mostly because, to her, it wasn't a temptation at all.

When they passed through Silverthorn's front gates, Tipp wanted to stop every few steps to look at something new, but Kiva urged him on. Relief filled her when she saw Rhessinda sitting on the familiar bench in the sanctuary, because she realized that if the healer accompanied them on their task, it would lessen the chance of suspicious eyes.

"Who's this?" Rhess asked, smiling at Tipp as they approached.

Kiva thought it was kind of her not to mention that she'd seen Tipp before—the night of the abduction, when he'd been dosed with a moradine tonic and snoring on the queen's couch.

"I'm T-T-Tipp," he said, offering his hand.

"Rhessinda," she said, with a firm shake. Winking, she added, "But friends call me Rhess."

Tipp grinned, the lighthearted expression proving he was quickly bouncing back from the previous night.

"I came looking for you yesterday," Kiva told Rhess. "I forgot you only work mornings."

"Everything all right?" Rhess asked, her ashy brows furrowing.

"I just wanted to see if you were free for lunch," Kiva said, and Rhess's forehead smoothed. "But today . . . I need something else." She pulled the empty vial from her pocket. "I have to make a potion. Can we go back to the apothecaries' garden?"

Rhess sighed loudly and rolled her eyes toward Tipp. "Sounds like Kiva wants to steal from Silverthorn again."

"A-Again?"

"Not steal," Kiva defended. "Just . . . borrow."

"Without permission," Rhess said pointedly.

Kiva crossed her arms, ignoring Tipp's snicker. "Will you help me or not?"

Rhessinda jumped to her feet. "For you, my friend, anything."

And then the healer linked their arms together, one through Kiva's, one through Tipp's, and began frog-marching them dramatically across the sanctuary, eliciting a delighted giggle from the young boy. For that alone, Kiva knew she'd made the right decision in bringing him along. Rhessinda's contagious personality was enough to brighten anyone's day.

Soon arriving at the gardens, Kiva recited the ingredients she'd seen on her grandmother's bench, along with the ones she'd detected by scent, rattling them off to Rhess and Tipp: tilliflower, silverwheat, garrow, mirkmoss, tumumin, and hogweed. They then consulted the map before traipsing through the numerous rows collecting the desired samples.

The only hiccup came when they realized that the mirkmoss was located inside the greenhouse, until Rhessinda pointed out that there might also be a workspace inside where Kiva could make her potion.

Her lack of certainty didn't fill Kiva with confidence—nor did her lack of a key, though she surprised them with her impressive lock-picking skills—but once they were inside, all of Kiva's reservations fled.

The greenhouse wasn't large, but it was bursting with rare plants, herbs, berries, and flowers the likes of which Kiva had only ever heard about in wondrous tones from her father. If she hadn't been so desperate to make her potion, she would have lingered for hours, breathing in the earthy, fresh scents and basking in the humidity of the air.

"It smells f-funny in here," Tipp said, wrinkling his nose.

"That's called nature," Rhess said, wrinkling hers, too.

Hiding a smile, Kiva hunted down the mirkmoss before moving to the wooden workbench at the back of the room. There she found an assortment of apothecary tools, including blades, chopping boards, and vials large enough to hold much more than the three stingy mouthfuls Delora had provided her.

"How can we help?" Rhess asked, wiping brown sap from her white robes.

Handing the empty vial over, Kiva said, "I need to replicate this. I think I've identified all the ingredients, but I'm not sure about the quantities."

When Tipp held out his hand, Rhess handed the vial to him and admitted, "I'm not great at making complicated potions, but I'm pretty handy with a blade." She indicated the chopping boards. "I can prepare anything you need."

Kiva had hoped Rhess might be able to offer more help, but she'd also known replicating the potion would be tricky. She'd just have to follow her healing intuition from years of having to scrape together life-saving treatments using limited resources. If she could do that, she could do this.

Resolved, Kiva laid out her ingredients, carefully considering what she knew of each, before giving instructions to Rhess and Tipp, with them slicing as directed. All too soon Kiva was combining the mixture and grinding everything together, then waiting for the garrow and mirk-moss to begin weeping, thinning the solution into a liquid.

"Is that h-how it's meant to look?" Tipp asked when Kiva poured the potion into a clean vial.

"I think so," Kiva said. She'd done everything she could to reproduce it perfectly, and she was certain that it looked and smelled the same as Delora's. All that was left was to taste it and see. "Here goes."

Tipping the vial to her lips, Kiva downed a mouthful, a thrill of pride hitting her when she realized that it tasted exactly the same as what she'd been ingesting for the last three days.

And yet, nothing happened.

Her magic didn't vanish—it didn't even *fade.* It was still there, whispering just beneath her skin, waiting to be released.

"Did it w-work?"

Kiva shook her head, disappointment—and fear—filling her.

"What was it supposed to do?" Rhess asked, eyeing Kiva closely.

Kiva just shook her head again and, in a hoarse voice, said, "It doesn't matter. I'll just—I'll have to figure something else out."

She'd been so certain—*so certain*—that she'd recreated the potion, enough that she knew there was no point in trying again with different measurements, because the taste, smell, and texture were all perfect.

Which meant, there was something missing.

A secret ingredient, most likely. Perhaps more than one, undetectable to taste, sight, and smell.

There were too many things it could be, a world of options, and while Kiva wasn't someone who gave up easily, she knew it could take *years* of trial and error to figure it out.

Anger welled in her toward her grandmother, but before it could turn into full-blown fury, she stifled it, knowing it served no purpose. Delora had encouraged her to learn control, so that was what Kiva would have to do. She'd already managed to repress her magic for a decade —surely she could figure out how to use it safely now. Especially since it was clear she had no other choice.

"You look like you could use a chocabun," Rhessinda commented, still watching Kiva carefully, and therefore seeing all the emotions play out across her face.

Having vomited up yesterday's chocabuns, Kiva felt queasy at the thought, but Tipp jumped in and asked, "What's a ch-chocabun?"

Rhess made a melodramatic gasping sound. "We need to rectify this situation *immediately*."

And just like that, Rhess was leading Kiva and Tipp from the greenhouse and guiding them away from the gardens—and from any hope Kiva had for a potion. She'd known it would be difficult, but still . . .

Her disappointment was hard to shake.

Her fear, even harder.

But she buried them both, knowing neither would help.

She couldn't, however, keep from mulling over why the potion hadn't worked, before considering ways in which she might gain control of her magic, perhaps training it like Caldon was training her body. All of this and more flitted through her mind as she followed the chattering Rhessinda and Tipp out of the academy and down toward the river.

Lost in her thoughts, Kiva didn't even see their attackers before Tipp's cry and Rhess's shout met her ears. An automatic instinct had her yanking Naari's dagger from her boot, but it was knocked out of her hand as a cloth slammed over her mouth, its pungent, unfamiliar fumes causing everything to turn black in an instant.

CHAPTER THIRTY-ONE

Kiva was going to kill her sister.

That was her first thought when she began to rouse.

Her second thought was that she was going to be sick, the lingering scent of whatever had knocked her out remaining like a bad aftertaste. No matter how much fresh air she gulped in, it refused to fade entirely.

But when she opened her eyes, coughing and gagging and struggling against the ropes tying her hands behind her back, one look at where she was had her trying hard to ignore her rebelling stomach.

She'd smelled it in the air, the sea salt and brine, the distinctly *fishy* smell, combined with musty old wood and faint traces of wine and spice, but it was only as she glanced around the building she'd been dragged into that she realized she was inside a warehouse at the docks.

The space around her was piled high with leaking barrels and bulging sacks. Ceramic jars lined the shelves, wooden crates were stacked precariously on top of each other, and only the smallest of slitted windows at the top of the lofty walls let in any hint of sunlight. The floor was largely empty, the stored items arranged in neat piles closer to the walls, but the room was bursting with enough goods to hide Kiva's line of sight to the door, indicating that she'd been carried deep into the warehouse. Even so, escape wasn't on her mind. Not when she assumed this was her sister's sick attempt at getting her attention again, the staged abduction too similar to her first to be a coincidence.

Only, this time Kiva wasn't alone.

Lying on the ground beside her were both Tipp and Rhessinda, their hands also bound behind their backs. The young boy was bleeding from a head wound—causing Kiva's pulse to skittle with alarm—and the healer was bloodied and bruised, though she was slowly returning to consciousness, pulling herself up into a seated position and looking around with a grim expression.

"I can explain," Kiva blurted when Rhess's eyes came to her.

"Are you hurt?" the healer asked.

"I'm fine," Kiva answered. "But I need to tell you —"

Before she could apologize for their predicament, two of the largest men she'd ever seen walked out from behind a row of stacked boxes, one covered in tattoos, the other pale as milk.

"Which one of you is Kiva?" the tattooed man asked.

His strong accent made Kiva still, her mind clearing as the pungent drugs left her system, enough for her to remember that, according to Caldon, her sister hadn't been the only one to try and abduct her nearly a fortnight ago.

"I am," Rhessinda answered.

Kiva gaped at her and quickly said, "No, *I* am."

Rhessinda shot her a look and hissed under her breath. "Shut up, and let me handle this."

The words startled Kiva into silence. Looking at Rhess, there was no trace of the fun, friendly healer whom Kiva had come to know and adore. In her place was someone new, someone different, her face hard and her eyes staring at the two men as if her gaze alone could incinerate them.

"You put up quite the fight, dollface," the pale man said to Rhessinda, his voice also thickly accented. He pointed to a long scrape down his forearm, then a deep scratch across his cheek.

"Loosen these ropes, and we can go for round two," Rhess said sweetly. There was no fear in her voice, as if she was *eager* to fight him.

Something wasn't right here. Something Kiva didn't understand. Something she —

The pale man slashed his equally pale eyes to Kiva, cutting off her train of thought. "You're here for two reasons, girlie, one of which is to remind your sister that our king is growing impatient. The Rebel Queen might be dead, but Navok still expects her side of the bargain to be fulfilled. Zuleeka Corentine has a debt to pay on her mother's behalf. On *your* mother's behalf. Make sure she knows that debt is overdue."

Kiva felt the blood drain from her face, her sister's words from Oakhollow returning with a vengeance: *King Navok was more than happy to make a deal with the Rebel Queen.*

Everworld help them, what had their mother *done?*

But Kiva didn't have time to dwell on it, not when she now had confirmation that Zuleeka wasn't behind this kidnapping. And perhaps worse, the burly man had just revealed exactly who Kiva was — and who her family was — to Rhessinda.

Dread flooded her, but when she turned to the healer with a denial on her lips, Rhessinda didn't seem the slightest bit alarmed.

Or surprised.

"Gods," Kiva rasped out as realization hit her, "are you —"

"The second reason you're here should be obvious," the tattooed man interrupted loudly, kicking her boot. It didn't hurt, but it did make her scramble backwards until she hit a wooden crate. "You're the bait."

"Last time some of our people tried to take you, they weren't prepared, but today things are different," the pale man said with a dark grin. "Even so, it could be a while before your handsome prince discovers you're missing, so if you want to keep that face pretty for him, you'll hold your tongue. Once he and his guards arrive, we'll have our own party. It won't be a masquerade, but it'll be just as unforgettable."

You're just very tasty bait for a much larger fish.

Caldon had been right all along, Kiva realized. King Navok had sent his people to capture her after the River Festival, for this very same purpose — to lure the crown prince. They knew how much she meant to Jaren; they knew he'd come for her.

Caramor and Mirraven are frothing at the bit to launch an invasion, waiting for the slightest hint of weakness.

Kiva was Jaren's weakness.

The pale man's grin widened as he saw understanding flood her face. "Mirraven has big plans for Evalon," he declared. "Today we'll be offering a taste of what's to come."

Kiva shut her eyes as if it would help block out the words.

She should have kept them open.

Because if she had, she would have seen the hand reaching for her face, the approach of the pungent cloth that slammed over her mouth again, right before the tattooed man said, "This'll help pass the time. Sweet dreams, girlie."

"Wake *up*, Kiva!"

A hand was tapping Kiva's face, and she groaned, wanting to shove it away, but her arms were still bound behind her.

"Good. Now open your eyes."

Kiva groaned again, recognizing Rhessinda's insistent voice pulling her from her unnatural sleep. A renewed surge of queasiness had her fighting the urge to vomit all over again.

Coughing and gagging once more, Kiva opened her eyes to find she was still in the warehouse, but the sunlight filtering through the windows was much weaker than before, the shadows across the ground longer, indicating it was now late afternoon. Combined with her time spent at Silverthorn, Kiva had been gone for hours, but with the plans for the masquerade in full swing, it was entirely possible that no one yet knew she was missing. That *Jaren* didn't yet know she was missing.

Casting her gaze to one side, she saw that Tipp was still unconscious, but in a different position, as if he'd woken and fallen back under again. On her other side, Rhessinda was kneeling next to her, the healer's wrists bloodied after having torn her way out of her bindings. She immediately shifted to start working Kiva free of her own ropes.

"Who are you?" Kiva mumbled, her numb fingers tingling painfully as Rhess plucked at her wrists. Despite being knocked out again, she hadn't forgotten what had happened with the burly men, nor Rhess's reaction — or lack thereof — when learning about her family.

"You know who I am. I'm Rhessinda Lorin."

"I didn't ask your name," Kiva said. "Who *are* you?"

This time, Rhess didn't try to avoid the question. "I'm Torell's second."

Kiva's mind blanked. "You're *what?*"

"His second," Rhess repeated. "As in, second in command. Of the rebel forces."

"I know what second means," Kiva hissed, struggling to process this news. "But — But you're a healer! A *Silverthorn* healer!"

Rhess shook her head. "That was just my cover. Tor wanted you to have someone nearby in case something happened, and since we knew you'd be tempted by the healing academy, it made sense to send me in undercover. My parents were healers, like I told you, and I sometimes help the rebel medics, so I had the best chance of maintaining the guise." She paused. "After Zuleeka's abduction, it was simple enough for me to steal some robes and intercept the message from the palace. Dressed like that, I only had to show the royal summons to the guards and they let me right through the gates. It was all too easy to get to you, cementing a position in your life almost as soon as we learned that you'd arrived in the city."

Kiva thought back over every interaction she'd had with Rhessinda, wondering why she'd never suspected anything to be amiss. Even yesterday, when no one at Silverthorn had heard of her. Hell, even last week, the Matron Healer herself hadn't recognized Rhess's name. And—

I'm here every day for the morning shift.

Whenever Kiva had found Rhess, she'd been *waiting* for her. Just sitting on that same bench in the sanctuary, a coincidence Kiva had never bothered to consider, always too happy to have found her friend to question why she wasn't *working*. Never mind how she'd conveniently offered up herself as a tour guide to Oakhollow, and—*gods*—she'd even *seen* the magic burst out of Kiva and had said nothing.

Because she'd already *known*.

"Was any of it real?" Kiva asked hoarsely.

The healer—*not* a healer, Kiva reminded herself—paused her tugging, shifting to meet Kiva's eyes.

"Everything between us was real," she said solemnly. "Please don't doubt that."

"You've lied to me about who you are, from day one," Kiva said, anger rising in her.

The look Rhess sent her spoke volumes. "You can hardly talk."

Kiva's anger dampened, but she held on to as much as she could, saying, "That's different. You knew who I was all along."

"But you still lied to me that whole time," Rhess argued, her attention returning to Kiva's ropes. "So why don't we call it even, and instead of fighting each other, focus on getting out of here?"

Any lingering anger fled from Kiva. Rhess was right—they'd both lied to each other, and they were both in this mess together. They could work out their differences later, once they were safe.

"Those were King Navok's men, weren't they?" Kiva asked, already knowing the answer, but showing Rhess she was willing to let everything else go, at least for the moment. "They're after Jaren?"

"So it seems," Rhess answered. "They said a few things after knocking you out again—they spoke in Mirravish, thinking I wouldn't understand, but the village I grew up in was close enough to the border that I was raised bilingual." As an aside, she said, "That's where I met your brother, by the way. He saved me from those mercenaries who attacked my village five years ago. He's been my best friend ever since."

Kiva remembered what Rhess had shared about her tragic past, and how she'd been adopted by a new family.

She'd been talking about the rebels all along.

Frustrated anew at missing all the signs, Kiva forced herself to stay on topic. "What did the men say?"

"They want to make a swap," Rhess answered. "Prince Deverick—Jaren—for us. They think he'll go for it, especially with you here."

"We need to escape before he does something stupid," Kiva said, stating the obvious.

"I'm working on it," Rhess said, continuing to pluck at the ropes.

Thinking about everything else the men had said, Kiva asked, "Do you know what bargain they were talking about? The debt they said is overdue?"

"*That* was particularly worrying, I'll admit," Rhess said. "I have no idea what they meant by it, but I don't have a good feeling."

"Are you *sure* you don't know anything?" Kiva pressed, shifting her hands. The bonds were loosening, but she was nowhere near free yet. "You're a rebel. And Tor's second, or best friend, or—whatever."

"He tells me everything," Rhess said, doing something to the ropes that had Kiva wincing. "If he knew about some deal your mother made, I'd know."

"I'm pretty sure Zuleeka knows," Kiva said, recalling her sister's veiled words again, and the way the Mirraven men had said her name so boldly.

Rhessinda's voice changed to one of displeasure. "How shocking."

Kiva couldn't keep from asking, "You and my sister . . . ?"

"My allegiance is to Tor," Rhess declared firmly. "I don't give a damn about the rebel cause, but I'd give my life for him. I owe him that much after everything he's done for me. So where he goes, I go. And if that means I have to put up with your scheming snake of a sister, then so be it." Pulling away from Kiva's ropes again, she quickly said, "Maybe don't mention that last part to her."

Kiva hid a smile. "My sister and I aren't on the greatest of terms, either." She thought about what Delora had said, how Zuleeka had kept the truth of their mother's dark magic hidden, and their tainted family history. But then she remembered how Zuleeka had apologized for her behavior, how she was trying to mend their relationship, as she'd promised she would. Quietly, Kiva added, "But we're working on it."

"Good luck with that," Rhess muttered. "Just don't forget that vipers have fangs."

"You really don't like her, do you?"

Rhess sighed and gave a particularly vicious tug to Kiva's ropes, after which came the sound of threads snapping. Still, Kiva wasn't yet free. "I'm sorry, I know she's your sister. Tor and I made an agreement long ago not to talk about her. He's very committed to his family, no matter what choices they make."

They.

"If you've been with them for five years, does that mean you knew my mother?"

Rhess said nothing, before clearing her throat and replying, "I did."

Those two words were loaded with feeling, very little of which was good.

"I didn't know her well," Rhess went on. "Tilda was very . . . fixated. On her goals. By the time I joined the rebels, she wasn't around much, leaving the camp often with Zuleeka. Tor was miserable. He felt like he'd lost both his sister and his mother, but he channeled that into his training, growing stronger and more skilled, and making the rebels fall in love with him in the process. I think that, without him as their general, they'd crumble under Zuleeka's leadership. She's the cunning, he's the heart."

Another snap of ropes, and Kiva could wiggle her hands more.

"Nearly done," Rhess said.

Determining to think about her messed-up family later, Kiva said, "Once I'm free, we'll have to hurry." She looked toward Tipp. "Has he regained consciousness?"

"For a few minutes. He knew his name, remembered what happened, asked about you. But then he passed out again."

Relief swept over Kiva at hearing he'd been lucid enough to talk. "We need to get him away from here and properly looked at. Any ideas for how we avoid our abductors on the way out?"

"We'll just have to wing it," Rhess said. "Tor will know something is wrong by now, so he should be looking for us. I was meant to meet him just after lunch, and that was hours ago."

"Tor's in the city?"

"Him and Zuleeka," Rhess said. "For the party."

In the turmoil of everything else, Kiva had forgotten that Mirryn had invited her siblings to the masquerade, and she cursed inwardly at her unending nightmare of a day.

"If we can get out of here, we can find him and—" Rhess cut off with a triumphant sound, and an instant later, the ropes around Kiva's hands were gone.

"Thanks," she said, grimacing as she rubbed feeling back into her fingers.

"You carry Tipp," Rhess instructed. "I'll need my hands free in case we have to fight our way—"

She stopped abruptly at the sound of heavy footsteps approaching, her wide eyes telling Kiva to return her arms around her back and act as if she were still bound.

"Oh, look, lover girl is awake," the tattooed man said after reappearing from behind the same stack of crates with his pale companion. "No word from your prince, yet. We're having trouble getting our messages through with how busy the palace is. You better get comfortable, girlie, because—"

Whatever he'd been about to say was interrupted when Rhess launched herself at him, barreling the full weight of her body directly into his gut. He doubled over and snatched for her, but she pulled back quickly, his sword in her hands and slicing through the air.

She was fast, but his pale companion intercepted her blade with his own, returning with a thrust that barely missed slashing open her throat.

Despite having next to no training, Kiva couldn't let Rhess take on the two massive men alone, so she scrambled to her feet. She'd barely made it three steps before Torell came flying out from behind the crates, his Jackal mask on and a sword in each hand, shouting, *"Stay there!"* to Kiva as he dived straight into the melee.

The clash of blades rang in Kiva's ears as Rhess and Tor faced off against the Mirravens, the sound drawing more men and women, all of them wearing the same gray fighting leathers as their abductors.

Kiva lunged for Tipp, dragging him as far away as she could, stopping only when they reached a cluster of wooden barrels pushed into the corner of the warehouse, where she hovered protectively over him, watching the battle unfold.

Tor and Rhess were outnumbered—by a lot.

And yet they were holding their own, fighting back to back, their swords blurring in the air, bodies falling in their wake.

They'd done this before.

It was clear in the synchronized power of their attacks, in the way they covered each other's vulnerable sides and yelled instructions to each other— *"Duck!" "To your left!" "On your right!" "Jump!"*

Kiva watched in awe as their enemies continued to fall. Her confidence grew with every slain body, but she still remained on edge, fearing the two rebels, no matter how good, couldn't keep up their defense against such an unrelenting force.

But then the Mirravens started to thin, with more of them on the ground than were standing, many groaning, many more still. Rhess and Tor were moving slower now, numerous cuts and slashes over them both, but still, they fought on.

Until, suddenly, there was no one left to fight.

Their chests heaving, Tor and Rhess stood in place for one long moment, staring at the mess around them. Rhess shook herself out of it first, moving toward where Kiva and Tipp remained in the corner. Kiva thought she might have heard the slightest of moans from the young boy then, as if he were waking, but just as she turned to him, something caught her eye.

The tattooed man had faked his defeat.

He rose silently behind Tor, unnoticed by her brother or Rhess, both of them looking in Kiva's direction.

"TOR!" she screamed. *"BEHIND YOU!"*

Tor whirled too late to mount a defense, the Mirraven already upon him.

But then Zuleeka was there in her Viper mask, appearing from behind the crates and slamming into the burly man just as he thrust his blade toward Torell. The three of them were locked together, their bodies so close that it looked as if they were embracing. A loud gasp of pain met Kiva's ears and the tattooed man sank to his knees, before he collapsed entirely, with Tor and Zuleeka standing above him.

For a moment, no one moved.

And then Tor was falling.

"Torell!" Rhess cried, reaching him just in time to stop him from slamming onto the hard ground.

Zuleeka was staring at their brother in horror.

As was Kiva.

Because the Mirraven's blade was lodged in Tor's chest.

For one terrible second, Kiva couldn't move, couldn't *think*, but then Rhess looked to her and screamed, *"HELP HIM!"*

And Kiva remembered.

She *could* help him—she could *heal* him.

Just like she'd healed Tipp.

Sprinting over to them, Kiva battled back a wave of fear and forced herself to remain calm.

"K-Kiva," Tor said, his emerald eyes clouded with pain beneath his mask.

"Everything's going to be fine," she said, using her most soothing healer's voice. "But this—" She reached shakily for the hilt of the sword. "This is going to hurt a little. Just a bit of a pinch."

With no further warning, she ripped the blade from his chest.

Tor's body buckled, his mouth opening in a soundless, agonized scream, and then his eyes rolled into the back of his head.

"Tor? *Tor!*" Rhess yelled. "Wake up! Kiva, *wake him up!*"

"He's better off unconscious," Kiva said, her hands covering the blood spurting from his wound. "Dammit, I think the blade nicked an artery."

"You have to help him," Rhess begged, her voice catching. "Kiva— *please.*"

In the back of her mind, Kiva marveled that the other girl had slain numerous bodies and was coated in bits of each of them, and yet it was the blood pouring from Torell that was her undoing. He was her best friend, she'd said. Kiva couldn't help wondering if perhaps he was more than that.

"Hold it together, Rhess," she said quietly. "And give me some space."

Throughout all of this, Zuleeka continued to look down at them in muted dread, but Kiva didn't have time to coddle her sister. Instead, she closed her eyes and reached for her magic. Her grandmother was right — she should have spent time learning how to use it, rather than stuffing it away and relying on it in desperate times only. But hindsight wouldn't help her right now, not when her brother's lifeblood was gushing through her fingertips.

"Please," Kiva whispered, having no idea what she was doing but urging her magic to come forth. *"Please."*

And then she felt it. The tingling in her fingers, the burning in her hands, the rush of power leaving her as long-buried intuition kicked in, directing the magic to heal the fatal wound. She opened her eyes to see the familiar golden light flooding into Torell, his blood flowing less and less until it stopped completely, his skin sealing shut. His face was pale, his lips nearly blue, the amount of blood he'd lost concerning but not catastrophic. He would recover, Kiva knew, as her magic began to withdraw, the golden light fading. He would live.

A sob left her, and she wasn't alone in her relief, with Rhess clutching desperately at Torell.

"Is he—"

"He's fine," Kiva said weakly, raising a hand to her suddenly dizzy head. "He just needs to sleep it off."

As did Kiva. She'd felt equally exhausted after healing Tipp, but she'd been in the middle of a prison riot at the time and hadn't had the luxury of taking a nap.

Unfortunately, she wasn't in the position to do so now, either, so she pushed past her lightheadedness and raised her eyes to her sister, wanting to reassure Zuleeka that Tor would be all right.

But Zuleeka wasn't looking at Kiva. Her eyes were focused on the corner of the warehouse.

With a sick feeling, Kiva turned slowly to follow her sister's gaze, already knowing what she would find.

Tipp was awake.

And judging by the look on his face, he'd seen everything.

CHAPTER THIRTY-TWO

Leaving the unconscious Torell in Rhess's hands, Kiva approached Tipp, keeping her movements slow.

"You j-just—you just *healed* him," he breathed, his blue eyes wide, his face white but for the streak of blood coming from his temple. "You w-were *glowing*. Y-You have *magic*."

"Not just any magic," Zuleeka said, having followed Kiva. She removed her Viper mask and declared, "Corentine magic."

Kiva looked at her sister in horror.

"It's not like he won't figure it out," Zuleeka defended.

With his hands still tied behind his back, Tipp rose on wobbly legs, his lips trembling as the betrayal hit him.

"Tipp," Kiva whispered.

"You're a *C-Corentine?*" he rasped. "As in T-Torvin Corentine? And —And *T-Tilda* Corentine?"

Still whispering, Kiva said, "Tilda was my mother."

Tipp gaped. "The Rebel Queen w-was your *mother?* But—what d-does that *m-mean?*"

"It means the whole time you thought she was cozying up to your friends at the palace, she was actually plotting their ruin."

"*Zuleeka,*" Kiva snapped. "*Shut up!*" She then hurried to tell Tipp, "It's not like that. That's not the whole story."

But the damage was done. There was no taking back what Tipp had seen, what Zuleeka had said, and Kiva didn't have the first clue how to prove she wasn't the villain.

Because that was certainly how Tipp was looking at her, his eyes filling with tears.

"I can explain," Kiva said, her voice—and her heart—breaking at the look on his face.

"Unfortunately, we don't have time for that right now," Zuleeka said. And in one quick move, she lunged forward and slammed the hilt of her sword against the back of Tipp's head.

Kiva caught him before he could crumple to the ground, her gaze furious as she looked at her sister and shrieked, *"What the hell?"*

"He's a liability," Zuleeka said unapologetically.

"He's an eleven-year-old boy!"

"Exactly," Zuleeka said. "Until we figure out what to do with him, he'll need to stay with us. With the rebels. We can't have him telling your royal friends about you, can we?"

Kiva was so enraged that she couldn't form words, and instead she reached for her magic again, wanting to heal Tipp's concussion—his *second* concussion—but Zuleeka touched her arm, breaking her focus.

"Don't," she said. "It'll be easier to move him like this."

"He's not going anywhere with you," Kiva spat.

"*Think*, Kiva," Zuleeka said, losing patience. "If he goes back to the palace, do you really believe he'll keep his mouth shut? You trust him that much?"

"*Yes,*" Kiva said without hesitating.

But then she recalled the way he'd looked at her, and the doubts began to creep in.

Caldon had discovered her identity before he'd ever really known her, so he'd never felt betrayed, since he'd been aware all along. Tipp, however . . . Kiva had kept her secret from him for three years. And worse, he now knew she'd been planning to hurt the Vallentis family—people he loved enough to paint them into his family portrait. If made to choose, Kiva wasn't sure what Tipp would do, not while he was so upset.

"I can see you're working this out, sister," Zuleeka said, her voice gentling. "Don't worry, he'll be safe. And tomorrow you can explain everything and see where his loyalties lie."

"Tomorrow?" Kiva croaked.

"The masquerade starts in less than an hour. We intercepted the Mirravens' messages, so no one at the palace knows what happened today, but if you don't want your prince to start wondering where you are, you need to get back to the palace."

"I'm not going to a stupid party while Tipp—"

"I suggest you avoid mentioning any of this to Jaren," Zuleeka spoke over Kiva. "I imagine you'd have a hard time explaining how you escaped. And it's best if he doesn't know our northern friends are in town. *Were* in town," she corrected, looking at the bodies lying around them. "They've been dealt with, so any immediate threat to him has passed."

Her words caught Kiva's attention enough that she stopped arguing and demanded, "What did Mother promise King Navok? The men who abducted us said you have to pay her debt—that it's overdue."

Zuleeka looked to where Rhess remained crouched over the still-masked Torell, heedless of the bloody carnage surrounding them. "It's none of your concern."

"It damn well is," Kiva ground out.

Zuleeka turned back to meet her gaze, noting how angry she was, and relented, "I'll tell you, but not here. Next time we're somewhere safe —and alone."

Kiva wanted to push for an answer, but her sister was resolute, so she gave a sharp nod of agreement. Despite her capitulation, she wasn't letting Zuleeka off the hook yet. There were other answers she still needed.

Jerking her head toward Tipp, Kiva asked, "Did you steal the Book of the Law?"

If Zuleeka was startled by the subject change, she didn't let on. "Not personally."

"Zul—"

"I might have had a hand in it," Zuleeka admitted.

Understanding hit Kiva. "Perita Brown was a rebel. She was your palace spy."

"One of them."

"Did you *kill* her?" Kiva gasped.

There was no softness in Zuleeka's expression when she answered, "She didn't want this one"—she indicated Tipp—"to get in trouble and was planning to confess. I did what I had to do."

Kiva recoiled. "But *why?* Why take the Book?"

Zuleeka wiped her bloodied hands on her pants. "Educational reasons."

At the look Kiva sent her, Zuleeka huffed and explained, "You mentioned that hidden clause the other night, the Royal Ternary"—Kiva's heart skipped a beat—"and it got me thinking: What else might be in there? What if there's another secret clue that could help us?" Zuleeka shrugged. "I figured it couldn't hurt to take a look." She offered a sheepish look and said, "I'll return it once I'm done. I swear."

Kiva was appalled by the lengths her sister had gone to, but even so, she loosed a relieved breath at her response.

Before she could ask any follow-up questions, Zuleeka put her mask back on and pressed her fingers to her lips, giving a loud whistle. Seconds later, rebels started flooding into the warehouse. Many were splattered with blood, indicating there had been more fighting beyond the stacked crates. Just how many Mirravens had Navok sent? Kiva shuddered, realizing how gravely the northern king had intended to harm Jaren—and Evalon—today.

Another whistle, and the rebels started dragging bodies away, clearing up the mess. A few approached Rhess and Tor, listening as the young woman gave them quiet instructions before they took off again behind the crates.

"What about Mother?" Kiva asked, swinging back to Zuleeka.

"I already said I'll tell you later about her bargain with—"

"No, what about her magic?"

Zuleeka stilled. "What about it?"

Kiva rearranged Tipp's weight in her arms, before acknowledging there was no point in holding him anymore, so she gently lowered him to the ground. Meeting her sister's gaze, she said, "Delora told me about what Mother did—how she used her magic to hurt people. Just like Torvin Corentine. *That's* what killed her, not some rotting illness."

"Mother made sacrifices for our family that you can't begin to imagine," Zuleeka said, her honey-gold eyes darkening. "Don't for one moment think you can judge her."

"Are you *defending* her?" Kiva asked. "She *killed* people."

"Look around you," Zuleeka said, waving to the bloodied space. "These people died today because of you. How is that any different?"

Kiva spluttered, "It's *completely* different. They wanted to hurt us. From what I heard, Mother attacked innocents. A wave of her hand and they were *dead*."

"Grow up, Kiva," Zuleeka snapped. "No one is innocent. Not in this world."

Kiva flinched at her sudden wrath.

Realizing she'd lost control of her temper, Zuleeka sighed and touched her forehead over her mask. "I'm sorry. I just—I didn't like seeing Tor like that. I've *never* seen him like that. If you hadn't been here . . ." She met Kiva's gaze, her eyes haunted. "Thank you, Kiva. I don't know what I would've done if I'd lost him."

Kiva released a long breath, understanding her sister's terror, if not her poor reaction. "I just wish you would stop keeping so many secrets from me."

"Can you really blame me?" Zuleeka asked, sounding weary. "Tell me the truth: are you truly willing to turn your back on the Vallentis family? I saw how much they care for you, and you can deny it all you want, but I saw how much you care for them, too. Jaren, especially. Are you truly willing to take everything from them? From *him?*"

Kiva's heart started picking up speed again. She could lie, she probably *should* lie, but she didn't want to. Not to her sister, not to herself.

Not anymore.

"I was," Kiva whispered. "When I left Zalindov, I was prepared to destroy them."

"And now?" Zuleeka asked, her expression open beneath her mask.

Feeling lost, but somehow certain at the same time, Kiva said, "You're right—I *do* care about them. But I care about you, too. You and Tor—I love you both. But I just—" She inhaled deeply and made herself admit, "I don't want to be a rebel." Quickly, she added, "I won't stand against you, but I . . . I don't want to help you. Not anymore."

The exhaustion Kiva had felt after healing Torell swept over her again, along with a heavy dose of fear. But Zuleeka's expression didn't change. There was no hint of the anger Kiva had expected, none of the outrage. If anything, she looked—well, not *pleased*, but finally happy to have the truth laid out before them.

"I figured as much," Zuleeka said quietly. "You never were very good at hiding your thoughts. Even as a child."

Kiva looked at the ground. "I'm sorry."

"You can't help how you feel," Zuleeka said, before opening her arms and drawing Kiva into a hug. "We'll figure it out. I promise."

Kiva nearly cried as Zuleeka curled one arm around her waist and the other around her neck, holding her close as she repeated her promise that they would work it out, somehow. That she didn't blame her, that she understood.

They stood like that for a long time, as if making up for ten years' worth of lost embraces, only pulling apart when a whistle from across the room caught their attention. Kiva wiped under her damp eyes, noticing with some surprise that the bodies had all been cleared, and the men

Rhess had given instructions to had returned with a stretcher for Torell. Carefully, they shifted him onto it, before vanishing with him beyond the crates. Rhessinda alone remained, striding toward where Zuleeka and Kiva stood above Tipp.

"Kodan just told me there's a shift change soon," Rhess said, her voice still hoarse with worry. "This warehouse is due for resupply, so it'll be swarming with dockworkers in a few minutes."

Zuleeka nodded. "We need to go." She looked at Kiva. "And you need to get back to the palace."

"But Tipp—"

"I'll look after him," Rhessinda said. "I'm sorry, Kiva, but I overheard what Zuleeka told you, and I agree with her. If Jaren learns what happened today, he'll want to know how you escaped—and who helped you. We still need to uncover what's really going on ourselves." She shot a pointed look at Zuleeka, clearly intending to interrogate her about Tilda's bargain with Mirraven as soon as possible.

Turning back to Kiva, Rhess continued, "That means you need to go to the princess's masquerade and act like everything is normal. And it also means Tipp needs to stay with us, at least until you have a chance to talk to him. You'll have to come up with an excuse for his absence, just for tonight. And then, as soon as you can sneak out again, you can explain everything to him." She lowered her voice to finish, "I swear I won't leave his side. He'll be safe with me."

Kiva hated this. But the logical part of her knew Zuleeka and Rhess were right—Tipp needed to be watched. She still didn't fully grasp why Jaren couldn't learn about the Mirraven abduction, but she did know that if he learned she'd been in danger, he would only blame himself, and she didn't want to place that burden on his shoulders.

"Fine," she said, albeit reluctantly. "But first thing tomorrow, I want to see him."

Rhessinda pulled Tipp up into her arms, grunting slightly at his weight. "We have a safe house in the city. Until Tor is—" Her throat bobbed. "Until Tor is awake, I don't want to risk moving him back to Oakhollow, so we'll spend the night in Vallenia. One of us will meet you at the palace in the morning and bring you to Tipp. Does that work?"

Kiva nodded, stopping herself from grabbing the young boy and refusing to let go. "Please take care of him."

"You have my word," Rhess said. "For both of them."

Kiva offered the slightest of grateful smiles—that being all she could manage—and then watched the young woman walk away with Tipp in her arms.

"He'll get over it," Zuleeka said. "The boy clearly loves you."

Kiva had trouble responding around the lump in her throat. "I just hope that's enough."

Zuleeka placed a comforting hand on Kiva's shoulder. After a moment, she said, "I feel dreadful asking this now—I know the timing is terrible, and we both need to leave, but I have to know."

"What?" Kiva asked.

Zuleeka looked torn, but finally asked, "You said you spoke with Delora—I take it you went back to her as planned?"

"She didn't help me." Kiva looked at the bloodstained floor where Torell had been lying, turning cold as she realized, "But Tor would be dead if she'd given me more potion, so it worked out for the best." She shuddered, then finished, "I'll just have to learn how to control my magic without her help."

And she would. Kiva was determined to learn every facet of her healing power, to be the very opposite of what her mother had become. Helping people, not hurting them.

"I was hoping she'd be more generous toward you," Zuleeka said.

"Yeah, well, she really doesn't like our family." With a pointed look, Kiva added, "You, especially."

Zuleeka shuffled on her feet. "I might have visited her more than I let on."

"She wouldn't give me the dagger," Kiva said, figuring that was what Zuleeka really wanted to know. "I tried, but she was adamant."

Zuleeka's shoulders slumped. "I knew it was a long shot. I'd just hoped . . ." Shaking her head, she said, "Never mind. It doesn't matter now." She jerked her chin in the direction of the exit. "We really do need to leave."

And then she started leading the way out of the warehouse, around more boxes and crates and barrels than Kiva could count—the building was much larger than she'd thought—before they finally stepped outside to find the sun setting in the distance.

"I need to grab something before the party, but I'll meet you at the palace," Zuleeka said.

"You really don't have to come," Kiva said, hoping her sister would stay away.

"Tor's already not going to be there. It might seem odd—even rude—if both of us ignore the princess's invitation."

Frustratingly, Zuleeka wasn't wrong, so Kiva blew out a breath and said, "I'll see you soon, then."

CHAPTER THIRTY-THREE

By the time Kiva finally made her way back to the palace, her feet felt like lead, her head was pounding, and she desperately needed a nap. But with the clock ticking down to the masquerade, she made herself wash quickly, scrubbing off Torell's blood—amazed no one had noticed it—and donning her gown.

Mirryn had delivered her a mask, as promised, and while the shimmering delicacy of it was beautiful, it was nothing compared to the masterpiece that was Kiva's dress.

Fashioned entirely out of a pale gold silk, the bodice cut low across Kiva's chest and fit tight to her waist, before flowing out like liquid to the floor. What truly made it spectacular was the luminium beaded into it, like little specks of sunlight, leaving the dress—and Kiva wearing it—looking nothing short of radiant.

Coupled with her intricate mask and glittering slippers, when Kiva peered in the mirror before leaving her room, she had to do a double take, barely recognizing herself.

"What am I doing?" she whispered, frozen to the spot. But then a knock on her bedroom door had her jumping and hurrying across her room to answer it.

On the other side was Jaren, dressed in formal black from head to toe, with whirls and eddies of gold embroidery dancing along the collar of his shirt and the seams of his jacket, begging for Kiva to reach out and run her fingers over them. Over *him*.

From his boots to his black-and-gold mask, he was utterly magnificent, and try as she might, Kiva couldn't take her eyes off him.

Not that she tried very hard, especially when she saw the look in *his* eyes as he stared shamelessly right back at her.

Heat pooled in her stomach at the desire on his face, at the sheer *hunger* that only deepened as his gaze raked slowly over her, like the softest, sweetest of caresses. Her skin felt like it was melting right off her bones, every part of her suddenly throbbing with want, with *need*—

And then Naari walked into the room.

Kiva leapt backwards, as if she'd been caught doing something wrong. She was panting lightly, feeling as if she'd run a lap around the training yard, embarrassed by her reaction but also still experiencing the magnetic pull toward the prince.

"Ready for the party?" Naari asked, oblivious to the tension in the room. "Where's Tipp?"

Kiva shook off what she could of her stupor. "He's, uh—" She fumbled for a response, having been so preoccupied on the walk back to the palace that she hadn't considered what excuse she might use. It was on the tip of her tongue to say he was sick, but Naari and Jaren would want to check in on him, and they'd also know Kiva would struggle to leave his side if that were the case.

"He went to Silverthorn with you, didn't he?" Naari pressed, reminding Kiva that there were guards watching the River Road—but apparently their eyes had been elsewhere today, missing the abduction that had occurred on the road up to the academy. "Did you come back together?"

It would take Naari all of two seconds to discover if Kiva lied, with numerous people—including the gate guards—having seen her return alone. Licking her lips, she answered, "It was his first time there, and he wanted to stay longer. Rhessinda—my healer friend—offered to show him around while I came back to get dressed."

Naari frowned toward Tipp's open bedroom door, before shrugging and saying, "I'll keep an eye out and let you know when he returns."

Kiva's stomach knotted, but she murmured her thanks. She only had to stall until morning. Then she could talk to Tipp and, hopefully, convince him to keep her secrets.

"You look nice, by the way," Naari said to Kiva.

Jaren made a strangled sound, the first noise he'd uttered since arriving, but Kiva kept her eyes on Naari and replied, "So do you."

The guard was wearing her customary black, but she'd traded her leathery armor for a pantsuit, the cuffs and collar threaded with the barest hint of gold, like an added afterthought for meeting Mirryn's color scheme. To finish, Naari wore a simple but still dainty mask, the golden flecks standing out in stark contrast to her dark skin.

"I don't like these events," Naari said, running her hands down her sides. "I can only conceal so many weapons in this outfit."

Kiva's eyes bugged out, since she couldn't see *any* weapons on Naari, and she was afraid to wonder where, exactly, she'd managed to conceal them. Jaren, she knew, was wearing a dagger at his waist, a glint of steel having peeked out from beneath his jacket when she'd first opened her door to him, but aside from that, he appeared unarmed as well.

"But since every Royal Guard we have is on patrol tonight," Naari continued, "and Mirryn ordered me to take the night off, I *suppose* I'll just have to put up with it." She pulled a displeased face. "Never mind. Shall we go?"

She didn't wait for them to answer before striding back toward the door. Kiva made to follow, but Jaren's hand caught her forearm, halting her.

"Naari's wrong," he said, his voice husky, his blue-gold eyes blazing a path of flames everywhere they touched her skin. "You don't look nice." He leaned in, causing Kiva's breath to hitch as he pressed his lips just beneath her ear and whispered there, "You look exquisite. You *are* exquisite."

Shakily, Kiva said, "It's the dress."

Jaren chuckled, his breath against her skin causing goose bumps to rise. "Trust me, it's not the dress."

"Are you two coming?" called Naari's voice from the hallway.

Jaren pulled back with a muted oath. "Do you think anyone would care if I murdered my own Golden Shield?"

Kiva bit back a smile. "Hypothetically?"

"Sure. Let's go with that."

"I can hear you!" Naari called.

Jaren sighed and placed a hand on Kiva's back, guiding her toward the doorway and muttering under his breath, "Maybe not so hypothetically."

Upon arriving at the masquerade, Kiva discovered the circular ballroom had been fully transformed. People were everywhere, dressed to perfection in shades of blue and gold, delicate masks hiding some of their features better than others. Multiple luminium chandeliers sparkled from the golden ceiling, a string orchestra played from a balcony high above their heads, and at their ankles swirled a layer of misted cloud—kept in place by elemental magic, no doubt, as were the floating specks of light dotting the air, like starbursts hovering among the dancing couples. On the far side, the glass wall had been opened to a reveal a balcony beyond which the Serin lay, its surface dusted with enough luminium candles to make it sparkle brighter than the moonlight shining down on the city.

"*Oh,*" Kiva couldn't keep from gasping quietly.

"My sister is a lot of things," Jaren mused, "but she certainly knows how to throw a good party."

Kiva nodded mutely, too stunned for words. She tried to spot Mirryn in the crowd but only saw the king and queen holding court near a large cluster of guests, young Oriel remaining obediently at their sides, Flox squirming in his arms.

"There are far too many people here," Naari stated, looking unhappily around the packed room.

"Half of them are guards," Jaren said. "And the other half are people we know. You're off duty, Naari. There's no danger to me here."

"But I—"

"Mirry ordered you to take the night off," Jaren reminded her. "If she sees you clucking around me like a mother hen, you know she won't be pleased. So grab a drink, get some food, and have some fun." When Naari continued to hesitate, Jaren smirked and added, "Unless you want to three-way dance with Kiva and me all night?"

The look on the guard's face was comical enough that Kiva normally would have laughed, but instead she looked at Jaren and repeated, "Dance?"

A devious grin stretched across his lips. "I thought you'd never ask."

And then he was tugging her deeper into the room.

"No—Jaren—*I can't*—"

But she didn't finish her protest before he twirled her into his arms, one of his hands landing on her waist, the other gently clasping her hand.

"I don't know how to dance," Kiva said quickly.

"Then it's a good thing I've been dancing all my life," Jaren replied, his eyes sparkling. "You just have to trust me." His forehead dipped until their gazes locked. "Do you trust me, Kiva?"

The way he said it, Kiva knew he wasn't just talking about as a dance partner.

And when she held his gaze and whispered a breathy, "Yes," she knew he realized she was answering with the same level of meaning.

His face lit with such hope, such *joy*, that for one moment, Kiva could only stare, but then he pulled her closer and whispered back, "Then follow my lead."

Kiva had no idea what she was doing, but she let Jaren guide her around the dance floor, spinning and twirling to the music. He didn't care when she stood on his toes, or that it felt like everyone in the room was watching them. He only cared about her, and the way his eyes never left her—not *once*—told her as much. It was all too easy for her to fall into the same enchantment, forgetting her troubles and sinking into the moment. Into Jaren.

When the song ended, he smiled, wide and glorious, and led her straight into the next dance.

And the next.

And the next.

They didn't stop until they were interrupted.

"All right, cousin, I think it's time you let someone else show your girl how to *really* dance."

As if being pulled from a dream, Kiva's eyes fluttered when Caldon's voice drifted to her during a pause in the music.

"Sunshine, may I?" the prince asked, offering his hand.

Jaren held her tighter for a moment, before sighing and loosening his grip. "I'll go wish my sister a happy birthday," he said, drawing Kiva's fingers to his lips and placing a perfunctory kiss on the back of her hand —something that felt anything *but* perfunctory to Kiva, leaving tingles in its wake.

"Good luck with that," Caldon said dryly. "Dearest Mirry hasn't graced us with her presence yet. My guess is she's waiting to make a grand entrance." He tilted his head toward Ariana, Stellan, and Ori, his voice lowering. "Your father's looking a bit peaky, though. You might want to suggest they retire early. Ori's miserable anyway since they won't let him leave their sides, and Flox keeps escaping to play in the mist, scaring the life out of the guests when he curls around their feet."

Kiva coughed to hide her laugh, but she sobered quickly when Jaren's concerned gaze shot toward his family.

"I'll go speak with them," he said, before offering a gentle smile to Kiva and sending a meaningful look to his cousin. "Take care of her."

"Goshdarnit, there go my plans to toss her in the Serin," Caldon deadpanned.

Jaren didn't deign to reply and took off into the crowd.

Caldon snickered, drawing Kiva into his arms as the music started again. "I like him like this," he said. "It's so easy to rile him up these days. You've been a real gift to us all, you know that?"

Kiva deliberately stood on his foot and smiled sweetly as she replied, "I'm so pleased to be of service."

The prince hummed an amused sound, spinning her away, then back into his arms. "I've been looking for your brother and sister." His teeth flashed in a grin. "Mostly your brother. But no sign of them yet."

Kiva's stomach tumbled. "Tor's not coming."

Caldon's brows rose above his golden mask. "Oh?"

Weighing her response, Kiva realized that if there was one person she could tell about her abduction — without having to lie about how she'd escaped — it was Caldon. And at least *someone* at the palace would know Mirraven had attempted to trap Jaren. But that wasn't the only reason Kiva decided to share.

She quickly — and quietly — summarized her day, before finishing with, "So I could really use your help. With Tipp. Maybe if you come with me tomorrow, you can be there when I explain?"

Caldon had cursed multiple times during her tale, but none so creatively as when she'd shared about Tipp learning who she was.

"I don't know which part worries me the most," Caldon murmured, guiding her around another dancing couple. He didn't answer her question, instead saying, "I'll have Veris double the city patrols to make sure there are no more Mirravens lying in wait, but you need to push your sister for details about the bargain your mother made with Navok."

Kiva nodded. "I will. But right now, Tipp takes priority for me. So will you help?"

Caldon led her into another spin. "I don't know how much good it'll do, but yeah, I'll come with you."

Kiva wilted with relief. "Thank you."

"Are you sure he's safe wherever he is tonight? I don't like that——"

"I know, I hate it too," Kiva interrupted, chewing her lip. "But Rhess promised to watch over him."

Caldon looked skeptical now that he knew the truth about the other girl, but despite Rhessinda's treachery, Kiva trusted her, especially having witnessed how deeply she cared for Torell.

"I'll help you cover for his absence tonight," Caldon offered. "But if things don't work out the way you want tomorrow, you're going to have to make some tough decisions, Sunshine."

Kiva blew out a breath and looked away. "I know."

Caldon moved their joined hands to tip her chin up, meeting her gaze. "Speaking of tough decisions, I'm really proud of you for telling Zuleeka you're done with them. That can't have been easy."

"It wasn't." And yet Kiva recalled how understanding her sister had been, with no hint of anger, no sign of judgment. It was enough for her to wonder if maybe Zuleeka felt a little like Torell, at least deep down.

Or perhaps she simply realized that after a decade in prison, Kiva deserved to make her own choices.

Marveling at the thought, Kiva moved into one final spin as the music came to a close, and then, barely a second after they stopped, Jaren materialized at their sides, eliciting a huff of amusement from his cousin.

"It was touch and go," Caldon said, his voice grave, "but she survived being parted from you for a whole seven minutes."

Jaren ignored him and reached for Kiva, linking their hands and leading her off the dance floor.

"Don't mind me!" Caldon called after them. "I'm fine by myself!"

At first, Kiva thought Jaren might have been taking her to his family, but a quick glance revealed he'd been successful in convincing them to leave. Mirryn hadn't yet arrived, so they weren't heading toward her, nor were they en route to the gilded refreshments table. Instead, Jaren was guiding her around masked men and women, many of whom called greetings, all of whom looked at Kiva in unabashed curiosity, and none of whom Jaren paused for, his attention wholly focused on their destination.

That being, to leave the ballroom.

"Where are we going?" Kiva asked as they stepped through the ornate doors into the hallway and then ascended the nearest red-carpeted staircase.

"Somewhere quiet."

The two words had Kiva's heart giving a leap, which turned into multiple leaps when she realized they were approaching the River Room.

The very empty River Room.

Situated directly above the ballroom, the music filtered through the walls, but there were no crowds of people, no prying eyes or lingering looks. The luminium chandelier cast a golden glow over the room, the candle-dotted Serin stretched out beyond the windows, the space nothing short of romantic, especially when, with a wave of Jaren's hand, mist tickled at their ankles and floating specks of light burst into being, a perfect recreation of the ballroom—just smaller, more intimate. And for the two of them alone.

"I know it's selfish," Jaren said, leading Kiva toward the windows, "but I don't want to share you with anyone else tonight." The orchestra launched into another melody. "May I have this dance, Kiva?"

Her throat suddenly dry, she answered by stepping closer. He didn't lead her into a waltz this time; instead, his arms encircled her waist, guiding her to sway gently in place, his eyes never leaving hers.

. . . Eyes that were full of emotion, revealing everything, hiding nothing, his heart laid bare.

Kiva's pulse grew erratic.

"Do you remember that night in the garden?" he asked quietly.

Kiva swallowed. They'd only ever been in one garden together — her medical garden back in Zalindov. And they'd only ever been out there once at night, when Tipp had fallen ill. But before they'd found him —

"I wanted to kiss you that night," Jaren murmured.

Kiva's breath lodged somewhere in her chest.

Jaren leaned down, his lips by her ear as he whispered, "And I think you wanted to kiss me, too."

A shiver traveled along Kiva's spine. "A lot has happened since then," she breathed, her voice different to her ears. Low, husky.

Jaren's eyes darkened at the sound. "It has," he agreed, one of his hands moving slowly, languidly, up her side and across her shoulder, before whispering up her neck to cup her face.

Flames ignited beneath Kiva's skin at his touch, her stomach dipping, molten heat pooling in her core.

Gently, Jaren pulled off her mask, and a moment later, his own was gone. The full effect of his unconcealed expression — the desire, the *longing* — made Kiva's knees weak.

"A lot has happened," Jaren repeated her words in a whisper, his thumb stroking her cheek. "A lot has changed." He leaned in so close that she could feel his breath on her skin. "But the one thing that hasn't is how I feel about you."

Kiva's fingers clutched at his chest, her breathing turning shallow.

Jaren angled his head to the side, his nose brushing hers. A quiet sound left her lips, the noise making his already-dark eyes darken even more, the gold rims like circles of fire in a twilight sky.

The sight was too much for Kiva, and she closed her own eyes, achingly aware of what he must be able to read in her expression.

His mouth moved back to her ear as he murmured there, "I know you're scared." He pressed a whisper-soft kiss against her neck.

Kiva whimpered.

"But I promise you don't have to be." Another kiss, this one at the edge of her jaw. "You're safe with me, Kiva. You'll always be safe with me."

Her shallow breaths turned into panting.

"Open your eyes, sweetheart," Jaren whispered.

It took her a moment, her heart pounding, pounding, *pounding*, but when she looked at Jaren again, everything in her stilled at what she saw radiating from his expression.

And then she *erupted*.

Kiva didn't know who moved first, but suddenly his lips were on hers, his hand tangling in her hair, his other arm drawing her chest flush against his. At the flick of his tongue, she gasped, her mouth opening automatically. He moaned as their kiss deepened, the sound causing her legs to buckle enough that his arm became a steel band around her waist, keeping her upright. She leaned her whole body against him, her hands sliding up his chest to his neck and into his impossibly soft hair, holding his face to hers, never wanting their kiss to end.

But then he shifted slightly, and the dagger at his belt dug into Kiva's side, the jolt of pain enough that she drew back with a quiet, *"Ouch."*

Jaren looked dazed, his hair mussed and eyes glassy, but with clear effort, he asked, "Are you all right?"

Unable to help herself, Kiva touched his face, tracing a finger over his kiss-swollen lips.

Heat flared in his eyes again, that same heat filling every part of her, but before he could lean toward her once more, she reached for his dagger, pulling it from his belt.

"Can we get rid of—" Kiva's words halted as she stared at the weapon.

"I'm sorry, I forgot all about it," Jaren said, prying the dagger from her suddenly numb fingers. "It's ceremonial, something I'm encouraged to wear to formal events. The blade isn't even sharp." He ran his finger along the edge to show her what he meant.

But Kiva wasn't looking at the blade.

She was looking at the hilt.

And at the clear gemstone embedded into it.

Kiva pointed a shaky finger at the jewel, a horrible feeling growing within her as she asked, "What is that?"

"Remember the Eye of the Gods? The gift they gave Sarana and Torvin?" Jaren tapped the diamond-like jewel. "It came forged into a dagger—so I guess a more accurate name would be the Dagger of the Gods, but that's a bit morbid." He cocked his head to the side. "Didn't I tell you?"

Kiva shook her head. Then shook it again.

No.

No, no, no.

"This one is just a replica." Jaren tapped the jewel again. "As I said the other day, Ashlyn has the real one."

He was wrong.

So, so wrong.

Because Kiva had seen the real one.

In her grandmother's cottage.

The one Ashlyn had was a fake. It had to be, or Delora wouldn't have been so determined to hold on to hers—and to keep it from the rest of their family.

"All the legends are different," Jaren went on, not noticing how pale Kiva had become, "but while some stories claim Sarana attacked Torvin with her magic, others claim she used this very dagger, nearly killing him with it. Or, well, not *this* dagger. But the one Ashlyn carries."

Kiva barely heard him. Instead, she was thinking about how Zuleeka had coveted the weapon for years, believing it symbolic to the rebels but having no idea of its true value.

Until two nights ago.

When Kiva had stupidly, *stupidly* shared about the Royal Ternary.

Ice filled Kiva as she realized that one of the two other objects was already in Zuleeka's hands, her explanation for stealing the Book no longer seeming so trustworthy.

In fact, Kiva was positive Zuleeka had lied.

It wouldn't have mattered if the Eye really had been hundreds of miles away, the Ternary incomplete without it, but now . . .

I need to grab something before the party, but I'll meet you at the palace.

Zuleeka's words from that afternoon all but shouted in Kiva's ears, a terrible premonition coming over her when she remembered her sister had tried to get the dagger many times, but had never succeeded, claiming Delora kept it hidden.

It is *hidden,* Kiva's own voice echoed in her ears. *She keeps it in a hollowed black book called* 1,001 Pies and Pastries.

Staring in dismay at Jaren, Kiva choked out, "I have to go."

Jaren's eyebrows shot upward. "Go?"

"Bathroom," she blurted.

"I'll wait for you here," Jaren said.

"No, no, you should rejoin the party," Kiva insisted, trying to keep her panic from showing. "See if Mirryn has arrived yet."

Jaren leaned in to kiss her cheek, his voice rumbling with meaning as he repeated, "I'll wait for you here."

Kiva ignored the desire that rose anew within her, scrambling instead for anything that might excuse how long she would be gone. "I need to track down Tipp and make sure he's not getting into any trouble, so I may be a while."

Jaren chuckled, misreading her anxiety and assuming it was about what they'd just done. With the memory of his kisses still on her lips, she wished she could stay and continue what they'd started. But her mind was focused on a cottage in the swamp, her blood pulsing with desperation to get there.

I'd rather die than see that dagger in your sister's hands, Delora had declared, the memory only adding to Kiva's dread.

"Take as long as you need, sweetheart," Jaren said. "I'll be waiting for you." He pressed his mouth to hers, the lightest of touches and yet so full of promise, before finishing, "I'll *always* wait for you."

His words washed over her, the warmth of them nearly chasing away the cold that had swept in upon her first seeing the dagger.

Nearly—but not quite.

And because of that, Kiva forced a wobbly smile to her face and turned from him, keeping her steps even until she was out of sight around the corner.

Then she ran.

CHAPTER THIRTY-FOUR

Kiva didn't waste time changing into clothes better suited to riding, instead running straight out of the palace, her slippered feet sliding on the path. She swiftly intercepted a stableboy leading a guest's horse away, taking the reins and exclaiming, "Family emergency!"

The prepubescent boy gaped as she mounted, silk skirts and all, and tore off toward the gates and out into the city.

Her previous two ventures to Blackwater Bog had taken twenty minutes at a sedate pace, but with urgency thrumming within her, Kiva galloped recklessly along the moonlit road, every part of her screaming to *hurry*.

If Zuleeka had gone for the dagger . . . If Delora had tried to stop her . . .

Kiva didn't know which of her fears was the worst, but all of them led to what might happen if Zuleeka retrieved the Eye, leaving only one part of the Ternary—the queen's Signet—between her and the entire kingdom.

She would become Queen of Evalon.

And the Vallentis family—

Jaren—

Kiva couldn't finish the thought.

She reminded herself there was no point in worrying about a future that hadn't yet happened, especially when their elemental magic was more than enough to keep them safe. Each of them, even young Oriel, was a force to be reckoned with. Panicking about undetermined events would help no one.

So Kiva focused only on staying on her horse, on riding faster than the wind.

She reached the swamp in half the time it would normally take, her horse panting as she leapt from the saddle and bounded up the porch steps, her heart lodging in her throat when she saw the door to the cottage cracked open.

"Delora!" she called, sprinting through the doorway and into the living room. There she came to a dead halt, taking in the mess of books and ornaments strewn all over the floor, the shelves stripped and bookcases overturned, the entire room looking as if it had exploded.

Zuleeka was nowhere to be seen.

But at the center of it all, face-down on the ground, was Delora.

"No!" Kiva gasped, lurching forward to kneel beside her grandmother, gently turning her over.

One look and Kiva recoiled, her hands flying away in shock and uncertainty. But then Delora moaned and Kiva realized the old woman was still alive. She just didn't know what was wrong with her.

A shadowy mist had settled over her abdomen, like a swirling black cloud. Kiva had no idea what it was, just that it was hideously unnatural. She was loath to touch it, but she made herself lay trembling hands on Delora's stomach, once again calling upon the healing magic in her veins, begging it to come to her grandmother's aid.

Her fingers started to tingle, her skin burned, her power rose to the surface . . . but the golden light didn't appear.

Something was wrong.

Her power *wanted* to heal, she could feel it there, ready and waiting for her to release it, but something was blocking it. Something that, for once, had nothing to do with Kiva.

Delora coughed and her eyes fluttered open. She seemed unsurprised to see Kiva, and equally unsurprised by the darkness that eddied along her torso.

"It w-won't work," Delora said in a weak voice, eyeing Kiva's hands hovering above her. "Don't waste your strength."

Kiva ignored her and pushed harder, again urging her magic into the woman. But still, nothing happened—aside from a wave of dizziness hitting her, the force of which made her reach out to steady herself on the ground.

"The she-devil came for the d-dagger," Delora said, her wrinkled face pinched with pain.

"What did she do to you?" Kiva breathed, reaching for the hem of her grandmother's tunic. If magical means were beyond her, she still had mundane healing skills.

But Delora raised a fragile hand and stopped her. "I t-told you, she's as dangerous as your mama. The same evil is in her." She coughed again, a rattling, wet sound, her fingers tightening around Kiva's. "This is what h-happens when you yield to Torvin's darkness. When you turn from healing to hurt."

Kiva's stomach bottomed out. "But—Zuleeka doesn't have magic. She's *never* had magic."

"She lied. Your mama—" Another wet cough. "Your mama taught her everything she knew. They learned together."

"No." Kiva shook her head. "You're wrong."

But then she heard Torell's voice, whispering across her mind: *She and Mother were really close, especially toward the end. They spent every minute together.*

Could it be true? Did Zuleeka have magic? Had she hidden it from them all? The evidence lay before Kiva, and yet, she still had trouble believing it, even seeing the darkness with her own eyes.

Delora coughed again, this time violently enough that her whole body buckled, a thin trail of blood leaking from her mouth.

Kiva cursed and demanded again, "What did she *do* to you?"

"My organs are sh-shutting down," Delora whispered. "There's n-nothing you can do while her power is working in my body, so you n-need to listen."

"This is my fault," Kiva moaned. "She came for the dagger because I—"

"*Listen,*" Delora urged, as more blood trickled down her chin. "The dagger—"

"I know it's the Eye of the Gods," Kiva said, wanting her grandmother to stop speaking, to rest. "I know Zuleeka can use it to take the throne."

"No, you d-don't understand," Delora said, before launching into another coughing fit, pressing her free hand to her abdomen, her other still holding Kiva's in a death grip. "The dagger—Sarana used it on Torvin. It's how she s-saved the kingdom."

Jaren had mentioned that before she'd fled the palace—how some of the legends claimed the queen had used it against the king, nearly killing him.

"It doesn't matter," Kiva said soothingly, dabbing the blood off Delora's rapidly paling face. "We need to get you some—"

"*Kiva,*" Delora snapped, a burst of frustration strengthening her voice. "That dagger can take away magic. It was a gift from the gods —a gift for Sarana to use against Torvin. A gift to *stop* him."

Kiva rocked backwards, her ears ringing in the wake of Delora's damning words.

That dagger can take away magic.

"I don't—" Kiva breathed, unable to finish her horrified sentence.

Delora released Kiva and lifted her hem to reveal a jagged scar across her stomach, the death magic still swirling around her pale skin.

"You wanted to know how I repressed my magic?" Delora asked, her voice growing weak again. "I s-stabbed myself with that blade. The Eye drew every scrap of power out of me, eliminating any chance that I'd ever use it to hurt someone. I d-didn't want to live with that fear."

Kiva stared at the scar, even as realization hit her. "The potion—I tried to recreate it, but it didn't work because—because—"

"It was n-never about the ingredients," Delora confirmed. "I used the dagger to make it. *That's* what stopped your magic." She took Kiva's hands again, both of them this time, her aged flesh cold and clammy. "You're different from them, Kiva, the light to their darkness. Your magic is pure, your heart is true. I c-can sense it."

A tear leaked down Kiva's cheek, not just at the words, but because she could feel Delora fading. It wouldn't be long now.

"But you m-must be careful," Delora went on weakly—so very weakly. "One mistake is all it will take, one p-poor choice. You have to fight it. Don't become like them." With a final pained gasp, Delora summoned the last of her strength to whisper, "Be the light in the dark, Kiva."

And then her eyes closed, the black mist vanishing into nothing as she breathed her last.

Kiva bowed her head, tears dripping off her chin. She'd barely known her grandmother, and yet, she knew Delora didn't deserve to meet this end.

This was Zuleeka's doing.

She'd killed their grandmother.

Murdered her.

And she had the dagger—a weapon that could steal not only Jaren's kingdom . . . but also his magic.

Kiva lurched to her feet, scrubbing a hand over her face. Delora needed to be buried, but Kiva would have to return for that later. Right now, she had to get to the palace and warn Jaren, even if it meant revealing the truth about who she was. Too much was at stake to risk keeping the danger to herself. They needed to guard the queen's Signet and prepare for Zuleeka's death magic however they could. Because while Kiva had seen the strength of the Vallentis's elemental powers, they had no idea what Zuleeka was capable of. And if she were to attack without warning . . . *especially* with that dagger . . .

Kiva cast one final glance at her grandmother, and then ran from the room, determined to keep her sister from harming anyone else that night—or ever again.

The ride back to Vallenia was just as harrowing as the journey to Black-water Bog, but Kiva pushed her mount faster, terror and desperation brewing within her, along with a rising dread that she was already too late. There was no telling how long ago Zuleeka had left Murkwood Cottage, but Kiva hadn't passed her on the journey. She could already be at the palace and—

Enough! Kiva mentally screamed, unwilling to travel further down that road.

When finally the palace gates rose before her, Kiva nearly wept, sweat coating both her and her mount as they sailed right past the guards and along the manicured garden path. She barely came to a halt before leaping off her horse, thrusting the reins at a manservant, and bounding through the pillared entryway. Her lungs burned, her sides ached, but on she ran, taking the stairs two at a time as she sprinted directly for the ballroom, bursting through the ornate doors to find—

Dancing couples. Laughing faces. Boisterous conversations.

Nothing had changed.

Nothing was wrong.

Kiva loosed a relieved sob and searched frantically for Jaren among the crowd, certain he must have given up waiting for her in the River Room by now.

She couldn't see him anywhere, nor could she see Mirryn, but she spotted Caldon dancing with a dark-haired woman. Fearing it was Zuleeka, Kiva's heart arrested, before a quick spin revealed her to be someone else.

Kiva tore across the ballroom toward them, her disheveled appearance eliciting gasps and murmurs from those she passed. When Caldon caught sight of her, he halted mid-dance, offering an apology to his partner before striding to meet her partway across the room.

"What the hell happened to you?" he asked, eyeing her from head to toe.

"Where's Jaren?" Kiva panted.

Caldon rolled his eyes. "Seriously? You two need to—"

Kiva grabbed the lapels of his jacket, shaking him fiercely. "Caldon, *where's Jaren?*"

The prince turned alert. "Last I knew, he was with you."

Kiva closed her eyes, wondering if Jaren *had* waited for her, just as he'd promised. "Have you seen Zuleeka?"

"She was just here, asking where to find you," Caldon said. "Someone told her they saw you and Jaren heading to the River Room a while ago." Seeing Kiva pale, Caldon added, "Naari followed her—she can't get into any trouble."

Kiva didn't need to hear more, already turning to sprint back the way she'd come.

"Hey—*wait!*" Caldon called, his long steps catching up easily as she bolted out of the ballroom and toward the nearest staircase. Keeping pace at her side, he demanded, "What's wrong?"

"Zuleeka's dangerous." Kiva didn't slow as they climbed to the next floor and barreled along the hallway. "She has magic. Evil magic. And she has a dagger that—"

Kiva and Caldon burst through the doors of the River Room before she could finish her warning. And then she couldn't speak at all, because the moment she saw her sister standing with Jaren by the window-wall, a wave of blackness speared toward her, rooting her feet to the floor.

It wasn't like when the queen had encased Kiva's ankles in ice. Instead, it was as if her very *bones* had fused together, her legs forced apart, her arms stretched out to the sides, her mouth sealed shut, pain tearing through her as Zuleeka's dark magic manipulated her muscles and tendons to her will.

Beside her, Kiva was aware of Caldon locked in the same position, the two of them entirely trapped by Zuleeka's magic—as was Jaren across the room, his body immobile while his eyes blazed with fury.

But Jaren wasn't looking at them. He wasn't even looking at Zuleeka.

His gaze was fixed on the floor.

Where Naari lay.

Eyes closed.

In a pool of blood.

Kiva's heart stopped. But then she saw the slight rise and fall of the guard's chest.

Alive—she was *alive*.

If Kiva had been in control of her own body, she would have buckled with the weight of her relief.

And then she realized something else: Naari had felt Zuleeka's magic before.

Darkness swirled in my vision and my limbs just wouldn't obey me, the guard had said when recounting the day she'd lost her hand. *It was terrible, not being able to control myself.*

If only Kiva had known about the dark magic sooner; if only she'd—

"Sister, so good of you to join us," Zuleeka purred, interrupting Kiva's woeful thoughts.

A fireball surged from Caldon, making Kiva wonder why Jaren wasn't using his own magic. Her terror flooded anew, but he didn't appear to be injured—nor was there any sign of the dagger.

Before Kiva's alarm could grow, Caldon's fire hit Zuleeka square in the chest—

And did absolutely nothing.

Zuleeka slashed a grin, fishing something out from beneath the high collar of her navy ballgown.

Kiva's remaining breath fled at the sight of the amulet.

Her amulet.

But how —

Inhaling sharply, Kiva recalled the long embrace she'd shared with Zuleeka that afternoon, when her sister had been whispering assurances in her ear, her hand on the back of Kiva's neck the whole time.

Working at the clasp.

Kiva hadn't realized. Even when she'd donned her ballgown and looked in her mirror, she'd been so startled by her transformation — and so exhausted from healing Torell — that she hadn't noticed it missing.

"Thank you for the gift, sister," Zuleeka said, stroking the powerful crest. "I never would have made it this far without its protection."

Jaren's eyes shot to Kiva, disbelief and uncertainty emanating from him. She wanted to scream that Zuleeka was lying, to even just shake her head, but she couldn't move.

"I don't have long," Zuleeka said, returning the amulet beneath her dress. "I have business in the western palace." Another slash of a smile, and then she pulled up her skirt and removed a dagger — *the* dagger — from her thigh holster.

Kiva made a panicked sound in the back of her throat, and Caldon launched another fireball, but it just bounced straight off Zuleeka again.

"Recognize this, Prince?" she said to Jaren, tapping the jewel. "Unfortunately for you, the blade your general possesses is a fake. *This* is the real dagger gifted by the gods. It's been in my family for hundreds of years, passed down from generation to generation." Her eyes flicked to Kiva's, a smirk growing as she corrected, "*Our* family. I think it's time you and your beloved were properly introduced."

Kiva made another distressed noise, but Zuleeka merely gave a poisonous smile and said, "Deverick Vallentis, meet Kiva Corentine—Torvin Corentine's descendant and my dear rebel sister, who has been working tirelessly to bring you and your family to your knees." Zuleeka winked at Kiva. "Well done, sister. I couldn't have done this without you."

Kiva barely heard Zuleeka, her gaze locked on Jaren, allowing her to see the devastation ravishing his features, his heart breaking before her eyes.

"It's a stinging betrayal," Zuleeka went on mercilessly. "But it gets worse."

She dragged the tip of her dagger over Jaren's chest, his breathing turning shallow—whether from fear of the weapon or from the pain of what he'd just learned, Kiva wasn't sure.

"You see, my dear sister helped me steal the Book of the Law," Zuleeka went on.

SHE'S LYING, Kiva wanted to scream.

"And coupled with this"—Zuleeka indicated the dagger—"I now have two items from your not-so-secret Royal Ternary. That leaves only one left." She cocked her head. "Tell me, Your Highness, have you seen *your* sister today?"

This time it was Caldon who made a strangled sound.

"With so many people coming and going for the party, it was almost too easy to steal her away," Zuleeka said, grinning. "The poor little princess is having the most awful birthday, but I daresay your mother will give me anything I want in exchange for Mirryn's safe return, don't you think?"

Gods, *gods,* Kiva thought, recalling what Mirryn had said about Ariana just yesterday: *I know she'd bring down entire kingdoms if anything ever happened to Jaren or Ori or me. She wouldn't hesitate to do whatever it took to make sure we were safe.*

The queen was going to hand over her Signet—there was no way she wouldn't.

This was all Kiva's fault.

And she couldn't let it continue.

You're different from them, Kiva, the light to their darkness.

Delora's words fueled her desperation, stirring the magic in her blood and urging it to rise. It hadn't worked around whatever Zuleeka had done to their grandmother, but Kiva refused to let that stop her. She would try, and keep trying, drawing on every drop of golden power in her veins to break free of the darkness trapping her. Trapping them *all*.

"As helpful as it's been," Zuleeka continued speaking to Jaren, "I've heard the power in this amulet has an expiration point, and you've certainly already tried to speed it along, given how much magic you threw at me when I first arrived. That must have been exhausting."

Jaren had fought her—of course he had. Naari, too, given the state of the guard. But neither of them had succeeded. Not with Jaren's own magic protecting Zuleeka. Magic he'd given *Kiva*.

"I'm glad I had a warning from my sister about that," Zuleeka went on slyly. "All four elements—it's far too much power for one person. I knew that the moment she told me about your secret."

Jaren's eyes slashed to Kiva again, and again she wished she could scream that it wasn't true. Kiva *hadn't* shared about his magic. But then . . . how did Zuleeka *know?*

"Fortunately, I have a way to fix that," Zuleeka said, waving the dagger. "I've been trying to get my hands on this for years—not because it's part of your Ternary, *that* came as a pleasant surprise—but because the Eye has a much more useful power, one that my mother told me all about. *Her* mother had the audacity to hide it from us, but as you already know, Kiva has been a wonderful spy in so many ways. She might as well have handed it right to me."

Zuleeka had lied about wanting the blade as a symbol to the rebels. Lies upon lies. But Kiva couldn't dwell on them now, instead strengthening her attempt to summon her magic, straining against the darkness that held her at bay.

"In all the legends you've heard about Sarana and Torvin, did you never wonder why Torvin didn't return to take back his kingdom?" Zuleeka asked conversationally. "It's because of this." She touched a finger to the glittering jewel. "The Eye of the Gods—their gift to Sarana." With a gleeful smile, she revealed, "A weapon forged to take away her husband's magic."

Jaren's face turned white, and Caldon sucked in a sharp breath.

"I'd always intended to use it on you one day, taking *your* magic away," Zuleeka declared, "but this opportunity is too good to resist. Why take your magic when I can just kill you?"

Kiva stopped breathing, her power slipping away like water through her fingertips.

Zuleeka pressed the blade up against Jaren's heart, looking back and asking, "Any final words, sister?"

Kiva's mouth loosened, but she didn't speak, forcing aside her terror and concentrating, *concentrating* on the burning beneath her skin, the tingling at her fingertips, pulling power from the very essence of who she was. But still, the blackness swirled around her, no sign of her golden light even though she could feel it *right there,* just out of reach.

Your magic is pure, your heart is true. You have to fight it.

Kiva didn't need Delora's encouragement, already fighting with everything she had. Sweat dripped down her face, mixing with her tears —which only flowed faster when Zuleeka shrugged and resealed her lips, turning back to Jaren and crowing, "I guess she doesn't care enough to say goodbye."

You're different from them, Delora had said, *the light to their darkness.*

Zuleeka drew back her dagger arm.

Be the light in the dark.

"Farewell, Prince," Zuleeka said, her snake-smile growing.

Be the light in the dark.

Zuleeka's dagger sliced through the air—

BE THE LIGHT IN THE DARK.

—and with an almighty scream, golden light burst from Kiva, the darkness vanishing under its sheer force, releasing her, releasing Caldon, releasing Jaren, leaving no trace of her sister's corrupt magic to be seen.

But then Zuleeka's blade stabbed into Jaren's flesh.

Right into his heart.

A wave of power erupted from him, sending Kiva and Caldon flying into the wall, the windows shattering, the chandelier crashing to the ground. Zuleeka alone remained standing as Jaren slid to his knees, his mouth open in a gasp of pain, his now-free hands clutching at the dagger lodged in his chest.

"NO!" Kiva shrieked, her ears ringing, head pounding, not just from the strength of his shockwave, but also from how much it had cost her to banish Zuleeka's magic.

She tried to get up, a sob leaving her when she couldn't stand, but she needed to get to Jaren—*she needed to get to Jaren.*

Caldon was groaning, bleeding from his head, barely conscious. He couldn't help her. She had to—*she had to*—

Crawling on hands and knees, heedless of the broken luminium shards cutting her skin, tearing her dress, she scrambled toward Jaren, reaching him just as Zuleeka viciously tore out her blade and declared, "Save him, or stop me. The choice is yours, sister."

And then Zuleeka was gone, donning her mask—her *Viper* mask—and sprinting out of the room to go make her bargain with the queen.

But Kiva didn't care.

Zuleeka could have the kingdom.

Just as long as Jaren lived.

His eyes were already fluttering shut, blood gushing from his chest. And yet, at seeing Kiva hovering over him, he still managed to lock his pained gaze with hers, whispering in a ragged, agonized voice, *"How . . . could . . . you?"* before he lost his battle for consciousness.

The accusation in his words broke something inside Kiva, but right now she had greater concerns than how much he — deservedly — hated her.

"No, no, no," she cried, pressing her hands against his wound.

He couldn't die.

He couldn't die.

And even though Kiva had nothing left, even though it had taken everything in her to free them all, she still closed her eyes and called to the deepest recesses of who she was, begging for even the smallest speck of power to come forth, to *rise.*

"Please," she croaked. *"P-Please."*

For one terrifying moment, nothing happened.

But then she felt it.

Her fingers tingled, her skin burned — and the golden glow poured from her hands, straight into Jaren's wound.

Kiva sobbed, laying her head on his bloodied torso, unable to hold her own weight as her healing light flooded him.

She heard another groan from Caldon, sensed him crawling across the room toward them, but she didn't look, pushing all her remaining strength into her magic until the glow finally faded.

And when Kiva sat up, she sobbed anew at the sight of the wound sealed shut.

But then another sob left her, this one not from relief, but with sorrow as she recalled how Jaren had once explained his power: *My magic is a part of me. Like an arm or a leg.*

Zuleeka had stabbed him with the Eye of the Gods.

When Jaren woke, his magic would be gone.

Kiva had done that to him.

She might have saved his life, but she was the reason he'd lost his magic.

And soon, his entire kingdom.

He would never forgive her.

She would never forgive herself.

"You need to run."

The dead-sounding voice came from Caldon.

Kiva turned woodenly to him, finding his eyes locked on Jaren's chest.

"He's going to be all right," she croaked, just in case Caldon didn't realize.

"You need to run," he repeated, his cobalt eyes darkening to ink. "Before he wakes. Before *she* wakes." He nodded to Naari.

"I didn't know," Kiva rasped, needing him to believe her. "I *swear* I didn't—"

"Don't," he said, whip-sharp, holding a hand to his bleeding head. "Not right now. I need to—I need to think. And you need to leave before they toss you in the dungeons. Or kill you outright."

Kiva swallowed, more tears flooding her eyes.

"Cal—"

"Run, damn it!" he roared.

Seeing the raw pain in his features, the grief, the heartache—for *her*—Kiva staggered to her feet.

And then, with only a single look back—just enough for one final glimpse of Jaren's pale, unconscious face, committing every line of it to memory—she bolted from the room.

Faster and faster Kiva flew through the palace halls, her golden dress bloodied and torn, tears streaking her cheeks, but she didn't stop, even as waves of exhaustion and grief pummeled her, as dizziness threatened to topple her.

She had to keep going.

Because as soon as Jaren woke and realized what had happened, what he'd lost, what she'd *done*—

Kiva had to keep going.

Torell—she had to find Torell. He might have been the rebels' general, but Kiva knew deep down that he'd had no knowledge of Zuleeka's true plans—or her death magic. Once she explained, he would help her. Some way, somehow, he would—

"Going somewhere?"

Kiva came to a screeching halt in the entrance hall, mere steps from the front doors.

She spun in place, nearly collapsing with relief at the sight of Mirryn standing there, her ice blue gown and mask perfect, not a hair out of place.

"Mirry," Kiva gasped, reaching out as if to prove she was real, that she was safe.

"Sorry about this," the princess said nonsensically. "It's nothing personal."

Before Kiva could question the warning, two bursts of air slammed into the sides of her head, the pressure like twin daggers stabbing her eardrums.

Sheer, inconceivable agony had her screaming out, the pain unlike anything she'd ever known . . . until it became too much, and everything faded to black.

CHAPTER THIRTY-FIVE

Kiva awoke in a cell.

Panic hit her, raw and hard, and she jumped to her feet, a hand flying to her aching head. But her pain was secondary to her fear, her eyes struggling to see in the limited light. Disoriented as she was, for one petrifying second she wondered if she was back in the Abyss, before her wits returned. It took weeks to travel to Zalindov from Vallenia—she was still at the palace.

In the dungeons.

Trembling all over, Kiva approached the iron bars blocking her escape, wrapping her hands around them and giving a useless tug.

"Hello?" she called, her voice echoing down the shadowy passage. "Is anyone there?"

Footsteps sounded in the distance, heels clacking on stone. Kiva expected a guard to appear, but instead she found herself face-to-face with Mirryn, her appearance just as perfect as before, not a scratch or tear or anything to indicate she'd been in a struggle.

Kiva's hands shook on the bars, her voice barely a whisper as she said, "Zuleeka never abducted you, did she?"

The princess held her eyes. "She didn't need to."

Four words, and Kiva's world crumbled.

"Your sister and I have been allies for some time," Mirryn revealed, smoothing the front of her dress. "We realized we both have the same goals, and that we'd reach them faster if we worked together."

Mirryn was Zuleeka's spy in the palace, Kiva suddenly understood. The one who had told Zuleeka about Jaren's magic, and gods knew what else. She'd betrayed her own family, had helped orchestrate everything that had happened tonight.

Afraid of the answer, Kiva asked, "What goals?"

"To rule Evalon, of course," Mirryn said.

But—Mirryn *already* ruled Evalon. She was a Vallentis. A princess from birth.

Kiva's brow furrowed. "I don't understand."

"Do you seriously have no idea?" Mirryn huffed out a laugh. She shifted forward, wrapping one hand around the bars, nearly brushing Kiva's fingers. "You see my brother just like everyone else—perfect and wonderful and amazing in every single way. Can't you imagine what it's like growing up beside *that?*"

Kiva's exhausted, throbbing mind was scrambling to follow. "You're —You're jealous of Jaren?" she asked. "*That's* why you're helping the rebels take the throne? *Your* throne? Just so he doesn't inherit it?"

Mirryn snorted. "You're finally starting to catch up. But you're only halfway there." Her angry blue gaze locked with Kiva's as she explained, "It was *never* my throne, but it always *should* have been. I was the first-born child—it was *my* birthright until precious Jaren came along, his magic considered so much more powerful, as if that meant something. Everything was taken from me the day they decided he should rule in my place: my title, my future, *everything.* I was raised in his shadow, always second best, always the *spare.*"

Her face twisted, the knuckle of her hand turning white against the bars, but then she visibly relaxed. "When I met your sister, she told me we could work together to get back what belonged to me, what belonged to *us.* It was a proposal too tempting to resist." She paused, then admitted, "That said, it's only been in the last few weeks that I really dedicated myself to our work. I helped provide information before that, but I wasn't in a rush for action. Now I am."

"Why?" Kiva croaked. "What changed?"

"Navok." Mirryn spat the Mirraven king's name like a curse. "He said I'm not good enough, that I'm 'just a princess'—can you believe that? We were so careful to keep our relationship secret from him, but somehow he found out. And now he's forcing the woman I love to marry Voshell, knowing that one day he'll be king, and she'll rule Caramor at his side."

Kiva blinked, realizing Mirryn was talking about King Navok's sister, Serafine. But that meant—

Her family got involved. They didn't think we were a good match.

Princess Serafine was Mirryn's girlfriend. *Ex*-girlfriend. They must have been forced apart because Navok wanted his sister to marry an heir, not a spare.

Kiva almost felt sympathy toward Mirryn—but only almost.

The princess leaned closer, her eyes fevered. "This is the only way I can get Serafine back—by becoming Queen of Evalon. Navok promised he'll terminate her betrothal the moment I'm on the throne. Then she can be mine."

"Where does Zuleeka fit into that plan?" Kiva asked hoarsely.

"She and I will rule together," Mirryn said. "We've already agreed— we'll be two queens the likes of which this world has never seen. A Corentine and a Vallentis, the way it was always meant to be." A slash of a smile. "And it's all thanks to you."

Kiva shook her head in denial even if she knew the princess spoke true.

"The Royal Ternary," Mirryn mused, raising her free hand. On her finger was a ring—the queen's Signet, Kiva realized with a sinking heart. "We never would have known about that clause if not for you," Mirryn went on. "That saved us *years* of planning." Another flash of teeth in the low light, stretching into a beaming grin. "Thank you, Kiva. You have no idea how happy you've made me. And Zuleeka."

Kiva felt hollow inside.

"Unfortunately," Mirryn said, her grin fading, "it'll take time for us to figure out how to make the announcement and enact the change of rulership. Even with the Ternary clause, the citizens of Evalon could still revolt. They may not care that we have a legal right to the throne, despite the Royal Council having no choice but to confirm it." Mirryn's lips tipped upward again as she added, "But your sister has a backup plan, just in case. I'll let her explain when she gets here. She wants to say goodbye."

Goodbye? Kiva wondered.

"In the meantime," Mirryn went on, "we've ordered Mother to act as if nothing has changed, even though she's fully aware that she's no longer in charge. The Royal Council will be informed first thing in the morning. We'll then discuss the most effective way for my family to abdicate."

"Jaren won't abdicate," Kiva said, everything in her hurting from just saying his name. "Royal Ternary or not."

Mirryn's face tightened. "He won't have a choice. Once we find him—"

She broke off suddenly, as if realizing what she'd said.

Kiva latched on to it, hope welling within her. "Find him?"

Scowling down the dark corridor, Mirryn shared, "Caldon got him and Naari out before we could secure them. But they have nowhere to go, and Jaren has no magic. We'll find them soon enough."

For the first time since she'd awoken, a smile touched Kiva's lips. "Don't count on it."

Mirryn's scowl deepened. "You look much too pleased for someone locked in a dungeon."

"You obviously have some plan for me," Kiva pointed out, "or you wouldn't have dragged me here." She'd already noted the lack of guards, making her think Mirryn must have levitated her into the cell without anyone seeing, everyone too distracted by the party. "If you're hoping to use me to lure Jaren back, it won't work. Not now that he—"

Not now that he knew who she was. Kiva couldn't finish the sentence, her voice cracking on the words.

"That's not actually our intention. But don't worry, you won't be staying here for long," Mirryn said, humor threading her tone. "Just until—ah, here she comes."

Another set of footsteps was echoing down the passage, and then Zuleeka was striding into view, still dressed in her navy gown but now with a dark cloak over it, her face solemn.

"Hello, sister," she said, stopping beside Mirryn. "You've had quite the day."

Kiva swallowed, unable to reply.

Zuleeka turned to the princess. "Give us a moment."

Mirryn looked like she was about to object, but then dipped her head and relented. "Call when you're ready for me. I'll be right outside."

Kiva didn't know what the words meant, but an anxious knot swelled in her middle as Mirryn walked away.

Zuleeka waited until the princess was out of hearing range before she said, "I told you I'd explain some things the next time we were alone."

"Do you really think I want to hear anything you have to say?" Kiva rasped, unable to hide the depth of her pain. "All you've done is lie to me."

Zuleeka was unmoved. "I'm not the one who betrayed our family."

Kiva pressed closer to the bars. "You're such a hypocrite," she hissed. "You're angry at me for everything with Jaren, when you've been working with a Vallentis all along."

"You don't know what you're taking about," Zuleeka shot back. But she said nothing more.

Glaring at her, Kiva said, "Tell me what you came here to say, then leave. If I ever see you again after that—"

"You'll what?" Zuleeka asked in a taunting voice. "What will you do, Kiva? Will you hurt me with that healing magic of yours?" She raised her hand and summoned a tendril of darkness. "I'd like to see you try."

Kiva recoiled at the memory of what it had felt like to be trapped by that awful power.

Zuleeka snorted, dropping her hand again. "You're pathetic. Mother never should have bothered trying to get to you in Zalindov. But if she hadn't, I wouldn't have Mirraven in my pocket, so at least her sacrifice was worth something."

Kiva froze. "What?"

"The bargain Mother made with Navok—I said I'd tell you, and believe what you want about me but I rarely go back on my word." Zuleeka brushed invisible dirt from her shoulder before revealing, "Mother allied the rebels with Mirraven. With Caramor, too, since they're so tightly joined, though her deal was with King Navok only." As if to herself, she murmured, "*He's* not going to like what happened in the warehouse today, but he should've had more patience. Those idiots could've ruined everything."

Heart pounding as Zuleeka's words repeated in her ears—*Mother allied the rebels with Mirraven*—Kiva ignored everything else to ask through numb lips, "What deal?"

"Evalon's defenses are too strong for the northern territories to invade without inside help," Zuleeka said. "So we—the rebels—will be the help."

Kiva struggled against her growing alarm. It sounded like Zuleeka was planning to aid Navok in taking over Evalon. But—

"Why would Mother make that promise if she wanted the kingdom for us?" Kiva asked, confused.

"Her anger was enough that she would've been happy just to unseat the Vallentis family, even if she couldn't take the throne from them herself," Zuleeka said. "When she left us to make the deal with Mirraven, she'd been working for years with little to show for it, and she was becoming sick enough that she knew she had to make a choice. She decided that allying with Navok would be the fastest way to get vengeance. But despite that, she still did everything she could to make sure there would be a Corentine ruling by his side."

It took a moment for Kiva to understand, but when she did, she gasped aloud. "Are you saying—are you *marrying* King Navok? Was that part of the deal?"

Zuleeka's hands clenched into fists, the only indication of how she felt about the arrangement. But all she said was, "Mother didn't know about the Royal Ternary—she didn't know there might be another legitimate way. Even with it, there could still be problems, so Mirraven's forces will guarantee the citizens of Evalon fall into line. The armies, too. Either way, a Corentine will be on the throne. That's what matters."

The backup plan Princess Mirryn had mentioned—it was *Mirraven*. Gods. *Gods.*

Jaren had been right all those nights ago when he'd shared his concerns about the northern kingdoms.

But he'd been wrong to underestimate the rebels.

"Does Tor know about this?"

Zuleeka barked out a laugh. "What do you think?" She shook her head, then looked down before quietly admitting, "I felt awful about stabbing him today, but I couldn't risk him getting in the way—I knew he'd try to stop me if he figured out what I was planning tonight. I've known for some time that his loyalty has been wavering. And much more so since you returned."

Kiva gaped at her sister. "*You* stabbed him? But I saw—"

Arms, legs, three bodies tangled. That was all Kiva had seen, no proof of who had plunged the Mirraven's sword into her brother.

"I had to make it look real," Zuleeka stated, stepping back and reaching into her cloak. "And I knew you'd be able to heal him. The only question will be what he remembers when he wakes, but I'll deal with that in the morning. *You,* however, won't know for some time how all this plays out."

"What do you—"

Before Kiva could finish, Zuleeka blew a handful of golden dust into her face. She coughed and spluttered as a rich caramelly taste overwhelmed her senses.

Along with absolute, blinding dread.

Angeldust.

The highly addictive drug was all over her, had gone straight down her nose and into her opened mouth.

"What the *hell,* Zul—"

"You took Mother from me," Zuleeka interrupted, her face hard. "In ways you don't even know about. Ways you'll *never* understand. She always believed in you so much more than me. The golden child, she called you. So much power, she said. So much potential. But look at you —you're nothing."

Zuleeka made a scoffing sound, but Kiva was beginning to have trouble focusing around the quick-acting drug, fighting to comprehend her sister's anger. Fighting to comprehend *anything.*

"You took *everything* from me," Zuleeka hissed. "And now I'm taking it from you."

"I don't—" Kiva tried to say, but the words mashed together before leaving her lips.

Zuleeka waved the pouch of golden powder in the air, her voice much calmer as she said, "Consider this a gift for all your help. The last gift you'll ever receive from me. That, and this."

With her vision moving in and out of focus, Kiva watched as Zuleeka removed the amulet from beneath her gown, reaching through the bars to slip the chain over Kiva's neck.

"The last of its protective power faded when I went to get the Signet from the queen," Zuleeka said. "She and Prince Oriel put up enough of a fight to drain it, so it's useless now, but I want you to have it as a reminder of tonight—of everything you helped make happen. We'll send along orders to make sure they don't remove it with the rest of your possessions. I want you to remember, every day, until you no longer can."

Kiva swayed on her feet, the iron bars swirling before her, every word from her sister's mouth like a hazy, nonsensical dream.

Zuleeka gave a sharp whistle, much like she'd done in the warehouse earlier that day, then waved the angeldust pouch again and said, "This really is a gift—something to help you survive the long journey back. You won't notice a thing, not even the passing of time."

Zuleeka's face was melting into colorful shapes as the hallucinogenic drug pulled Kiva into its embrace, but somehow she managed to slur a single word: "Back?"

"To Zalindov," Zuleeka said. "I can't have you running around helping your prince get in the way of my grand plans. Or Torell, if he doesn't cooperate." She leaned toward the swirling bars and whispered, her face tinged with a hint of madness, "There's so much more happening here, so much you don't understand. Mother was thinking too small. I won't be making the same mistake. And I won't risk you being free to stop me."

In the back of Kiva's mind, she knew she should be upset, even terrified, but instead, her limbs loosened as she relaxed, a humming sensation overtaking her body, the pain in her head fading and her troubles disappearing.

Zuleeka was saying something else, something Kiva couldn't hear around the pleasant chiming sound in her ears. She watched through a foggy cloud as her sister turned to look at someone—Mirryn, who rematerialized at her side, summoned by the whistle—and handed over the golden pouch.

"She's already so out of it," the princess commented, her amused voice coming to Kiva as if from far away. "I'll go make sure the prison wagon is ready and give the rest of this to her guards. They've agreed to keep her dosed until she reaches Zalindov. She won't cause them any problems that way."

The fuzzy outline of ice blue silk disappeared from Kiva's vision, her head lolling to the side. Somehow she'd ended up on the ground without realizing it.

"Goodbye, sister." Zuleeka's words were nothing more than a distorted whisper of sound. "I wish things could have been different."

What happened next, Kiva couldn't say, the angeldust pulling her under, its grip swift and powerful. She was aware of Mirryn's blue dress returning again, of the dungeon cell opening and then her body floating. She laughed at the sensation, feeling lighter than air, but then she was outside in the cold and lying on a hard surface, her limbs cramped tight as more iron bars surrounded her, caging her in.

And then she was moving.

The following minutes, hours, days, weeks became a blur of crunching gravel and clanging bars, broken only by the briefest moments of clarity, just enough time for her transfer guards to blow more of the caramelly powder into her face, sending her under all over again. She dreamed of golden palaces and glittering rivers, of rooms full of windows and mist-covered marble. She saw Jaren's face, his hands, his lips, as he touched her, held her, cherished her. And she whispered to him, telling him everything she'd never said aloud, all the truths she'd bottled up inside, too afraid of what they would mean if she let them out.

I know you're scared. But I promise you don't have to be.

His voice washed over her like pure sunshine, and she wanted to tell him he was wrong. She wasn't scared anymore.

Because she loved him.

More than anything.

And when she finally awoke one crisp morning and found herself surrounded by familiar limestone walls, the first thing she did was murmur his name, reaching for him.

But he wasn't there.

Reality crashed down on Kiva, even as the angeldust still flooding her system sought to regain control of her mind. She fought it, remembering how Jaren had looked after he'd kissed her — and then the pain in his features after he'd learned of her betrayal.

A sob left her, but her anguish was muted by the drug, as was her fear when Warden Rooke's dark face appeared, staring triumphantly through the iron bars of her prison wagon.

"Pity we filled your position in the infirmary," he said, "but there's always plenty of work in the tunnels." His lips stretched into a smile. "Welcome home, N18K442."

And that was the last Kiva knew before the angeldust pulled her under again, leaving her with one final conscious thought:

If Rooke was sending her to the tunnels, she would have six months left.

A year at the most.

And then she would be dead.

ACKNOWLEDGMENTS

I wrote this book in the middle of a global pandemic, while recovering from surgery, after being diagnosed with an autoimmune disorder, and then, halfway through drafting, my beloved grandmother passed away. So to say it was challenging is a vast understatement.

But.

Something I've learned is that the best things in life rarely come easy, and the toughest battles reap the greatest rewards.

Writing and editing *The Gilded Cage* might have been one of the hardest experiences—*of my life*—but because of that, it's also the book I'm most proud of. And I have so many people to thank for helping me along the journey.

First, I have to thank God, my family, and my friends for being my strength and offering me hope, even during the darkest of times. (We've all certainly had our share of those in the last year or so.)

I absolutely have to thank my agent, Danielle Burby, for fighting my battles and keeping me sane—all while somehow never losing your mind over the bazillion emails I send you (daily). You are my greatest champion, and I can't tell you how much that means to me. Thank you also to the entire team at Nelson Literary Agency for being so awesome and continuing to help make my dreams come true.

Huge amounts of gratitude go to my foreign rights agent, Jenny Meyer (and your whole team!), for continuing to wow me with new international offers, despite the challenging state of the world. You once joked about global domination, but I'm no longer sure you were kidding.

To my editors, Emilia Rhodes and Zoe Walton, I genuinely can't express how grateful I am for all your hard work on this book. The difference between the first draft and the finished version is astounding, with so many more layers than I ever would have thought to incorporate without your insight and guidance. And more than just the editing, thank you for advocating so strongly for this series in every single way possible! (Cue warm-and-fuzzies.) I'd also like to thank Gabriella Abbate and Mary Verney for your added wisdom, and, of course, my copyeditor, Ana Deboo, and proofreader, Ellen Fast—this book truly was a group effort!

I definitely have to offer a wholehearted *thank-you* to the entire publishing teams at HMH Teen (especially John Sellers, Julie Yeater, Lauren Wengrovitz, Mary Magrisso, David Hastings, Samantha Bertschmann, Taylor Navis, and Jim Tierney), PRH Australia (especially Dot Tonkin, Tina Gumnior, Jess Bedford, Adelaide Jensen, Michael Windle, and Kristin Gill, plus, of course, legends Julie Burland, Laura Harris, and Angela Duke), and Hodder & Stoughton (especially Molly Powell, Kate Keehan, Maddy Marshall, and Sarah Clay). Big, squishy virtual hugs for all of you.

Thank you also to my foreign publishers and their teams at Intrínseca, Sperling & Kupfer, Znanje, Maxim, Szeged, Loewe Verlag, Eksmo, Albatros/Fragman, and De Boekerij. I can't wait to see all your beautiful translations!

To my author friends, as always, thank your for your continued support and encouragement. There are too many of you to name, but I'm so honored to know you all. I'd especially like to thank Sarah J. Maas for being so incredibly generous and just downright amazing. I'm so, *so* blessed by your friendship. (Six years and counting—can you believe it?!) And Jessica Townsend, our attempted weekly beach walks are absolute highlights for me—partly because of the doggos, but mostly because I get to hang with your "wundrous" self. (See what I did there?)

I'm certain I've forgotten people here (can we blame pandemic brain?), but I'm going to finish by offering my unending gratitude to everyone who read *The Prison Healer* and loved it enough to shout it from the rooftops — book reviewers, booksellers, librarians, teachers, kids, teens, adults, parents, grandparents, *everyone*. I hope you're satisfied with this continuation of Kiva's tale, but, uh, sorry for yet another cliffhanger. My bad. *Hides face.*